GUNS

PHIL BOWIE

Gold Imprint
Medallion Press, Inc.
Printed in USA

DEDICATION:
For Aaron Roberts.

Published 2006 by Medallion Press, Inc.
The MEDALLION PRESS LOGO
is a registered tradmark of Medallion Press, Inc.

Printed in the United States of America
Typeset in Adobe Caslon Pro

10 9 8 7 6 5 4 3 2 1
First Edition

ACKNOWLEDGEMENTS:

My thanks first and always to my parents, Edith and Erol, and to my sister, Nancy, for unflagging faith and encouragement. I owe Lee Child one for his support. Ken Gruebel has been an incisive critic. Bud Aldridge contributed good ideas. The hard-working folk at Medallion have done a fine job.

THE RINGING PHONE WAS TRYING TO COMPETE WITH THE keening of the wind outside the cottage when Sam Bass untangled himself from the sheets and reached for it in the gray light. "Damn, what time is it," he mumbled, sitting up groggily.

"It's oh six hundred, Sam. This's Ruben. Listen, we got us a situation here I thought you'd wanna hear about. You know the Stilleys pretty good, right? They got that big ketch the *Osprey*?" The voice sounded hollow and scratchy, as though the caller was shouting from the far end of a long tunnel.

Sam turned on the bedside lamp and reached for his jeans hanging on a straight chair. "Yes," he said loudly. "Is something wrong?"

The caller was Ruben Dixon, a grizzled Coast Guard boson's mate stationed on the island, and a casual friend. Ralph and Adele Stilley were much closer friends, retirees in their middle sixties with an expensive new home on the sound side of Ocracoke and a shiningly restored fifty-foot vintage wooden sailboat they were supposed to be bringing back home after visiting family and taking a shoebox or two full of summer snapshots along the New England coast.

"This storm has blowed up into a real nor'easter overnight, Sam. Gale warnings up all over the place. Seas offshore here are fifteen feet and more. We got a weak distress call from the *Osprey* an hour ago, from Miz Stilley. She was pretty shook but she gave us a fix from their GPS. Put 'em about fifteen miles south of Hatteras. Said they got hit by a real big wave. Busted the aft mast. Taking on water and her husband's hurt real bad. Haven't been able to raise them since and no EPIRB signal. Now here's the deal. One Jayhawk chopper out of Elizabeth City's down for repairs. The other's out hunting a sinking trawler that maydayed off Oregon Inlet. We got us a Herc assigned but they can't take off for another two hours. This blow's caught everybody with their pants around their ankles and it's Sunday to boot. The crew and me set out in the motor lifeboat forty-five minutes ago. It's rough out here but we're makin' good way. Thing is, I don't know how long the Stilleys can wait for, like, an organized search, you know?"

"What you're asking is will I go out and see if I can find them, right?"

"Naw, I couldn't ask a civilian, even a hot rod like you, to do anything for us, even if it ought to be a piece of cake. Something went wrong it'd mean my ass, you know?"

"Dammit, Ruben. That wind outside is fierce." He switched ears so he could pull on yesterday's paint-stained denim shirt. "What exactly *is* the weather, anyway?"

"One of our people checked with Flight Service. Visibility's not too bad. Between rain squalls you got up to four miles. Surface wind's a little stiff, though. About twenty-nine out of zero one zero, with gusts to thirty-eight or so. Ceiling's from eight hundred scattered to twelve hundred solid. Forecast through mid-day is about the same except for the winds maybe to shift and blow more out of the east, ease off some.

"Ruben, what I've got is a hundred-eighty-horse Cessna." Sam stuffed his feet into his tall hand-made goatskin ropers, a five-hundred-dollar extravagance from six years and another life ago, scuffed and worn now, but still fitting like a second skin. "What you just described is marginal visual flight rules at best. No visibility at all in those rain squalls. Winds aloft I don't even want to think about, and a bad thirty-degree crosswind on the Ocracoke strip. Picture trying to launch a kid's kite out there now."

"Well, like I said. There's no way I could ask a civvy to help out in a search. I mean specially if it could be a little risky. I just thought if you was, say, out for a spin this morning anyway, and you happened to spot anything, you could maybe give us a call on your av band at what, one twenty-two point seven-five? Boat's number is four three two five two."

A little risky.

"Okay, okay. Maybe I'll give it a try. I'll need fifteen minutes to top off and preflight. What was that fix Adele Stilley gave you?"

Ruben read off the latitude and longitude and Sam used a pencil stub to copy the numbers onto a pocket pad on the bedside table. He put a number one in a circle beside the fix. A blast of rain rattled against the cottage's tin roof. The light coming in the window was a dingy gray and the window banged softly in its frame. "How far do you guys think they could have moved since this fix?"

"That's a tough one," Ruben said. "Do they have the engine? A good bilge pump? If he's out of action how much does she know? Hold on, here comes a real big bastard . . ." The phone crackled for ten seconds. "Okay, anyway, would she try to take the seas on her bows and run for an inlet? Or take it on the stern and make for deeper water, steer clear of the shoals? You got to make some assumptions or it's just a crapshoot. So figure that rogue wave really hammered them. Figure no power. The current's tryin' to push them northeast while the wind's driving 'em southwest. Anyway, you consider all that, we put them maybe thirty miles east southeast of Ocracoke Inlet now. Coordinates might be . . ."

Ruben read the numbers off and Sam copied them, putting a circled number two beside them. He wished Ruben good luck and hung up. He knew that riding the bucking rescue boat through the confused seas out there would be no picnic. Ruben had given him a tour of the Coast Guard station and the boat two months back.

The forty-four-foot motor lifeboat, with its squarish fiberglass passenger cabin perched on the aft deck and its high amidships steering station open to the weather on three sides for visibility, was self-bailing and self-righting. Though it was not nearly as fast as a cutter, with a top speed of only fourteen knots, it had been designed to handle the roughest water and was virtually unsinkable, but the ride for the crew of four on a day like today could be sheer hell despite all their training.

Sam used the bathroom, raked his thick black hair back with his fingers, and crammed an old ball cap on to hold it there, pulled on a light jacket, and grabbed a stale donut from a box on the kitchen counter.

Then the power went out, the ancient refrigerator wheezing to a stop. *Great.*

There was no avgas on the island, so whenever Sam couldn't fill up at Manteo or some mainland airport, he burned auto gas, laboriously using five-gallon cans to lug it to the plane. No power meant the pumps at the village station would not be pumping. So, no fuel. He tried to remember exactly how much was left in the plane's tanks. He usually kept the plane topped off but this one time he had neglected that chore after his last flight two days ago.

Outside, the wind pummeled him, almost snatching the ball cap away. Ragged gray rolls of cloud scudded low overhead and the tough, wind-stunted wax myrtles around the cottage were shuddering. As he drove his rusted Jeep Wrangler down the sandy lane on the outskirts of the village and squealed onto the deserted main highway, rain spat inside through several old rents in the soft top, soaking the seats. The tall marsh grasses on both sides of the road rippled wildly as though in sympathy with the restless sea out beyond the dune line.

He hoped the *Osprey* was still afloat. It was August and the ocean was plenty warm so the Stilleys would not soon die of hypothermia if they were in the water, but the odds against finding them quickly would increase exponentially without the boat to spot. And Ralph had a mild heart condition. The man definitely did not need the stress of a foundering boat added to whatever injury he had suffered from the big wave.

He had met the Stilleys eighteen months ago when they had been supervising the construction of their two-story contemporary home and had chartered Sam several times to fly them to the mainland so they could select wallpapers, appliances, and furnishings, and to take care of bank business. Though they were twenty-five years older than Sam, the three of them had hit it off immediately. Ralph was a big, weathered, bald man with a faceful of smile lines, and Adele was a perky redhead barely five feet tall with an infectious shrieking laugh that often caught the amused attention of bystanders. They had made some real money together in their own long-haul trucking business. They were absolutely devoted to each other and shared a quirky sense of humor. He called her Red and she often called him Chromedome. Ralph knew enough dirty jokes to have written a blue encyclopedia, and could somehow deliver the worst of them inoffensively and almost always hilariously. They had invited Sam to their housewarming and after the party had wound down, the three of them had sat out on the brand-new rooftop deck under the stars. With the stubby Ocracoke lighthouse winking lazily over by the inlet they had poured salty dogs from a huge sweating pitcher, had devoured the remains of the hors d'oeuvres, and had laughed, at times tearfully, into the small hours. Sam always enjoyed watching the two of them interact and he valued their friendship.

There was nobody at the airstrip. Five light planes were in a line on the small parking apron, all of them rocking their wings and straining at their tiedowns, wanting to fly. At mainland airports, tiedowns were most often just worn ropes. Out here, twenty miles from the mainland, where many a fierce storm had blown some common sense into the natives, they were stout chains. Sam's twenty-year-old blue-and-white Cessna, three niner zero Whiskey Sierra, was the farthest away from the single open-walled shelter that housed only a pay phone and some benches. He parked the Jeep on the grass behind the plane just as a squall hit. The cold gray rain drenched him through to his skin while he did a fast walkaround, pulling out the rudder gust lock and unhooking the chains as he went. The agitated surf thundered out beyond the dunes that ran alongside the strip.

He unlocked the cabin and climbed into the left seat, using a paper towel to wipe his face. He pulled the master switch and watched the needles jump up to just under half tanks, knowing that light plane fuel gauges were notoriously unreliable, realizing that fueling up from cans would be next to impossible in these conditions anyway. *So figure a maximum of two hours flying time with no reserve.* He punched the two fixes from his pocket pad into his GPS and started the elapsed time clock. The plane rocked on its gear and the wind whistled in the vents. As an afterthought he dug under his seat for a yellow inflatable life jacket and put it on. He clicked on the seat and shoulder belts, snugged them up tight, pulled on his headset, gave it two shots of primer, clamped the foot brakes, released the hand brake, and keyed the starter. The engine stuttered to life and the prop became a fluttering gray blur, blowing the rain back off of the windshield in quick little runnels. He switched on the radio but left the transponder off.

The fixes were close to the Atlantic Defense Identification Zone line, or ADIZ. Prowling around out there could trigger the coastal warning net and some bored non-com from Seymour Johnson Air Force Base might mark him for an enemy bomber from Grenada or a flying saucer from Mars and scramble a pair of Tomcats to bounce him just for the sport of it. Flying in low-level search patterns, without his transponder, there was less chance of him being painted on anybody's radar and having to take the time to explain what he was doing. Also, the weather might legally be IFR, in which case he was not even supposed to take off without filing an instrument flight plan with Air Traffic Control. ATC was not likely to grant him clearance to conduct a search offshore in these conditions. If anybody wanted to know later, he would just have to say conditions were basically VFR, with at least three miles visibility and at least a thousand-foot ceiling. There wasn't anybody out here checking.

The windsock, starched by the gale into a rigid cone, danced about ten degrees side-to-side in the gusts. The brutal crosswind was from the left about thirty degrees to the strip on average. He had never taken off in a light plane in such a wind, much less a crosswind. He checked the gauges, noting the oil pressure in the green, set the altimeter to zero, and taxied out onto the narrow runway, holding the yoke full forward to keep the buffeting gusts from getting under the tail. He back-taxied the length of the strip and swung it around to line up into the wind. He held the brakes while he did a run-up to check the magnetos and the carb heat, and cycled the flight controls to their stops. Then he lined up on the centerline and let it fast idle and warm, the wings rocking, while he talked to the plane, an old habit since his student days two decades ago.

"Okay, old girl. The best way to do this is a short-field takeoff but with no flaps. As soon as our wheels are off we crab full into the wind. Hold the rate-of-climb down and be ready for those gusts." He rehearsed the takeoff mentally for a few seconds, then said, "Okay, let's do it." He clamped the brakes tighter and pushed the throttle smoothly to the panel, watching the windsock for the most favorable wind direction and hoping for a lull. The engine was bellowing at full power, the brakes slipping. The wind seemed to let up somewhat and he cranked in full left aileron to keep the wind from lifting the left wing during the early part of the roll, and released the brakes. Then he was moving, picking up speed, easing off gradually on the aileron, and a sudden gust shoved the left wing up, hiking the left main gear clear of the pavement despite his immediate return to full aileron deflection, the right tire yelping as it skidded sideways, the sand at the right edge of the strip getting close, and he reached for the throttle to chop power but the gust eased and the left wheel bounced back down and he was accelerating so he left the throttle firewalled. He tested the elevator and then pulled the plane up off of the pavement, immediately lowering the nose to stay in ground effect and build flying speed, pushing left rudder to crab into the wind.

The airspeed indicator inched up to eighty miles per hour and he let her climb at full power into the wind, fighting the gusts to keep reasonably level, noting the island stretching away to the northeast to quickly disappear in the sand-and-salt spray and the rain mist. The shelter and the dunes crawled by below. A sudden lash of rain sounded like gravel flung against the Plexiglas windshield.

At seven hundred feet he was already in dirty wisps of scud and he leveled off and began a cautious turn across the wind, the left wing lurching up wildly in gusts. He fought around to a heading of one hundred and twenty degrees, the violent bucking easing off somewhat. The turbulence was bad but manageable, not quite exceeding the limits of his flight controls. The island quickly fell out of sight behind and there was only the angry sea below. The dark waves looked monstrous and malevolent, with violently breaking tops and chiseled foam-streaked flanks.

Within ten minutes, off to his right he caught sight of the white Coast Guard motor lifeboat, with its diagonal orange slash on the bow. The boat punched obliquely into a breaking wave and burst in a welter of wind-blown spray out the other side, only to slam down into the trough and bury its nose into the next wave.

Sam thumbed the push-to-talk switch on his yoke and said, "Coast Guard vessel two five two this is Cessna three niner zero Whiskey Sierra more or less airborne on a heading of one two zero. I have you in sight. How do you read?"

"Five by five Cessna Whiskey Sierra. Got you in sight. Jesus, you look like a rodeo bronco. Two five two more or less same heading," Ruben said.

Sam was crabbing considerably to allow for wind drift and he had to keep fighting the turbulence. He began scanning ahead to the limit of his visibility, back and forth, glancing at the GPS frequently as it counted down to the number two fix. He reduced the power another five percent and leaned it out as much as he dared, conserving fuel.

In another ten minutes he was at the fix but there was no sign of the ketch. He rolled into a thirty-degree banking left turn and tried to gradually increase the radius in order to fly outward in a spiral from the fix, scanning.

Nothing but ranked mountainous black waves. Nothing . . .

Nothing . . .

Nothing . . .

After a frustrating ten minutes he flew back to the fix and took up a heading to the number one fix, the position Adele had radioed. "Okay, Red, where the devil are you, girl?" he said to the wind.

Within minutes the GPS told him he was at the number one fix and he tried the spiraling scan pattern again, making his turns steeper when he flew away from the wind, lessening the bank angle as he flew into it, trying to keep the spirals from elongating despite the gale.

No luck. Nothing.

Turbulence forced him to fight the controls constantly. He wiped his eyes with his fingers and strained to see into the mists. Twice he flew into rain squalls and had to go on instruments until he broke out again. The boat could be under one of these squalls and he'd never see it. He had to believe it was still afloat.

Maybe the ketch hadn't drifted as far as Ruben had estimated. He assumed they would have taken down or at least reefed any sails on both masts as the storm had intensified. So, without much sail up, such a boat was low to the water, with minimal surface exposed to the wind and a heavy keel to slow its drift. Maybe it was somewhere between the two fixes, then. He tried to fly a loose, wide zigzag course along the line between the fixes. Scanning all around. There was nothing but empty crumpled foam-streaked sea.

He flew back to the first fix and orbited, thinking furiously. *Where. Where.* The wind was warring with the current, but the wind was far stronger. Ruben had to be right. The boat had to be downwind of this point, but farther to sea or closer to shore? *Pick one and try it. Okay, closer to shore, then.* He struck out on a more westerly spoke from the fix and gave himself ten minutes by his watch before he would backtrack and try another spoke.

And he found it.

He was looking at a breaking wave crest that seemed to suddenly solidify and realized there it is. *Yeah, dammit. There it is.* He flew over it, banking, and saw Adele in the cockpit looking small in a yellow slicker and orange life jacket, holding onto the big chromed wheel with one hand and waving at him animatedly with the other, her hair plastered down. The wooden rear mast had snapped and smashed down onto the center cabin, denting and splintering it deeply, and it was now trailing the wallowing boat in a tangle of rigging. He banked into a circle with the boat at the center and thumbed the push-to-talk switch.

"Coast Guard vessel two five two. This is Cessna Whiskey Sierra. I've got the *Osprey* and I'm orbiting. Wait one for a fix."

"Coast Guard two five two. Nice goin', hot rod."

Sam flew directly over the boat and punched present position on the GPS, memorizing the numbers. He relayed them, slowly and clearly, to Ruben, who would lay out a line from the number one fix and figure a position to intercept the drifting sailboat.

"What's *Osprey*'s condition?" Ruben asked.

"Cabin is badly damaged. Trailing the broken mast. No power. Boat looks heavy and very low in the water. Adele looks okay." She was still waving excitedly at him. "No sign of Ralph. Give me an ETA when you can, Ruben. I'll try to orbit until you get here. Whiskey Sierra." He looked at the panel clock and was amazed to see that an hour and twelve minutes had gone by. *Maybe forty-five minutes of fuel left then.* He hoped.

After two more orbits Ruben called. "Cessna Whiskey Sierra. We're making all the knots we can. ETA's twenty minutes."

"Okay two five two. I'll be parked here." The ceiling was lowering, and he had to let down to five hundred feet to keep clear of the roiling clouds. He tightened the orbit to make sure he could keep the ketch in sight. Adele had both hands on the big wheel now, hanging on, but was still tracking him. At times she and the boat almost disappeared in the wind-blown spray.

After what seemed an hour but was only seventeen minutes, the motor lifeboat plunged into view a mile off and altered course slightly toward the plane. When the two boats were a quarter-mile apart, Ruben called and said, "Okay, Whiskey Sierra, we got her in sight. We'll take it from here. Meet us at The Privateer when you can. We'll buy the beer."

"I'll hold you to that, two five two." Sam rolled out of the bank and struck out for Ocracoke. Before he'd taken off, he'd had some vague idea of landing at Manteo on a wider runway that was more into the wind, but Ocracoke was closest now and both fuel needles were wobbling between the one-quarter marks and zip. He was flying crosswind again, the right wing bucking up in the gusts. Why couldn't the gods for once have granted him a tailwind when he needed it? He licked his dry lips and crabbed right to stay on course. He pulled off another hundred rpm and leaned it fractionally more. *I'd give about a thousand dollars a gallon for just five more gallons right now,* he thought.

Then the sky began to close in on him. It was no squall, but a wide band of heavy rain that stretched as far as he could see to the left and right and he went on instruments before he flew into it and all visibility vanished in a gray pall, the rain blasting against the windshield. There were no lights at the Ocracoke strip but there were three published instrument approaches, the best of which Sam thought was the GPS, which he had memorized.

Long minutes later, as he drew closer, he set up the

GPS to provide the approach numbers while he kept up his instrument scan and fought the turbulence to maintain five hundred feet and stay on course. Both fuel tank needles were bouncing on empty now. He figured he needed only about fifteen more minutes of power to make it. He could catch only an occasional glimpse of the sea below, and did not dare to interrupt his instrument scan for very long to keep checking outside.

If this rain band extended over the strip the visibility might well be next to nothing all the way to the surface, but he had no choice now except to try shooting the approach anyway and hope the wind had shifted enough to the east to be more aligned with the strip. At least there were no buildings with people in them anywhere within a half-mile of the strip so there was little worry about hurting anybody else in a crash.

If he even had enough fuel left to make it that far.

He tried to gain a little altitude. Time seemed to slow down and he was hypersensitive to the regular drumming of the engine, listening for the first cough of a starved cylinder. He could sense those big waves below, reaching up to swat him from the sky like an insect. His first approach would have to be perfect. There would be no fuel left for a second try.

Finally the GPS told him he was close.

Still no letup in the gloom outside. Still the constant lashing of the heavy rain.

He grabbed the yoke with his right hand so he could flex the cramps out of his left. He wiped his left hand dry on his jeans and took a new grip on the yoke. With his right hand he aligned the directional gyro with the wet compass, turned up the lighting on the GPS, and then rehearsed the approach silently, keeping up his instrument scan the whole time and making control corrections automatically, trying not to over-control in the jolting turbulence.

As he began the approach he spoke to the plane again. "Okay, old girl. We've done this before, what, twice? So what if we didn't have anything like this much wind then and so what if we broke out at eight hundred feet or so both times. Hey, it's still no sweat."

It was darker than ever outside. He knew the letdown would go slower than it had before, both because he was flying into a savage wind and because he was intently anticipating every foot of the glide path. He kept the power on and noted he wasn't having to crab too much to hold course, which could only mean the wind must have become more favorably aligned with the strip after all.

Finally a small lucky break.

He was letting down and theoretically aligned with the phantom runway ahead in the murk now. He put down ten degrees of flaps.

Four hundred feet. Three hundred feet . . . two hundred . . . one hundred.

Seventy feet.

And then he sensed something outside and glanced aside to see the hump of a dune below. Suddenly it lightened up some ahead and he could make out the approach end of the rain-slicked strip. He was slightly right and he corrected, all his attention focused ahead now, pulling off a little power but just as the engine sputtered anyway, now willing the glide to stretch out just enough to get him there please and the engine died, the prop solidifying in a ten-to-four position. The Cessna was settling and it was going to be too short. His instinct was screaming at him to haul back on the yoke but he eased the nose down slightly to maintain all the airspeed he could.

The mains pounced down softly in the sand, then clipped the end of the strip pavement with a loud bang and the plane bounced and slewed wildly once and then he was down and rolling out, aligned with the centerline dashes, the nose wheel touching down, his feet gentling the brakes. It was a short rollout because of the wind and he sat there for thirty seconds after the plane had come to a stop, the wings rocking madly in the gusts and the rain slashing loudly against the aluminum skin. His left hand felt like a rigid claw and he massaged it with his right fingers.

He would walk to the Jeep and use it to tow the plane to the tiedowns. He set the hand brake, took off the inflatable vest, and climbed out. He knelt down on each side of the fuselage to inspect the gear but could see no damage. He walked along the centerline, watching the angry clouds race by low overhead, the rain drenching him to his skin again but it didn't bother him at all this time.

He held out a cupped hand and then licked the rain from his palm and smiled.

It tasted sweet.

IRA COHN WAS STRETCHED OUT NAKED ON THE MOTEL BED, his hands behind his head, his hairy legs crossed, looking at her. Even standing there in profile half wrapped in the badly wrinkled sheet, her glossy blond hair in disarray, no makeup on, glaring out at the storm, Samantha Blackstone was absolutely stunning.

"I guess this means you don't want to make love this morning," Ira said.

She didn't turn away from the window. "I want a cigarette."

"You quit smoking yesterday, remember? Threw your last pack off the back of the ferry. A seagull grabbed it. Probably dead by now from nicotine poisoning."

"You drive me halfway across the state in your rattling rust bucket to the end of the world here," she said with her flawless diction. "The so-called restaurant doesn't know the meaning of medium rare. The damned cable goes out. And now *this*." She flung an elegant hand in the direction of the storm outside, parting the sheet to give him a picture of that perfect body.

"Look, why don't we go down and have us a good breakfast," Ira said. He was starving. "Some French toast, maybe. Hot coffee. A little Everest of scrambled eggs. Some really greasy sausages."

"The damned *power's* out, Mr. Investigative Reporter? Anyway I don't *want* breakfast. I'm on a *diet* remember? I want a *cigarette.*"

"A tall glass of orange juice, then. And a big bowl of corn flakes Real crispy, with cold milk and about four spoons of sugar. You speak in italics, you know?"

"You go get me a damned pack of Salems *now.*" And she stamped a foot on the carpet.

"Okay, okay," he said, swinging his long legs down and using his toes to hook his boxer shorts up from the piles of hastily-shed clothing scattered around the bed.

When he was dressed he said, "How about a fond kiss?"

She aimed her squinted eyes at him and said through clenched teeth, "I'll be ready to leave by the time you get back."

So he trudged down the outside wrought-iron stairs, the wind howling and the blown rain spattering him as he jogged to his beat-up Toyota Corolla and got in quickly. He sat there for a minute thinking.

He had not quite believed it when Samantha had accepted his invitation for this getaway weekend, she the gorgeous co-anchor of the Channel Six news, he the slim, casual, bearded, rising-star reporter for the Raleigh *Sentinel*. He thought of himself as slim and casual. His mother called him an anemic hippie and constantly goaded him to eat more—even though he always ate like a horse right after galloping through the Kentucky Derby—and to go visit this certain decent men's shop in the Crabapple mall, where she worked as a security guard. He could use her mall discount card.

He had run into Samantha a number of times over the past three years while they were both covering some story or other, and she had always treated him as a princess might treat, say, her royal dung-shoveler. They were both of the same kingdom, you might say, but Ira was clearly the tabloidal digger-of-dirt, whereas Samantha performed a type of high docudrama.

So when she had agreed to let him buy her a few drinks one day last week, after they had both covered the release on bail of the deputy state treasurer, and then when she had further agreed to this weekend tryst, he had been more than a little incredulous at his sudden good fortune. And the thirty bucks for flowers, the ninety-eight for the big third-floor room overlooking Silver Lake Harbor, and the seventy for last evening's dinner and drinks, plus gas and oil and ferry tickets, had seemed as nothing, even though he figured if he were to hold his VISA card up to the light just so he'd probably see little wisps of smoke rising from it.

Then, after they had made love with abandon, at one point him likening a particular pose of hers in the glow from the bedside lamp to the way she smiled at you intimately out of your TV, clutching the microphone close to her lips . . .

Anyway, after all that, when they were sprawled panting in the shadows, her slender fingers lazily twisting his chest hairs, she had asked, "So, what's the real story on Senator Farcotton?"

Aha. I should have known, Ira thought. *It wasn't that she has a thing for slim and casual, after all.*

He offered her a tidbit. "Well, he had a little affair with Wanda Williams, the state attorney general's daughter, the one who's married to that big paving contractor Ezra Williams who sort of lucked up and got the Raleigh beltway improvement job last year..."

It was like trying to offer a cheeseburger to a great white shark. Nothing less than clear up to his shoulder was going to even come close to satisfying her.

"*Everybody* knows *that*, silly," she said. "I mean about the excess campaign contributions from the Tobacco Institute."

It was a story that Ira had been working on for three weeks now and his first installment was due to break on the front page of the *Sentinel* in four days. He'd heard that even the point people from "Sixty Minutes" had been sniffing around and he should have been more on guard against local reporters.

"Campaign contributions?"

"Oh, come on, Ira. You can *trust* me. I won't breathe a word of it until *after* your piece comes out, next week is it? I *promise*, darling."

They had sparred verbally for twenty minutes before she had yanked out two of his chest hairs and rolled over to put her back to him.

He started the Toyota and rattled around the harbor toward the Ocracoke General Store to get the Salems for her and two or three of those big Butterfingers for himself.

He knew from last night that she wasn't a real blonde. He would bet one of his inevitable Pulitzers that Samantha Blackstone wasn't her given name, either.

Inside the dim, dusty, and cluttered general store an attractive young black woman with intricately braided and silver-beaded hair was behind the old-fashioned mechanical cash register, talking to an older couple who looked like island natives.

"The boat sank not long after they got the Stilleys off," the young woman said.

Ira's antennae bristled like those of a just-launched satellite.

"Mrs. Stilley is okay," the young woman said. "Mr. Stilley's pretty badly hurt but stable, they say. This wind is letting up some so they're going to send a medical helicopter to fly him over to Pitt Memorial in Greenville. The motor lifeboat is supposed to dock any time now. It's been pretty rough out there."

"Good thing they found them fast enough," the man said.

"Sam Bass really found them," the young woman said. "He heard about them early this morning and he flew out there in that little Cessna of his and found them almost right away."

"Excuse me," Ira said. "I'm Ira Cohn with the Raleigh *Sentinel*. Are you saying somebody flew a light plane offshore in this storm?"

"Hello," the young woman said pleasantly. "I'm Danielle. Yes. Sam Bass. He's a friend of the Stilleys'. That's his flyer right there in the brochure rack, there on the top left. My boyfriend Melvin Stanton is in the Coast Guard.

He runs the Ocracoke Station. I just got off the phone with him."

Ira picked up one of the rack cards. It was cheaply done in dark blue ink on white stock, with a muddy blue aerial photo of Ocracoke Village. It said Sightseeing Flights across the top and below the photo said Reasonably Priced and Safe Air Charters Anywhere, with the pilot's name, phone, and beeper numbers, and an Ocracoke address. Ira thought the name Sam Bass was somehow familiar.

Ira always carried his very expensive Nikon F4 in its Tamron bag on the floor in the back seat of his Toyota, where it was always close to hand, amid the discarded Coke cans and burger wrappers. He had a white towel over it to keep it cool and hide it from any nocturnal cruising powdery-nosed camera buffs. The bag also contained polished wide-angle and telephoto lenses, a powerful flash, a small Sony tape recorder, and a thick six-by-nine notebook.

"Do you think Melvin would let me interview him if I went over there now?" Ira said.

"Oh, sure," Danielle said, smiling. "In fact I'll call and let him know you're on your way. Mr. Bass is over there, too."

"Thank you, Danielle."

He was halfway out the door when she said, "Did you want to buy something, Mr. Cohn?"

"No, thanks. I was after a pack of Salems but the lady who wants them ought to quit anyway."

As he was rattling back around the harbor at speed he was thinking *find out the exact weather numbers from earlier today, get the model number and specs on the light plane, find*

*out if the Stilleys are anybody and what kind of boat they had,
what they were doing out there. If he's conscious grab a quote
from him before they chopper him off to the hospital. Talk to her,
talk to the boat crew, maybe get an aw shucks quote from this
idiot Bass—hey, why couldn't the Coast Guard have done the
aerial search? Get a few shots of her giving Bass a big hug . . .*

Melvin Stanton met him at the door of the small station quarters carrying a thick coffee mug in one hand. Ira
had his camera bag slung from his shoulder. They shook
hands and Stanton led him down a hallway. The quarters
were immaculate, with vinyl floors waxed to high gloss.
The door to a radio room was open, a crisply uniformed
young woman wearing a headset seated in front of the lit-
up equipment. Somewhere out back a diesel generator
hammered noisily at high rpm. Stanton ushered him into a
small conference room decorated with a large nautical chart
of the mid-Atlantic coast and framed photos of cutters and
motor lifeboats and their assembled crews. A fit, lean man
wearing a paint-stained denim shirt was slouched at the
table. He had a mass of black hair resembling a charcoaled
mop. Early forties. He looked damp. His jacket and cap
were drying on the back of the chair beside him.

"You must be Sam Bass. I'm Ira Cohn, with the Raleigh *Sentinel*."

Bass looked immediately defensive, but leaned across the
table to take the offered hand and shake it once, unsmiling.

Stanton said, "We've got coffee in a thermos and a
couple dozen donuts there in the corner. Help yourself."

"Thanks, I sure will." Ira turned over a mug bearing the
Coast Guard emblem and filled it with steaming coffee. He

piled six donuts onto a paper towel and took the feast over to sit at the table with the other two men. He got out the recorder and notebook and began asking questions between large mouthfuls of donut and sips of the aromatic coffee.

Stanton was smilingly cordial and helpful, filling him in on the weather and sea conditions, what facts he knew about the Stilleys and their ketch *Osprey* and the procedures of the rescue, the capabilities of the motor lifeboat and its crew chiefed by an old hand named Ruben Dixon, volunteering information about how many distress calls they got annually and about the Ocracoke Station in general and its long proud history. Bass volunteered nothing, just sitting there quietly with his hands wrapped around his mug, gazing down into his coffee. Ira let the tape run and used the notebook to supplement it, jotting impressions and ideas as they came to him.

"So, Mr. Bass. I understand it was you who found them. In your plane."

Bass didn't look up. Just nodded.

Ira flipped back a page to some notes he'd already written on Bass. Not handsome. Somehow striking, though. Might have been a cowboy in an earlier time. What the hell's bugging him about me?

"How did you learn about the Stilleys being in trouble?"

Bass gestured at the recorder and said, "Maybe we could do without that for a minute."

"Sure thing," Ira said, and switched off the recorder and put down his ballpoint. He didn't need them anyway. He had a memory like a Gateway computer. He used the notebook and recorder mostly to help him think, to make interviews appear semi-formal, and so interviewees would remember they had been recorded when they sometimes later might want to decide they really hadn't said that. *Bingo*, he thought. *Now we're getting to what's bothering him.*

Bass leveled penetrating gray eyes at him. *There's a hell of a lot more to this guy than shows on the surface*, Ira thought.

"I hope you'll understand, Mr. Cohn. I'm not associated with the Coast Guard in any official way. I do have a couple of friends here at the station, though. I was talking with one of them on the phone early this morning and he mentioned the Stilleys."

So somebody in the Coast Guard had asked him to conduct the search, but they're not supposed to do that.

"Please. Call me Ira. I understand. Suppose we just say you heard about the Stilleys from a friend. How's that?"

"Good," Bass said, but something sizable was still bothering the man. Ira could sense it. He switched the recorder back on. "Flying a light plane out there this morning had to've been pretty rough, to put it mildly."

Bass looked into his coffee again and said, "It was turbulent but not all that bad, really. Visual flight rules conditions, basically."

Aw shucks time. And bullshit. I'll have to dig at him, Ira thought.

Then things began happening fast. There was the whapping of an approaching helicopter outside and the young woman called down the hall, "Chief, the motor lifeboat's coming in the inlet."

Stanton pulled on a slicker and Bass stood and grabbed his jacket and cap, Ira noting that Bass matched his own height of six two. Ira gathered up his own gear.

Outside, the wind had lost some of its punch, the rain had all but quit, and there were ragged bright holes in the overcast. The helicopter, a Bell JetRanger rigged for EMS, its strobe lights flashing, approached the pad slowly, the pilot obviously cautious in the still-brisk gusty wind. It settled onto its skids and throttled back to cool-down rpm. Two white-clad EMTs climbed out and ducked under the rushing blades to be greeted by Stanton. One of them carried a large metal case and the other a light-weight fold-up stretcher. Stanton walked with them from the pad three hundred feet to the dock and told them the lifeboat was due within just a few minutes. One of the EMTs signaled with a rotating forearm back at the helicopter pilot. Keep them turning.

Ira had the Nikon out and had already ripped through one roll.

They all watched as the motor lifeboat rounded the harbor entrance and rumbled up to the dock, Stanton effortlessly heaving coiled lines to the life-jacketed crew who tied them off expertly. Ruben stepped from the salt-flecked wheelhouse as soon as the boat was secured and shut down, gesturing for the EMTs. They climbed on board and went down into the aft passenger cabin. Within a few minutes they came out with Ralph Stilley strapped to the stretcher, his left arm encased in what looked like an inflated pillowcase, his color gray, his eyes closed. Adele, who seemed to Sam to have suddenly aged a decade, trailed them, helped off the boat by Ruben and one of the crew, a young freckled woman with short brown hair.

Adele had a haggard, agonized expression and looked childlike in her yellow slicker and orange life jacket. She saw Sam and gave him a strained, distracted little smile, her attention totally focused on her husband. She tugged at the sleeve of an EMT and said, "But I want to go with him."

"I'm sorry, lady," the EMT said. "There's just no room. It's a serious fracture but he's going to be fine, I promise. We've given him something for the pain. Call the hospital in about two hours. We really have to leave now."

"It's all right, Adele," Sam said, walking over to stand beside her. "I'll fly you to Greenville as soon as I can get some fuel." He was thinking *I'll get permission to drain the fuel out of Phil Saxton's plane if I have to. Or just drain it and tape a note to the windshield.* Phil had an unlisted phone and was only on the island when he was not out to sea on a trawler for weeks at a stretch.

Adele clasped her hands under her chin, nodded meekly, and watched them load up her husband and then take him away, moving fast to the west.

Ira changed rolls quickly.

Sam put a hand lightly on her shoulder and said, "Dammit, Red. You look like holy hell."

Ira realized it had been exactly the right thing to say as he watched her turn her face up to Bass and that lost-little-girl look was slowly fading, replaced by a tired grin and a glint in her eye.

"What," she said, "I don't look like I'm ready to party?"

Sam smiled and squeezed her shoulder.

"Oh, Sam," she said. "It was bad. We thought it was just going to be a rainstorm. Then it got worse and worse through the night and we took down all the sail. Ralph was in the cabin fiddling with the radio and I was out in the cockpit and this monster wave came out of nowhere and hit us. We heard the rear mast crack and then it just . . . it just crashed down on the cabin. It smashed all of the electrical stuff and broke Ralph's arm. The *bone* was sticking out and I didn't know what to *do*. He was bleeding and he was in horrible pain. I managed to get the radio to work and Ralph said give them the numbers off the GPS and then it all quit. The mast was floating alongside all snarled in the rigging and every once in a while it would slam into the boat. I got Ralph tied into a bunk and went out and tried to steer the best I could. The motor ran slow for a while and then it stopped, too. It seemed to go on forever and there was just nothing I could *do*. Then I heard the engine and I knew it had to be you. And there you were, bouncing around up there while we were bouncing around down in the waves and it was almost funny and I cried and I knew you'd lead them to us. They shot a rope to us and came over in a raft and got Ralph and then came back and got me. And then I looked back and *Osprey* was gone. Just gone. If you hadn't found us when you did . . . who's this?"

"Ira Cohn, with the Raleigh *Sentinel*, Mrs. Stilley." He had the tape recorder going in his shirt pocket.

"Really? Well, look, take a picture of *this*," and she grabbed Bass by his jacket, pulled his head down, and planted a kiss full on his mouth, hard. Bass actually blushed.

Then she clamped him in a side-hug, her damp head barely coming up to his armpit, and smiled widely at the camera as Ira shot away.

"Did he tell you he's a cowboy at heart?" she said.

Bass was unsmiling and trying surreptitiously to shade his face with the brim of his ball cap, but the fill flash would wipe out the shadow nicely.

What the devil, Sam was thinking. *It's only the Raleigh paper. Who's going to see it? Don't worry about it.*

Since the helicopter had arrived Ira had not had to ask a single question. *Sometimes you just plain get lucky*, he thought.

Then he remembered Samantha Blackstone.

3

SAM WAS FLYING BACK ACROSS PAMLICO SOUND AT TWENTY-five hundred feet in the fast-gathering night, the sunset afterglow behind him. He had left an exhausted Adele at the hospital with her suitcase to spend the night with Ralph, who was in a massive cast and resting comfortably.

The air was scrubbed clean and silk smooth, the air-plane just about flying itself on its own inherent stability. A large Carolina moon was climbing into the cobalt sky, a billion shavings of pure silver adorning the wide sound and the limitless sea beyond. The Outer Banks formed a slender black band fifteen miles ahead, broken by the inlets in several places, curving gently away as far as the horizon to the left and to the right. In the center of the broken band straight ahead the lighthouse winked slowly and Oc-racoke Village sparkled in the darkness. So the power was back on. There were only scattered feathers of high cloud lightly veiling the emerging stars. It was a night fit for the slumber of the gods.

Ma Nature's way of apologizing for losing her temper

in the storm earlier.

Legally, nobody was to use the unlighted Ocracoke strip beyond one-half hour past official sunset. Which had occurred about forty-five minutes ago. *Well*, Sam thought tiredly, *once you start violating aviation commandments I guess you just get on a roll.*

He was on a frequency with Cherry Point Marine Corps Air Station because he was transiting one of their several coastal restricted areas, and was squawking their assigned transponder code. He thumbed the push-to-talk switch and said, "Cherry Point. Cessna three niner zero Whiskey Sierra. I have Ocracoke in sight," thinking *now don't go getting all technical about the time, son.*

The bored controller came right back, "Roger Whiskey Sierra. Radar service terminated. Frequency change approved. And have a good *night*, sir."

"Thanks, Cherry Point. You too. Cessna Whiskey Sierra." He changed the squawk to the VFR 1200 code and switched over to the silent unicom frequency.

He had all his night vision and the moon was nearly full so the landing posed no real problem. In a few minutes he came in over Ocracoke Village at a thousand feet, the lights like a baroque necklace all around Silver Lake Harbor, set off by the dim anchor lights of several moored boats, the *Osprey* not among them tonight.

He waited until he was on a long final for the shadowy strip before turning on his powerful landing lights, recalling the old joke about what you do if you lose your engine on a night cross-country. You set up for best glide and go through your emergency checklist, and when you get close to the ground you turn your landing lights on. If you don't like what you see, you turn them off.

He made one of those rare absolutely perfect landings during which you could not feel or hear just when the tires kissed, and taxied slowly to the tie-downs. He stood out on the apron for a few quiet moments taking in the night sky. The wind sock hung limply on its pole, worn out.

"I know just how you feel," he said to it.

He had topped off in Greenville so he would be able to drain the avgas from his tanks to replace what he had borrowed earlier from Phil Saxton's Lark, an older high-winger that looked like a Cessna until you saw those knobby-kneed gear and a few other peculiarities. Phil refused to even think about burning auto gas. Sam's note was still taped to the Lark's windshield. Transferring the avgas and then refilling the Cessna with auto gas was a chore that would have to wait for early in the morning. Then he would try to look up Phil and tell him what he'd done.

When he parked on the sandy patch in front of the cottage the phone was ringing persistently inside. He hurried in and grabbed it.

"My hero," she said.

"Hi, Val."

"I heard you drive up. Don't you think you should get a muffler for that antique Jeep before the tourism committee has it condemned? On second thought, you can probably get away with it for a while yet. The whole island is talking about how you rescued the Stilleys practically single-handed."

"Aw shucks," Sam said.

"I have two rewards for you. The first is one of your favorite suppers. I called the hospital to find out how Ralph is and what time you left, so everything's just about ready. I'm putting the corn muffins in as we speak."

He pictured her moving about in her warm steamy kitchen deftly doing amazing things to magical concoctions that would render them delicious, her cordless phone clamped between her shoulder and her ear. He could barely do instant oatmeal right, so what Valerie Lightfoot did in her kitchen held an aura of the mystical for him.

"What's the second reward?"

"After we put Josh to bed we'll get comfortable and discuss that one at length."

"Do you hear that sound?" he said. "That's me coming in your back door."

He hung up and took only long enough to get into fresh underwear, jeans, and a decent shirt. He could shower at Val's. Maybe the two of them could. It would conserve soap and rain water.

He went out the back door and used the sandy path they had beaten into the grass over the past year, winding through a grove of gnarled wax myrtles and yaupons, to the back door of Valerie's cottage. Both his and her small houses were old rentals on the fringe of the village with metal roofs and gutter systems that drained rain water into large cisterns, shallow wells anywhere on the Banks tending to be brackish at best. Maybe one day the three of them would live in one cottage or the other. It would save rent and utilities. But neither he nor Valerie had raised that subject yet, both being stubbornly independent by nature and neither wanting too much baggage just now for a number of private reasons.

She met him at her door with a kiss on his cheek and a lingering hug. Her long black hair was done back in a pony tail.

Returning the hug around her narrow waist, he sniffed and said, "Meatloaf."

"Nope," she said. "Vanilla Fields. Fourteen dollars for a little spray bottle at Wal-Mart. I only wear it for special occasions like rewarding a hero."

"Come to think of it, you do smell pretty good, too. And feel pretty good."

"Careful, there are small eyes watching."

Five-year-old Joshua Lightfoot stood in the doorway to the living room with two fingers in his mouth, watching solemnly.

Sam stepped aside, went down on his haunches, held out his arms and said, "Come here, Curly."

Joshua lit up and ran barefoot across the kitchen, nearly knocking over a chair, flung himself at Sam, and administered a breakneck hug. "Come in my room and play Star Wars," he said. "You can be Hanz Olo."

"That's Han Solo," Valerie said. "Uh, uh, Mister Skywalker. Go wash your hands. You too, Chewwy. And then both of you can set the table. Supper's almost ready."

"Can we light the candles and turn out all the other lights?" Joshua said.

"Okay, now go."

Sam carried him into the bathroom and set him on his feet. Joshua turned on the water and Sam stood behind him and reached around the small shoulders to lather their four hands together vigorously while the boy giggled.

The cottage had only two bedrooms, a living room, a bath, and the kitchen, so they sat in candlelight at the rickety kitchen table, which Valerie had burdened with her version of meatloaf casserole, the recipe for which Sam thought ought to be kept in a bank vault, steaming foil-wrapped sweet potatoes, a vegetable concoction that even Joshua always devoured, her own ginger iced tea, and hot corn muffins with honey butter.

Under the table Joshua propped one small bare foot on Sam's knee as usual, Valerie quietly and sincerely said grace as usual, and they all dug in.

Halfway through the meal Valerie asked, "What are you doing tomorrow?"

"I've got a chore at the airstrip first thing. Then I'll go pick up Adele Stilley at the hospital if she wants me to. I've got a lot of finish work left for Brad Meekins on that newest rental cottage he built, but he doesn't seem to be in any great hurry for me to get it done. No charters scheduled. Why?"

"I wondered if you could pick Josh up from kindergarten at three. I don't get off until nine and Mrs. Bradley has to go up to Nags Head and won't be back in time to watch him."

"Sure. We'll find something to do. Go bungee jumping, maybe. Or skydiving. We'll grab foot-longers and milkshakes at the Burger Box. Maybe rent a good old western from the General Store later and fix up some popcorn. If he's bad I'll spank his backside."

"Oh, sure you will," Valerie said. "Whenever the two of you get together it's not real easy to tell right off which one's the five-year-old. Just remember his bed time is eight."

"I'll spank *your* backside, Sam," Joshua said with a dimpled grin. "Sam, did you know that girl lions have to go out and get all the food and the boy lions just lie down under a tree? For real. I seen it on TV."

"You *saw* it on TV," Sam said. "And that's exactly how things ought to be."

"You're warping my kid, you know," Valerie said.

After the events of the day Sam felt especially privileged to be here with the two people he had come to care most about in the world, sharing the meal and each other, and he saw them with a newness.

Valerie glowed primitively in the candlelight. Her Cherokee blood, thinned only by two generations, gave her fine skin a dark sheen. Her cheek bones were high, her carriage was unpretentiously proud, and her long dark hair was satin black. She thought her breasts were much too small but Sam considered them to be perfect. Lightfoot was her family name, Joshua's father having died in a brutal car wreck near Johnson City, Tennessee, just two weeks before the date that had been set for their marriage, never having seen his son. Her relatives were scattered up in the North Carolina mountains. At thirty-two, she was nine years younger than Sam.

Joshua was slender like his mother, with her large shining dark brown eyes, but he was light-skinned. His face was lean, his chin faintly prominent, his lips full, and his hair a tumult of light brown curls. *He'll break a heart or two when he's grown*, Sam often thought.

Over bowls of her peach cobbler, Valerie said, "I've been talking with Pam a lot at work when it's slow about a new line of products she's selling."

Uh oh, here she goes again, Sam thought.

Valerie worked as a waitress at Sonny's Seafood, and always had a little left over at the end of each week for her savings after promptly paying all her bills, but she was continually on the lookout for some scheme that would greatly expand her income and help make her dreams of what she called a real house and of a good college education for Joshua come true. Sam knew she had tried Tupperware, which now filled two of her limited cabinets, and lines of cosmetics—although she seldom wore any makeup herself—and vacuum cleaners, and Beanie Babies, not to mention envelope-stuffing and home crafts assembly for some company based in Minneapolis.

"Val, please don't take this wrong, but I don't think you're cut out for sales. The way you cook you could open your own restaurant and get rich. You know that business."

"But these products practically sell themselves once people understand the principles behind it all," she said, starting to clear the table. She turned on the overhead light and let Joshua make a wish and blow out the candles.

Joshua ran into his room and came back with an armload of worn miniature *Star Wars* figures and created an imaginary alien planet on the kitchen table while Valerie and Sam washed and dried the dishes.

"The way Pam explains it, there are all kinds of toxins in our bodies. If we can help our bodies get rid of them we'll be healthier in every way," she said seriously.

"So how do we go about doing that?"

"Magnets," she said.

"Magnets."

"I know it sounds a little far-fetched but Pam swears it really works. This company has all kinds of products. Small disc magnets about this big." She made an O with her soapy thumb and forefinger. "Car seats with multiple magnetic pole lines embedded in them. Vests. Pads that you sleep on. Wrist bands. I'll show you something in a minute. Pam's mother-in-law used to have severe indigestion and painful arthritis. She's been sleeping on one of those pads for just a week and taping the discs on at specific locations and her symptoms are all gone. Pam's husband had a bad back from working construction so he started using one of the car seats and now he says he feels ten years younger. It's a Japanese thing. Pam has a tester that lights up and beeps when it senses a magnetic field. She can tape a disc on your back and pass the tester near your stomach and it will go off. That demonstrates how the force field passes right through your body. The field stimulates the nerves internally to increase your blood flow and when you have increased blood flow you're getting rid of toxins and you have healing, don't you? Pam goes to monthly meetings that the company puts on over in New Bern and she's invited me to the next one. You'd be welcome too, of course."

"Now I know why you feel so good when you're around me," Sam said. "Go ahead, ask me."

"Okay, why?"

"It's my animal magnetism."

"Pam *said* your friends won't believe it at first. Wait, I'll show you."

She finished washing the last glass and Sam dried it and put it away while she rummaged in her oversized purse and came up with a thin pasteboard envelope, from which she extracted two knobby-looking black shoe inserts. "One size fits all," she said. "Sit down and take your boots off."

He sat and worked off his ropers.

She slid the inserts inside. "Okay, put them back on."

"How much do these cost?"

"They're not inexpensive, but what price do you put on your health?"

"About how much."

"Sixty dollars. Well, plus tax and shipping, of course."

"Sixty dollars."

"There," she said. "Now walk around a little. That's it. Don't your feet feel better already? Pam wears them and her feet don't bother her at all anymore, and you know how we're on our feet all the time, with that cement floor in the kitchen and only a thin layer of vinyl on it."

Sam had to admit the insoles seemed to stimulate his feet somehow, either the knobs or the magnets evidently at work, thinking maybe she's not such a bad sales person after all.

"Mmmmm," he said. "Not bad."

"Go ahead, wear them for a day or two. Pam said to give them a good fair trial. You let me know what you think and then I'll try them."

"Is this my second reward?"

She smiled slyly and said, "Not hardly."

They played a game of Monopoly at the kitchen table, Joshua winning with only a little sneaky assistance from Sam. Then they sat on the couch, Joshua snuggled in the middle, and laughed uproariously together through an old episode of "The Angry Beavers"—the one in which Norb fakes illness and wears his concerned brother Dag out waiting on him, trying to satisfy an endless list of increasingly outrageous requests, but Dag finally manages to turn the tables. They watched a chatty Australian naturalist in his baggy shorts picking up deadly snakes in the wild and tickling alligators and eating something he scraped off of a stump, all much to Joshua's delight. Then Valerie decreed it was bed time.

"Do I have to take a shower?" Joshua asked pathetically.

"Well, you had one yesterday, so I guess we can skip tonight," she said, "but you still have to brush your teeth. *All* of your teeth."

They hugged him and both tucked him in. He called Sam back into his room for a drink of water. Then he called him in again to turn on the night light. The third time Sam went into his room he was sitting Indian-style in the middle of his bed.

He said, "Sam look, I can almost snap my toes." With his thumb he folded his second toe over the top of his big toe and flicked them. "See? Almost a snap. I bet you can't do that."

"Good goo. I sure can't. That's a pretty good trick. Now, what say you hunker down under these covers and think about having the best dream ever." Sam sat on the edge of the bed. "About Luke and Han and Leia, maybe. What kind of adventure do you think they're having right now? Maybe they're flying the *Millennium Falcon* down, down, down to a planet that's glowing in the light from its star. Its great oceans glimmering even from way out in space. Pure white swirls of cloud hundreds of miles across. The sensors showing thousands of incredible life forms below . . ." He talked on quietly for five minutes, weaving a fantasy about a miraculous planet not at all unlike Earth, watching the boy's eyelids flutter and his breathing slow, until he finally drifted off on a smile.

Sam and Valerie sat on the couch with cups of hot green tea.

Valerie looked at him evenly and said, "Sam, tell me about yourself."

"What do you want to know?"

"Everything there is to know. Start with when you were zero and give me an autobiography."

He couldn't bring himself to tell her what she probably had every right to know by now, yet he didn't want to lie to her. He had fully intended to tell her all of it, but had just kept putting it off.

He said, "Well you pretty much know it all. I grew up in Massachusetts, in the Berkshires. My parents died three months apart when I was eighteen. I was always interested in flying. There was enough money to pay for most of my training. Then I didn't want to go the airlines route so I started flying charters. Hauling freight. Towing banners with Super Cubs. You know, 'Meet 'N Eat At Pete's Pizza.' I worked as a corporate pilot. Saved up enough to buy the

Cessna. Found my way out here to Ocracoke. You've been right there for the rest."

She gave him an exasperated frown and said, "You know if you tried harder you could probably be even a little more vague."

"What do you mean?"

"There's something else, isn't there? A big something else you're not telling me."

He could feel her starting to withdraw from him.

"Why do you say that?" he said lamely.

"You have nightmares and you mumble things."

"Val, I . . ."

She shook her head quickly and said, "No. Never mind. I don't mean to pry or nag. Some day when you feel you can trust me to handle it, you'll tell me."

He said, "Look, all that matters, really, is that I found you and Joshua here on this island and since then things couldn't be much better, as far as I'm concerned."

He used the remote to switch on the news. They both watched in uncomfortable silence for a while.

Then a report came on about a new eruption of violence outside Kosovo. There was hastily-shot footage of masked men boldly brandishing what looked to be new AK-47 assault rifles and shouting. Sam abruptly grabbed up the remote and cut the TV off. He sat there staring at nothing. Brooding.

She studied him searchingly, but gradually her frown faded to be replaced by a resigned smile. She canted her head, raised an eyebrow, and brought her fingertips up to trace the line of his jaw.

For a dreamlike time they touched and caressed like

teenagers, Sam gradually drifting back from wherever he had gone in his mind.

Then she got up, pulled her heirloom turquoise and silver clip off to let her long hair swirl free, and tugged at his hand.

"Take me to bed," she said.

He cleared his throat and said, "I was wondering."

"What," she said a little breathlessly.

"Well, should I keep my magnets on?"

"I'll slap you. I swear I will."

Not long later, in the low light from a single candle on her bedside stand, with the blue moonlight softly tinting the sheer window curtains, while he held himself up on his forearms to just brush her nipples with his chest, his fingers loosely splayed in her hair, both of them willing themselves still for a long moment, freezing time, she said,

"Those gray eyes. Sometimes...like a wolf."

"Do I frighten you?"

She gave him a feral smile and whispered, "Not hardly."

And she pulled him down to kiss him hungrily.

4

THE DAY WAS BRASSY, WITH THE TEMPERATURE IN THE high seventies, so Sam had the top off of the Jeep when he picked Joshua up from kindergarten. A frayed flight bag on the back seat held a bag of corn chips and a thermos of ice-cold root beer, the boy's favorite snack fare, along with other items purchased that morning at the General Store. Willie Nelson and Waylon Jennings were on the tape player doing "If I Can Find A Clean Shirt," the Mexican trumpets harmonizing soulfully in the background, so Sam and the boy sang along loudly as the breeze flailed their hair.

He drove to the airstrip and parked by the Cessna.

"We goin' flying?" Joshua asked.

"Nope. Your mom doesn't want the two of us to go up unless she's with us."

"Why?"

"It's just the way moms are. Sometimes it's hard to understand them. Tell you what, though, as moms go I think you got lucky and got a really good one."

"I know."

"I thought I'd clean this old plane up a little. Why don't you look in that blue bag there? Whatever you find inside you can keep."

Joshua unzipped the bag and came up with a yellow dozer with a backhoe attached and a Ford Explorer towing a runabout on a trailer that had a working winch. "Hey, cool," he said. "Thank you, Sam." He immediately put the dozer to work on a sandy patch behind the plane.

Sam got out a gallon of dry wash, towels, and a three-step folding ladder. He turned the Jeep's player back on with a tape that was a compilation of his favorites. Ray Charles and Willie doing "Seven Spanish Angels". Waylon and his Jessi Colter doing stuff from their old *Leather and Lace* album like "Waltz Across Texas" and "Wild Side Of Life". Willie and friends again doing "Slow Movin' Outlaw" and "Are There Any More Real Cowboys" and "Tryin' To Outrun The Wind".

He set to work swabbing on the dry wash, letting it haze, then wiping it off to leave a fresh luster and a protective coating. The constant sun and the salt air were taking an inexorable toll on the paint job despite his efforts. Twice a year he removed all the inspection plates and used a pump garden sprayer to mist expensive corrosion proofing into all areas to fight the sea air. Then, for weeks he would have to swab away black streaks that seeped out between the aluminum skin overlaps. The dry wash did a good job of removing stubborn black stains, chalking, and leading-edge bugs, but required a considerable amount of elbow flexing to scrub all the surface area on the plane.

When Willie's rendition of "Honky Tonk Woman" came

on he did some fancy footwork on the top step of the ladder and sang along, and Joshua jumped up to dance enthusiastically as well, giggling when Sam nodded his approval.

When the tape ran out Joshua made construction noises for a while and then said, "Becky Sampson said there used to be horses on Ocracoke. Is that so?"

"Yup. That's why that motel in town is called the Pony Island."

"How come there was horses here?"

"A long time ago men used to ride along the beaches looking for wrecked ships, to help save the people and to salvage the cargoes."

Over the decades the 125-mile stretch of the Outer Banks—despite six lighthouses, the most famous of which was the spiral-painted brick Hatteras light, tallest in the nation—had claimed some seven hundred known vessels, earning the title Graveyard Of The Atlantic. Once in a while the sands here or there would shift to expose the ribs of some old wreck, only to soon shift back and cover them up again. The elements reminding Bankers, hey, don't forget what we can do.

"The men stopped riding the beaches but some of the horses stayed on and became wild," he told Joshua. "They learned to take care of themselves. There haven't been any on Ocracoke for a while, but there's still a small herd down on Shackleford Bank where there aren't any people. I've seen them lots of times from the air." The shaggy animals resembled the wild mustang, and Sam always enjoyed spotting them running free among the dunes whenever he happened to be flying down that way.

"What do they eat?" Joshua asked. "And what do they drink? 'Cause you can't drink the ocean."

"Good questions. They eat the marsh grasses and they drink rain water or they use their hooves to dig down to get water that's fresh enough. Once a year some people have a roundup so a vet can look the horses over for any that need doctoring, and they rope a few and sell them to keep the herd small enough so all the horses that are left have enough to eat."

Joshua thought for a while and said, "Sam will you help me buy a horse? I got money in my bank."

"Now, where are you going to put a horse? In your bedroom?"

"We could build a big fence right here near the airport and then I could sell rides on him like you sell rides in your airplane and there would be a horse on Ocracoke again."

"Hmmm. Not a bad idea. Maybe some day. We'll see."

"You know, Sam, grown-ups always say maybe and we'll see. I think they really just mean no."

"What you need there is a house on the top of that hill you just built," Sam said, changing the subject. "Take a look in the back of the Jeep. There's a small empty box in there you can use."

Sam finished the tops of the wings, the vertical stabilizer and rudder, and the top surfaces of the horizontal stabilizer and the elevator, then stood back and said, "What do you think of the old girl?"

"Good goo, she's shiny. Can I please sit inside?"

Sam lifted him up onto the pilot's seat and put the headset on him. "You push here to talk and let go to listen.

Do you remember what I told you about the instruments? Which one tells you how high you are?"

Joshua pointed at once to the altimeter.

"Which one tells you how fast you're going?"

He reached over to tap the face of the airspeed indicator with a small finger.

"Which one lets you know if you're upside-down or right side up?"

He pointed at the attitude indicator.

Sam described what some of the other instruments and gauges were for and the boy paid rapt attention. Then he gripped the yoke and made airplane noises.

"You know it's getting on toward supper time," Sam said. "Maybe we should call it a day. I can finish up here tomorrow."

"Sam, can we go for a little walk on the beach?"

"Sure, you bet. Let's pick things up first, though."

They walked along the access road through the dune line and headed northeast alongside the lazily breaking rollers, Joshua stopping frequently to investigate a glinting shell or a ghost crab den. There were several four-wheel-drive pickups and sport utilities parked on the beach, rods propped in PVC pipe sections hammered into the sand, monofilament lines like spider strands angling out into the surf, people sitting patiently in comfortable old clothes on tilted canvas chairs and gazing out to sea as the nearest star slowly rolled aflame down the sky behind the island.

They stopped to watch a small gang of porpoises loping along out in the glassy swells. They had a baby with them, and it would come almost all the way out of the water as it surfaced frequently to breathe, two adults never more than a few feet away from it.

Something over by the dune line caught Joshua's attention and he ran ahead to investigate, stopping to look closer and then turning to shout, "Sam, Sam. Come here quick."

It was a Bonaparte's gull, trapped in one of the holes of a translucent plastic six-pack retainer, fluttering and flopping, trying to free itself and move away from them.

Joshua looked up at him with an anguished expression and said, "You gotta help him, Sam."

"Let's step back a way so he'll calm down. We're in his space here. Why don't we both help him?"

"I don't know how. Oh, please, Sam."

Sam took off his denim shirt, walked up to the bird very slowly and spread it out all the way over him, and the covered bird settled down.

"Okay. Now you feel through the cloth and hold him. Try to watch out for his wings. Try to fold them back against his body and then hold him still."

"Sam, I can't do it."

"Yes, you can. Just take your time and be careful."

After considerable nervous fumbling Joshua managed to do it. Sam got out his pocket knife. "Now, what we'll do is work the cloth back enough so we can see that plastic around him. Hold him, and let's do it slowly."

When the plastic was exposed Sam slipped the blade in deftly and slit the plastic. He stepped back. "Okay, Josh. Let him go," thinking *let's hope he didn't break a wing trying to get loose earlier.*

When Joshua stepped away the gull fluttered and

screamed raucously, trying to regain some of its avian dignity, then it flapped tentatively and took off, faltering a little but flying.

Joshua wiped his hands on his pants absently and grinned widely, watching the bird fly away.

"Good job," Sam said.

"Yeah," Joshua said.

Sam stuffed the plastic in his back pocket and picked up his shirt.

The fourteen-mile-long Ocracoke beach was generally less plagued by litter than most mainland beaches Sam had seen—there were lengthy stretches where on most any given day you would not find another human footprint much less a discarded Bud bottle—but there were always some don't-give-a-damn sun worshipers finding their way out here. Back one day in July when a hard blue sky had been crowded with magnificent cumulus clouds with dazzling sunlight shafting down among them, turning their fringes into liquid light, dappling the sand and the sea with shadows, Sam and Valerie had been sitting side-by-side on a plaid blanket in one of the cool cloud shadows, loosely hugging their knees, watching rain veils drift along the horizon, and tasting the clean breeze, Joshua industriously excavating some imaginary dinosaur bones nearby.

A young couple with a baby had a sheet spread out thirty feet away. When the couple got up to go they left a loaded diaper, three empty Coors cans, several cigarette butts, and a crumpled yellow chip bag on the sand. She was carrying the baby, her purse, and a diaper bag. He had the big cooler and the wadded-up sheet.

Valerie brushed some sand from her dark sculpted calf, got up, and walked over to stand in front of the departing couple, halting them. "You see my friend over here?" she said in a friendly tone, pointing back at Sam. "He's a captain in the Environmental Rangers. He's off duty right now, but if you leave that mess back there on the beach he won't have any choice. He'll have to issue a citation and I think the fine can go up to three hundred dollars. Especially with the diaper. That would make it a Class Two offense."

Sam sat on the blanket trying to think mean and nasty behind his sunglasses.

The young woman shifted the baby to her other arm and said, "He was gonna go back and get that in just a minute. Wasn't you, Jack?" The young man went back and picked up all the trash and stuffed it inside the cooler. They left in a hurry, looking sullen. Damned law was everywhere these days.

Sam drove Joshua into the village. They ate heaped-up foot-long dogs washed down with vanilla milkshakes at a picnic table on the grass outside the Burger Box, Joshua then asking for a butterscotch sundae and sharing spoonfuls with Sam as the boy demolished it with efficiency. Sam took him home.

They played a game of Monopoly at the kitchen table, Joshua getting gleefully wealthy as Sam cheated carefully in the boy's favor, and then Sam ushered him in for his shower, helping him towel off and climb into clean pajamas.

Joshua made popcorn in the countertop microwave, dragging his stool over so he could reach, and they settled in on the couch. Sam had rented *Heidi* mostly for the boy and *Rooster Cogburn* mostly for himself. He never tired of watching the interplay between the aging John Wayne and that most noble of ladies, Katharine Hepburn.

When Valerie came home she found them asleep on the couch in the darkened living room, one of those old shoot-'em-up tapes that Sam liked so much playing in the VCR. Sam had his boots off and his feet crossed on the coffee table, his head thrown back and his mouth open, snoring mildly. Joshua was curled in under Sam's protective arm, his head pillowed on his small hands against Sam's rib cage.

She leaned her shoulder on the door jamb, her arms folded, and just watched them for a while, the light from the TV playing over them.

My men, she thought.

IRA COHN SAT DOWN NAKED IN A STRAIGHT CHAIR AT THE doorway of the book-and-file-piled closet he called his home office for IRS purposes and booted up his Micron, which occupied one whole shelf. He logged onto the Internet quickly, thinking *I knew it would come to me.*

He ran a search under "the wild west", got a long list of sites, scrolled down a few pages, and clicked on "Outlaws". Bingo. There it was.

Sam Bass.

He picked up a half-eaten Milky Way from the mouse pad, took a bite, and started reading fast, automatically condensing and editing as he went.

Born 21 July, 1851, Indiana. Parents died when he was small. Raised by a skinflint uncle who worked him like a dog and denied him an education. Ran away by building a raft and floating down the Mississippi to Rosedale. Worked hard as a teamster, driving supplies to Texas. Bought a fast sorrel mare which he raced, winning enough bets to quit his job.

Discovered hard liquor.

Took up with Henry Underwood, who had fought with Jennison's Jayhawkers against Quantrill's guerrillas and obviously knew guns. They got into a minor scrape and lit out, chased perfunctorily by the sheriff. Bass became a partner in a freight company and later in a mine, which failed, whereupon he fell in with a pack of serious gunmen. They robbed seven Deadwood stages in the Black Hills in 1876 and '77. In the fall of 1877 the gang boarded a train at Big Springs, Nebraska, and relieved it of $60,000 in newly minted twenty-dollar gold pieces, collecting another $1,300 from the startled passengers.

The gang split up but Bass gathered another group of hardcases to establish an enterprise of robbing Texas trains. Among his business associates were old friends Henry Underwood and Frank Jackson, along with apprentice thief Jim Murphy. Subsequent train robberies soon made Sam Bass the most notorious and most wanted outlaw in Texas—dead or alive—but he eluded a small army of lawmen by moving from one hideout to another in the back woods of Denton County.

There was the inevitable shootout, at Salt Creek, and Bass had to escape with others on foot, which only increased the rewards posted for them.

Turned out Jim Murphy was working for the authorities, hoping to get himself and his old man extricated from certain previous charges, and hoping for at least a goodly chunk of the posted rewards. Even some members of the hardened Texas Rangers would later revile Murphy for his betrayal of the Bass gang.

Murphy was present in July of 1878 when the Bass gang met to plan a robbery of the Round Rock, Texas, bank and he got a message out to the Rangers, who were waiting in force when the gang rode into town.

There was a big-time gunfight. A deputy shot Bass through the hand. Then he was trying to calm his skittish horse when a Ranger knelt in an alleyway, took deliberate aim, and shot Sam in the back. Frank Jackson spurred his horse and grabbed the reins of Sam's mount. They rode hard, Bass hunched over and bleeding but still trying to shove cartridges into his pistol, down an alley, up a rutted street, and on out of town.

Jackson, also wounded, managed to guide his friend's horse for several miles. Near Bushy Creek, Bass told Jackson to stop. Jackson helped his friend down onto the grass under a tree. Bass told Jackson to leave and take what gold they had between them. Jackson reluctantly obeyed and rode away, vanishing. The Rangers found Bass that night, still alive, and carried him back to Round Rock.

They questioned him at length about his associates but he gave them nothing of value and on 21 July, 1878, at the exact age of twenty-seven, Sam Bass passed into history.

Could be one of two things, Ira thought. Either it's just a coincidence. Most likely that. Or, for a guy who thinks of himself as a cowboy—Mrs. Stilley had volunteered as much—for a guy who even *looks* like a cowboy, for a guy like that, Ira thought, Sam Bass could be an alias.

This was two days after he had returned to Raleigh from Ocracoke, three days actually, it being two in the morning now. It had been the previous afternoon before he had found time to tap out a draft of the piece about the rescue. He had handed a hard copy to his wrinkled editor along with the stack of contact sheets, asking about the possibility of submitting an expense voucher for the past weekend. The editor had ignored the expense plea, had skimmed the piece, had used her loupe to quickly scan through the photo proofs, circling just four possibles with her fat felt-tip, then had grunted once and nodded, which Ira had taken as high praise. She wanted him to use a digital camera, but he stubbornly preferred to use print film, developing and printing it himself in the newspaper's darkroom. The piece would run the following Sunday as a half-page spread with a single photo on the front of the *People* section, above the fold.

Ira Cohn was stark naked.

Whereas Samantha Blackstone was stark nude, standing there now in the doorway of his bedroom down his short apartment hallway, hipshot and wearing only an extremely exasperated expression, her arms crossed under those Olympian breasts.

"You tell me I remind you of some Greek sculpture in some old ruin called The Porch Of The Maidens," she said. "Well, all right. Then you jump up and tell me, hey, hold it. *Wait* a minute. Now you're playing with your *computer*? You have about *five* more seconds before I hold my nose and go into your filthy kitchen and try to find a *nutcracker*." She pointed an elegant finger inside the bedroom and stamped her foot on the carpet. "I suggest that you shut that thing *off* and get your skinny, hairy butt back in here right *now*."

"Okay, okay," Ira said, shutting down the Micron.

Within twenty minutes the scene in his cluttered bed-room did indeed resemble certain aspects of the wild west, and he had clean forgotten all about Sam Bass.

6

LOUIS STRAKE STOOD ON HIS HIGH DECK, HIS GLASS WALL
at his back, looking down at the evening traffic that flowed
in perpetual two-way streams along the Tappan Zee Bridge
stretched across the darkened Hudson. The house was in
deep shadow and the last of the sunset torched the tops of
buildings across the river, lights coming on all over. Behind
him in the dazzling chandeliered dining alcove off of the
huge indirectly-lit great room, Dorothy was preparing the
large glass table for him, his wife, and his daughter. He
was still wearing his newest double-breasted light gray
suit that had been tailored for him in London, and a dark
blue silk shirt with matching tie, having returned home
just under two hours ago from an art scholarship benefit
luncheon that he and his young wife Elaine had hosted at
the Strake Gallery of New Age Art in the city. The gallery
was Elaine's private passion, a gift from him, and it had
even required a little creative bookkeeping on the part of
his accountants to keep its profit minimal this year.

He was fifty-one and an even six feet tall, with a

once-muscular build now just beginning to show signs of softening, but he worked hard to keep kept himself toned and trim, and he had his thick silvered mane of hair brushed high and straight back and sprayed in place.

His glass wall was constructed of five massive French doors with a row of fifteen-foot-high Palladium windows above, and the view from up here on the Palisades—the house half-cantilevered from sheer rock two hundred feet above the river—was spectacular. He especially enjoyed it at night, when he could look across toward the glitter of White Plains, and see the awesome sky-glow downriver that was being sprayed up from Manhattan.

Gazing out on all those lights made him feel a part of the sprawling, intricately-tentacled economy that nourished one of the greatest urban concentrations on the planet, and for a time he could almost forget that he often moved in a much darker world.

He also maintained another immaculate house in Vancouver and what he called his getaway cottage in the Bahamas, a neutral place where he often conducted business. His gleaming seventy-two-foot Hatteras was cruising down the Intracoastal under the guidance of his captain and two crew people to Fort Lauderdale. It would stay there for an electronics upgrade before moving to the Bahamas, where it would be constantly ready for him and certain of his associates throughout the winter.

One of the French doors opened behind him. "Excuse me, sir," Dorothy said quietly, "I believe Mr. Montgomery just drove up."

"The man's name is Montgomery Davis. I've told you

that before, dammit. It's Mr. Davis. When will dinner be served?"

"Yes, sir. In twenty minutes."

Strake walked erectly inside, strode across the high-gloss oak floor to the vaulted entrance foyer, and opened one of the heavy stained-glass doors. Davis, looking bear-like in a black windbreaker, was coming up the lit walkway, having parked his maroon Mercedes with its dark-tinted glass.

"You're late," Strake told him.

"The traffic was bad."

"That's something you allow for. Keep your jacket on. We'll go out on the deck."

They crossed through the great room. Strake opened one of the center French doors, and they walked out onto the deck, Strake closing the door behind them. He moved over to put his hands on the rail and look down.

He knows I hate heights, Davis thought.

Davis was a big man in his late forties with the face of a football coach set off by a razored black goatee. He had seen much violence in his long career and feared few humans or circumstances, but heights made his head light and his breathing rapid and shallow.

"Come here," Strake said. There was a breeze picking up. There were no poles under the deck, just big struts angled back into the rock. The traffic on the bridge far below moved in beaded strings of light. Red one way, white the other.

Davis walked over to stand near the rail, not touching it. Controlling his breathing.

The deck was softly lit from built-in fixtures under the railing and from the glow of the lights spread out down there. Davis thought he could feel the deck boards shifting slightly under his feet.

Strake reached into the inside pocket of his immaculate suit jacket and took out a newspaper clipping. He held it out to Davis. It was carefully folded to show a photo of a lanky man standing in a side-hug with a short woman. Davis took his time studying it, bending slightly to hold it down under the railing lights, and unfolding it to scan the article. The piece was actually an abbreviated version, though Davis couldn't know that. Picked up by the Associated Press Syndicate, it had run in one hundred and twelve different papers across the country, mostly as filler on slow news days. Davis straightened and said, "It's the Cowboy. On some island in North Carolina."

"Yes. Keep the clipping."

"Louis, are you sure this will be worth—" But Strake cut him off with a quick stop-it gesture.

"We have the transaction in Miami next week," Strake said. "That should take no more than three days."

Tina, Strake's chubby three-year-old daughter, wobbled across the floor of the great room all by herself in her fluffy pink slippers and Pooh pajamas, clutching a yellow-dressed doll in one arm. She stopped, slapped the window with her free hand, and waved. Slapped and waved. Slapped and waved. Slapped and waved. Leaving finger marks on the glass.

Strake smiled and waved back. Elaine hurried over, not looking out onto the deck, took Tina by the hand, and led her quickly away.

"When we get back from Miami," Strake said, absently watching his shapely young wife and his daughter through the glass wall, "I want you to go down there and kill him."

Davis was still for a moment. Then he said, "All right, Louis."

Strake turned back to rest his hands on the railing and look off. "I'm telling you now so you can think about it. Take Winston and the new one, Donny. The son of a bitch knows you and he may have seen Winston, so Donny will be useful, and the young man has his specialties. The pay will be thirty thousand. Half up front. I don't care how you split it. You pay your own expenses. Be careful. Set it up. And, Montgomery . . ."

"Yes."

Strake turned his head to look intently at him, those black eyes glittering now in the up-light.

Like a pissed-off wharf rat, Davis thought, *or a rabid Doberman, standing there stock still just before it charges you.* He wondered, not for the first time lately, why he had worked so long for this guy who wanted people to think he was high-class but who was really no better than any number of other men who lived in Davis's world of shadows and violence. Strake tried to talk like a lawyer but Davis thought he wasn't fooling anybody. He was like two different men, one this fake slick talker and the other basically just a street thug like himself.

"I want him to see it coming," Strake said, speaking slowly. "You listen to what I'm telling you. First, I want you to break him. Take your time doing it. I want him to hurt. I want him to see it coming."

"We'll take care of it, Louis."

"Now, you'd better be going. I'm sure you have some young lady waiting. You always do. And the traffic is bad."

7

SAM BASS WAS IN THE PRIVATEER WAITING FOR VALERIE to get off work, nursing a draft at the bar and watching a "Gunsmoke" rerun on the muted TV, the jukebox belting out "Wild Thing" at the eardrum-splitter setting. The back bar above the multicolored ranked bottles was decorated with plastic muskets, a draped Jolly Roger, and crossed sheet-metal cutlasses.

He had visited the Stilleys that morning. Adele had driven Ralph back home the day before. The hospital had been holding him to monitor his heart condition. Over Adele's fresh-ground coffee in their gleaming much-gadgeted contemporary kitchen the three of them had gotten into a discussion about their favorite old dirty jokes, one on Ralph's top ten list being the quickie about the man who walks into this book store and asks the buxom young lady at the counter, "Excuse me, do you keep stationery?"

"Well, right up until the end," the young thing replies demurely, "but then I just go all to pieces."

Sitting there in the chrome-plated kitchen, Sam had

suddenly realized that it wasn't so much the jokes but the way Ralph's face wrinkled up and he chuckled and wheezed wholeheartedly to himself that set you off. Sam had promised to come back one evening in a week or so with Valerie and Joshua so Adele could serve a royal feast to all of them.

Mrs. Bradley was watching Joshua. Valerie would meet Sam here tonight and they would dance for a while and he would have one or two drafts while Valerie had a vanilla Coke and they would talk with their friends who drifted in. If Ruben Dixon happened by with his Coast Guard comrades Sam planned to coerce them into lightening their wallets considerably buying rounds for the house.

A sunburned muscular man in his thirties with shaggy blond hair and a dimpled grin walked up to stand beside Sam and shouted, "You Sam Bass?"

Sam nodded.

"How about we go in the back, have a little talk."

Sam shrugged, got off the stool, carrying his draft, and followed the man into the pool room where there were somewhat fewer decibels in violent collision. They took a corner booth. The room was decorated with more mementos of that era when the difference between a pirate and a privateer had been only a matter of one's political alliance. In other words, Sam often thought, things haven't changed all that much since then. *Same old thing; different century.*

There were framed plaques on the walls summarizing the exploits of buccaneers Stede Bonnet, Henry Morgan, Jean Laffite, and Calico Jack Rackham, and of buccaneer-persons Anne Bonny and Grace O'Mally. In a central place of honor on the back wall in a large ornate frame there was somebody's acrylic rendition of the infamous Blackbeard, dressed all in black, his fists resting on his hips and his booted feet set wide, wearing a ferocious expression, his pigtailed beard wild, smoldering hemp fuses sticking out from under the brim of his tri-corn hat, a brace of black powder pistols behind his wide belt.

Blackbeard—Edward Teach to his mother and his business associates—had owned a big house on Ocracoke, often called at the time Blackbeard's Castle, and another house up the Pamlico River in Bath, where he entertained neighboring planters and certain politicians lavishly and kept one or two of his fourteen wives. The hefty Teach had finally been wounded twenty-five times and then be-headed in a savage fight just off Ocracoke in November of 1718 by a crew sent on the mission by an angry Virginia governor, North Carolina's Governor Charles Eden by all accounts having been a well-paid friend to the pirate.

One legend had it that on certain dark nights you still might catch a glimpse of Blackbeard's eerily glowing body swimming in the sea near the island in search of its head, and indeed, on murky nights when phosphorescence made the breakers burn green and the wet beach sand lit up mag-ically if you ran on it—a glowing disc at each footfall—the legend was a bit harder to disbelieve.

There were lingering rumors of buried treasure here-about or thereabout along the Carolinas coast and as far north as Tangier Island in the Chesapeake Bay, certainly not dis-claimed by regional tourism interests. A research company had recently discovered what were most probably the remains of Teach's biggest vessel, the forty-cannon *Queen Anne's Revenge*, in shallow water just down the coast near Cape Lookout, where it had rested for going on three centuries, and there was already a popular exhibit of rusty barnacled shot, a blunderbuss, and other artifacts set up in a Beaufort museum.

There was a small sign nailed to the booth wall that said: HAVE YE FLOGGED YER CREW YET TODAY?

"Bo Brinson," the man said, extending a large callused hand across the much-pocket-knifed booth table.

Sam shook it and said, "You need a pilot?"

"Why I'm here. I'm only a plain fisherman. Tryin' to make a livin'. Like my daddy and his daddy. From over to Pantego. You want another beer?"

He signaled the waitress, an attractive young brunette dressed like a wench in a full burgundy skirt and white peasant blouse, and she blushed coyly when Bo turned the full force of his white-toothed dimpled grin on her. "Lord, but you're a pretty thing," he said. "Would you please bring this gentleman here and me two drafts? I'd be obliged if you'd put that on a tab for me."

When the waitress was out of earshot, Bo grinned at Sam and said, "You ever done any fish spotting?"

"No. But I suppose there's always a first time."

"That's the attitude. Me and Spud, my partner, ran my boat over from the mainland this afternoon. She's a twenty-three-foot skimmer. Beamy, with a flat bottom and square bows, a tower in the center, and a jet drive. Built for the shallows and to run out a corral net in a jiffy. She's tied up at the public dock and we got us a room at the Pony Island. We'll be goin' out before daybreak. We're after sea mullet. Fish about three foot long. Speedy. You find them in schools anywheres from a dozen to a whole bunch. It's the time for 'em. Over in Japan they like their caviar, you know? Well, sturgeon's harder to net every year all around the world and I guess mullet roe don't taste half bad if you go ahead and call it caviar, so the price of sea mullet's gone up ten times what it was. There's some good money to be made. Thing is, now everybody and his white-haired grandmother is after 'em. Fisheries got so they can't sleep at night worryin' we'll net every last one of them poor sea mullet in just a week or two. So now they say you can't spot 'em from a plane. You with me so far?"

"I think so."

The waitress came over with the drafts. It seemed as though the top of her peasant blouse had slipped a bit since her last visit. She took enough time wiping off the already clean booth table so that Bo, and incidentally Sam, absolutely could not fail to notice she was most generously endowed and unfettered by a bra.

After she left, Bo said, "See, I figure what Fisheries don't know won't hurt 'em. Say you was to spot for us, Sam. We'd use a radio—I expect you got a spare hand-held for us or you can borrow one—but we never say fish or hey, there they are or like that. We use a code. We meet someplace tomorrow morning off behind the island here and you fly around, take a good look. Right now you'll find 'em in around the marshes on the sound sides of the Banks, sometimes in no more'n two foot of water. No problem for us. We can get 'em if they're swimming in dewey grass. Easy to see from up there. Not near so easy from down here. Okay, you spot a school you say on the radio, 'I think I'll take a aerial picture of this interestin' feature here.' Or whatever. And you circle. We blast over there and you fly right over that school and wag your wings." He illustrated by wiggling a meaty hand in the air above the salt shaker. "We get close enough to see 'em from my tower and then circle 'em with the net. You go off and gas up or whatever. Drink a beer. Give us no more'n thirty minutes to get 'em in the boat, ice 'em down in boxes, and re-rig the gear. Then we do her all over again. We get all our boxes full to the top, we hightail it for the fish house over to Hobucken. We meet right here tomorrow night and you get paid cash money. I'd say a fair share of the take, but you got no way to know how much that will be, so let's just say a straight fifty an hour, from the time you crank her up until you shut her down."

"Even if you don't catch anything?"

Bo turned up the wattage on his dimpled grin. "Now, there's about no chance of that at all, with you spotting and us netting. I'm flat the best there is around here. You just ask my old gray-haired momma. I figure we could use you regular for the next two weeks. Maybe longer. We all make us some money. What do you think?"

Sam's kitty was getting skinny. The Cessna was coming up for its annual inspection in a month, and needed new tires. His rent would soon be due and he was running up a fuel tab at the village station. With fall coming on there were fewer tourists on the island so his sightseeing business had dropped to almost nothing. The motels were filling up with anglers drawn by the excellent seasonal surf fishing, but they seldom booked a charter other than an occasional emergency sortie to bring in a load of fresh bait. He'd been working on the new rental cottage for Brad Meekins but had been waiting for two days now for Brad to take his pickup over to the mainland on the ferry and bring back sheet rock, paint, wallpaper, and moldings that were needed.

"I think you could talk the varnish right off of this table," Sam said. "The best thing would be for me to give you GPS coordinates, but that's out because any bureaucrats listening would be able to home in on the spot, and so would any of your competitors who figure out what's going on. There's a way it could work fairly well, though. You could get one of those day-glow-orange ball caps. They've got some over at the General Store. I've got a cheap old square radio at home that has four bands on it, including the aviation band. You can't transmit but you won't have to. I'll give you a frequency to monitor. That way, if anybody asks you can just say you've been listening to George Strait on the FM band; nobody can say you've been in touch with an airplane. We meet at some location like you said. I fly over you and say something. If you hear me you put on the cap. Also, when you're wearing the cap it means you haven't seen, or heard about, over your marine radio, any kind of law boat nearby. I may have trouble sorting out one kind of small boat from another up there. I'll go look for the fish. If I seem to be moving too far away you start up and follow along. If I spot a school I won't circle. I'll climb up where I can see both you and the spot where the school is. Then I'll say 'downwind for one-nine' or some other number. That means you steer a compass heading of one-ninety. When you get within a hundred feet or so of the school I'll say 'final for one-nine.' These are common phrases that could be coming from anywhere in the eastern part of the state. Except I won't be giving my aircraft number, of course. I want to sound like some farmer who's lazy about his radio procedures, maybe flying near some dirt strip. You take your hat off when you want to quit for the day. If I disappear it will probably be just to get fuel at Manteo or somewhere. Stay where you are until I come back. If I don't show in, say, an hour and a half you know you're on your own. Tomorrow night you come here, but I won't be around. Talk to Tony, the bartender. He'll tell you my hours flown and you pay him. He'll get some money for his trouble. You give me a number where I can reach you or get a message to you if you're not still at the Pony Island."

"You came up with all that just now? Sam, I like the way you think. What we could do is we get one of those hats for Spud, too. That way if we both got 'em on it means one thing. If just one of us's got it on it means something else. If the one who's got the cap on is standing in the bow it means something else, you see? If he's in the stern—"

"Let's keep it simple, Bo."

"Maybe you're right. So. We got us a deal?"

"We'll give it a shot. One thing, though. Since this is illegal, I couldn't shut my conscience up for anything less than seventy-five an hour."

"You sure you ain't a lawyer, Sam? You're a bandit. But, okay. Far as what's illegal it's all how you look at it, ain't it? Over in the South China Sea they go fishin' with bombs they make from fertilizer and fuel oil, or they use cyanide. Kill *every* damn thing in a couple acres of water, including the coral. Go around after and pick up what they want and leave the rest. All we're trying to do here is put a little food on my gray-haired momma's table and maybe pay some on her QVC bill."

"Sure."

"Look, Sam, how many people you know always drive the speed limit? Nobody, right? They sell a lot of radar detectors. Come April fifteenth after supper how many people shave a little on their taxes? Everybody, right? Tell Uncle Sam they been givin' fifty a week to their favorite church. They got to go look one up in the phone book. That trip to Busch Gardens or Mickeyworld with the kids and the mother-in-law was really a job interview. Waitresses only make about seven bucks a month on tips. Everybody's got a real short memory about any cash they take in, don't you? Hell, I do. The smart ones, they get some bookkeeper with a real good pencil sharpener knows all the rich man's tricks, and he helps 'em shave even more. Then the bookkeeper lays a big flat fee on 'em but his secretary really only spent two hours ticklin' her computer mouse to work it all out. The secretary herself's doing a little thing with the petty cash the bookkeeper don't know about. You give the lawyers and the doctors and the politicians and the inboard motor mechanics half a chance, what are they gonna do? Carve just as big a slice out of you as they can make off with, is what. Here's another one.

"How many people you believe have cheated, or thought

about cheating, on the little lady, or on the hard-workin'
hubby? Everybody, right? It ain't been that long ago the
President's getting laid in the War Room, sayin' hey, no,
baby, don't touch them *red* buttons over there and the next
thing you know there's a half-dozen cruise missiles headed
for some empty mountain in Afghanistan. President says
later hey, honest to gosh, I wouldn't think of even trying to
spell Lewbowski, much less prod one.

"Hell, Sam, there's outlaw in us all. And we like our
big-time outlaws, too. Look around. If Blackbeard was
nothin' but a cold-hearted thievin' killer, why's he treated
like some kinda hero up and down this coast? He walked
in here right now his money'd be no good and everybody
would want his damn autograph. You know that's so. Who
got more write-ups, Mother Teresa or that asshole Gotti,
what'd they call him, the Dapper Don? They did what,
half a dozen movies on the godfather thing. Just about
everybody in there was a stone killer, but we sit down and
watch it all on TV with the kids, see do they discover hap-
piness in the end. What was that most popular series on
TV for a while there? The thing about the mob jerk with
his wife and kids and his shrink, right? What's the most
important thing in this whole country? Money, right? And
the more you've got the less everybody else cares about how
you got it. Where did the money come from to build Las
Vegas? How did the Kennedy millions get started? Who's
been in control of the big labor unions for so long? Who
gives a damn, right? You get rich enough you get to live by
the rich people's rules, and they're not the same as for you
and me. Not many rich men in prison. You're poor like us

you just got to bend the law a little once in a while so you can afford your oatmeal. Oh, yeah, there's a touch of outlaw in us. We can't help it. Just makes life interesting, you ask me. And like I say, all you and me are trying to do here is put a few beers on the table."

He watched the wench collecting empties from booths across the room. He grinned broadly, appraising her, and said as an idea evidently firmed up, "Yessir, there's a bit o' the pirate in us all."

"You know," Sam said thoughtfully, "there was a movie called *For A Few Dollars More* some years back. Clint Eastwood and Lee VanCleef are fast-draw bounty hunters. They team up to go after a pack of killers led by a psychopath called Indio. Over a drink they settle on the terms of their temporary partnership and VanCleef tells Eastwood they don't want to be shooting each other in the back."

"Meanin'?"

"Like I said, I think you could talk the varnish right off of this table in about twenty minutes, or the skirt right off of that waitress over there in about two, but we don't want to talk about our temporary deal here to anybody. It's just you, Spud, Tony the bartender, and me. Let's not even tell your gray-haired mother, okay? I won't talk about it, either. We don't want to be shooting each other in the back, do we?"

"Hey, sure thing, Sam," Bo said, thinking *you know, the son of a gun even looks like a cowboy*.

Later that night, back at the Pony Island, Spud having been asked to take a walk for about an hour, Bo and his companion having done serious damage to a fifth of Jim

Beam chased by a quart of beer, Bo, still wearing his new orange hat and his underpants, managed to turn off all but one of the lights. Step two of his three-step plan. The wench, by now minus both peasant blouse and skirt, stood unsteadily there in her panties in front of him, pushed down his tight jockey shorts, and said woozily, "Wow."

Bo, looking down at himself, said, "What you just done 'minded me of that movie."

"Which movies zat?" the wench said.

Grinning dimpledly, Bo said, *Free Willy*.

The wench fell over onto the bed giggling.

And across the village, as they lay sleepily side-by-side in the darkness, just holding hands now, Sam said, "Val, do you declare all your tips?"

"What brought *that* up?"

"Just wondering."

"Of course I do."

"Thought so."

She was quiet a moment, and then said, "Well, you know, almost all."

DAYBREAK FOUND SAM BASS RUNNING NORTHEAST ON the Ocracoke beach, not another soul in sight, no sign whatsoever of other human habitation on the planet. The pain had left him three miles ago as he'd gotten his second wind and his fluidly pistoning legs were moving easily on their own now, his sneakers hardly touching down, flicking small regular sprays of sand up behind him, his forearms swinging slightly in perfect rhythm in front of his chest, the clean cool air flooding his lungs and softly brushing the light perspiration from his forehead. He could picture his endorphins and all his other little blue-jeaned peptides in there tumbling out of the bunkhouse raring to have a real old-fashioned rodeo. Who needed a sixty-dollar set of magnets?

The stark nightmare had visited him again last night, filling him with the same sickening hollow hopeless feeling of being rooted to the spot, unable to do anything, and he had jolted awake sweating in the dark room with Val stirring but not awakening beside him.

With the light of day it had all receded into what now seemed a distant past.

The stars had faded and the eastern horizon was afire, long motionless ropes of cloud flaming up crimson and scattering sparks onto the sea. The clear new sky overhead might have been from a perfect day a thousand years ago. The sea birds soared and cried, greeting the day around him. He ran on for another two miles beside the glossy swells that each curled and broke with that ancient sustained sound that, if you closed your eyes, could be the exhalation of some magnificent coruscating serpent risen up from foraging the deeps. Then he turned back, never slowing until forty-five minutes later when he drew abreast of the line of early anglers parked on the sand near the cut through the dunes onto the access road near the airstrip. He walked to the plane feeling loose and refreshed.

He did a leisurely walk-around, singing Waylon Jennings' "Good Hearted Woman" and thinking of Valerie.

He climbed in and went through start-up, the airplane trembling alive under his hands. He taxied out onto the strip, lined up, went through the run-up checks, and pushed the throttle smoothly all the way to the stop. The Cessna faithfully gathered up her skirts, the prop invisible now, and sprinted nimbly down the faded dashed line, faster and faster until Sam felt the familiar little shot of euphoria as she broke free and left the world of groundlings behind. The dunes fell away below and they climbed into the morning, the cool air rushing in through the wing root vents, the four-cylinder Lycoming bellowing strongly and the prop slapping the breeze smartly. The Cessna's previous owner

had fitted her with a 180-horsepower engine, thirty horses
more than she'd been born with, giving increased speed and
useful load capacity, and Sam had often had cause to bless
that fact when he was hauling three well-fed adults or getting out of a short strip somewhere.

The sea was hammered gold off to his left and the wide
Ocracoke Inlet was spread out ahead. Beyond lay the narrow twelve-mile-long stretch of uninhabited Portsmouth
Island. He flew low over the ghost town of Portsmouth
at its northern tip, a jumble of old overgrown buildings—
crumbling cottages, the tiny post office, a boarded-up
store, the shuttered abandoned Coast Guard station off by
itself—and the one pristine structure left, nestled up near
a cluster of yaupons, the small white chapel that a few volunteers from Ocracoke kept painted and in good repair,
also tending the little fenced cemetery in a shady grove out
behind it.

Earlier that year Sam had visited there with Ralph,
Adele, Valerie, and Joshua, in a borrowed eighteen-foot
flat-bottomed outboard skiff, picking their way through
the maze of shoals for what seemed ten miles—although
the dead town was actually only five miles as the pelican
flies from Ocracoke village—backtracking twice, nudging
aground three times, and finally tying off to the crazily
tilted Coast Guard station dock, a loose shutter up on the
old gray structure banging a slow unsettling cadence in the
hot light breeze.

They had explored the silent town for only fifteen
minutes before the big seasonal deer flies had found them.
Capable of inflicting a bite like a sudden match burn, the

persistent maddening flies had driven them from the island in haste, Sam trying to keep them brushed away from
Joshua until they could get the boat clear.

Portsmouth had once long ago been home to inlet and
sound-side pilot skippers, seamen, fishermen, and their
families, but the spreading shoals had gradually choked
the island off and now it was left to its birds, its tough
scrub trees, its dunes cloaked with shivering sea oats, and
to its ghosts.

Bo and Spud were in the skimmer, anchored where
Bo had said they would be, two miles southwest of the
inlet, three hundred feet from the back side of Portsmouth
Island. There were stacked boxes in the skimmer and
some big coolers. There were other small boats scattered
out but none near them. Sam flew over them at six hundred feet, thumbed the yoke switch, and said, "I have the
traffic in sight."

A bright orange ellipse appeared atop Bo's shaggy head
and Spud started hauling in the anchor line. It was hard to
tell for sure from this altitude, but Sam could have sworn
Bo was suffering from a pirate-class hangover. He flew on
and let down to three hundred feet, searching along the
ragged back side of the island, but the bottom was colored
in many hues, shadowy and grassy here, rippled lighter
sand there, sky glare all over the surface, and it was difficult to see much, though he thought that twice he caught
glimmerings in among the marsh grasses.

This wasn't going to work. So he let down to a hundred feet, and the details below began to sort themselves
out, although they of course appeared to be going by much

faster. He slowed and put down ten degrees of flaps. Right there, by a small grassy hummock. A tight school of good-sized sleek gray fish. Maybe ten or fifteen. Had to be them. He climbed up in a long arc, taking a quick fix on the hummock, noting that it was roughly aligned with a particular notch on the island shoreline. He flew back over the skimmer at five hundred feet, thumbed the switch, and said, "Downwind for two zero."

The skimmer sprouted a white feather at the stern and bounded away on the heading, Bo's bright orange hat prominent. Sam watched the boat's progress but then checked around for any other airplanes and waited until it was almost too late, the boat no more than seventy-five feet from the school, so he said quickly, "*Short* final for two zero." Bo got the message and immediately chopped his throttle, Spud kneeling in the bows pointing toward the hummock. The boat sped up smoothly again, curving out in a neat fast circle, net tumbling off the stern over an upright H-shaped support, quickly surrounding the whole hummock. Bo was good, give him that.

Sam flew off down the Banks for a few minutes, then came back. The skimmer was waiting by the hummock, the net piled neatly back inside, and Spud was icing down what looked like a fair number of fish in boxes. When Sam went over, Bo took off his hat and swept it wide as he bowed deeply like a Musketeer.

It was working like a charm. Sam found another two small schools over the next hour and a half, then while they were boating the most recent load he flew down to Michael J. Smith Field in Beaufort—named for the commander who lost his life aboard the *Challenger* in 1986 and who had first learned to fly here—to get a Coke and top off the fuel.

By early afternoon the skimmer was heavily filled and Bo took off his hat. The boat looked overloaded and too low in the water, but when Bo poured the coals to her, she labored up onto a sluggish plane and headed west across the sound for the fish house in Hobucken. Sam flew over a last time, climbing, and both Bo and Spud looked up and pumped their right fists enthusiastically in the air. Sam smiled to himself and banked away for Ocracoke.

That night Sam went to The Privateer just before closing and sat at the bar. Tony drew a beer for him and gave him a greasy envelope. Sam took the cash out and counted it, leaving two twenties on the bar top. Tony nodded and said, "Bo says how about five miles up the back side of Ocracoke from the ferry docks at eight tomorrow."

It went well for three days, Bo and Spud hauling large loads off to Hobucken each day. On the morning of the fourth day it was overcast but the ceiling was above twelve hundred feet and the wind was light. Sam met the skimmer in the gray light farther down the islands where the sound narrowed to just four or five miles across between the Core Banks and the waterfront hamlet of Sealevel on the mainland. Sam had only been flying for half an hour when he saw Bo wave his hat in agitation and then stuff it away out of sight.

Sam scanned the few other small boats in the area. There were two more skimmers, a runabout with two men in it using rods, and what looked like a very old couple in an ancient outboard skiff working crab pots, but there was no boat that he thought might be law. Then he looked around in the sky and there it was, another light plane at his altitude, a Cessna about two miles back and closing. It looked to be another Skyhawk. Good. It likely had the smaller engine.

Sam kept at five hundred feet, making a shallow left turn to see if the other plane followed. It did, as though it were on a tether, so he straightened out, heading west, retracting the ten degrees of flaps he had out and fire-walling the throttle. He picked up even more airspeed as he put her into a shallow descent, flying inland over the desolate salt marshes of Carteret County, bearing left because there was a Marine Corps bombing range not far off to his right now and he didn't know if it was currently hot, keeping the transponder off and leveling out at two hundred feet, looking back.

The trailing Cessna was losing the race, falling farther and farther behind into a gathering haze until finally it was out of sight. Sam turned northeast along the mouth of the Pamlico river, skirting the bombing range, then let all the way down to fifty feet, below Cherry Point's radar, and headed east across the sound for Ocracoke, pulling the power back to normal cruise.

After he landed he went to the Burger Box and treated himself to a Monster Special with a thick slice of Vidalia onion and a goodly slathering of their excellent chili on it, along with a large root beer float. He topped off the plane with auto gas using the cans in the back of the Jeep, did some more on the dry wash job, then stopped in to talk with Brad Meekins for a while. Brad planned to go over on

the Cedar Island ferry the next day for materials, so Sam
said he would be available for work the day after that, intending to call Bo that night and strongly suggest they cool
it for a few days anyway until the coast seemed clear again.
He stopped at The Privateer to tell Tony his services would
not be needed until further notice, and to have two leisurely drafts while he watched the national news on Fox, then
he went shopping for a few things he needed at the General
Store. After all, he had a few dollars in his jeans, although
they smelled a little fishy, and his kitty was no longer so
undernourished.

When he got back to his cottage in late afternoon
there was a spotless Dare County Sheriff's car parked in
his yard.

He parked the Jeep alongside and got out. Deputy
Thomas Mason, a very black man in his fifties with a dust-
ing of close-cropped white at his temples showing under
his squared-away billed cap, got out of the patrol car and
adjusted his tie minutely. "Somebody ought to cite you for
the muffler on that thing," he said, not smiling. "But that's
not why I'm here. Hello, Sam."

The crisply-uniformed Mason gave the impression of
being starched top to bottom. Not a large man, he never-
theless projected a certain aura that warned those nearby
not to try anything dumb. Sam had done a favor for him
a few months back. He'd been in Manteo dropping off a
charter party when the distraught Mason had asked him
which way he was headed. Sam had asked where do you
want to go, and Mason had explained that his brother had
been in a wreck in Wilmington and was in poor shape at

the hospital, so Sam had flown him down there, refusing any fee, and had grabbed a courtesy car at the FBO to drive them to the hospital at some speed. They had been too late, but Mason had been grateful to at least get there to offer immediate comfort to his sister-in-law and three nephews.

"Good to see you, Thomas."

Mason leaned back slightly against the fender of his car and crossed his well-toned arms. "The reason I'm here, Sam, is because I've got a certain lady friend with Fisheries. Do you know a man named Bo Brinson? He's a real charmer who might have been an award-winning con man, or one ace of a used car salesmen, if he wasn't a fisherman."

"Well, you know, Thomas, I meet a lot of people—"

Mason held up a palm and said, "Never mind. Wrong approach. I'm sorry. Let's do it this way. My friend in Fisheries called me this morning. She's been calling around asking questions of several people on our side of the legal fence in the coastal counties. She told me that they—the good people at Fisheries—think that an aircraft, coincidentally marked a lot like yours and with a last tail letter that could possibly be an S for Sierra, may well have been spotting sea mullet recently, specifically for this one Mr. Brinson. It seems he's been uncommonly fortunate to have hauled in big loads of mullet for several days now, earning for himself and his partner respectable sums."

"Thomas, I—"

"No, now, let me finish my little story here. It's just getting interesting. It seems that spotting for the big mullet is very much against the law. Fisheries would dearly love to hook somebody perpetrating this particular crime in order to gaff him, string him up, and take an eight-by-ten of him to serve as a clear example that will cause all potential sea mullet rustlers out there to perhaps get religion. With any kind of proof, they can cause an offending aircraft to be grounded and levy a fine of up to five thousand dollars against its hapless pilot."

"That much."

"Yessir. That much. The thing is right now they have no real proof of any such nefarious activity, other than Mr. Brinson's rather sudden good fortune and the fact that when a Fisheries patrol plane happened upon a suspicious aircraft this morning the aforesaid aircraft hightailed it for the hills, so to speak, like a turpentined tabby cat. That's the end of my story, and I believe I told it well."

"Yes, you certainly did."

"I'm gratified you agree. Now, of course, if anybody should ask, the reason I put off serving several warrants today and drove all the way down here from Nags Head, waiting for fifteen minutes to catch the forty-minute Hatteras ferry ride and waiting for another thirty-two minutes right here with only that shabby cottage to look at—with the result that even if I use the lights and siren on the way back I will probably still incur the wrath of my wife when I am late for supper yet again—was to ask on behalf of my lady friend that if you should happen to stumble over any information about mullet spotting in the Ocracoke environs would you be so kind as to let the good people at Fisheries know?"

"Sure thing, Thomas. I'll be on the lookout. Always

glad to help the forces of justice."

"Yes. Well, it's been good talking to you." Mason tipped the bill of his khaki cap and with a creaking of highly polished leather got back into his car. He started up, then rolled down the window. "One other thing," he said.

"Yes, Thomas?"

Mason said, "That was a damned stupid stunt you pulled about the Stilleys."

"I know."

Mason extended his hand out the window and Sam shook it.

"I'll see you, Thomas, and thank you."

"Don't mention it. And I mean that."

As the patrol car pulled away briskly the phone started ringing in the cottage.

"I'm callin' for Beaufort," the female caller said.

"Excuse me?"

"Well, yor his new pilot ain't you? Sam Bass? Beaufort Brinson from over to Pantego?"

"I'm his new pilot?"

"What I just done *said*. I didn't figure you could stay a pilot if you got hard of hearin'. Or maybe you just plumb forgot you was his pilot."

In North Carolina the town of Beaufort was pronounced Bo-fort, while a city of the same spelling in South Carolina was called Bew-fort. Sam had only heard of something like the latter version ever being used for a man's first name, that from an older movie about a real-life southern sheriff by the last name of Pusser who, as he recalled, did not walk softly and who did carry a very big stick.

"You must be Mrs. Brinson, Bo's mother?"

"Lucinda Brinson. That's me. Think you can remember that?"

"Bo has a message for me?"

"Only reason I'd be callin' you, ain't it? 'Less you notion I want a date at my age. Mr. Sam Bass, maybe you want to go get a checkup, see if *they* think you're slippin', too. Beaufort says—lessee, I got it wrote down here somewheres—Beaufort says you ought to lay low for a few days. He'll get over there in a day or so to pay Tony what's owed for this mornin'. That's it."

"Mrs. Brinson, would you please tell Beaufort something for me?"

"If it ain't too much. This's long distance and it's my seventy-five cents, though I can surely remember when it used to be a quarter."

"Just tell him he needs to hang up his orange hat. He'll know what I mean."

"He done said you might talk in some kinda code. That's it, then?"

"Well, ma'am, you could tell him I might be in touch one of these days about going into the used car business."

"Don't hardly think so, mister. Beaufort's daddy done that sorta thing on the side. It's what got him locked up in the end." And she hung up.

Sam could hear it now. A story would soon be circulating among all of the six or seven other double-wides that constituted most of Pantego that there was this dim-witted pilot over to Ocracoke, who was also likely a car thief, trying to get their good ol' Beaufort into trouble.

9

ON TUESDAY EVENING, THE LAST DAY OF THE ILL-FATED sea mullet caper, Valerie said, "I've got an unexpected day off tomorrow and I don't think playing hooky for one day will hurt Josh, so what about you?"

"I don't have much that really needs doing," Sam said. "What do you have in mind?"

"Josh has never seen Kitty Hawk and I haven't either. Could we fly up there and maybe bring along a picnic? This warm weather isn't likely to last much longer and we might as well enjoy it while it's here."

"A pilgrimage to aviation Mecca. Haven't been there in a while myself so I guess I could use a fix. We can spread a blanket by the airplane for the picnic. How about half a dozen two-inch-thick chicken salad sandwiches and a quart or so of your ginger iced tea? You might want to bring something for Joshua and yourself, too."

"Aye, aye, sir."

"You don't say that to your pilot."

"What do you say?"

"You say chicken salad, ginger tea, or me?"

"And you get to say all three, is that it? Uh-uh. What if I said you have to pick one?"

"Let me think on that for a minute."

"I will slap you."

"What are you two talking about?" Joshua asked.

Later that same evening Montgomery Davis walked into a smoky Newark, New Jersey, tavern called Little Italy. He recognized Winston in the shadows by the sheer mass of the man, sitting at a small back-corner table lit with a single candle. Davis went over, sat down, and ordered a Heineken from the waitress.

Winston weighed two-eighty and his immense strength matched his size. He normally moved slowly, never smiled, and had the flat face of a bulldog, which always made him look angry. There was a vague resemblance to the famous prime minister and he smoked fat cigars, hence the name that many had come to know him by. At 48, he was a year older than Davis and had similar experience. Davis had used him as extra security a number of times and on con- tracted hits twice.

"We have a contract," Davis said.

Winston lit a cigar from the table candle and said, "Where and when?"

"Down in North Carolina. I'm driving. We'll leave early on Friday morning. I'll pick you up at four in front of your house. Bring two changes of clothes and a piece.

There'll be one more along with us."

"What? We taking out some crew?"

"Just one man. They used to call him Cowboy. I don't think you know him."

"What's so special about this guy it takes three of us?"

"Strake just wants to be sure. And he wants this one bad."

"That's what you said about the last one. Look, you want a plate of pasta?"

"No, not here. I had food poisoning once and that will make you picky."

"Fuck it. You gotta die of something," Winston said, and signaled the waitress.

The next morning was a study in the infinite, the sharp ocean horizon off Ocracoke seeming so far away that the shores of timeless Africa had to be just beyond, the sky so transparently deep in the early sun dazzle that you could sense the panoply of diamond-hard stars out there across the light years.

Sam, Valerie, and Joshua took off in the cool air and climbed to three thousand feet, where the view was soul-filling. Beyond the blue sound the flat mainland spread away westward, its shores a lacework of bays and river mouths and marshes giving way to great swaths of pine forest and scattered cultivated fields. The sea outshone any precious metal, and the narrow Banks curved away northward. Below, the surf fanned the miles of sand in its patient eons-old rhythm, and there were long swatches of beach elder that would turn butter yellow with the onset of the cooler nights and the winter quietly amassing to blow southward, planning to hitch a ride on the jet stream. Kitty Hawk lay 90 miles ahead and Whiskey Sierra cruised smoothly at 120 miles per hour.

Valerie was in the right seat beside him and Joshua was belted into the back seat on one of Valerie's throw pillows so he could see out well. They all wore headsets. Joshua's forehead was pressed against the right rear Plexiglas and he was looking down absorbed in his own thoughts. Sam was keeping to the sound side of the Banks so both Valerie and the boy could have a good view of them down to the right.

They passed over the inlet at the northern tip of Ocracoke, a white ferry grinding north with a load of cars heading for the docks on Hatteras Island, trailing a long scarf of gulls. The 208-foot black-and-white spiral-painted lighthouse looked stately standing on Cape Hatteras, whose spear shape pointed toward the ship-tripping shoals that ran out under the swells.

They flew past the three settlements of Salvo, Waves, and Rodanthe, with wide Oregon Inlet eighteen miles ahead now, spanned by its long, graceful high-rising bridge.

"Why don't you fly for a while?" Sam asked, so Valerie took over the dual controls. Sam had been acquainting her with the plane in the hope she would begin formal lessons one day soon, provided he could find a way to pay for them. He knew a semi-retired flight instructor based at the Billy Mitchell strip on Hatteras and believed that she and Valerie would fit well together. So far Valerie had shown a cautious enthusiasm for the idea, and she had a natural ability for it, handling the yoke smoothly and confidently, never over-controlling.

After she had been flying for a few minutes, banking through a few mild S turns, she said, "How do you do a loop?"

"Yeah, Mom," Joshua said. "Do one, do one, please."

"Your mother's just kidding, Josh. Or just joshing, kid. Looping isn't listed anywhere in this airplane's owner's manual."

"Oh, come on, Sam," Valerie said over the intercom. "You were a lot more adventurous last night."

"I don't remember doing any loops."

"Well, you sure made *me* do a few."

"What are you two *talking* about?" Joshua said.

Past Oregon Inlet the beach began to look like most others, crowded with cottages, condos, motels, restaurants, beach wear and souvenir shops, and strip malls with the ubiquitous robot teller machines. Within a few short decades, Sam had thought, shopping will be so damned convenient we'll just stay right at home and a truck will pull up out front each month with all the stuff they think we ought to have and just draft the money out of our accounts. After the thirty trial days we'll ask them to please come in and pick up the one or two items we've discovered we can probably live without. For those new offerings remaining that will require some choice, fourteen shopping channels will be beamed directly into our frontal lobes.

Ahead at Whalebone Junction a road ran over to good-sized wooded Roanoke Island and from there on over to the mainland. Roanoke was where Virginia Dare had been spanked to life, the first child born to English parents in America. It was also from Roanoke that Sir Walter Raleigh's deposited 1587 colony had vanished without a trace, and it had been re-vanishing nightly in season for the last six decades now in an outdoor drama called *The Lost Colony*.

Sam thought old Walt might easily have solved the mystery way back then had he but chatted in sign language with some of the Indians who maybe tended to look on these islands as their own turf and on the white man not as an innocent colonist but as an overdressed arrogant invader. What would the English have thought of a 1587 gang of painted breech-clouted Indians who piled out of their seagoing canoes carrying their weapons and set about erecting a walled village on the outskirts of London? Would they have been wholeheartedly welcomed as colonists with lots of wampum to spend? Or diced up and dumped in the Thames?

There were other examples of olde-tyme English arrogance not far away. Inland over in New Bern back in 1770, Royal Governor William Tryon celebrated the completion of the lavish home meticulously designed and erected for him on sufficient appropriated acreage. It was a home reminiscent of the finer estates in grand old England, replete with manicured decorative gardens wherein one could stroll for an afternoon contemplating one's superiority, and so having worked up a royal appetite, perhaps then pausing long enough to instruct one of the kitchen persons to put some extra creature to sleep and serve it up as a side dish with that evening's usual feast.

While the Tryon family was thusly roughing it in the

new colony, their extensive complex maintained at considerable effort by a goodly staff of sweating servants, the homespun-clothed people of New Bern, many of whom were practically eating dirt just to stay alive, derisively called the pretentious piles of bricks "Tryon's Palace". Today, restored to all its original splendor, what was now proudly called Tryon Palace drew gaggles of videotaping tourists while in areas of the city not on the official tour routes, only blocks from the Palace, some of the citizenry still practically ate dirt.

Roanoke was also the home of the Dare County Airport at Manteo, so Sam called them on unicom to advise that he was transiting their air space to land fifteen miles beyond at the small First Flight strip. Down on the right was the 140-foot-high khaki-colored Jockey's Ridge dune, with three multicolored Rogallo hang gliders poised along its crest looking like prehistoric butterflies. He talked Valerie all the way down to entering a right downwind at eight hundred feet for the runway two-zero end of the narrow unattended strip. It was not the easiest place to land, Sam's *Flight Guide* listing a road and unmarked power lines on the runway two approach and a tower, tank, and trees near the runway two-zero approach, the listing also cautioning to watch out for deer. But a small challenge was probably appropriate considering the location.

Sam took over and concentrated on making the best landing he could, aware that the shades of the famous duo might be standing in their habitual suits and ties nearby atop Kill Devil Hill watching. Wilbur runs a hand over his bald pate and says, "What do you think brother, a six?"

And Orville tugs his handlebar mustache and says, "Aw heck, let's give him an eight, Curly. One or two of our landings that day back in oh-three weren't all that great either, remember?"

Sam parked the plane on the apron and set the hand brake. There were no facilities at the strip, and no other planes.

They walked along a narrow paved footpath that wound up the broad grassy flank of Kill Devil Hill, Valerie in front followed by Sam and the boy. Joshua was holding Sam's hand and skipping. Appraising Valerie, Sam quietly sang Waylon's song about a good-looking long-legged Nashville woman with a sexy wiggle in her walk.

Back over her shoulder she said, "Well I'm from Cherokee, mister, but you got the rest right."

"Why did you leave the reservation, miss?"

"Find me a handsome rich white boy. Make all my dreams come true."

"Well," Sam said, "I'm white."

"What am I?" Joshua asked.

"You're a wild Indian," Valerie said.

The sixty-foot granite monument atop the low summit carried a beacon on its top. It had been years since Sam had been here—way back before what he thought of as his other life—but this place still held almost a religious significance for him. They took in the view from the hilltop. A warm breeze was building and a few fair-weather cumuli were gathering in the western sky.

A re-creation of the original rustic wooden camp, where the brothers had slept nightly in burlap slings hung from the rafters above their workbenches, lay below on the plain. Near that there was the contrast of the glassy modern memorial building. Small rough granite boulders marked the distances of the four powered flights made on December 17, 1903, the first just twelve seconds long and covering 120 feet, the fourth and longest lasting 59 seconds and going 852 feet.

"Come on," Sam said. "Let's walk down to the memorial building."

"Good goo, those are big kites," Joshua said as they walked inside. Replicas of the 1902 glider and the 1903 powered Flyer were perched behind ropes in the center of the building.

"They sure do look like kites," Sam said, "but if you look closely you'll see they're built a whole lot better than any kites you've seen." Crafted of spruce and ash braced by wires, with wings covered by finely-sewn muslin, the Flyer achieved roll control by means of a hip cradle that was attached to wing-warping cables, the cradle strapped onto the pilot who lay prone on the lower wing of the stacked pair. The pilot controlled pitch with a vertical wooden lever in his left hand that changed the tilt on the biplane elevator extending from the front. The landing gear were simple ski-type skids. A twelve-horsepower four-cylinder gasoline engine spun twin pusher counter-rotating propellers through a simple chain-and-sprocket drive. The Flyer had a forty-foot wingspan and weighed 600 pounds.

It was a sophisticated creation based on hard-won theory and solid scientific fact, and Sam explained the finer points to Joshua, who paid rapt attention.

Exhibits behind glass around the walls displayed the

engine design, yellowed notes and calculations, and various mementos. There was a wooden wind tunnel that the brothers had built.

There was a single photograph of the first powered flight. It had been snapped with Orville's camera by their volunteer helper John T. Daniels, who knew little of photography, but Ansel Adams could hardly have done a finer job of it.

Sam pointed at the image and said, "Look at that, will you? Talk about a Kodak moment."

The priceless old photo showed the Flyer going away two feet above the far end of the rail, Orville prone on the lower wing, the elevators canted to begin climbing free of the shadow on the sand, the props blurred as the engine belted out all it had, the big wings tilted only slightly to the left, and Wilbur standing tensely to the right, his right elbow bent, his suit jacket blowing back in the wind, watching his brother and their creation intently, and every fiber of him obviously projecting go . . . go . . . go . . .

Sam, standing there imagining the staccato clatter of the four-banger engine and the icy wind in his face and the brace wires thrumming as the Flyer came alive, knew he had often felt much the same flush of elation that Orville had certainly felt at that moment captured so dramatically on that two-cent rectangle of emulsion a century ago.

Outside, Sam spread a blanket on the grass near the plane, anchoring it with two quart containers of aviation oil, and they shared a late lunch, Joshua asking questions about the Wrights and Sam trying to answer them accurately.

"It's all because of avian envy, you know," Valerie said.

Sam, his cheeks full of her excellent chicken salad, raised an eyebrow.

"Well," Valerie said, "what if there hadn't been any birds around to show us it was even possible in the first place? People watched them for centuries, and envied them. Right up there on top of that hill, on top of that monument, on top of that beacon, there ought to be a sculpture of a little sparrow in flight."

Out over the beach, the gulls seemed to cheer raucously in agreement.

When they took off from the narrow strip and banked away southward, Sam could easily imagine the wraiths of Orville and Wilbur standing there side by side in their suits and stiff white collars and ties on the summit of Kill Devil and, in the manner of every pilot everywhere, shading their eyes with their hands and looking up as an airplane went by.

* * * * * *

"It's about time you got back to me," Davis said. "Are you at a pay phone?"

"Yes," Donny said in his childish voice.

"All right. Hang up and call me back in ten minutes at . . ." Davis gave him the number of a pay phone in the parking lot of the convenience store at the corner of his street.

When Donny called exactly ten minutes later Davis said, "We have a contract. One customer. Some way out of town. I'll be driving. Bring two changes of clothes and your own tools; everything you described to me two weeks ago."

"Do I know the customer?"

"No."

"What's the pay?"

"We'll talk about that later. I'll pick you up at your place at four-thirty Friday morning."

"That's pretty short notice."

"You should have called me back sooner. Do you want to go or not?"

"Hey, I'll be ready," Donny said. "Hell, I'm always ready."

Sam kept a rusty bicycle on the small back porch of his cottage and, like many other people on the island, often used it to run errands. That early Thursday morning was chilly and dew-damp when he rode through the village to the new rental cottage.

He unlocked the place, checked over the materials Brad had left inside, and spent the morning hanging sheet rock and taping joints, whistling to himself.

At eleven-thirty he dusted himself off and rode the bike over to the school. Joshua had secured his promise to have lunch with him. Valerie was at work. The boy lit up when he spotted Sam waiting outside the classroom that contained the combined kindergarten and first grade classes. Outside on the wall near the door there were twelve crayoned sheets of paper taped up in a row. The theme was obviously outer space, going by the multitude of stars and fiery-tailed rockets. Sam found Joshua's rendition and immediately judged it to be the best of the lot.

Joshua's teacher, a pleasant woman just shy of 50, greeted

him with a smile. "I'm Belinda Jameson," she said. "So you're the famous Mr. Bass. We've heard quite a lot about you. Joshua ranks you right up there alongside Spiderman."

"He's a pretty neat kid."

"He surely is. They all are. They keep me young. No matter what happens, they start out each day as brand new. They don't hold any grudges and everything they learn carries a touch of magic for them. Their imaginations are just boundless."

She led the line of them down the hall to the small cafeteria, Sam walking along beside Joshua, who proudly held his hand. They went through the food line, Joshua slipping an extra two peanut butter cookies onto Sam's tray. Joshua gave his lunch number to the woman at the end of the line and Sam paid for his own tray.

Trying to fold his frame up enough to sit beside Joshua at a table on one of the somewhat undersized chairs was a project, but he managed by keeping his legs out to one side.

"What have you been doing today?" he asked the boy.

"Miz Jameson showed us how to make paper-bag puppets. I made a bear. And I'm in the count-to-fifty club. Sam, you can take one of those cookies with you for a snack this afternoon."

"Thanks, I will. I saw your space drawing. Good job."

Joshua smiled and took a bite of cookie and a gulp from his small carton of chocolate milk.

A little girl across the table frowned, squinted, and said, "You're all dusty, mister."

"Oh, yeah, well, he's been working," Joshua said.

"My favorite color is purple," the girl said. "Are you

Joshua's daddy?"

"No, honey, I'm just a good buddy."

"Where *is* Joshua's daddy?"

"He can't be here."

"Does Joshua *have* a daddy?"

"Eat your broccoli," Sam said.

The girl made a face and said, "I think broccoli's ahs-gusting."

A hefty freckled boy at the table behind them tugged on Sam's sleeve and said, "Listen, listen. My Mom got this at a yard sale." The boy pushed a button on his plastic watch and the watch said, "A baby's gotta do what a baby's gotta do."

"Well, I hear that," Sam said.

The smiling teacher walked by and said, "It's nice to have Mr. Bass here with us today, children, but we still have to eat our lunches, now, don't we?"

Sam took a sporkful of his broccoli.

After lunch he stopped at the General Store and looked over their small faded stock of movies. It wasn't exactly Blockbuster. He picked out the gritty Elmore Leonard story *Last Stand At Saber River*, with Tom Selleck as a rancher fighting to reclaim his land and the love of his wife after the Civil War.

He chose another one he hadn't watched in some time, Larry McMurtry's *Streets Of Laredo*, a sequel to *Lonesome Dove*, about the flinty Texas Ranger Captain Coll, played by James Garner, who goes on a hunt for a blond, blue-eyed Mexican boy filled with an icy killing rage and wearing the chilling aura of a cocked pistol, loose on a murderous rampage with a scoped rifle. Sissy Spacek plays a two-dollar whore gone good who eventually saves Coll after the ruthless boy killer leaves him for dying. Sam liked to watch the intense tale to study the ribbons of honor and raw courage running through it. That was probably the distilled reason he liked to watch most of the great westerns. He remembered two particularly powerful lines from *Streets Of Laredo*. Commenting on the fallen Coll, Sheriff Goodnight says, "Life's but a knife edge, anyway. Sooner or later a man slips and gets cut."

"Mr. Bass, I think you're the only one on the island who rents those old westerns," Danielle said, "so why don't you just keep these for a week or so? No extra charge."

"Waaal, I'm surely much obliged, ma'am."

"That's a terrible John Wayne."

"Hey, you recognized him, didn't you?"

He worked until dusk, stopped in at The Privateer for a cheeseburger plate and a draft, and then rode home in the early darkness to clean up. Valerie would be working until nine and Mrs. Bradley was watching Joshua. He might as well spend a while doing much-postponed paperwork while he watched one of the movies.

At eight-thirty his beeper went off and he called Val at Sonny's. She asked if he'd eaten and he said more or less, so she told him she would grab a bite after work and then head home, inviting him over for coffee and some of her date-filled cookies at about nine-thirty.

"Talk about an offer I can't refuse," he said.

Joshua was in bed asleep by the time he got there, and Valerie had just bid goodnight to Mrs. Bradley, who always walked to and from her house two sandy streets away.

"You know, I wouldn't mind watching Josh on nights like this," he told her.

"No. It's not right to expect you to do that on a regular basis and besides, Mrs. Bradley needs what little I pay her."

She lit three clustered candles on the coffee table and set up a classical CD to play low on her stereo. She arranged a plate of date cookies, poured fresh-brewed coffee, and they got comfortable on the couch.

"How was your day?" he asked.

"Bearable. I found out the Geo's heater won't work but you know I bought the car from Fred, Sonny's brother-in-law, so Fred says he'll fix it. I'll go over to his place in the morning, he'll bring me back here, then take the car to work on it. Josh can ride the school bus. So, no problem. It's my regular day off and I know you need to work, so I'll spend it cleaning up around here and making something really special for our supper."

She turned toward him with a serious expression. "I've been thinking, Sam. I can get a few days off around Christmas when Josh is out anyway. What would you think about us going up to the mountains? I want you to meet my people. Especially my grandfather and my uncle and his family, but the others, too."

"What if they don't approve of me?"

"Besides the facts that you're a white cowboy and they're at least part red Indians, and you pilot a machine that's only about the size of that Wright Brothers' string bag, and you do a really bad John Wayne, and if left to your own devices you'll eat like a junkyard dog, and you drive

a Jeep that sounds like a stock car race, what's to not approve of?"

"You Indians can be cruel. I should have known. I've
seen enough westerns. I guess this means we're getting serious here."

"If you're saying you haven't *been* getting serious, mister, you can put that cookie right back on that plate."

Sam smiled and took a bite of cookie and a sip of coffee.
"All right. We'll fly if you want to. Maybe get them to pick
us up at the airport? Maybe there'll be snow. Josh would
like that. Me, too. We can build us a snow person."

"Uncle John has a pickup I know he'll let us use. Don't
worry, you'll like them all. Grandfather will probably ask
you a lot of questions. He's from a generation when the
elders were supposed to seriously question a young man
who was courting one of their young women."

"Tell me about the Cherokee. And tell me about your
family. And about what it was like growing up on the reservation."

She drew her legs up and sat sideways facing him, leaning her head slightly onto the couch back, her hair glossy in
the candlelight and her dark eyes bright, looking off into a
distance, and her voice became mesmerizing.

"Cherokee was never an Indian name. We were the
Tsalagi, and we went back ten thousand years to the first
people who wandered here from Asia. When DeSoto
came in 1540 there were twenty-five thousand of us and
we claimed as our hunting grounds an area that's now parts
of eight states. We were the strongest of all the Southeast-
ern tribes. We never lived in teepees. Our cabins were

made of poles woven with split river cane, covered with smooth plaster that was mixed from clay and grass. We had a chief and he had a right hand man and a speaker. The center of government and ceremonial life was a seven-sided council house that held five hundred, and there were seven clans. Seven women sat among the council members and their opinions were always respected. The fire in the center of the council house was kindled from seven woods. The council held court and made laws, but most crimes were avenged by members of the wronged family. If we had to fight against the Creek or others the *Kalanu* or war chief would take over, there would be a ceremony, and the warriors would vow never to stain their weapons with the blood of children or old people or those who couldn't defend themselves.

"Each family had a hothouse for ceremonies and for keeping warm through the coldest nights. A family would gather around the fire in the hothouse and a myth-keeper would recite the sacred legends. One of my favorites that my grandfather told me when I was a little girl, by the fireplace in his house, was about *Ataga'hi*, the magic lake. Way back up in the high mountains, beyond the headwaters of the Oconaluftee River, there's a place where if you listen carefully, mingled with the whisperings of the wind in the trees you can hear hundreds of birds in flight. If you fast and you say all the right prayers and you keep a vigil through the night, at dawn you might catch a glimpse of *Ataga'hi*. Its waters are violet, fed by springs in the cliffs, and there are many birds and fish and the tracks of animals are all around. If a bear is wounded by a hunter and if he can make his way to the lake and go in, when he comes out his wound will be healed. It's the medicine lake of the animals, so they keep it invisible from humans."

She told him how, in 1738, half their number had died of white man's small pox. And how, in 1838, 7,000 soldiers had driven 17,000 Indians from their mountain homes to the Oklahoma wastelands, 4,000 dying on the way from exposure and brutality.

"That was the Trail Of Tears," Sam said.

"Yes. About a thousand had hidden back in the high woods of the Smokies. An old man named Tsali was one of the last to be rounded up, with his wife and two sons and his brother-in-law Lowney. As two soldiers were pushing the small group along a trail one of them prodded Tsali's wife with a bayonet. Tsali talked to his sons and Lowney quietly in the old tongue, setting up a trap for the soldiers at a bend in the trail. Tsali feigned tripping. Lowney and Tsali's son Ridges grappled with one of the soldiers and Tsali swept the other soldier's legs from under him. As the soldier fell his gun went off and he shot himself in the head. He was dead. The other soldier ran, and Tsali and his family went way back up into the caves. The Army put out word that if Tsali and his family would give themselves up the remaining Indians would be allowed to stay in the mountains. Old Tsali surrendered and they sentenced him, Ridges, and Lowney to die."

She took a sip of tea and said, "The soldiers stood them against three trees. Tsali said if he was to be shot he would rather it be by his own people than by the white soldiers. They gave guns to three Indian men and Tsali told them to go ahead and do it. So because of Tsali and his son and brother-in-law, we have that scrap of land in the most rugged part of the mountains. The Qualla Boundary.

"It was beautiful and strange growing up there. You have this wonderful ancient culture always pulling at you, and then you have a friend whose father earns extra money by letting tourists take his picture standing beside a little tin teepee, wearing a plastic war bonnet from Taiwan. Some of the teenagers have this current of anger running in them. The reservation is dry because liquor really does poison something in us, but bootleggers near the reservation sell bonded booze and moonshine so there's alcoholism. There's depression. But there are also some of the finest wood carvings and jewelry and pottery and crafts you'll find anywhere. We still have a chief and a tribal council, all elected now. Some of the people try to preserve what was best about the old ways. And it's so beautiful up there, the worst of the land for cultivating when they let us keep it, but some of the most attractive, it turns out, for the tourists. There's a big casino. Draws white men and their money from all over. I'd like to think it's the Indian way of getting even, but the place carries a white name and I'd be willing to bet that if you took a close look at the books you'd find the profits are mostly white, wouldn't you?

"No bet from me," Sam said.

"You know my parents died when their pickup slid on a patch of ice on a mountain road, and I went to live with my grandfather, Wasituna. He taught me a lot. He's an expert with the blowgun, and one of the last who knows how to make the best kind from river cane and the darts for it from locust feathered with thistledown. He can still kill a running rabbit with it at sixty feet. His father, Goingback Lightfoot, lived to be a hundred and five, and was said to be a witch, maybe the last of the *Tskilegwa*.

"Grandfather Wasituna tried to teach me *Kituhwa*, the old language. I can understand it but I'm not fluent. I have a book by Mary Chiltoskey and I'm teaching Joshua a little of it, trying to relearn it myself. So many of the words have a simple beauty in them. *Talutsa* means basket. Bluebird is *tsaquoladagi*. Colt is *aginasoquili*. Wolf is *waya*. Candle is *ukanawiatsvsdodi*. Don't attempt that one." She smiled. "A white man can tie a knot in his tongue just trying it."

"Why did you wind up out here on the Banks?"

"When Joshua's father was killed in a car wreck, in the same way my parents died, I just had to get away. At least until I could go back some day and really see the beauty in the mountains again. I drove east until I couldn't go any more. And it's beautiful here, too, in a different way. Open and vast and most often serene. But now I want to go back to visit, and I want them to meet you."

"I'll be proud to meet them, Val."

"Good. We'll make plans tomorrow, then. Right now . . ."

"What?"

"You know, there's a last time for everything we do in life," she said quietly with a sadly wistful smile and with the candle flames burning like a long-ago council fire in her *Tsalagi* eyes. "We ought to live with that in mind but we never seem to. Let's go into my bedroom, Sam Bass, and make love like it's for the very last time."

BEFORE DAYBREAK ON FRIDAY THE SILVER BLAZER MOVED south on I-95 at no more than five miles per hour over the posted limit. It was rigged for surf fishing with four expensive rods standing upright in plastic tubes mounted to the front bumper. The four-wheel-drive vehicle had oversized all-terrain tires and had, in fact, been used frequently for surf fishing jaunts by its owner, D.J. Arguillio, brother-in-law to Montgomery Davis. Tonight it was wearing a different plate, though.

Davis was driving. He had a stainless Bodyguard Airweight .38 Special in a soft oiled-leather shoulder holster under his black windbreaker. With only a five-round cylinder and a two-inch barrel it was strictly for close-up. It had a shrouded hammer that would not snag if you had to get the gun out fast. He favored revolvers because, although they tended to be inherently loud and could not be effectively silenced, they left no brass behind. You didn't have to rack a slide back to chamber the first round and cock it like with most autos, either, and it never jammed like a lot of the autos could. Just snatch it out and pull the trigger.

Winston was in the front passenger seat wearing voluminous jeans, a red plaid flannel shirt, and a dark blue windbreaker. He was left-handed. He had a compact blued-steel nine millimeter Smith auto that fired twelve rounds and had an ambidextrous external safety. It was in its nylon clip-on belt holster, with an extra magazine in an attached pocket, slid under the seat now because it made him uncomfortable to wear it. There was a silencer for it in his suitcase. He was looking idly out the side window into the passing glare of Newark Airport. The bright landing lights of three huge airliners were spaced out maybe two minutes apart floating down the glowing night sky. Four big jets were single-file on a taxiway awaiting takeoff clearances, their tall tails lit up like billboards.

Donny was in the back seat studying a North Carolina map with a Mini-Maglite. He was of average height and thin with a blond military buzz cut. He wore desert fatigues. All of his gear was behind the backseat in a black leather sports bag, along with their suitcases, a yellow plastic tackle box, and a metal tool box. Wrapped in an old blanket there was a stubby Heckler and Koch MP5 SD2 submachine gun with a fixed butt stock and a built-on silencer, with two 30-round box magazines full of 9mm Parabellum.

Donny was twenty-nine but he spoke in a little-kid voice that irritated Winston. He said, "How about we stop for coffee?"

"All right," Davis said. "After we get on the turnpike I think there's a service area not far along. Past Rahway. We could use gas anyway. We'll talk there. I want to spread out the map."

"There are some things I don't like about this setup," Donny said.

Davis said, "We'll talk at the service area."

"The first thing I don't like it's an island and there's no bridges."

"You hear the man?" Winston said laconically, still looking out the side window. "Shut the fuck up."

At the service area Davis parked under a light close to the fast food restaurant. There weren't many other cars in the lot. He got a ten by thirteen manila envelope out of his suitcase and told Donny to bring the North Carolina map. Inside he pointed to a booth well away from the few other people, near a window. He told Donny to go get the coffees and some donuts or whatever else looked fresh. When he got back Davis spread out the eastern three folds of the North Carolina map and used his finger to trace the highway.

He spoke in a lowered voice. "We'll take I-95 all the way down here to Rocky Mount, then go east on sixty-four, about a hundred and twenty miles to Roanoke Island and on over to the islands. There's only one road, route twelve south. At Hatteras, maybe sixty miles down, there's a free ferry over to Ocracoke. Then it's fourteen miles to the town at the bottom end of the island. The town and the island have the same name. Once we're on the island there are three ways off. About every three hours there's a toll ferry out of the town harbor southwest to Cedar Island here, a two-hour-and-fifteen-minute run. There's another toll ferry from the harbor three times a day east over to

Swan Quarter on the mainland. A two-and-a-half-hour run. Last ferries leave from the harbor at five-thirty in the afternoon. The other way is back over on the Hatteras ferry at the north end of the island, only a forty-minute run and it's free. No ticket people to deal with and probably more cars, so we're less likely to be remembered on that one. Last one leaves seven-thirty at night. Then nothing leaves until five in the morning. The schedules are in here." He tapped a big finger on the manila envelope, which bore a label from the North Carolina Division Of Travel and Tourism. "I've got a room reserved two nights at a place called the Pony Island under George Harvey, paid up with a money order, in case we get stuck outside the ferry schedules. It's possible they could seal off the island by shutting down the ferries, but there's no law of any kind on the island, just a few Coast Guard people."

He folded up the state map and drew another small map out of the packet in the manila envelope. It was of Ocracoke Island and the village. He spread it out. "The town is grouped around the harbor pretty much. Airstrip's about a mile from the town center. He lives right there, on Teach's Lane. There's a picture of him here in the envelope. Strake had it. It was taken at some party in Vancouver. There's another recent shot in a newspaper clipping. He's using the name Sam Bass. Strake found out he drives an old Jeep Wrangler; the plate number's in here. I want you both to study it all—the pictures, the notes, the layout, the ferry schedules. You've got time. We won't be there until at least late afternoon. So get it all in your heads."

Winston nodded and took a sip of his coffee, which was

so hot it scalded his upper lip. It smelled like battery acid and tasted like something worse, like electrically-burned plastic. "There oughtta be a fuckin' law," he said.

"What?" Davis said.

"This coffee's poison."

Donny said, "I don't like the part about drawing it out. This is a small town of what, how many people?"

"About six hundred and fifty," Davis said. "But there'll be a lot of surf fishermen on the island right now, too. A lot of strangers."

"Okay, this is good cover we've got with the fishing thing. But it's still just a small town. Everybody knows everybody. We take too long at it somebody finds out and calls the law. Maybe they come in a chopper. It's no damned place to get stuck, out there. I say we go in, do it quick and quiet, and get out."

"We'll have to see how it plays," Davis said.

"Another thing, Strake's not paying all that much," Donny said in his little kid voice. "You said fifteen, right?"

"That's right," Davis said. "Five each when it's done. He pays me. I pay you."

"There's a thing we could do," Donny said thoughtfully. "That's your brother-in-law's tool kit in the back?"

"Yes."

"Well, I've got a small pair of wire strippers and they might work but better would be a pair of side cutters. I'll take a look in the tool kit. We do the job, then take off a finger. With the cutters it's just a quick clip."

Winston raised a thick black eyebrow and said, "You want like a fuckin' souvenir?"

"We put the finger in a clear Ziploc bag I've got. Easy to get rid of any time if we have to. Don't get any prints on it. Just throw it out the car window with a paper towel.. We bring it back to Strake. Tell him we took a few fingers off before we did the job. The guy begged and screamed his head off and like that. Strake sees the finger, he'll believe it."

Winston said, "Why?"

"Because he wants to," Donny said.

Winston said, "They teach you this in the damn Marines?"

"No, but they taught me a lot of ways to kill a man. No matter his size."

Winston tensed and sat a little straighter, leveling an unblinking pit bull glare at Donny.

"All right, that's enough," Davis said. "Let's get some gas and get back on the road."

AT ONE-THIRTY ON THAT FRIDAY SAM TOOK A BREAK from hanging more sheetrock in a bedroom and hand-sanding the joints and screw head depressions in the living room that he'd compounded the day before. He wore a fine coating of white dust everywhere except around his mouth and nose where the protective mask had been. He dusted himself off as best he could and rode the bike over to the Burger Box to order a Monster with homemade hot relish and a quarter-inch-thick slice of Vidalia onion on it, along with an old-fashioned vanilla milkshake, which he carried to the picnic table outside where an old man was polishing off a cheeseburger.

"Hello, Pops," Sam said, sitting down on the other side of the table.

"Sam. Ain't this day a doozy?"

"Sure is that."

"These Yankees here sure know how to fry up a burger, you know?"

"Tell me about it," Sam said, and took a good-sized

crescent out of the Monster, enjoying the crunch of the sweet onion and the tongue-sting of the relish.

The sunshine felt clean and good. Although it was getting chilly in the nights, the temperature during the days was holding unseasonably warm and several of the people Sam had seen this day seemed to be smiling slightly to themselves and had a lift in their steps.

The old man finished up, shook his head once, and said, "Yessir." He lobbed the balled-up wrapper neatly into a bright red trash can over by the small garish building, got up with his Coke can, and gave Sam a grin that lacked a few teeth. "Guess I'll go home, get drunk, beat up one a my girlfriends, an' kick the dog. Y'all take care, Sam."

"Hey, you too, Pops."

Sam sat at the table for a time after he had eaten, appreciating the random ethereal mares' tails way off to the west and probably five miles up. At that altitude they'd be laceworks of powder-ice crystals. He thought about how it might go meeting Valerie's people up in the Smokies and about when and how he was going to tell her about himself.

The silver Blazer moved south on I-95 with the cruise control set five miles an hour above the limit, just now crossing the line from Virginia into North Carolina. Davis had his driver's side window down. He noticed the high-up clouds way off to the left looking like somebody who didn't know crap about painting had taken a barn brush to it. Donny was in the back seat reading a war paperback.

"I think maybe I've seen him," Winston said. He was holding up the newspaper clipping, trying to keep it from fluttering, and studying the image intently. "I don't know, maybe one time in Miami. Wasn't many times I was around where Strake and the others like you were. But I think maybe I've seen this guy."

"Then you better watch it when we get there," Davis said, "because he may remember you. Stay in the car or in the room mostly, until we're ready to make a move. If he gets one look at me he'll be gone. He'll know what I'm here for. If he gets away we're not likely to find him again."

"It may be he's home with his feet up," Donny said. "We just go in there and do him quick and quiet. Get out. That would be the best."

From experience Davis knew these things seldom went as you hoped. Never quite the way you tried to plan it. "Or he could be going to a barbecue tonight with friends. Or he could be flying a charter someplace. Not even on the island. We'll have to see how it plays."

Donny said, "How about we get something to eat?"

"All right," Davis said. "We've got time. I'd just as soon not get on the island until about dark, anyway."

****

Sam was absorbed with the sheetrock work as the day ticked on. By late afternoon he had only three sheets left to hang in the back bedroom and he took a break to drink a warm Coke. He didn't plan to be at Valerie's until seven-thirty so there was plenty of time to put up the sheets and get a coat of compound on them and on the rest of what he'd hung that day if he kept his nose to it. He stretched his back muscles, picked up one if the heavy sheets, lined it up against the studs, and held it with his knee while he drove the first few of the screws with the cordless driver.

The silver Blazer was in a line of cars that had rolled off of the Hatteras ferry. After the nearly die-straight drive down Ocracoke as the sunset glow was beginning to fade to the west, Davis spotted the shadowed tails of light planes lined up, just showing above some dunes alongside a broad right-hand bend in the road. He put on the signal, slowed, and pulled off onto the short access road near the strip in the fast-gathering darkness. Nobody else was there. He stopped the Blazer beside the shelter and let it idle, looking around in the headlight glare. Six light planes were chained down on a small apron, three of them with high wings, one of the low-wing jobs a small twin-engine. The open-walled shelter had benches around the inside. A pay phone in one corner. A rutted cut through the dunes led out onto the dark beach. An orange wind sock twitched in a fitful breeze.

Looking over the planes Winston said, "Which one of them is his?"

"No way to tell," Davis said. "Maybe none of them. Maybe a couple. But probably just one. Stay put. I want to know if that pay phone works." He could feel himself focusing in now, his senses sharpening, a kind of cold

familiar clarity taking over. He left the Blazer idling with
just the parking lights on and got out. He consulted a small
pocket pad, wrapped three layers of handkerchief over the
mouthpiece to help alter his voice, and dialed the number he'd been given earlier by information for Sam Bass,
thinking *make sure he's alone, set it up to meet at his place to
talk about a charter, then just go in there and do it.* He let it
ring nine times before hanging up. Then he dialed the
number for the cell phone that was in a console pocket in
the car, to be sure it worked. Winston answered it.

"Okay," Davis said.

Back in the Blazer he said, "Donny, you'll go get the
room key but we'll leave everything in the car for now.
Don't give them a plate number, of course. We'll try not
to even let them see the car. I'll go in, mess up the bed,
make it look like somebody stayed in there in case we don't
wind up spending the night. I'll leave it clean, no prints,
and leave the key inside with the door unlocked or wedged
a little. That way we can either go back to it if we have to
or just leave it like it is. There's no answer at his house,
but we'll make a run by there to take a look at the layout.
Maybe he'll be home by then. If not, Donny, then you can
go in one or two of the stores. Maybe he's got business
cards out with a beeper number, or a flyer that shows a shot
of his plane. We know which one it is we can disable it."

"Or maybe plant a charge in it," Donny said. "I could
do that. Then we catch the next ferry."

"No. We're here for him, not for any of his customers.
We can slash a tire on it."

Winston loosened his belt a notch, slid his auto holster

out from under the seat, pulled the gun out and checked it for a chambered round, put it back in the holster, and arched back in his seat, grunting, to clip the holster inside his belt on the right side. The jacket would cover what little of it showed. When they stopped at the motel he would get the silencer from his suitcase and carry it in his zippered right jacket pocket.

He pulled a short fat cigar out of his shirt pocket, stripped the wrapper off and dropped that out the window, and stuck it in his mouth, leaving it unlit.

As Davis drove into the outskirts of the village Donny said, "Yeah, a real hick town." He reached back over the seat and unzipped his leather bag. He took out a big Model 226 Sig Sauer and screwed a silencer onto it. Checked that it was ready to go. Put it on the seat beside him under a towel. Fifteen rounds of nine millimeter Parabellum. Enough firepower right there to kill half a dozen assholes, even if you missed a lot.

Which he did not.

DONNY PICKED UP ONE OF SAM'S FOUR-BY-NINE CARDS from the brochure rack in the General Store and took it to the register along with an oversized bottle of Pepsi and a pack of Nabs. He was wearing his billed camo cap to cover his hair and shadow his eyes. He put the brochure card down on the counter and tapped it with a finger. He smiled pleasantly and said to the black girl behind the antique register, "I tried to call this man a little while ago but couldn't get any answer. I'd like to set up a sightseeing flight for my girlfriend and me for in the morning. Would you happen to know how I could reach him?"

She smiled. "Well, I'd say chances are pretty good he's over at Valerie Lightfoot's place for supper. He forgets his beeper sometimes. Here, just a second and I'll give you her number." She reached under the counter and pulled out a phone book and began looking it up, paging through and then tracing down the column of names with a half-inch-long glossy fingernail.

Sam was riding his bike along the dark main road when

he decided to stop at the General Store to pick up a small pack of jelly beans for Joshua. The boy could be made to squeal in delight when Sam caused each bean to magically appear from some improbable place—from behind his small ear, or from his belly button, or from Sam's boot top, or plucked from one of Val's house plants—though Val always gave him the devil for letting Josh have so much pure sugar. He propped his bike on its stand at the edge of the lit parking area as a noisy red pickup whizzed by too fast on the road. Across the area there was an idling silver Blazer nosed into a space, the only car there. The man in the passenger seat behind the rolled-up window had a cigar in his mouth and was looking at him intently.

Sam stopped dead in his tracks and felt a lance of ice stab his gut. He watched the man take out his cigar and mouth the word "fuck". Sam turned around quickly, toed the stand up and got back on the bike, riding away fast toward the village center, not looking back. He took the first right on a street, standing on it, speeding up, the rusty chain protesting.

"*Fuck*," Winston said. "Right there. That's him. On a beat-up bike. Going out of sight now. He made me."

Davis said, "Are you sure?"

"Yeah. It's him."

Donny was coming out of the store. Davis gestured urgently for him to hurry it up. Donny ran to the back door, yanked it open, and jumped inside, and Davis had it backing up before Donny could get the door closed, one wheel yipping as it slipped on a sandy patch. He braked hard in the road and drove ahead, saying, "Where?"

"There. First right," Winston said. "He's got some kind of white dust on him, what got my attention. I stared at him like a fool and he made me. Fuck."

Davis turned the Blazer into the street, flicked on the high beams, and slowed. The headlights caught only a white cat crouched near a bush, suddenly uncoiling into a loping run off into the shadows. The houses were sparse here, with a lot of vegetation between them. Most showed lights but some were dark—good hiding places.

The Blazer crept along.

There was a left turn and Winston said intently, "There, there, turn left," just as Davis started taking the turn anyway. They all tensed, but it was just some little old lady with a bandanna on her head on another bike caught in the headlights, wobbling along, a handlebar basket filled with something in plastic. Davis flicked down to the low beams and stopped until she was past them.

Nothing else showed anywhere.

"The ferries," Winston said.

"Not from the harbor," Davis said, checking his watch quickly. "The last harbor ferry is long gone."

Donny held up the brochure card on which he had jotted Valerie Lightfoot's number and said, "This is his flyer. No shot of the plane, but I've got his girlfriend's number here. Her name's Valerie Lightfoot. What do you want to bet he's headed there?"

"No, I don't think so," Davis said. "I don't think he'd want to draw us down on her. But I can use her number." He reached for the cell phone with his right hand and flipped it open, still driving, still scanning in the headlights. "We're pretty much between him and his house here, and he was moving away. He's probably smart enough to assume we've already got his place spotted out. I think the only reason he's going this way is because he's got some place to hole up. What's the number?"

Donny used the Mini-Maglite to read off the number and Davis punched it in with his thumb. It rang three times before she answered. He said, "Yes, Ms. Lightfoot? I was told you might know how I could get in touch with Mr. Sam Bass. I'd like to book a charter for tomorrow but I haven't been able to reach him at his business number."

Valerie had the cordless phone clamped between her shoulder and her cheek. She was in the bathroom doorway bent down, holding Joshua's pajama bottoms so he could climb into them after his shower, his wet curls flattened onto his head. He was looking in the hallway mirror at his tongue, and licking droplets off of his upper lip where he had failed to dry himself completely. She said, "Sometimes he goes off and forgets his beeper. You could give me your name and number and I'll have him call you. Or you could call back here any time after seven-thirty." Joshua put his hands on her shoulders to steady himself while he stepped into the pajama bottoms. He started humming "If I Can Find A Clean Shirt" off key.

"All right, ma'am. Thank you. I'll do that, then."

He was moving the phone down, just about to flip it closed, when he heard her say, "Or I guess..."

He brought the phone back to his ear quickly. "Yes, ma'am?"

She knew Sam wouldn't be very presentable after

working with the sheetrock all day, but she also knew he would want the charter. "Well," she said. "He's been doing some finish work on a new cottage for a friend and he's most likely still at it. You could probably catch him there, if you'd like to. He's on his bicycle."

"That would surely help, ma'am, if you could give me directions."

Joshua was asking through flying and shooting gestures if he could go get his Star Wars toys. She nodded yes. "Okay, on the main road into the village, do you know where The Privateer is?"

"Yes, ma'am, I believe I passed it on the way in."

She gave him the directions starting from The Privateer and he memorized them.

"Look for an old Jeep in pretty bad shape. He might not still be there," she said, "so why don't you give me your number and I can have him call you as soon as he gets here?"

"That's not necessary," he said. "Thank you again, ma'am." And he hung up.

"I know where he is," Davis said as he put the phone back into the console pocket. He began driving faster, but it wasn't far.

He parked the Blazer on the sand by the end of the street, killed the headlights, and switched off the ignition, putting the keys in his jacket pocket and zipping it up. Like all the other sparse streets, there were no sidewalks or street lights, just an occasional yard light. There were only two lit houses that showed from here as the street curved away to the right, three cars parked on the shoulders.

"All right," Davis said. "It's the third cottage on the

right. New construction. He's been working on it. Donny, work your way along over there, get behind the place. Winston, you and I will come up on the front from both sides. Give me three minutes to get across to the other side, then you move in."

Winston was screwing his silencer in place. He would conceal the gun partially by just holding it down alongside his leg. He had the cigar clamped in his mouth again.

Donny said, "Is he likely to have a piece?"

"I don't think so," Davis said, "but try not to be an easy target, anyway. You two have the suppressors so it will be up to you unless I can get my hands on him. All right, let's go."

Donny walked away quickly toward the brush, holding the Sig inside the front of his camo jacket. Davis waited a few seconds and then moved off. Winston gave it a three-minute count and followed. They each carried a pocketed filtered Mini-Maglite but would use them only if necessary.

Sam had gone back to the cottage because it was the closest place that came to mind where he would not be drawing them down on people he knew, and to buy some time to think. He had left the bike close by the side of the cottage, partially concealed behind a dead bush. There had been two of them in the Blazer. The one with the cigar and the driver. He was standing in the living room in deep shadow, where he could look out onto the street through the bay window that still had stickers on the corners of the panes and had not been cleaned.

He thought, *I've got to draw them off, away from the island*. He was close to the harbor here, but if he just grabbed a boat and left they would still be here, still be a threat to anybody, everybody who knew him as Sam Bass.

Maybe there was a way to draw them along, make sure they would see him go away in a boat, would know it was him and know beyond doubt he was running away. Then they would either try to steal a boat and chase him or leave by the Hatteras ferry. He could go a ways up the back of the island and then hide in the marsh grasses. If they managed to get a more powerful boat going and got too close he could always beach the outboard and run for it. There was no way they were going to catch him on foot. He knew of a small old outboard boat at a dock he could take without much trouble. It would not need a key. It had only a pull starter.

A wind was picking up outside, the strong light on a pole in the yard of a home across the street two doors down spraying through the trees and creating crazily cavorting shadows.

He saw a movement off to the left across the street. A shadow out of place. There. A lumbering figure. How could they have found him so fast? He scanned along the street, and there was the other one to the right by a tree, pointing at the side of the cottage, at the bike, and both of them moving up through the shadows faster now.

He spotted the lump of the tool box in the corner, bent down and felt over it, picked up a big pipe wrench, and moved quickly to the back of the house. He eased the back door open and spent five seconds scanning all around. There were only about fifteen feet of cleared area between the cottage and an expanse of low brush and grass with a few scattered trees. He went out the doorway low and fast, making for the brush.

Standing under a tree forty feet away Donny instantly
froze and leveled the big auto two-handed, his right on the
grip and his left palm already firmly under the butt, not
seeing the gun really in the darkness but knowing where
he was aiming, the wind making the shadows dance, and
pumped off five fast rounds at the furtive low shadow rac-
ing across the uneven dirt patch and into the brush, the
Sig making hardly much noise louder than the wind rustling the leaves, the wind masking both sound and motion
and confusing the shadows, but he heard a slug hit something. Maybe the big thigh bone. He listened intently and
scanned the brush but saw nothing.

He walked over to where the shadow had entered the
brush and used the end of the silencer to lift a branch out
of the way. He got out the red-filtered flashlight with his
left hand, made sure the beam was set narrow, and played
it over the ground. There was a big red pipe wrench in the
sand with a smear on it from his slug. No blood anywhere
that he could see.

Behind him, near the side of the cottage, Davis said
quietly, "Donny."

"Over here," Donny said. "He bolted. He's gone. He's
not armed."

Davis and Winston walked up and Winston rumbled,
"Well, you had your shot, jarhead, and you missed him."

In his irritating falsetto, Donny said, "It's too dark back
here and he was fast. I hit a pipe wrench he was carrying."

Winston snorted.

"All right," Davis said. "He'll try to get off the island

now, I think. Let's get back to the car fast."

Davis drove the Blazer not much over the limit the short distance to the village fringe, then he floored it. He slewed to a stop on the gravel area by the shelter at the air strip. There was nobody in sight. The wind sock was standing out in what was now a heavy gusting breeze. "Winston," he said. "Take the MP5 and get in the shelter. Take the big Maglite. Keep a watch on all the planes. Nobody besides our man is likely to come along. I don't think they're supposed to use this strip after dark. Anything happens, use the pay phone to call me."

Winston grunted and got out. He went around to raise the back glass and get the five-cell and the submachine gun, keeping it wrapped in the blanket. He closed the glass and Davis had the Blazer moving away fast. Winston stuck his cigar in his mouth and walked up the steps and across to the far side of the night-blackened shelter. He used the flashlight, filtered by his fingers, to insert a clip into the MP5 and then rested it on the bench close beside him, covered by a single flap of the blanket. It was a little bulky with the fat silencer on the end of it, but it was not heavy so you could handle it fast and it hit damned hard where you aimed it. It was possible to lay the small-headed Maglite alongside it to light up a target, holding both it and the gun, but Winston had found that cumbersome and preferred to rely on his excellent night vision.

There were plenty of stars and a sliver of moon. The dunes and the planes were silhouetted against the dark sky already, after only a few minutes of acclimation. The auto was back in its belt holster, the silencer in his zippered jacket pocket. He leaned back against a post watching the planes and waiting to get his full night vision, which he usually acquired within twenty minutes. A few cars were moving north out on the main road but their lights were not a problem.

Davis was driving fast back toward the village. He said to Donny, "Keep an eye out for that Jeep. He might chance going for it now. He's running. I can feel it."

Davis killed the lights and parked by the end of Teach's Lane, which was dark except for a yard light about ninety feet beyond the Bass place and on the same side of the street. He kept the engine idling. A Jeep was parked there, the cottage dark, lights from another cottage showing out behind it through a grove of trees. A white Toyota Camry went by slowly, but the couple in it did not seem to pay them undue notice.

Donny said, "You told us he drives an old Wrangler so that's his Jeep, right? You want me to rig it?"

Davis was silent for thirty seconds. Thinking. Looking all around. The Jeep had the right plate. "All right. First check out the house. Then do it. I'll keep watch out here."

Donny reached over the seat and grabbed his leather bag and was getting out when Davis said, "Wait."

"What?"

"Can you set it so you can get it back off fast if you have to?"

"No problem."

"Okay, do it that way, then. Make it quick."

"Give me ten minutes from right now." He was wearing thin rubber gloves. He went away like one of the shadows.

Davis never spotted him near the cottage or the Jeep. He was back in eight and a half minutes. He got in the back-seat and said, "Easy. It's small to keep the noise and flash down, but it will turn that metal dash into shrapnel. Hell, just the concussion ought to take his head off. For a while most people will figure it's only somebody's propane tank or maybe a transformer. No sign of anybody in the cottage. The back door was unlocked, can you believe that? I don't feel him anywhere close, you know? I don't think he's holed up near here."

"No. I think he's running," Davis said as he backed the Blazer around and got moving.

Davis was quiet for half a minute, intently watching the road ahead and to the sides and then he said, "What is it?"

"Good old C-4. Sky-hi. You can't beat it for this work."

Davis checked his watch. He wanted to catch that last Hatteras ferry now, if at all possible. There was still well enough time. He drove toward the harbor. He had both front windows down and Donny had both rear windows down, the auto ready in his hand, resting on the seat beside him. They were both scanning.

Sam was running full-out in the wind, across the sand through an expanse of waist-high marsh grass thinking *I'll fly low over the village at full power. Keep all the lights off. Head west. They'll have to know it's me. That will draw them away.*

Winston was standing in the shelter with his hands on his hips, staring intently into the shadows outside, chewing lightly on the end of the unlit cigar. The chilling wind had picked up even more, blowing at his back, carrying sprinkles of sand with it, moving the bushes and rippling the grasses, making it harder to spot any wrong movement out there.

But it was like deer hunting. You could walk real careful through the woods with a cold wind in your face and the dry leaves and the brush noisy thinking, *I'll never see or hear one* but then all of a sudden there's a movement or a sound not like all the others and there she is and you whip the Winchester up and blow her fuckin' heart out with a hundred-seventy-grain soft nose.

Better than twenty minutes with a seventy-five-dollar whore.

More cars went by north on the main road.

Keeping low, Sam unhooked all three tie-down chains and gentled them down onto the pavement. He opened the cabin door slowly and climbed in, easing the door closed. Took out the yoke gust lock. Slipped the key into the ignition. He gave it two shots of primer, let off the hand brake and clamped the foot brakes and said, "Come on, old girl." He pulled on the master switch and keyed the starter. Before the prop had completed one revolution the engine stuttered alive and he immediately gave it throttle and let off on the brakes, heading for the midway entry onto the strip, all of the lights off.

Winston grabbed up the MP5 and lumbered for the near end of the strip. The plane was taxiing away fast, not a good shot from where he was, the other planes in the way, and at first he thought it was going to take off in the other direction, but then as he made it out onto the strip the plane swung around into the wind down at the far end and the motor revved up. It was aimed right at him. He used his left hand to cover his left eye tightly, waiting, squinting through his right eye, and there it was, the bright light coming on in the wing. Then two seconds later another bright light right beside it. *You smart fuck*, he thought. *Spotted me right off and you figure to kill my night vision. We'll see who's smart.*

You smart son of a bitch, Sam thought, watching the big man caught defiantly like a bear in his lights at the other end of the strip, carrying what looked like a submachine gun in his right hand and holding his left hand over that eye, the wind blowing his hair around wildly from behind him, striding heavily over to the side of the strip now and going down onto his left knee in the sand. *You're saving the night vision in that eye*, Sam thought. *And you're left-handed.*

Sam was keeping his own right eye shut to preserve his own night vision in all the glare of both his big landing and taxi beams. He kept the throttle fire-walled and pulled it up off of the pavement as soon as it was ready to fly, immediately then dousing the lights and opening his right eye. Now he would be only a fleeting shadow against the dark sky.

As soon as the lights died Winston opened his left eye and shouldered the MP5. His first burst missed just ahead of the big cross-shaped speeding shadow but then he was getting good hits all over the belly of it, he knew, rapping out quick little bursts as it banked up away from him, the engine and prop loud, aiming then right at the nose, leading it a little, and hearing with satisfaction the engine right away begin to miss and chatter bad just as his ammo ran out.

He grasped the MP5 with his right hand and drew out the auto and emptied it, firing fast but each shot aimed and deliberate as the shadow went away, banking right and then leveling out but real shaky at maybe a hundred feet, going out over the ocean, that engine sounding good and sick.

He waded through tall grass up onto a windy dune to watch, breathing hard, the empty MP5 in his right hand and the empty auto hot but unnoticed down against the side of his left leg.

Sam fought to control the Cessna. One cylinder was trashed, he knew, and the resultant violent vibration from the juddering engine was threatening to tear the wings off, so he pulled back on the power, just trying to maintain altitude. He had only maybe a hundred feet. His right hip burned and felt warmly wet. The left wing kept trying to hike up, something wrong with the aileron, then he felt a *spang* in the yoke and the aileron control became all but nonexistent, so he got on the rudder trying to keep the wings level. If he could just ease back to the right maybe he could put it down on the beach.

The windshield was starred and cold air was spouting into his face. He had full rudder in and it wasn't enough to control the bank and she slowly rose up into a steep right bank and then buffeted and stumbled in the air and fell. He saw the black sea coming up and tried to brace for it but the tremendous impact wrenched him sideways, throwing him against the belts, his head slamming into something numbly, and he lost his grip on the yoke. He felt a pang of regret that Whiskey Sierra was dying. She had served him well and faithfully, trying to keep flying until she just couldn't any more.

There was only a loud sustained rushing sound in his head and he was cold. *Cold.* Water was coming in everywhere. He felt for the seat belt latch and fumbled with it in slow motion but it was tight and he finally managed to free it and then fell straight ahead and again hit his head on something. *She's upside down* he thought idly. He was in almost total darkness, so he felt around, got a grip on the seat and felt up under it. There. His hand closed on the inflatable life jacket and he got it out and tried to pull it on right, telling himself to wait until he could get outside to yank the lanyard. There wasn't much air space left in the cabin and he choked and tried to suck in a supply of air, his lungs already burning.

His door was jammed so he turned and kicked weakly at the window twice with his left foot until the latch gave and a sudden cold flood of water filled up the last of the air space. He tried to swim out the window but he was caught on something and he could feel himself rapidly getting dizzy and hopelessly disoriented, his lungs on fire.

Winston used the pay phone.

Davis said, "Yes."

"It's done," Winston said. "Pick me up."

When Davis got there Winston had the MP5 wrapped in the blanket again as he walked up to the driver's window. "He took off but I shot the fuck down. Climbed up on a dune and watched him go into the water a good ways out there." He pointed back toward the ocean. "Did like a big cartwheel."

"You sure it's done?"

"I put most of a thirty-round magazine right into him and I'd bet even a few nines from my auto. The slugs must have punched right on through that aluminum, tearin' up whatever on the way. A couple turned his engine into scrap. Even if I didn't hit him solid I don't know how he could've come out of that crash."

Davis thought for a few seconds. "All right, we can get out of here clean. Put the MP5 away but keep the flashlight. Go pick up your casings. Donny, you help him. Try to get it all but make it fast." He checked his watch. "We've got to go get that charge off of the Jeep and maybe we can catch that last ferry."

* * * * * * *

Valerie said, "Josh, go put your sneakers on and get your light jacket. We have to make a quick run to the store. I forgot to get cornbread mix and you know how your Sam likes his biscuits and honey butter."

"Yeah, me too," Joshua said as he looked for his sneakers under the couch.

There was a knock at the front door. It was Mrs.

Bradley. Valerie smiled and said, "Oh, of course, you've come for your check. Come on in. Could you keep an eye on Josh for just a few minutes? He's already in his pajamas and I have to make a last-minute run to the store."

Mrs. Bradley said, "Surely. Where's your car, honey?"

"Fred hasn't finished working on it yet. Sam's on his bike, so I'll just run over and use the Jeep. He keeps the key under the floor mat but I don't know why he just doesn't leave it in the ignition. Who'd want to steal it? Josh, you could set the table while I'm gone, please?"

Josh said, "Can we light the candles and turn out all the other lights?"

"Sure," Valerie said. "Mrs. Bradley, I'll write your check as soon as I get back." And she hurried out the door.

The silver Blazer was moving fast toward the village when they saw the bright orange flash and a second later heard the quick double detonation. Davis braked hard to a stop and glared back over his shoulder at Donny.

Donny held up his palms and said in his little-kid voice, "Hey, no way it went off by itself. I'm telling you. No way. Somebody tried to start it and it took the gas tank, too. I can't help that."

"*Dammit*," Davis said, slamming a hand onto the wheel.

Then he took a deep breath and checked his watch, the Blazer sitting there in the dark road idling. He did a squealing U-turn and headed north. Fast. "All right," he said. "We have fifteen minutes to make fourteen miles. Get all the hardware out of sight."

When they got to the ferry docks the big white steel boat was nosed up to the pilings in the glare of the parking

area pole lights, rumbling. There was a long double line
of cars, the first of them being beckoned aboard by the
ferry hands.

Winston said, "It looks like a hell of a lot more cars
than the boat can hold."

Davis said, "Donny, dig that ferry schedule brochure
out of that envelope back there. Then get out and go over
to that machine and get me a Coke. Count the cars."

When Donny came back and got in he said, "We're
number twenty-nine. How many does the boat hold?"

Putting his finger on a line in the schedule brochure
Davis said, "Thirty."

THE OLD CLAW HAMMER THAT HANK HAD FOUND TO LIFT aside the lid so he could replenish the pot-bellied stove with good dry wood slipped and the lid clanged shut.

"Hank," she said in a low scolding voice, "I reckon you've just got it set in your mind to go ahead and wake Roy up."

"Sorry, Hattie. She slipped. Maybe the next time we go over we can find us a proper stove lid handle."

"Yes," she said. "Let's put that on my buy-or-borrow list before we forget it. Now, where did I put that list?"

"I'll just go in there real quiet and check on Roy. Now, if he wakes up it ain't going to be me. It'll be 'cause he smells this good breakfast you're fixing."

He came awake in the musty bright light knowing he was feverish. He was on a low bed looking out a dirty window at clear sky, trees, grass, and a long sliver of blue water. He was naked under a sheet and a thin wool blanket. His head was wrapped with something and it pounded sharply as though it was about to crack. His right leg was hot and whitely painful. Didn't feel as though he could move it. His ribs and his hip ached and the teeth on the left side of his mouth felt loose. His tongue was like a wedge of un-sanded wood. He moved his head slightly. The ceiling was old-fashioned thick bead board, sagging in the center, water-stained, most of the paint having long ago flaked away. He eased his head over to the other side and looked up dizzily at a figure backlit in the doorway. Beyond a far-ther raggedly-screened doorway he could see breeze-bent grass and sand in the sunlight. "Walta . . . Maphau," he said with dry cracked lips.

"How's that, son?"

He scratched his parched lips with his wooden tongue. "You look . . . little like Walter Maf . . . Maffau. 'Cept you have . . . mo' winkles."

The skinny figure slapped its knee and hooted. "You hear that, Hattie? Roy says I got more wrinkles than Walter Matthau. Well, son, I reckon I earned every last one of them over the years since we seen you. Fifteen years it's been now, and that's a fact. Hattie, Roy needs him a cool drink of water here."

A little lady with her thin pure white hair in disarray showed in the doorway wearing a calico dress and a white apron. She carried a jelly glass half full of water with a straw, and his eyes fixed on it. She came over and held the glass for him to drink from it thirstily sideways, wiping a little overspill from the side of his mouth with her apron, then feeling his forehead with her palm. The water tasted far better than the finest wine could have. She was smil-ing and crying. "Roy," she said. "Oh, Roy. You just don't know how good it is to see you come home to us. She used her fingers to wipe at her pale blue eyes. Don't you worry, now. You'll be all right. I'll have your breakfast ready before you can think about it. I just put on a pot of tea."

"Hattie makes the best cup of yaupon tea on Portsmouth," the old man said as she left the room wiping at her eyes with the hem of her apron. "Don't you, Hattie?"

From the other room she called, "Hank, you'd best get the bucket and wash up for breakfast. Then you should get a towel and wash Roy's hands and face. We'll see he eats first. He needs to start getting his strength back."

"Okay, Mother."

"Hank?" he said weakly. "Listen. My name's not Roy. It's Sam Bass and . . ."

"It's dang sure good to have you home, Roy," Hank said loudly, holding a finger up to his lips. Then he came closer, nervously pointing out toward the other room, using his body to hide the gesture. His eyes were stern and he said in a rasping whisper, "Now, I don't think you want her to go and have another stroke, do you, son? This is her best day in fifteen years and we ain't going to spoil it for her. So I'll just be callin' you Roy and my wife can too, she wants to, you hear?"

Sam let his head ease back carefully onto the pillow, closed his eyes, and said tiredly, "Okay, Hank. God, that water tasted so good . . ."

After the old man had gone out to wash himself and had brought a wet towel back in to wash Sam's hands and face gently, Sam said, "How did I get here, Hank?"

"Roy, you're danged lucky I was out on the sea side

walkin' just then. I saw your plane go in. A real big splash it was, and like a cartwheel. Didn't float long, on its back, looked like. I took a sight on the shore so I'd be able to find the spot. I come and got the skiff and went out that inlet hell for leather. Sea wasn't too rough, thank the Lord. You had that yellow jacket about half on and blown up, and it just was holding your face above water. You was all banged up. Head looked the worst, but head wounds can bleed like the bejeesus. You was turnin' the sea pink when I got my flashlight on you, but I think maybe the sea was chilled enough to slow your bleedin' some. Out cold. I looked but I didn't see nobody else. I tied you alongside the skiff and brought you back to the old Coast Guard dock." He whispered again, "Come and got Hattie and right away she took it as a gift from God. It's Roy, she told me, come back from the sea like I prayed for so long."

He went on in a normal voice, "We rolled you up onto the dock in a low part of it, then dragged you along to where we could roll you off gentle into our cart, and then pushed you on home. We'd already borrowed a real good first aid kit and Hattie knows a lot about mending folk, so we cleaned you up and used two bottles of peroxide and got the bleedin' stopped in the worst places and bandaged you. Hattie thinks your right leg's broke but it's straight and we got it splinted good. You might of cracked a few ribs on that side, too. I wrapped a clean shirt around you and then bound you up good with duct tape. All you can do for ribs. Now, you can get some of her good food into you and start healin' up. Only thing, was anybody with you in your plane?"

"No. Just me. You two saved my life."

Hank smiled. "Glad it was only you. That was workin' on me, fact there might've been somebody else trapped down there in that plane. As for savin' you, if you could see the difference in Hattie, today from yesterday, from fifteen years of yesterdays, you might put that the other way around."

Hattie brought in a tray that was actually an old cookie sheet and put it on a small rickety table beside him. There was a big steaming bowl of grits drizzled with maple syrup along with two thick pieces of fried bread and a cup of tea. There were also four aspirins on a folded paper towel. Hank dragged in a rocking chair that had been repaired with splints, duct tape, and string lashings, and a straight-backed chair with a square of canvas nailed down where the caning had once been. Hattie took the rocker and Hank sat in the straight chair.

Sam raised himself slowly and painfully onto his elbow and Hank hurried over to prop him up with pillows.

"That smells delicious," Sam said. He managed to reach gingerly for the spoon and take a swallow of the grits, which were hot and sweet and immediately made his stomach feel better. "Ma'am, I appreciate this. I didn't know how hungry I was. He took a bite of crisp bread and then sipped the tea, which tasted wild and bittersweet. They watched him slowly put away the aspirin, the tea, and all of the food and then Hank helped him lie back onto the lumpy bed. He already felt a hundred percent better.

"Thank you, Hank. Thank you, ma'am."

"Have you forgotten what you used to call me?" Hattie said.

"Course not, Mother," Hank said. "He knows he always called you Flutter because you was always makin' such a fuss over him."

"You're the best of them, you know," Hattie said. "Your brother and sister never did understand Hank and me, although we surely tried."

"What they finally went and done, Roy," Hank said, "was go to the lawyers and they came to us with papers. Put us in Shady Grove down in Morehead City. A wonderful place to enjoy your golden years, they call it. We had a dinky place they call a villa. All the villas is connected by halls. Locked doors at the ends of the halls. Place don't look like a jail, but that's what it is. Villa had a dinky kitchen with what they call a intimate dining nook. A little bedroom, a livin' room about big enough for a TV and two chairs, and a bathroom full of chrome-plated rails. Like we're gonna get too light-headed takin' our showers. Hell, we been takin' showers together more years than we can count, ain't once fainted over it yet. Out the one window we could see a iron bench, a dead tree, and more villas across the cozy courtyard. You couldn't fart, sorry, Hattie, without drawin' the Lieutenant Witch down onto you. They tell you when to sleep, when and what to eat. You better eat your jello now, or let that butcher in a white coat poke you any damn place he feels like, or you don't get no allowance this week. They take your dentures out and then start askin' you questions. Mean spirited. People livin' there all got one foot on the shuffleboard court and the other foot in the grave.

"They got activity time. What do you think of that?

Activity time. Tell you who you're supposed to play check-
ers with for today's activity time. I swear I come this close
to takin' a shuffleboard stick to that Mr. Moser. A man
ninety years old ought to know when you can double-jump
and when you can't. I play maybe three bars on my fiddle and here comes the Lieutenant Witch, says, 'Now, Mr.
Gaskill, you know Miz Toomey right next door here is
tryin' to sleep.' Well, the fact is, you couldn't wake Miz
Toomey up if you was to crash-land Air Force One in the
parkin' lot. That woman will be dead a week before they
figure it out."

Hattie held a corner of her apron up to her mouth to
stifle a girlish giggle. She said, "So Hank and I ran away."

Hank took on a sly expression. "What we done, we
saved up our allowance until it was near fifty dollars,
packed our suitcases, then we borrowed the extra door key
from Private Witch's desk while she was outside smokin' a
cigarette, and when the coast was clear after midnight we
walked right on out of there real quiet. Spent the rest of
the night hidin' out in a little park. Hitched a ride over to
Beaufort early. We stocked up on a few things and then
we borrowed an old outboard skiff and come on out here.
Hattie read a book about Portsmouth once."

Sam said, "How long have you been here?"

"Goin' on six weeks, I guess. We got all we need right
here. This house nobody else wants anyway; doesn't leak
much. Set in here among the trees. Furniture and stuff we
found around the town. I got a tarp rigged to catch rain off
the tin roof. Dug a good latrine out back and put a bench
across it and a lean-to over it. By the way, don't you worry

none about that, Roy. I got an old cake pan you can use until you're up and around. I'll take care of it. Anyway, when we borrowed the skiff it had fifteen crab pots on it so we set those out in the sound. We eat some of the catch ourselves—Hattie makes a killer crab cake—and take the rest over to a fish house in Sealevel. We wade the shallows and dig clams for ten cent apiece. The man over at the fish house buys the clams and the crabs. Always fills up our gas tanks, too, and throws in a jug or two of fresh water if it ain't rained lately or if we ask, or some other stuff like a can of lantern fuel. I expect he knows we're fugitives but he won't say anything. He's eighty-three himself and his sons want to take over the business, run it their way, but he comes in to work every day, keeps his hands on that wheel. Hell, it's his wheel."

"We have that old stove out there to cook on and keep us warm on these chilly nights," Hattie said. "There's plenty of wood around. If we only run the stove with good dry wood and at night or when there's some breeze, we don't think anybody will see the smoke. We keep soft drinks cool in the gut out back, where I wash our clothes. I don't get groceries that go bad fast."

"We keep the skiff hid under the Coast Guard dock. We go over to the mainland once in a while to buy or borrow whatever's on Hattie's list. We borrowed the big cart. It was on a dock back of a fancy house. I guess they used it to carry stuff to their yacht. We call it our go-cart. It's good for haulin' wood and stuff. We borrowed the big first aid kit from there, too, and a few other things."

"I've got a list of the things we've borrowed." Hattie

said, "and about where we've borrowed them from, so later on it can all go back."

"You can gig a flounder in a heartbeat not three hundred feet from here," Hank said. "You walk along in the shallows at night with a flashlight and just use a long sharp stick with a barb whittled back of the point. Nothin' to it."

"We have the sand and the sea and a good clean breeze most always," Hattie said. "And even with the others out here it's so peaceful."

"Others?"

"Oh, there are the ghosts," Hattie said. "You can catch a glimpse of one sometimes, if you happen to move your head just right, over by a dune at sunset or in the shadow of an old house in the daylight. Sometimes you can hear one in a building, or they whisper when it's raining, but they don't mean us any harm at all. I expect we're good company for them."

"We can get out my fiddle and raise Cain anytime we want," Hank said, "and there's nobody around to give a dang."

Hattie gestured at a yellowed 1956 calendar hung on a nail and smiled. "When it's Sunday," she said, "Hank and I get dressed up and walk over to the church. We just sit for a time with the sunlight coming in those old rippled glass windows. Hank will take out his fiddle and play 'Ave Maria' or 'The Old Rugged Cross' or 'Silent Night' and we'll sing. We'll just fill up that little old church with singing. I'll read some words from the Good Book. Then Hank will take me for a walk on the beach. When we come home I'll maybe fry us two flounders that Hank gigged just before dawn and make some skillet corn bread we can have with molasses, and brew up my tea."

"I expect they'll track us down one of these days," Hank said, "and make us go back to Shady Grove or some other jail, but then we'll have all these good days out here to think about. This last free time."

"I think Roy needs to rest now," Hattie said, "so we'll go get our own breakfast and then do some chores. Come on now, Hank."

Sam was sleepy with the warm food in his belly and the aspirin beginning to dull the pains. "Thank you, Hank," he said. "And thank you, Flutter," seeing the way it made her smile. He closed his eyes and felt himself drifting off.

He woke briefly in the early afternoon to take a long drink of water and more aspirin, and Hank helped him use the cake pan.

When he woke up again it was dark. Outside the smudged window, bright stars were tangled in the trees and way off there was the lazy regular wink-flash of the Ocracoke lighthouse. He had a heavy black feeling that there was something terribly wrong over there and his mind shied away from it. He had drawn them away from the island. They must think they had killed him, and they had no reason to harm anyone else over there. They had to be long gone. Valerie and Joshua would be missing him and would be worried. They would think he'd just left the island in a hurry for some reason, he thought with a nervous hollowness, for some emergency, and would be waiting to hear from him, but he could make up for all of that.

Hattie set a hissing lantern on his bedside table and made him a supper of a large golden-fried flounder and fried bread with molasses, with canned peaches and a Mountain Dew. He ate every morsel of it and had another long drink of cool sweet rain water. If he had any fever left it could not be much.

After Hank and Hattie had eaten, they came in and sat with him. Hank said, "You feel up to a little music, son?"

Sam nodded, so Hank went out and came back with his violin case.

The instrument looked old, the grainy wood burnished in the lantern light. Around its bridge there was a powdery patch of rosin. Hank plucked the strings and tuned it by ear, then tightened up the age-discolored horsehair bow and drew it briskly across a small grooved rosin cake several times.

"Play 'Blue Eyes in The Rain'," Hattie said. "That one is so pretty to me."

Hank rested the back of the fiddle on his chest and sat erect in the straight chair. Hattie leaned her head back and got the rocker moving slightly. Hank drew the bow deftly across the strings, making them vibrate and setting the old wood to resonating richly, his scuffed boot toe tapping out the time, his weathered bent fingers pressing with sureness on the slim neck of the instrument, Hattie's small palm tapping the rocker arm softly in unison. He and Hattie sang in a harmony tuned to perfection from long practice, and Sam watched them and listened to the old song. He hadn't heard anybody else do it better.

Hank played a lively "Turkey in The Straw", double-stringing most of it, and then a haunting "Red River Valley".

"Here's one you ought to know, son. And you can sing

right along if you're up to it. I call it 'Me and My Hattie McGee'."

Hattie said, "I surely wish you had your guitar, Roy." She smiled and closed her eyes, rocking slowly.

Hank plucked the strings, using the pegs to fine-tune them, and then began singing Kristofferson's "Me and Bobby McGee", substituting "Hattie McGee" for Bobby, and Sam soon joined in weakly.

Hank gestured toward Hattie with his head. She was dozing off, her head canted on a thin pillow tied to the rocker back. He played "Love Can Build a Bridge" softly, not singing, then sat there with the fiddle resting on his knee.

"When I look at her now, son," he said quietly, "or when we're out in the shallows clammin' and she's got her skirt tied up above her knees and her straw hat on, I don't see all the years on her. I see her like she was forty years ago. It's the same spark in her blue eyes and the same way she carries herself and the same good light in her voice. That woman there has stuck with me goin' on fifty years now, like I really was somebody. When I never was."

Hank put the violin up on his chest again and played "Tennessee Waltz". Watching her sleep.

Sam closed his eyes and saw the ghosts of Portsmouth town standing out there among the trees listening.

Smiling contentedly to themselves because their island was alive once again.

If only for a while.

When Sam came awake at dawn he saw Hank asleep in the straight chair, his head on his shoulder and his arms folded. In his right hand he held a big squarish automatic pistol. Sam stirred, trying to raise his upper body and awkwardly stuff a pillow back there as a prop. Hank started and woke up abruptly, looking around.

Sam nodded at the gun and said, "What's that for?"

Hank said in a lowered voice, "You talk in your sleep, son. I know you've got some men after you. I never did tell Hattie but that rut along your hip looked like a bullet track whenever I first saw it, and then it matched up with the hole in your jeans. Took a chunk out of your belt, too. I don't know what your trouble is, son, but I'll do whatever I can to help."

"I have to go back to Ocracoke, Hank. A woman and her son are over there. They're my good friends and they don't know where I am. They'll be worried sick. But nobody else should know I'm here. It could be bad for them."

"You ought not to go anywhere for a while," Hank said,

not looking him in the eyes. "Hattie and I done all we can for you. I don't believe there's a hospital could do much more except charge you about a thousand a day. You're healin' just fine, Hattie says, and she knows. Hattie, she's dropped ten years off. Smiles in her sleep again. It's good to see. Yessir, the best thing you can do is stay right there and rest."

"Hank, you don't understand. I . . ."

"No, son. Now that's the last I'll hear of it today. We'll give it a week or so and then we'll talk." The old man's expression was determined.

Sam studied him for a moment. He said, "That's an Army forty-five you have there, isn't it?"

"Colt model nineteen and eleven. Still one of the best side arms there ever was, I expect." He looked down at it. The bluing was worn off in several places but it looked clean and oiled. The old man's voice took on a faraway tone. "This one saved my life. It was all I had left when a Jap carryin' a rifle with a bayonet on it caught me in a flooded ditch-bank. This gun was coated in mud but it fired when I needed it to. It saved my life."

"What was it like for you? That war."

"Something you don't ever forget, hard as you might try. Bunch of us was in Guadalcanal. They wanted volunteers so I signed on. We got secret orders and went to Bombay. Mountbatten himself inspected us there. We was led by General Frank G. Merrill. Not what you'd expect in a general. He wasn't a big man, wore glasses, didn't speak loud, but he damned sure had sand. He took three thousand of us into Burma from Ledo, India. We had

American Japanese with us. And Gurkhas. You don't ever want to square off against no Gurkha, son. Some of the best fighters I ever saw. We used mules for pack animals and it's sure right what they say about how stubborn those damned animals can be.

"It was supposed to be for three months but it dragged on to twice that. They needed to clear out Burma enough to get supplies through to the Chinese. I didn't know a man could be so scared for so long. Or so wet and dirty. It was the worst at night. They called us Merrill's Marauders. Besides all the Japs there was cholera, malaria, scrub typhus, beriberi, dysentery. Eight out of ten of us got bad dysentery, but we still fought like the devil. Had a fight at Shaduzup and by then a lot of us had took bad sick or been killed or wounded. We were tuckered out for sure, but we took the air strip at Myitkyina, and by then there was only a hundred of us left on our feet, and I was so bad off I could hardly pick up my carbine. Merrill had his second heart attack and they disbanded us in August of forty-three. Merrill went on back to New England and did alright after the war. Some said later we was one of the most heroic units in World War Two. I don't know about that. I just know when you're so scared you go all hollow inside and you watch a buddy not twenty-one yet in a stinking dirty red puddle twitch like a rabbit and try to hold his guts in and holler for his momma you don't feel like no hero. You just feel sick to your soul. But we always had our pride, no matter what. We might not be no saints, we said, but we damned sure was the Marauders. That was all a long, long time ago, son. Nobody cares now."

"What happened to Roy, Hank?"

In a subdued, barely audible voice he said, "He was a hand on a big trawler. One of the toughest, most dangerous jobs a man can have, I guess. I was worried for him, but proud, you know? He was makin' good money and savin' it up toward his own boat. Not pissin' it away like a lot of them. Got caught in a bad storm way out over the Grand Banks. Waves to fifty feet and more they said, enough to make even a good-sized boat pitch-pole or roll right over on her beam. All they ever found was some extra diesel barrels that'd been lashed to the deck. Hattie never gave up hope. It wasn't like Roy died. He just disappeared. And even when you know better you always kind of hope there'll be a letter or a phone call some day and it will be him. Hattie, she just never was the same after it. Until now."

"How did you two meet?"

He brightened. "Not a fancy story. It was after the war. I come to Pendleton down in South Carolina to visit my uncle."

They heard Hattie come in the front door, shuffling toward the bedroom. Hank quickly got the gun out of sight, jamming it behind his belt at his back, and raised his voice. "My aunt introduced Hattie to me in October of fifty-one. We went to a country fair. Stayed until it closed. She just couldn't resist my charms, I guess. I got a job helpin' build houses for GIs around Wilmington, and we ain't never looked back. But I know you heard all this before, Roy."

"What lies is he telling you, Roy?" Hattie said with a smile as she entered the room. She came over and rested a palm against Sam's forehead, nodding with satisfaction. "The fact is, I felt sorry for the man. I knew there was no other girl anywhere in this world who was likely to have him."

"Wasn't no other girl in this world I wanted, anyway," Hank said, grinning.

"First we'll see about getting a good breakfast into you, Roy. Then we'll change those bandages. I'm going to clean and mend your clothes today. Hank, you'll give him a sponge bath. Fresh sheets and pillowcases. Roy, I'll have to cut your blue jeans so they'll fit over that leg splint but I can sew them back up later. You'll need a warm jacket so I'll fit one of Hank's for you and maybe a sweater, too. Hank, you might as well set about making some crutches for him today so he'll be able to get around. Soon as possible there's no reason you can't be up and moving a little, Roy. You don't want your muscles to weaken any more."

Both men said, "Yes, ma'am."

By the afternoon of the next day the weather had turned cold, windy, and cloudy. Hank brought in a pair of crutches made from forked tree saplings. They had been crafted with care, the ends of the wood cut cleanly, chamfered, and sanded or scraped so there were no splinters, and the forks padded evenly with wrapped-on rags. Hank helped him dress in his clean salt-stiff clothes and a warm jacket that Hattie had let out for him. Hank tied on his sneakers for him and then Sam, aching all over, managed to get himself up off of the bed and onto the crutches unsteadily. His head felt light and airy but after a moment that passed.

Hank said, "You gonna be okay there, son?"

Sam smiled and nodded, taking an experimental step. The crutches worked well, sized to fit him perfectly. After a minute he made it out into what had once been the living room of the house and saw the sleeping bags rolled out near the far wall.

He said, "Dammit, Hank, I've been using your bed, haven't I? You just have these two rooms fixed up, don't you. The rest is closed off." Two doors leading off of the room were closed. Along one wall there was an old walnut wardrobe beside three stacks of shelving that the old man had obviously put up to store all their belongings and provisions neatly. There was a stack of wood—mostly pieces of driftwood and broken-up old gray boards—for the stove. There was a small table. The floor had been swept clean.

"Not a problem, son. Hattie and I like it out here by the stove, anyway, and them bags that we already borrowed in case it gets real cold are comfortable. You can even zip 'em together, you want to, make one big bag. Been tryin' to convince Hattie that'd be the thing to do. Conserve on body heat, I figure."

Hattie came in the front door, a sweater and a light jacket over her dress, a scarf tied around her head, and her nose pink from the cold. Hank had the stove crackling well and the room was pleasantly warm.

Sam sat down heavily in a mended straight chair. He said, "Okay, you two. Listen to me. Tonight I will take one of those sleeping bags and you will take your bed back. That's the way it's going to be."

Hattie said, "But, Roy, how will you get up and down with your crutches?"

"I'll manage. I can use this chair to help me, and I need the exercise, anyway. No arguments about it. Flutter, is that a pot of your famous magic tea on that old stove?"

She smiled and scurried to get him a cup.

He took a short walk outside that day, until Hattie sent Hank to retrieve him so she could inspect his bandages and make sure he still had no fever. While Hattie herself was outside later, Hank gave Sam his wallet back. "I dried everything in it," he said. "Hung it all on a wire where Hattie wouldn't see it."

Sam checked it over. His pilot's and driver's licenses were laminated and had suffered no real damage but they would be no good to him any more, anyway. There were fifty-seven dollars in water-damaged bills. He made Hank take the money. "Use it to get some of the things on Hattie's list," he said.

That night Hattie fixed them a big supper starting with sliced carrots and lettuce followed by corn pancakes with honey and maple syrup, and canned pears, with skillet gingerbread for dessert, and they all sat together at the table. Then Hank got out his fiddle and they sang some ballads, two or three Christmas carols, and two old hymns that Sam thought he had long forgotten. Sam drifted off in one of the sleeping bags as Hank was stoking the stove up for the night.

Over the next two days Sam spent longer periods hobbling around outside on the crutches. The long cuts on his head had crusted over and no longer hurt. His ribs, hip, and leg were painful but healing well, he knew, and he could feel some of his old strength returning as Hattie fed him her simple hearty meals. He spent some time doing curls with a full water jug and squeezing a short length of two-by-two in each of his fists. He found he could use one crutch and bring in small armloads of wood to replenish the stack, and he helped Hank better secure the rain tarp, rigging it so it would capture a little more water from the low-eaved roof. He washed the windows that they were using in the house.

On the morning of the twelfth day he'd been on Portsmouth he walked slowly on the crutches beside Hank along what had once been the main sandy lane of the town, now mostly overgrown with brush and grasses, Hank pointing out the tiny boarded-up post office, the ruin of the single store, and a cottage where he and Hattie had found several useful and repairable items, such as Hattie's rocker.

Later he asked Hank if there was a pencil and paper he could use and Hank got a ballpoint and a spiral pad for him. While Hank and Hattie were out on the sound in a chilly breeze tending the crab pots, Sam sat at the table and wrote them a long letter, trying to thank them, albeit grossly inadequately he felt, for saving his life, for all they had done, telling them he would send the skiff back to them within a day, that their secret was safe with him, and that he would come back to see them when he could.

He had changed his mind about going right back to Ocracoke. If word got out he was still alive it could endanger the people over there again and he couldn't stand the thought of that. He would get in touch with Valerie discreetly, meet her somewhere, and tell her all of it. When he got to the mainland he would call Bo Brinson and ask him to tow the skiff back to Portsmouth, swearing him to secrecy about him and about the Gaskills. When the letter was done he read it over, signed it Roy, folded it, and put it in his shirt pocket.

He went to sleep early that night and awoke well before dawn. He dressed quietly, left the letter on the table, and eased out the door. A gibbous moon was making a high thin layer of cloud glow like old lace, and the light breeze was clean and cold. He struck out through the shadows for the Coast Guard dock, placing the crutch tips carefully.

He was standing by the dock propped on his crutches figuring how best to untie the skiff and get into it when behind him in the darkness Hank said, "I got somethin' better than that right here, son."

He turned around. Hank moved closer, holding something out in his hand. It was a cell phone. "The man over in Sealevel loaned this to us," Hank said. "Wanted us to have it if there's an emergency. I got extra batteries for it. He swaps batteries for fresh-charged ones whenever we get over there."

Sam found himself hoping he could meet the old couple's benefactor over in Sealevel one day and shake that man's hand.

"Got a flashlight here, too. Why don't you sit on the dock there and call who you like. I'll take a walk."

"No, Hank. You stay here." He used the phone to call the number Bo had given him. Lucinda Brinson answered with sleep in her voice.

He said in a gruff tone, "Is Bo there?"

"A minute. Hey, Beaufort," she said loudly, "it's somebody for you don't give a damn what time it is. Get your butt up, boy."

In about thirty seconds Bo said, "Yeah."

"Listen, Bo. Don't let on who this is. It's important that only you know about this."

"Well, I'll be damned," Bo said, then lowering his voice, "You just disappeared, man. Where the hell are you?"

"I'm on Portsmouth Island. I need a couple of big favors."

"You say 'em, I'll do what I can."

"Do you know where the old Coast Guard dock is?"

"Sure do."

"Can you pick me up in your boat, then drive me to Raleigh? And Bo, you can't tell a soul about it. This time it's life or death."

"Give me three hours from now. I got to cancel what Spud and me had planned, and gas up. I'll be in the skimmer. How are you dressed?"

"Jeans and a jacket."

"It'll be cold as a witch's left tit out on the sound today, and choppy. I'll bring an extra slicker. You sit tight there, hear?"

Sam handed the phone back to Hank. "A man will pick me up here in three hours. I'll talk to him about you and Hattie, tell him to keep quiet. I won't tell anybody else."

"I know that, son. While we're at it I want you to take this." He brought out the old Colt forty-five auto. "Only reason I been keepin' it is if Hattie should go first. What I'd do, I figured, is put her there in a place out back of the church. She likes it out here so much. Then I been figurin' I'd use the gun for me. Except I know she really wouldn't want me to do that. So I'm askin' you to take it. Safety's right there. That's the slide latch. This is the magazine release. You got to pull the slide back to chamber the first round and cock it. Seven rounds. There's only the one magazine and the ammo's old so you'll want to get fresh, but the gun is right as ever. Hits like a mule kick. It saved me. Maybe it will help save you."

Sam hesitated, looking the old man in the eyes, and said, "Thanks, Hank." He took the gun and put it behind his belt at his back, hidden under the jacket.

"Now, let's go back," Hank said. "Along the way we got to cook up what to tell Hattie. She'll want to get a good breakfast in you. Then you can tell her a proper goodbye. I know she'll want to walk back out here with us to see you off."

The day was cold and clear, the sky decorated with ranks of low, fast-moving fair-weather cumuli. As the three of them walked back to the Coast Guard dock, with Sam in the middle on his crutches, a line of pelicans rode the breeze northward overhead, their wings almost motionless. Hattie was trying to smile. Trying not to cry. Sam had told her he had a job to do in Raleigh, helping to design a new kind of trawler that would be safer for the crews. He and Hank had made up the lie to give her some peace, and it seemed to be working.

She said, "Now, when you get back on the mainland, Roy, you have somebody take a good look at those cuts and change those bandages. I wish I'd packed you a lunch. You stop and get a good meal in you at noon, do you hear? Don't be working too hard for a while. Are you going to be warm enough?"

"I'll be fine, Flutter. You've just about healed me and you've fed me like a prince and filled me up with good music and good memories. I'll be back to see you both as soon as I can, and that's a promise. You take care of this old man while I'm away."

They stood together not far from the dock and watched the skimmer bounding in from way off, sending spray flying out to both sides, Bo big and bright in his yellow slicker. Sam asked Hank and Hattie to stay back a way while he had a talk with Bo, and he went down through the grass close to the water's edge. The skimmer floated easily in over the shoals, only slowing a little, and Bo chopped the throttle at exactly the right time so the big squarish boat rode in on its own swell and slid to a stop parallel to the dock and only a few feet from it. Bo deftly threw two lines around dock pilings and jumped out into the shallow water, wearing knee-high rubber boots. He waded up and shook Sam's hand, unsmiling. "Damn, man what happened to you?"

"My plane crashed," he said in a low voice. "Those two there saved me. They're Hank and Hattie Gaskill. It's a long story but she thinks I'm her son Roy, who was lost in a storm over the Grand Banks fifteen years ago. They ran away from a rest home in Morehead City a couple of months ago and they've set up a pretty good life for themselves out here. I've told them we'd keep their secret. I was wondering if you could look in on them once in a while until I can get back this way. See what they need, make sure they're okay, you know? I'll send you some money as soon as I can. There are things I'll have to do. There's a woman and her boy over on Ocracoke I need to get in touch with, but first I have to see people in Raleigh. I can't explain it all. It's just going to take some time, so I don't really know when I'll be back."

Bo was not smiling, not wanting to look Sam in the eyes, nervously rubbing his hands together. "No problem about that. Their story on a son, that's an old one here-abouts, sad to say. Lost a good friend that way myself. No need for any money. I'll look after these two. We know how to take care of our own around here. But you know this is all National Seashore out here. Pretty soon a ranger will find them, or somebody else will, then the bureaucrats and the lawyers will take over."

"I know, but I'd like to think they've got some more good days out here, at least."

Bo smiled thinly. "Ran away, huh? Can't say as I blame 'em for that. Wouldn't want to die in no rest home myself."

"Come on over and meet them. They're good people."

Bo forced a smile, walked over, shook Hank's hand and said hello ma'am to Hattie. "Roy's told me about you, how you got out here. I live not far away over to Pantego, and I'll just be comin' out here time to time to see how you're gettin' on, if that's okay. You need anything, Roy here says to just let me know."

"You won't be going too fast on the way back over, will you?" Hattie said. "Roy's hurt as you can see and he doesn't need a rough ride just now."

"I'll treat him like three dozen eggs, ma'am. We'll go slow."

"That's a slick rig you got there, son." Hank said.

"Next time I'm over this way we'll take a ride in her. I'll show you how she works."

"I'd like that, son."

"Mister Gaskill, Miz Gaskill, would you mind if I talk with Roy a bit now? There's a thing I got to tell him."

"Not a problem," Hank said. "It's gettin' cold out here anyway. What say we go back and get us a cup of your tea, Mother." She hugged Sam and then Hank led her away, both of them turning and waving twice before they were out of sight, Hattie wiping at tears.

"What is it, Bo?"

"Sam. Why don't we just walk over there to the church. Get in out of this wind. Talk a little."

Sam's belly was chilling with a creeping black dread. He followed Bo to the church and they went inside. Bo sat in the back pew and Sam propped the crutches against the back wall and slid awkwardly in beside him. There was a plain rough-hewn cross on the wall up behind the old pulpit. Dusty sunlight shafted through the rippled-glass windows. The rustling of Bo's slicker seemed loud as he used his hands to rake back his shaggy hair. "Lord, I don't know how to tell you this," he said, his voice loud in the small church.

"Just tell me, Bo."

"You got some good friends over to Ocracoke. When I heard you disappeared I ran the skimmer over there, see was there something I could do. Met a Coast Guard man named Ruben Dixon in The Privateer. We talked a while. Sam, the boy Josh, he's fine. But your lady, Miz Lightfoot. She's dead, Sam."

It didn't register. "No, that can't be. You're wrong, Bo."

"Lord, I'm sorry, Sam. Maybe if I had more school I'd know a way to say it so it wouldn't hurt so much."

He was numb. "Her parents and her man died in car accidents," he heard himself say. "God, it wasn't that..."

Bo shook his head. "They figured it was somebody was after you. They planted a bomb in your Jeep. She tried to use the Jeep. It had to have been so fast she never knew it, Sam. I hear the boy is with kin somewhere up in the mountains."

He squeezed his eyes closed tightly, trying to shut it out, but all he saw was her getting lithely into the Jeep, reaching down under the mat for the key, trying to start it, maybe thinking of some kid thing Josh had done that day, maybe even thinking of him, and the whole world suddenly flashing white...

He stared at the back wall of the church. The cross began to melt and hot drops fell onto his shirt front. He started to gather the hundreds of random thoughts of her. Those ancient dark and deep eyes. Her lustrous black hair. Her knowing smile and her electric touches and her satin skin in the candlelight. The unique timbre of her voice. Her neatness and efficiency and sense of humor. The dreams she'd dreamed for Joshua. He began to gather it all and to sear it into his memory so she would go on living there and he would never...never forget her love until his own dying day.

He whispered, "Joshua. He must be full of so much pain, Bo. They could have killed that good little boy, too. She didn't even know why. They were after me. God, I drew them down on her."

"No, Sam. I never knew the lady but I'd bet she'd never blame you. I don't know where you'll have to go from here, but I wanted to tell you, Spud and me, we're not half bad in a fight. If you need us to watch your back..."

"That's okay, Bo," he said in a raw, choked voice. "Thank you...thank you for telling me here, in this old church. That's eased it somehow. I knew, of course. I knew there was something badly wrong over there." He took a deep, shuddering breath and wiped his eyes on the stiff salty jacket sleeve.

He sat there for several more minutes in the quiet musty little church, the breeze shivering the brush outside, making small shadows skitter nervously at the windows, Bo sitting motionless beside him in the bright yellow slicker with his head bowed.

The world suddenly a profoundly changed place.

After a time he took a last look up at the cross and said, "Let's go now."

A YOUNG DOCTOR AND A NURSE WORKED ON HIM FOR
three hours in a small outpatient clinic on a Raleigh
side street. The doctor told him he would have minor
permanent scars on the side of his head and upper forehead
and a much more evident one along his hip, but that he was
healing well. They put a light-weight cast on his right leg,
which an X-ray confirmed had been broken, and re-taped
his ribs, three of which were cracked. They swabbed and
band-aided him here and there and gave him two small
bottles of pills to take at specified intervals, and a new pair
of crutches.

A Marshal took him to a plainly-furnished house
on a quiet street in the suburb of Wake Forest outside of
Raleigh, a small three-bedroom ranch indistinguishable
from hundreds of others in the area, in a sprawling development filled with young couples trying to make livings
and pay all the bills, most of them neither knowing nor
caring about their neighbors. Another Marshal followed
in another car. They used a radio-controlled door opener

and drove him right into the garage. One of the Marshals left to get some groceries and he sat with the other one across from him at the dining table.

It was eleven o'clock at night. Matthew Jensen was leaning back in his chair, balancing it on its back legs, with his arms folded, dressed in what seemed to be the regulation dark blue suit, white shirt, and a loosened muted burgundy tie. He was in his late fifties and was somewhat overweight and balding, wearing half glasses. He was ready to take notes on a small flip pad. There were foam cups of coffee and a box of donuts on the table.

"No, I'm afraid nobody has been arrested for it," Jensen said. "I understand they combed the island thoroughly. A woman in a store remembered some young man in fatigues with a high-pitched voice asking questions about you early that night, but she couldn't give any description beyond that. Apparently nobody else noticed anything unusual before or after the, ah, the incident. They know it was C-4 rigged to the ignition, but not much else. I'm really sorry, but if I were you I wouldn't expect any arrests soon, much less any prosecutions."

"I saw a big one. A face like a bulldog. Smoked a fat cigar. I'd seen him somewhere before."

"Yes. That might have been Walter Calzo. His street name is Winston. Lives in Newark. They tell me he's a known occasional associate of Strake's."

"I'm pretty sure that was the one who shot at my plane. He had a submachine gun."

"Yes. After you talk with them they'll bring him in and question him, maybe, but he's apparently an old hand at this game. It's likely he'll have two or three who will swear he was playing stud poker in Newark when you say he was on the island. I'm sorry, but that's the way this frequently goes. They'll either raise the plane or go down and take a look at it. We're debating whether the best thing to do would be just to leave it right where it is for a time. But with the lack of evidence and no real witnesses other than you, as I say, I wouldn't expect much to happen soon."

He unfolded his arms, letting the front chair legs thump down onto the carpet. He took a sip of coffee from the foam cup. "Anyway, there's nothing I can do about any of that. My job is to protect you. From my point of view the situation is good. As far as anybody knows or has to know outside of the law, except for that fisherman who saved you and brought you in this morning, Sam Bass is dead or vanished, and you say the fisherman will keep his mouth closed. Let's hope you're correct about that. All we have to do, then, is let Mr. Bass rest in peace. We'll fix you up with a whole new identity and significantly change your appearance this time. Tinted contact lenses would make a big difference for you, to start with. Color the hair and cut it close, part it, grow a beard or a mustache, maybe some plastic work around the eyes. We can put a little discreet pressure on the company that insured the plane if we have to. I think the policy was for forty-five thousand, and the plane was paid off, wasn't it? So I think we can get that for you, paid to Mr. Bass's estate, with our lawyer handling it. We'll get you established in some Midwestern state, maybe. That should be the end of it.

"Meanwhile you can stay right here while you heal

some more. Sturdevant will stay here with you. The house has an excellent security system. He'll see that you're fed well and he'll go out to get clothes and whatever else you need. There's some exercise equipment in the back bedroom. You need to do exactly what Sturdevant tells you to do. He's a good man. As I say, it's a near-ideal situation."

"No. I want to stay up in the Smokies somewhere. Western North Carolina or eastern Tennessee."

"Yes, well. You want to be near the boy. I can understand that. What *you* have to understand is the potential danger you pose for him."

"Believe me, I realize that. I don't plan to have any contact with him."

"That would be wise. I still would strongly suggest you get well away from the East Coast, but if you insist I suppose that if we handle it correctly, and as long as you'll follow our instructions, the mountains might be safe enough for you."

"How did they find me?"

"The story about you that ran in the Raleigh *Sentinel,* I'm sure."

"I never saw it."

"I didn't either, but somebody did. It was picked up by the Associated Press and it ran in something over a hundred papers all over the country. You should have let us know that was going to happen. We probably could have stopped it, or at least we could have moved you off of that island in time."

"It had been almost five years. You tend to forget, or to diminish the threat in your mind. I was getting careless."

"There's nothing we can do about that now. What we can do is build you a new identity that will have no holes. Do you have a preference for a name?"

He thought for a minute and then said, "John Hardin."

Jensen printed it on the pad and turned it so he could see it and confirm the spelling. "That sounds familiar. It shouldn't be even close to anyone you've known."

"It's nobody I ever knew."

"Okay. We'll get started on that, then. We'll help you set up a pilot's license with all the same ratings as before. We'll get photos later, of course, for the passport and driver's license. Meanwhile you're safe hidden away here."

"You get tired of hiding, too."

"Well, any time you do, take a minute to consider the options."

"I have. There's an old movie you ought to like," he said, staring at the wall with his gray eyes and speaking in a distant voice. "It's called *Cahill, United States Marshal*."

"I don't think I ever saw that one."

"It opens at night in a snowy woods near a campsite. John Wayne slowly rides in carrying a double-barreled shotgun in his left hand with the hammers cocked. There are five armed hard-cases at the camp, three in a fan in front of Wayne, two in the nearby woods, one of those with a shotgun, the other with a Spencer rifle. Wayne pins his Marshal's badge to the outside of his coat, then draws the side of the coat back with his right hand to expose his ivory-handled hog-leg. You know what he says?"

"I can't imagine."

"He says, 'Any of ya wanna surrender?' "

The Marshal looked at him for several seconds and then said, "Yes, well. Life can't be like some old western, I'm afraid."

"It can't?"

"That's Sturdevant coming back now. I'll be leaving. I'll be back late in the morning. We might as well start using your new name, John Hardin, so you'll get accustomed to it. How does it sound?"

"It will do," thinking *John Wesley Hardin.*

Fastest gun in the west.

Two days later when he and Grady Sturdevant had nothing particular to do in the afternoon they sat in the living room of the safe house drinking casually from a pint of Jim Beam, the Marshal limiting himself to two drinks. Sturdevant could have been a poster image for the Marshals. A neat young black man, he was burnished-healthy and rugged-looking. He had his suit jacket off but kept his tie on, and the leather of his shoulder holster gleamed. He had an interest in light planes. "I went for my license a few years ago," he said. "I soloed in an old Cessna one-fifty and passed the written, but I've never seemed to find the time to finish up. The wife and kids take up most of my free time these days. I'm not complaining, mind you. I'll get back to it one of these days."

"Do it," John Hardin said. "I've never done anything else that's given me the same challenge, the same satisfaction, and I've done some crazy things. I've never tired of flying."

"They never told me the full story of why you're in the witness program."

So over the rest of that afternoon John Hardin told him most of it.

IT STARTED THE DAY HE MET LOUIS STRAKE.

The big brick warehouse in Edgewater, New Jersey, was behind a high razor-wired fence alongside a ship dock across the Hudson from Harlem. A small brass plaque on the steel entrance door bore the raised name Worldarms Corporation superimposed on a logo that was a stylized peeled globe. A receptionist had him sign in and ushered him into a large room with a leather-inlaid conference table at one end that could seat ten. An oversized ornate desk at the other end looked to be a valuable antique. Everything was darkly immaculate, softly lit from recessed ceiling fixtures. The walls were crowded with lighted glass display cases that held scores of different weapons, mostly military. There was a medieval feel about the room and it smelled of gun oil. He moved along with his hands in the back pockets of his jeans, examining the exhibits. A large case labeled World War I contained old bolt-action rifles with bayonets affixed, gas masks, uniforms, sabers, and accouterments. None of it was dusty; all of it was well preserved.

A quiet voice behind him said, "Do you have an interest in weapons?"

He turned and said, "Yes, but I don't really know much about them, except for some of the western frontier guns like the Spencer rifle, the lever-action Winchesters, the early Colt revolvers."

"Have a seat at the table. Would you like coffee or a soft drink?"

"No, thank you. I had breakfast an hour ago."

When they were seated across the table from each other he studied Strake. The man was impeccably dressed in a tailored blue suit. There was something about his manner and his erect bearing, his aura, that made you see beyond the surface and realize you were in the presence of an intelligent, powerful man. He had a dark penetrating gaze even though he was smiling. There was a hint of menace about him.

Strake said, "Mr. Kensington at the Teterboro Airport recommended you to me. He said they call you Cowboy. I need a pilot. My former pilot now captains a seven-twenty-seven for a Kuwaiti."

"What kind of airplane do you have?"

"A Super King Air B Two Hundred. I'm told you know the airplane well."

He had flown one five hundred hours over the past three years for a New York financier until the man had been caught up to his elbows in a widespread insider trading scheme. The financier was awaiting trial and facing the prospect of doing modest time in an upstate country club prison, where he would have plenty of leisure to contemplate whatever small portion of his portfolio the lawyers deigned to leave him.

"Yes, I do know it well. It's an excellent plane. Probably the best turboprop twin ever built. It's certainly been popular."

"I like it because it has enough range to take me anywhere I want to go with minimal refueling stops," Strake said. "It cruises at over three hundred miles per hour, yet it can operate out of relatively short, unimproved strips. The one I have is seven years old but it's been well maintained and upgraded. GPS, color radar, an electronic flight information system, Collins autopilot and flight director. Virtual all-weather capability. I've owned it for almost three years. It's as good as—in many respects better than—brand new and I insist that it be kept that way."

"It sounds like a fine machine. I'd like to take a look at the logs, of course."

Strake's smile widened fractionally. "I tend to be rather more demanding than others you may have worked for. I need someone who will be on call every day at least from dawn until dark, someone I can reach within an hour so I can be airborne within two or three hours for any destination. I also require absolute discretion concerning my business affairs. I've had you checked out rather thoroughly and so have some assurance that you're a competent pilot and a man to be trusted. In return for what I demand I'm willing to pay fifty percent more than that Wall Street fool was paying you. There are other amenities.

"The company has a comprehensive benefits package. There are the best accommodations wherever I go. The best food. The opportunity to meet some of the most influential people in the world. I do a great deal of my business these days right from that desk, with the telephone, e-mail, and Fax, but there are still many occasions when I must travel to inspect a stock of weapons that I want to buy or to conduct a transaction that can't be handled any other way. Very often time is at a premium. I have a home in Vancouver and a getaway cottage in the Bahamas, so there are planned flights to those places. I take commercial flights most of the time to Europe, Asia, or Africa, although there will be times I will want to use the King Air for overseas trips. I have agents who work for me around the world and I maintain small subsidiary offices in London, Vancouver, and Panama. I ski in Vail and I go to Caracas and other South American destinations from time to time."

"This is quite some collection you have here, Mr. Strake," he said, looking around at all the weaponry. "No offense at all intended, sir, but I've been approached by certain potential employers who have offered tempting sums for regular trips that would have involved flying very low over the Gulf of Mexico and night landings in some out-of-the-way places."

Strake laughed dryly. "Tactfully put. The items you see here are only part of my collection. It's probably the highest-quality and most extensive private assemblage of light arms in the world. The sword in the case behind my desk belonged to Napoleon.

"Let me assure you. I'm a businessman, the sole owner of this company. Not so different from other businessmen and with more scruples than many. I've never defaulted on a contract and have always paid my debts in full. I have sterling credit. Worldarms is fully licensed in every country where I do business. I serve as agent for twelve different weapons manufacturers in five countries. Governments do by far the bulk of the world trade these days, supplying each other with jet fighters, tanks, missiles, the latest technology. At the other extreme there are always those idiots who sell Saturday night specials in back alleys or move a few stolen assault rifles or grenades to crazed terrorists. This company has always operated—and has always flourished—well within those two extremes. I do business as openly as the Pentagon does and often with their tacit blessings. I control something on the order of sixty percent of the private world trade in light arms."

"Again no offense, sir, but how do you make sure that the guns you deal in don't wind up in the wrong hands? People who'll use them indiscriminately?"

"I know enough about you to say that you're not that naïve. Over in that desk there's a gold-plated letter opener. You probably have a pocket knife. My wife has an expensive set of steak knives. All of those things are inherently dangerous. As potentially lethal as any of the bayonets on the rifles in this room or as the rifles themselves. I can't be responsible for how you choose to use your pocket knife or for how anyone chooses to use any weapon. Does Detroit feel responsible for how people drive their vehicles, vehicles that kill forty thousand people in this country every year with monotonous regularity? Do car dealers feel responsible? In any given eighteen-month period, by the way, more Americans continue to die on the highways than died in the entire decade of the Vietnam War."

It seemed like a set speech that had been delivered many times before. The man seemed to have a polished, practiced veneer, not allowing much of his real self to show through.

Strake went on, "Within legal limits I sell to anybody who can pay my price. The United States has sold complete air defense systems to both Israel and its Arab neighbors. The United States and Britain have sold weapons to both India and Pakistan, weapons that both those countries have used with vigor. The creation of Bangladesh has been one result, with attendant untold suffering. Surely you remember the Iranian hostage crisis. In the face of that crisis Israel blatantly sold military supplies to Iran that had come from the United States as foreign aid. Israel has never felt any affection for Iran but they always considered Iraq the far greater threat.

"The French have denounced America's imperialist policies in Central America but they have sold arms to South Africa and Argentina. The Czechs will sell to anyone, no exceptions, as will the new Russians. Why should I show any more restraint than those governments do? I have no interest in any of the past or current conflicts in the world. My only interest in governments concerns how they might affect my business. I have personal views, of course, but I don't take sides. That would be absolute professional folly. Politics change with the seasons. Leaders come and go but the items I trade will outlive all of them.

"There's a flintlock musket over there in the corner. It is two centuries old and it still functions perfectly.

Whatever political forces caused it to be created and employed have long since faded into murky history, but there it remains, and its value has increased steadily, if only as a collector's item.

"I don't sell to terrorists primarily because it's bad business. It would threaten my entire legitimate operation. They are unreliable people at best, and the quantities of items they want are minuscule; not worthy of my time. If anyone objects to what I do let them first object to what their own governments are doing routinely, and let them first go talk to Boeing, Lockheed, General Dynamics, Dassault, and the Royal Ordnance Factories. The weapons they produce are potentially far more lethal to far greater numbers of people than my trade items. My business is almost as old as gunpowder and it will always endure. Trying to control it is often foolish and almost always ineffective because there is a constant intense demand. Years ago when the United States and Britain finally bowed to African majority opinion and stopped selling arms to South Africa, they only lost the business. France and Jordan stepped in and profited hugely, and South African military strength suffered not one iota. If I were to go out of business tomorrow there would be no long-term measurable decline in violence worldwide. You know that to be true, intuitively."

"If you don't mind my saying so, Mr. Strake," he said with a smile, "I think you're a consummate salesman. And your business seems to have been very good to you."

"I has made me wealthy, yes. Worldarms grosses on the order of eighty million dollars in a good year. And my father started it all with only his own wits." He tapped his temple with a manicured finger.

"That must be quite a story."

Strake became pensive, gazing into a distance. "It is. It began with a trip he took as a young man through Europe right after World War Two. He had no money and no real idea of what to do with his life. The roads over there were lined with tanks and howitzers, many of them fully functional. Fields were littered with abandoned arms and war debris. Rifles, pistols, machine guns. There were piles of gravel by the sides of the roads where farmers were supposed to throw cartridges, grenades, and fragments for disposal. There were bleached skeletons of soldiers that the peasants wouldn't touch for fear of booby traps. It took the Russians two years to collect all the discarded ordnance along that front and it took the Allies even longer to clean up. A lot of it was simply dumped at sea. From field artillery pieces right down to Luger pistols and fine Mauser rifles.

"My father slept in abandoned bunkers where there were cases of rifles, grenades, and ammunition stacked to the ceilings. The people were sick of war, of course, and wanted nothing to do with the weaponry. But a lot of it was collected and stored. My father knew the demand would return and he began to learn who had what and where. Back in the United States he went to work for the CIA and when the Korean War broke out they sent him to Western Europe to buy weapons to arm Chiang Kai-shek, who they hoped would then distract the Chinese from their focus on helping North Korea. He learned a great deal more during that buying trip.

"In the early nineteen-fifties he left the CIA. He bought a load of weapons from Panama on credit, sold them to Eastward Arms at a one-hundred-percent profit, and never looked back. He bought hundreds of thousands of weapons in every caliber and millions of rounds of ammunition. He paid eighty-five cents each for bolt-action Mannlicher-Carcano rifles that sold through American chain stores to hunters for twenty dollars each."

"That was the rifle that killed John Kennedy, wasn't it?"

Strake ignored the comment and went on. "He sold thousands of rifles himself by mail order to sportsmen for ten dollars each. He sold M-1 Garands to Guatemala. He found a huge cache of weapons in a vast bunker in the Netherlands that even included V-1 rockets. He bought hundreds of the excellent German MG-42 machine guns there for twenty dollars each and sold them to Germany for three hundred and fifty dollars each. Within a decade of the end of World War Two Germany was re-armed, a fact most people don't realize. He even sold helmets, uniforms, and weapons to Hollywood in respectable numbers for the endless succession of mostly-inaccurate war movies. He dealt with Trujillo, with both Somozas, father and son, with first Batista and then with Castro, with Perez Jimenez of Venezuela. He taught me well and for the past eighteen years I've run the company myself. He died ten years ago in his sleep."

"That's a fascinating story. It would make a good movie on its own I would think."

Strake seemed to refocus. "That's something to

consider one day. But I've talked far longer than I intended. What I need to know right now is do you want the job I'm offering you?"

"With all respect there's one point I'd like to cover up front, sir. I had a friend who went down in a Navajo. He took three top executives from the same company with him. I happen to know they pressured him, to the point of threatening to fire him, to fly in extremely bad weather against his far better judgment, and they all died because of it. Your plane sounds well-equipped but there are some conditions, like severe icing or bad thunderstorms, that make staying on the ground, or at least diverting, the wisest course, and I'll have to retain the absolute right to make decisions like that, no matter what. I also have to abide by a lot of ATC instructions, FAA rules, aircraft limitations, and legal restrictions. It's in your best interests as well as mine that I be in command of the plane at all times."

"That's conditionally acceptable. If you refuse to take off, for example, I will probably need to know why in some detail."

"Not a problem. And I accept your offer."

Strake got up, went over to his desk, and pushed a button. "Margaret out there will help you with the necessary paperwork, sign you up for our insurance and the withholding."

A large man came in the side door to the room. "This is Montgomery Davis," Strake said. "He's in charge of our security here and at my homes and elsewhere. Montgomery, this is Cowboy, our new pilot. I suggest you two meet at Teterboro Airport this afternoon. Why don't you make it one o'clock. Montgomery will show you where the King

Air is hangared, give you a set of keys, and introduce you to the maintenance people I use. You will oversee all the maintenance and routine cleaning. Run any significant modifications or upgrades past me first.

"The logs and manuals are in the plane. Take it up for a checkout flight. Within sixty days I'd like you to select a backup pilot we can put on a modest retainer and use if you're ill or away for any reason. Give us the name and Montgomery will run a background check.

"I'd like you to wear black slacks, a white shirt with epaulets, and a black tie. A jacket will be optional except when we're carrying somebody important, then I'd like you to wear it. Margaret will give you the name of a tailor I've used. You can charge your first set of clothes to my account.

"Your apartment is already close enough to the airport. Margaret will give you a beeper. Do you have objections to any of that?"

"None."

"Shake hands with Mr. Davis, then. He'll be along on most of our trips, sometimes with one or two of his people."

Over the next few days Cowboy gave some thought to choosing the backup pilot. Duane Kelly was a casual acquaintance from his early training days. They had both had the same instructor for their commercial multi-engine ratings in Myrtle Beach, South Carolina, and had spent a night or two carousing in beach bistros. Kelly was darkly good-looking and attracted women with his good looks and cocky humor. Kelly had gone to work flying light twins for a freight hauler out of Macon and they had lost contact for several years. Then one day Kelly had called saying he had a proposition. They had met in a bar in Jacksonville, Florida, where Cowboy was flying a Super Cub towing banners along the beaches and flying an occasional charter in a Beech Duke.

Over cold beers, Kelly worked around to asking if he would be interested in a quick trip or two into Mexico. He smiled and made it sound virtually innocent.

"You're talking about carting drugs, right?"

"Hey, a little coke. The stuff is everywhere these days, right? Nose candy for the affluent. Hell, you can't go to a party now where there isn't a supply in the back bedroom or right out there in the open on the damned coffee table. The trips are probably safer than you flying that old Cub for the tourists. You go down, they load you up, then you fly back low across the Gulf and land in Mississippi, or maybe Texas, depending. You get twenty-five thousand a trip, a bag full of cash. They provide the plane, probably a Baron or something like a twin Comanche. I figure if we don't do it somebody else will, right?

"What you do is rig it so you can jettison the whole load over the water if you have to before you land. It's weighted to sink. No evidence, no problem. You quit when you want to. No hard feelings. I've already made two trips without a hitch. I told the money people I'm working for I'd try to find them another good man. They'd surprise you. They're not your typical movie image. These people are legitimate businessmen and professionals. They wouldn't chance it if it wasn't safe. The offer won't last long. What do you say?"

"Duane, how the hell did you get involved in this?

What if the plane turns out to be stolen? What if you're caught on the ground in Mexico? Or on the ground back here while they're offloading? What they're paying won't seem like nearly enough money if you wind up doing ten years in a federal prison. Think about it. Are these people—these money men—are they really taking any chances compared to what you're risking? Count me out."

"Hey, I was just asking, you know? You're not interested, that's cool. If you change your mind give me a call." He wrote his number on a bar napkin.

"Be careful, Duane. Those aren't any kind of people to ever turn your back on."

"Hey, two or three more trips and I'll have a real stake. Then I'm gone. Don't you worry about me."

A year later Cowboy heard that Duane had crashed an old DC-3 on takeoff from Amarillo but had walked away. The law had come close to charging him but he'd had a thin cover story about simply trying to ferry the old plane to a mechanic for repairs. The story had barely held up, so he had walked away from that, as well. He had showed up in Teterboro a year ago, down on his luck, contrite about his Mexican adventures, and vowing to turn his life around. He was working as a part-time charter pilot for a shoestring operation. Two days after he was hired Cowboy phoned Kelly and said, "I might have a slot for you as a backup pilot for the company I'm working for. Are you interested?"

Kelly said, "Buddy I appreciate that. I really do."

"You're not making any runs down over the border these days, are you?"

"No way. I can be a little dense, but that's one lesson

I've learned real well."

The next day Cowboy told Strake, "I might have a backup pilot for you. A man named Duane Kelly. He and I trained at the same place years ago. You ought to know some say he hauled a few illegal loads up from Mexico, but not for at least a year now. He's supposed to be a good twin pilot."

Strake said, "Give the details to Davis." Two weeks later Strake signed Kelly on for a modest retainer.

The first trip was one week later to Atlanta with Strake, Montgomery Davis, and an accountant named Chester Thurgood aboard, to evaluate a small company that made Walther pistols. The King Air was in perfect condition and the six-ton airplane handled like a much smaller docile twin, the PT6 turboprops delivering a total of 1,700 horsepower smoothly. At dawn they climbed strongly out of Teterboro at 2,300 feet per minute and 140 miles per hour in cool clear fall air.

The Newark controllers vectored them through their complex crowded airspace with rapid-fire instructions. There was a cold front angling west to east between them and Atlanta but it was dry except for some light snow well away to the west. As the King Air cruised southwest on autopilot at 26,500 feet over Virginia at 310 miles per hour, Strake came up and took the right-hand seat. He said, "Have you found anything concerning the plane that needs attention?"

Monitoring the instruments, he said, "Nothing at all right away. The maintenance people tell me we should think about tires at the next inspection. You mentioned using unimproved strips occasionally. In that case you might want to consider changing from the standard high-pressure tires to high-flotation ones. They're wider so they would protrude from the wheel wells slightly when they're retracted. The extra drag would cost you, for example, about four miles per hour at 16,000 feet, but the fat tires would ease operations on rough fields so the whole plane wouldn't absorb as much stress, and they'd be better than what's mounted on here if there's mud or snow.

"The other thing would be a set of wing-tip landing lights. Yours are mounted on the nose gear now. The wingtip lights would let me drag a strip at night to check it out without putting the gear down, supplement the nose gear lights in certain conditions, and light us up better in traffic areas when we're traveling at higher than gear-down speed."

"Go ahead and have it all done. Just let me know when and how long the plane will be down for it."

They made conversation to pass the time. Strake's knowledge of light weapons was encyclopedic and he obviously liked to discourse on the subject. "For decades the United States was slow to adopt new weapons technology," he mused. "And always at a cost of lives. There are many examples. Smokeless powder was developed by a Frenchman in 1884. Peter Paul Mauser was a genius and he designed a bolt-action rifle that used a cartridge with the new powder. His gun was highly accurate at long range and was rugged and reliable but the U.S. Ordnance Board ignored it and instead bought Norwegian Krag-Jorgensen rifles for the troops.

"The Krag used a black-powder cartridge, so the rifle needed frequent cleaning and every shot gave away the exact location of the shooter. So in 1898 in Cuba Spanish riflemen used their Mausers to easily pick off the smoking Yankees, breaking the assault at El Caney. At San Juan Hill it was the same, with 15,000 U.S. troops against 700 Spaniards. The famous heroic charge was really a slog through deadly Mauser sniper fire, and the Americans took ten percent casualties. They managed to rout the 700 Spaniards only with heavy Gatling gun fire. When they finally built the Springfield rifle they used a great deal of the Mauser design.

"The only thing more stupid than ignoring new technology in weapons is arming troops with known bad quality weapons. Italy has produced some trash. Their standard World War Two machine gun was the Breda Modello 30. It was heavy, just over four feet long, and was fed by twenty-round chargers. The extraction system was so bad it needed an internal oil pump to lubricate the spent casings, and the oil attracted dirt, of course, so it failed constantly. It had no carrying handles so the gunners had to wear heavy gloves to handle it hot in combat. Yet the Italians also produced the Beretta Model 1938A submachine gun. Collectors prize them today as a mechanical work of art.

"The Japanese also produced at both extremes. Their Nambu Type 14 was probably the absolute worst service pistol in history. It was so poorly designed it could accidentally discharge rounds before they were fully seated in the firing chamber.

"In World War One the British had the Vickers machine gun that vented steam from the barrel water jacket, so the clouds of vapor obligingly marked the precise location of the gunners for the Germans.

"They never seem to learn from such incredible blunders. After World War Two, during the race to make fully automatic rifles, while the Russians were producing the Kalashnikov AK-47 and Fairchild was producing the .22-caliber Armalite AR-15, both excellent weapons, the Pentagon, all on its own, came up with the .30-caliber M-14, which was much heavier than the Armalite, and when it was fired on full automatic even a trained soldier couldn't hold it steady.

"The first troops in Vietnam in 1965 carried M-14s. The Armalite AR-15 was a vastly superior weapon for Vietnam conditions because it had been designed to hose the enemy at relatively close quarters, from 30 to 200 yards, and it functioned superbly in dirty, humid conditions. The Army grudgingly recognized its merits only under extreme pressure from President Kennedy and Robert McNamara. The Pentagon still preferred its own demonstrably bad M-14. Army dogma held that a rifle should be accurate to 600 yards so before they would accept the AR-15, which became the M-16, they demanded modifications that had the effect of destroying its reliability. They insisted on a more powerful powder for more range. The powder was dirty so it fouled the rifle and it increased the rate of fire from 750 rounds a minute to over 1,000, which only aggravated the fouling and also tended to jam the mechanism, so soldiers died with

rounds jammed in their M-16s. A number of unmodi-
fied AR-15s had been sent to the South Vietnamese in
1962 and they had worked flawlessly. Later in the war
GIs bought those AR-15s on the Saigon black market for
$600 each to replace their M-16s. When the Viet Cong
won a fight they'd strip the bodies of everything and leave
the M-16s as worthless."

Cowboy said, "The same thing happened after the
Battle of the Little Big Horn when the Sioux stripped
Custer and his men but left their Army-issue rifles behind
because a lot of them had jammed."

Strake said, "The M-16 was eventually improved but
how many men were shot while they were working to free
up a jammed early model? If I had been in Vietnam I would
have thrown my M-16 into the jungle and picked up an
AK-47. It's made now in more than thirty factories around
the world. More than forty million have been produced.
The essential moving parts are made to close tolerances but
everything else is purely functional and cheap. It's rugged,
reliable, accurate, and all of its parts are completely inter-
changeable, whatever factory they come from. Worldwide,
it is probably the most popular service rifle ever built. It's
used in some seventy countries."

As they drew closer to Atlanta Cowboy was preoccupied with ATC communications, monitoring the aircraft
systems during the long descent, and studying the layout
for Dekalb-Peachtree airport in his *Flight Guide* for a final
time, and Strake fell silent, looking disinterestedly out his
side of the cockpit, absorbed in his thoughts.

Northeast of the sprawling city he entered a downwind

leg for Dekalb-Peachtree's runway two-zero left at 2,500 feet. Working with familiar assurance he armed the autofeather, turned off the propeller synchrophaser, selected approach flaps, reduced the torques to 1,000 foot-pounds per side, and slowed to 170 miles an hour. When he was abeam the runway numbers he turned off the yaw damper, put the gear down, pulled the power levers back to 600 foot-pounds, and banked onto the base leg and then onto final, descending, bleeding off the airspeed to 140 miles an hour, aligning with the runway centerline dashes. As the threshold drew closer he squeezed off another 200 foot-pounds, pushed the prop levers forward, and put down the final increment of flaps.

As the threshold rushed by underneath he started pulling back gently on the yoke, raising his gaze to the far end of the runway for better peripheral vision height judgment. The mains touched down with only a muffled chirp at 90 miles an hour. He let the nosewheel touch down, then pulled back on the power levers to put the props into reverse pitch, the deceleration hefty, and got on the brakes, slowing the big twin down to walking speed in well under a third of the 6,000-foot runway. He retracted the flaps, set the power levers back into forward pitch, swung off onto a taxiway, and guided the plane sedately to the Mercury Air Center, where an attendant directed him to a tiedown. Without comment Strake got up and went back into the cabin. Cowboy went back and opened the stairs.

They all walked into the executive lounge of the fixed base operation, or FBO, and the attendant took their order for fuel. The gun company had sent a limousine to pick them up. Cowboy was prepared to wait at the FBO.

Davis pointed a thick finger at him and said, "While we're gone, take a courtesy car and stock up the mini-bar in the plane."

After a moment's thought, Strake said, "No, he'll come with us."

Davis looked at Strake quizzically, glared briefly at Cowboy, then shrugged.

At the plant the accountant was left with the company comptroller and two members of the office staff while the CEO and his fawning assistant conducted a detailed plant tour for the rest of the visitors through the offices—the five-person engineering room, the machining and assembly areas, tool and die, inspections, the parts warehouse and shipping, the cafeteria, and the small test firing range.

The tour consumed the remainder of the working day because Strake stopped to ask many pointed and perceptive questions along the way and was not satisfied until he received exhaustive answers, sometimes to the obvious irritation of the gray-haired CEO. Montgomery Davis followed along like a temporarily tame bear several steps behind the group, occasionally aiming a dark look at Cowboy. Because time had run out they were invited to return the following day to hear several planned presentations, and Strake agreed.

They were all prepared with overnight bags. A secretary arranged rooms for them at the Atlanta Hilton and by eight that night they were enjoying a leisurely meal in the Russian four-star restaurant on the Hilton's top floor, the lights of Atlanta spreading away in an endless glittering carpet below. Cowboy ordered lobster in a wine sauce and found it to be easily the best he'd ever tasted. Twice he caught Davis eyeing him malevolently, but dismissed it. Traveling in this kind of style, he thought over brandy and excellent coffee, was a heady experience and could soon become addictive. Strake did not discuss his views on the company.

They took off late the following afternoon and when they were at cruising altitude Strake came up to take the right-hand seat. He said, "What did you think of the company?"

He was surprised by the question but tried not to show it. He thought for a minute and then said, "I think a lot of their machinery looked old and worn. I got the impression they were at the top of the industry once but time and technology have begun to pass them by and they're still trading on their old reputation. Too slow to update their machinery and systems. Increasing overhead. They seem to be top-heavy with executives, probably all promoted up from the ranks over the years. I think they still put out good quality and have a good name, but I'd bet their profits have fallen off from what they used to be. But I'm certainly no businessman."

Strake nodded and said, "It's entirely a family-owned business. The owner is the third-generation son and he rarely darkens the door of the place. It's a fairly common story. The old man who started the business came up out of the Depression and that made him tough. He put everything into building the business. His son saw what it took, at least, and carried on, though not with the same toughness and probably milking away too much of the profits. His son, in turn, the current owner who couldn't even be bothered to meet me, grew up expecting the best of everything as his natural right and has bled off most of the profits to get it all for himself and to maintain it, so updates in machinery and systems had to be put off. Couple that with the rising salaries and general overhead, and too many executives, and the business has begun to skid down a long slide. The owner most likely does not understand the reasons why it's happening, but he's feeling it begin to crimp his lifestyle.

"I can buy it, cull out the deadwood, upgrade some of the machinery, streamline the whole office system, use contacts I already have to market the products, and begin to make a good profit within three years. I'll wait three weeks and then make a low half-hearted non-negotiable offer directly to the owner through my lawyer, reminding the owner of the declining profits, the increasing overhead, the constant threat posed by competition, and other general headaches associated with business ownership.

"My offer will be structured so the owner is tempted by a good immediate lump sum, perhaps to take care of a new Mercedes and a few other daydreams, and in such a way that he can see the possibility of a secure income ahead for at least fifteen years that's equivalent to, or perhaps even slightly more than his last year's take, with no apparent headaches whatsoever. We'll do that by offering monthly payments with generous fixed interest, but there will in fact be a small rather obscure clause in the agreement that will effectively let me pay off the balance in full at any time. What do you think he will do?"

The promised interest would inflate the total deal price by three hundred percent, probably, but the interest would evaporate, of course, when Strake paid the deal off early in full. "I'd say he'll add up the fifteen years worth of principal and interest payments and the lump sum and then jump on it," he said with a genuinely appreciative smile.

Unsmiling, Strake said, "My lawyer will even help him do that addition."

THERE WAS A TWO-DAY TRIP TO DALLAS AND THEN THEY went on a three-day excursion to Miami. On a rainy Friday while he was fifteen feet up on a tall stepladder in the Teterboro hangar inspecting and polishing the King Air's T-tail his beeper went off and when he responded to the call Margaret told him, "Mr. Strake says for you to plan on leaving for Caracas, Venezuela, at any time within the next forty-eight hours."

On the following day he took off at three in the morning with Strake, Davis, and two withdrawn unsmiling men who obviously worked for Davis and looked hardened. He flew down along the coast and landed just after dawn in Fort Lauderdale for fuel. He filed an international flight plan with the FAA Flight Service Station on the field and they were airborne again within an hour, climbing through scattered clouds on a southeasterly heading to skirt Cuba, the Bahamas strung out off to the left. They passed over Andros at 21,500 feet and farther on Great Inagua slid by underneath them.

Strake again came up to sit in the right seat and seemed to take some interest in the view, which was spectacular. They were in clear tropical air three miles above a widely-scattered layer of cumulus clouds that cast phantom island-like shadows onto the water. There were real islands in sight all of the time and the sea glowed with all the improbable luminescent colors of the Caribbean, abstract areas around the islands clearly revealing the sand, grass, and coral bottom, white fishing boats and yachts dotting the deeper, darker areas. They flew on over Puerto Rico.

Strake said, "When Davis ran a check on Kelly he found a brief history of probable drug flights."

Cowboy said, "I mentioned that to you."

"I know. You also said you had been approached to do the same kind of flying. Were you tempted?"

He thought a moment. "Yes. The money can be enough to tempt a preacher."

"Then why didn't you do it?"

"Mostly too much risk all around, I guess. But some part of it was that I don't like what drugs do to people."

"People start with drugs by choice, just as they choose to drink to excess and to take unreasonable chances for recreation and to eat like idiots."

"And to fight each other."

"Yes."

After a few minutes Cowboy asked, "How much of the gun trade is black market?"

Strake stared at him intently, his black eyes bright. He said, "Why do you ask?"

"I've done some reading. I just wondered."

After a moment Strake looked out at the view and said, "Nobody really knows, but black market trade is certainly significant. When an AK-47 can be bought readily for a bag of maize in southern Africa and sold for a thousand dollars in Israel, there is ample incentive. Again, our governments are largely responsible for fueling the trade.

"The CIA, for example, supplied the Mujahideen in Afghanistan for their war against the Russians, sending, ironically, 400,000 AK-47 rifles, thousands of land mines, 8,000 light machine guns, Stinger missiles, 100 million rounds of ammunition. When the war ended nobody made any attempt to collect the weapons so they've been circulating on the black market ever since. Afghanistan, Pakistan, Angola, they're all open arms bazaars selling everything you can imagine.

"When the United States pulled out of Vietnam in that ridiculous mad scramble in 1975 they left behind a stupendous stock of weapons that had cost the American taxpayers over five billion dollars—800,000 M-16s, 600 M-48 tanks, 300 self-propelled 175-millimeter guns that had cost one million each, brand new F-5 fighters. It was probably the biggest war booty in history, and it's still out there, still worth several fortunes even at bargain prices.

"The Pentagon has routinely given away small arms—M-16s, M-14s, pistols, machine guns, grenade launchers—to Bahrain, Bosnia, Chile, Egypt, Estonia, Greece, Israel of course, Latvia, Lithuania, Morocco, and the Philippines. But many officials in those governments seldom play by American rules. A weapon knows absolutely no allegiance, and who can say how many of those arms are being traded on the black market?"

They were following a westward track along the chain of the Lesser Antilles leading in a broad shallow crescent over the horizon all the way to the northern shores of South America. The plane sped along powerfully in smooth air, all systems working flawlessly.

"How long will we be staying in Caracas?" Cowboy asked.

"My business should take no more than four days. Among other things, the day after tomorrow I'll be bidding on a large store of arms that includes a sizable private collection of antique weapons, part of the estate of a weapons manufacturer that specialized in military and sporting shotguns. I have it on good authority that my only serious competitor is a man named Charles Harrington from Liverpool. The man has been troublesome to me in recent months concerning two different African transactions."

"Do you know how he'll be coming into the country?"

"He'll be coming in on a commercial flight tomorrow afternoon. The stock of weapons will only be made available for inspection the following morning. The bidding deadline is noon."

Cowboy thought for a moment as he scanned for traffic. "How well is this Harrington known in Venezuela?"

"I don't think he has ever traded there before. His dealings have mostly been in Africa. Why?"

"I did some reading on the country yesterday. There's a recent history of serious trouble along the border, with Colombian guerrillas. If the customs people at the airport were to get an anonymous call claiming this Harrington is coming into the country with forged papers to buy guns that will be diverted to a Colombian guerrilla group, I would guess they'd detain the man for a while to check it out. If they should hold him overnight that might leave a clear field for your bid. It's just a thought."

Strake appraised him, his dark eyes hard. Then he nodded once. He said, "You will have considerable free time while we're there. Caracas is one of the most beautiful cities in the world. Take some time to see it, but I warn you it's like New York in many respects. There are areas you do not want to explore after dark, areas where even the police do not venture." He got up and went back to take a seat in the cabin.

Just over four hours out of Miami as they drew close to the verdant, wildly-rugged coast of Venezuela, he called approach control at Simon Bolivar airport—actually located in the coastal suburb of Maiquetia—and they gave him traffic advisories, altitudes, and vectors in only slightly accented English, the universal language for air traffic control.

He landed at the large modern airport and taxied directly to customs, where they were all cleared after a perfunctory look at their passports, visas, and luggage, and no inspection of the plane whatsoever. Two of the officials seemed to know Strake well and were smilingly accommodating. They re-boarded and taxied to an FBO where attendants tied the King Air down and chocked the wheels. A limousine met them by the plane to take on their luggage and then drove them for just over half an hour along a palm-lined freeway to the modern high-rise 780-room Caracas Hilton complex downtown in the center of the financial district, with the offices of companies such as GTE, 3M, and Fluor Daniel within walking distance.

After checking in, Davis called Cowboy's room and said, "Mr. Strake wants you to have a drink in the Orinoco Lounge for about an hour. Says he'll call you there if he needs you. After that you're on your own. You might want to watch where you go after dark. Some places you could get cut and rolled in a heartbeat. Be a real shame." And he hung up.

Cowboy showered and dressed in white jeans with a silver-studded belt, black boots, and a gaudy-flowered silk shirt he'd bought in Miami a year before. He went down to the lounge and took a seat at the bar. At this hour the only other customers were a young man and a woman engaged in low amorous conversation in a booth. Salsa music surged softly through the speakers. The bartender was a portly man with a ready smile and excellent, though thickly accented, English. He asked the usual get-acquainted questions as he polished glasses and slid them into racks above the high-gloss padded bar, and offered advice about what to see and do in the city.

After forty-five minutes a young woman in a white summery dress put a beaded straw purse on the bar and took a stool three down from Cowboy, smiling at him politely as he nodded to her and smiled, the bartender hustling to take her order.

"I think I want something that will make me just a little bit dizzy," she said playfully. "A big, big frozen margarita." Her skin was deeply bronzed and her black hair was pulled tightly back into a neat bun pinned with a single white flower. She wore large looping earrings made of delicate braided gold chain. Peach lipstick set off her white-toothed smile, and she had used eye makeup to good effect. Cowboy estimated she was in her middle twenties.

"Sir, you have the pallor of an American tourist," she said with a mischievous grin and a raised eyebrow. "Are you here with a group of overweight gringos covered with cameras?"

"No. Actually, I'm working."

"Oh, I *see*. And what kind of company employs you to sit and drink in the Orinoco Lounge? I would like to apply for such a position, I think. Do they have any openings?"

"I'm just a pilot for a gringo from New York. What brings you here?"

"An advertising convention. I am from Maracaibo. I arrived one day early to renew my romance with Caracas. I grew up here and I love my city."

"What little I've seen of it is impressive. Maybe you'll let me buy you that margarita and in exchange you could tell me what I should see and do this afternoon."

She appraised him as she ran a long-nailed clear-glossed finger around the rim of her glass, making it sing. "Do you know I am feeling just a little bit adventurous today? My name is Maria Elena Ortiz."

"They call this one the Cowboy," the bartender said affably.

"Aren't all American men cowboys at heart? Well, Cowboy, if you can take some time off of the busy schedule of your sitting-there-and-drinking job, and if you will promise to buy me a most huge dinner, I will be your tour

guide for this afternoon and show you some of the very best
things in Caracas. What do you say to that?"

"That sounds great. I can always come back here later
and put in some make-up time."

They began by walking across the street to the Teresa
Carreno Cultural Complex. Landscaped buildings in
the area included the Museo de Bellas Artes, which was
actually two museums in one, the National Art Gallery
featuring the works of Venezuelan artists such as Alejan-
dro Otero, and the Fine Arts Museum where there were
Goya etchings and a surprising variety of Egyptian pieces.
She took him on a whirlwind tour and as soon as she got
him interested in one painting she would pull him by the
hand along to another that caught her fancy. She was like
a happy schoolgirl.

Outside, they walked a ways in Los Caobos Park. "It
means mahogany trees park," she said. "Isn't it beautiful
here?" She flung her arms wide and pirouetted, her straw
purse swinging on its shoulder strap, swirling her skirt out
to display lean bronze thighs. There were profusions of
scarlet bougainvillea and richly-scented orchids amid the
tall trees and palms. The vegetation was sheened with the
vivid healthy greens of the tropics. "This place is a refuge
for joggers and for old people walking. And for lovers," she
said with a contrived shy smile.

"Do you know any Spanish?" she said, switching
streams of thought abruptly.

"Not really."

"Oh, but you should. It's such a pretty language. I will
give you a lesson. Repeat after me. *Hola* means hello."

He repeated it dutifully as they held hands and walked in the cooling shade. "Please is *por favor*. Thank you is *gracias*. You are welcome is *de nada*. Sorry is *disculpe*. Excuse me is *con permiso* or *perdon*. *Buenos tardes* is good afternoon. Repeat after me, please, and pay attention to the subtleties of accent. That's it. Very good, sir. Do you begin to feel the beauty of it? One of my most favorite words is *estralita*. Roll the R on the tip of your tongue and try to say it as I do. Yes. That is close. When I have a stunning daughter I will name her *Estralita*. My perfectly beautiful little star."

She tugged him out to the Avenida Colon to wave down a taxi. "You should get one with a fixed sign on its roof," she explained. "The others with stick-on signs are *piratas*." When an incredibly battered light blue cab stopped for them she held him back from getting in and she dickered with the gesticulating driver in rapid Spanish through the open window, finally nodding that they could climb into the shabby backseat. "You must set the price before you get in," she said in a low voice. "This one's meter is conveniently broken right now. The driver will put the money into his own pocket this time."

The ride was wild, the driver palming the horn frequently, swerving violently from lane to lane, narrowly missing other horn-blowing vehicles and driving much too fast the whole way. Somehow they were deposited unscathed at the Plaza Morelos, where the air was redolent of grilling meats and there were many stalls loaded with bright clothes, garish trinkets, and costume jewelry that glittered in the hot sunshine. From a grinning wrinkled old woman he bought Maria a delicate silver bracelet and she was inordinately delighted with it. She made him buy a felt *vaquero*'s hat with a red feather stuck rakishly in the beaded band for himself. "With those mysterious gray eyes you are a dashing mountain *bandito* leader," she said as she appraised him with her head cocked and her hands on her hips, a mix of happy *Caraquenos* and tourists milling around them.

She took him to Plaza Bolivar to show him the magnificent 1674 *Catedral Metropolitan de Caracas* with its graceful scroll designs on the exterior and the baroque altar inside gilded with 300 pounds of gold leaf, and to the *Panteon Nacional* with its ornate domed towers, enshrining the remains of Simon Bolivar, who in the early 1800s led ragged armies in a fourteen-year campaign to free Venezuela, Colombia, Ecuador, Peru, and Bolivia from Spain's colonial stranglehold, only to watch much of the freed territory dissolve into years of bloody internal conflict. But the memory of him was still vibrant and revered throughout the countries where he and his men had fought.

By the time the sun was low, setting the western flanks of Mount Avila ruddily aflame, they had worked up ravenous appetites so they went back to the Hilton and took a table in a dim corner of the well-appointed L'Incontro Restaurant. They ordered a lavish five-course meal and took their time enjoying it. They lingered over desserts with strong coffee and an excellent nut-flavored wine, both of them acquiring a pleasant glow. They laughed and touched hands and smiled knowingly and it seemed the most natural proceeding in the world for her to go with him to his room.

She showered and came out dressed in a hotel terry-cloth robe, her hair undone and brushed back. He went in to shower and before too long he heard her coming into the bath. She slid the frosted glass door aside, smiled mischievously, stepped out of her robe, and joined him. She took the soap out of his hand and began lathering his chest, humming some tune softly.

In bed she was laughingly energetic and fresh, teasing and prolonging, making of it a wonderfully innocent lark, and he responded strongly. It was close to midnight when they finally fell asleep exhausted in a tangle of bedding, a Latin ballad playing low over the stereo, the room washed softly by the bright lights of the city coming in the balconied sixth-floor window.

In the morning they enjoyed a hearty room-service breakfast and they made love again. Then she said she must go to register for the advertising convention and she quickly showered and dressed.

He said. "Will I see you again? Is there a number where I can reach you?"

She smiled brightly and kissed him softly on the cheek. "I will be very busy for the next few days, but we will see. I have much enjoyed showing you some of my city. *Hasta luego*, my *llanero*." And with a smile, a swirl of her skirt, and a wave, she was gone.

That evening as he sat in the Orinoco Lounge having a margarita, hoping she would show up, Montgomery Davis took a stool beside him and ordered a draft. He said, "How about that Maria Ortiz twist. She's something, isn't she?"

"What do you mean?"

"You must have done something Strake really liked. She was a little present to you."

"Are you trying to say she was bought and paid for?"

"Don't look so surprised," Davis said. "She's strictly a high-class whore. Probably clean enough. I think I might try her myself tonight, maybe tell her to bring a friend. Make it a three-way."

"Do you have some kind of problem with me?"

Davis shrugged and looked at himself in the bar mirror. "Why would I have a problem with you? You're just the pilot. From what I've seen most pilots are a little too cocky for their own good. Sooner or later they step on their own dicks."

He finished off the margarita and got up without a word, leaving Davis at the bar. He took a taxi—settling on the fare up front—to a *parrillera* that the bartender had recommended, a restaurant where he watched his steak cooked to perfection on a table-side grill and where he got mildly dizzy on margaritas.

Flights became more frequent over the ensuing months, mostly within the States but also several times to Central and South America—Panama, Argentina, Ecuador, and again to Venezuela. Strake would often take the co-pilot's seat and talk about various aspects of the business. Cowboy listened and learned.

On a Saturday morning Strake called him to the office. He placed a manila envelope on his desk and said, "I have to stay in New York for the next several days. I would like you to fly the plane to Chicago on Monday. I have a stock of bayonets in the warehouse, World War Two items for the most part. The complete list is in this envelope. Look it over. I've had samples drawn from inventory to take with you. They're in a briefcase in Margaret's office. Meet with the owner of the catalog company that is outlined in the envelope; he will be expecting you at one o'clock. He sells military surplus, collectors' items, and survival gear. There's also a list of other items we have in inventory. The catalog company might have an interest in some of them. Don't let anyone else see that list. Make the best arrangements you can. There are suggested retail prices in here. You're free to make a contract for us, but don't let anything go for less than the minimum wholesale prices listed. Do you have any questions?"

"Why are you trusting me to do this?"

"I believe you will show an aptitude for it."

He spent the rest of the weekend going over the inventory list and reading through books he got from a library. The bayonets included the model for the famous bolt-action M-1 Garand of World War II, a Swedish Mauser blade, the Soviet AKM, the 1907 Enfield that looked more like a sword with its 17-inch blade, the 1909 Argentine Mauser, an 1895 Chilean Militia blade made in Germany, the Yugoslavian K-98, and half a dozen other models, most with scabbards. There were tens of thousands of them in stock.

There was a sample catalog from the Chicago company in the envelope. They sold military field and camping gear, surplus camo outfits, stun guns and pepper sprayers, karate weapons, a wide selection of gun magazines and ammo, replica swords, holsters, paintball guns, black powder rifles, crossbows, and a variety of shooting accessories such as scopes, laser sights, and hearing protectors. The catalog was glossy, sharp full-color, and well designed. Somebody had devoted considerable thought to the photography, graphics, and copy writing.

At the meeting in Chicago the florid overweight owner of the company leaned back in the big leather chair behind his desk, lit a large greenish-looking cigar, and said through the smoke, "So why should I pay you people thirty percent more than I've been paying for some of the same items from other suppliers?"

"Our prices are fair for several reasons. First, we have a larger inventory than any other supplier so we can guarantee to fill all the orders you get. You won't be stuck with an item listed in your catalog and no inventory to back it up. All of these bayonets are packed in cosmoline. They're NRA rated to be in 'very good to excellent' condition and that's something you can put in your catalog listing. It's a good selling point. Let's take the M-1 Garand bayonet. You sell it with a scabbard and with a frameable certificate of authenticity that will cost you what, a few cents? You tell your customers these aren't replicas. These blades have seen real action from the Ardennes to Korea. The same bayonets their fathers or grandfathers carried. Put your catalog people to work on the certificate and on a good presentation for the bayonet, maybe with a genuine World War Two recruiting poster for a background. You'll get top dollar for them."

The big man blew a small mushroom cloud ceilingward, smiled, and said, "Where did Strake find a slick bullshitter like you? No offense. I like your style. The certificate's a good idea. Let's see those samples you brought. Then we'll get my manager in here and work out a realistic deal. You got any other ideas to help make my accountant happy? I don't need old uniforms or helmets; I've got plenty."

"As a matter of fact, I was looking over your latest catalog and thought of a possible cover item for your next one.

Something that will really command attention."

The man raised a thick eyebrow, squinting in the smoke, and said around his cigar, "And what will that be?"

"A machine gun. A Browning M1919 A4 .30 caliber machine gun, mounted on its tripod. You feature it big on the cover, with an actual greyed-out background combat photo showing it firing. Your graphics people can do a great job with it. We'll replace the receiver with a dummy so it's non-firing and can't be converted to fire, so it's entirely legal. You sell it as a show piece, a collectors' item, in this case with a framed certificate. You could even offer a two-foot belt of dummy ammunition for it as an extra. The gun and tripod should sell for a thousand dollars, maybe more. It's a genuine war relic that was used from the 1930s to the 1960s all over the world, even in the early days of Vietnam. It fired eight rounds a second, air cooled. It was an infantry favorite. They're rare today, but we happen to have a good stock of them. Again, they're all in excellent shape."

"You know you just might have something there. Even if we didn't sell all that many it would make a dynamite cover. Tell you what, you get tired of working for that thief Strake, you come see me. Let's get my manager in here."

The deal with the catalog company was profitable for Worldarms and was eventually expanded to include a stock of old Thompson submachine guns, modified with aluminum dummy receivers, that would list for $495 each in the catalog.

Strake sent him on other errands, several times in the King Air and twice on commercial flights. He surprised

himself with his own confidence and small successes, and
realized Strake was gradually feeding him more and more
details about how the far-flung business functioned. And
was testing him.

Strake scheduled a trip to an arms exhibition in Budapest. They left Teterboro before dawn on a humid summer
day with Montgomery Davis and another taciturn man who
was introduced only as Gordon and who looked like an ex-
prizefighter. They flew northeast in the gathering light over
New England and beyond the Bay of Fundy, the mouth of
the St. Lawrence, and Nova Scotia to land in lush and cool
Goose Bay, Newfoundland. After refueling, Cowboy set
a course for Iceland that would take them over the southern tip of Greenland, offering the possibility of a landing
at Narsarsuaq if any problem developed with the plane, but
the sleek King Air performed flawlessly and they passed
over the tip of the frozen continent at 23,000 feet.

Greenland was anything but. Clear air made the stark
white mountains blindingly brilliant. Giant blue-green
icebergs formed a defensive fleet around the shore and the
sea was a deep cold blue. Black rock showed through the
ice cap here and there and the coastline was scarred and
cracked with barren steep-walled fjords. It was a forbid-
ding land.

At Reykjavik the airport was in the middle of the town,
which was a random assortment of spaced-apart low buildings on a plain by the water. It was a perfect summer day
there with light winds, the temperature a balmy 59, and only
a few scattered fair-weather cumulus decorating the clear
hard sky. The approach end of Runway zero-two began

close by a rock wall at the water's edge. There were some grassy patches among the buildings, and purple mountains were strung out along the horizon. They ate lunch in the Loftleider Hotel right beside the FBO and then took off on the next long over-ocean leg to foggy Glasgow, where the King Air was refueled before they pressed on in clouds and light rain for an instrument approach into Budapest. The flight consumed the entire day.

The arms exhibit had an incredible variety of weaponry and accessories on display and was thronged with intently interested people from the European countries, Africa, and South America. They stayed for three days and Strake went off with Davis and Gordon for lengthy periods to handle business that Cowboy was told nothing about, which was not at all an unusual situation for a corporate pilot, most of whom certainly knew far less about their employers' affairs than he did about Strake's dealings.

A month after the Budapest trip, Strake told him to plan a flight to Vancouver. When the departure day arrived, Strake's wife Elaine came to the FBO at Teterboro along with Strake and Montgomery Davis and half a limousine full of luggage. It was the first time Cowboy had seen Elaine. She was a doll-beautiful blonde at least fifteen years younger than Strake, with shoulder-length hair, green eyes, and a remote smile. She wore a vividly multicolored skirt and a sheer ruffled blouse. She seemed subdued around Strake. There was no affection evident between them. He seemed to treat her as he would another of his prized possessions.

There was a scheduled stop at Denver so Strake could

meet briefly with a potential customer. As they approached the jagged horizon-wide belt of the Rockies on a cloudless morning Cowboy found himself wondering about those souls back in the frontier days who had plodded across the plains, day by day watching that formidable range grow closer and higher, undaunted by the prospect of crossing through those awesome peaks, some over two miles high, on steep rutted trails in overloaded wagons or on foot, drawn by the dream of finding some verdant fold of land beyond to claim as their own, or of discovering a long gleaming sprinkle of yellow flakes in the bed of some magical California stream. They had to have been some tough people, he thought as he began the descent into Denver, which from the air looked like just another smog-shrouded city, albeit this one perched a mile high.

At the FBO Strake and Davis took a courtesy car and left for the business meeting. After a half-hour of sitting in the FBO lounge with the quiet Elaine, both of them leafing through well-thumbed magazines, Cowboy asked her politely if she'd like to walk a short way to an on-field restaurant for an early lunch.

"No, thank you. I'd better stay here," she said, but gave him a slight smile.

"The man on the fuel truck told me they make the best egg salad and tuna salad sandwiches he's ever had, and cinnamon coffee, with homemade pies for dessert. We could be there and back within an hour. I'm buying. I'll just put it on my expense account. What do you say?"

"Well it *is* pretty boring just waiting here, and I didn't have much of a breakfast. All right, but we'd better not be gone too long."

The food was as good as promised and they both enjoyed the lunch. They made light conversation and he managed to draw her out somewhat.

"I grew up in Binghamton, New York," she said. "My father worked as a salesman for Louis's father."

"Mr. Strake is an impressive man."

She looked at him seriously, something hidden behind her eyes. "Yes. He's successful and likes to live well. So do I."

"Do you travel with him often?"

"Occasionally. We'll be going to the Bahamas sometime soon. It's very pleasant there. What do you do besides flying?" Her green eyes were cautiously appraising.

"Not much. I try to stay in shape. I like to read, and watch old movies. I like good music."

"Classical?"

"Yes, some of it."

"I studied fine arts at Syracuse," she said. "I paint abstracts in watercolor and acrylics. One day I hope to establish my own gallery in the city. A place for really unusual art. Where good unknowns can be showcased."

"I don't know much about fine art, but I have the impression it must be a tough way to make a living."

"It is. This is not a world where art of any kind, even the best of it, is easily successful. You have a few writers, sculptors, and painters making insane money way up there in the stratosphere, and then you have those starving thousands back down here on Earth. My gallery would be a place for talented artists to break in, and I believe it could be a commercial success."

"It sounds great. I hope it all works out for you."

They were eating wedges of hot apple pie crowned with melting vanilla bean ice cream along with refills of cinnamon coffee when Strake came into the small restaurant with Davis following. Strake's eyes were depthless black marbles and there was a tick in his left eyelid. He stood erectly and looked steadily at Cowboy but said, "Elaine, go get in the plane."

She dabbed at her mouth with her napkin, unhurried but obviously nervous, then got up without a word or a glance, leaving the food unfinished, and went out.

"Mr. Strake," he began, smiling, "we were just having a bite of lunch here—"

"Shut up. You listen to me very carefully. You are hired help. You are not to associate with my wife." His eyes glittered darkly. "Is that clear?"

He met Strake's glare with a steady calm gaze but said nothing. Standing off to the side, Davis smiled and idly inspected a thumbnail. A couple at a corner table stopped eating and looked their way. The waitress stopped wiping the counter. The room was still.

After several long seconds Strake motioned to Davis and said, "Montgomery, go pay the check. We will be leaving now." He turned and walked out of the restaurant as Davis went over to the woman behind the counter, tugging his wallet out. The couple at the corner table went back to their meals.

Cowboy watched Strake leave. He finished the slice of pie and the coffee, taking his time. Davis came over, grinned with a raised eyebrow, and said, "See? Like I said, sooner or later they all step on their own dicks. I think we better go now, hotshot. That is, if you want your job."

He wiped his mouth with a napkin and got up, leaving a good tip.

When he boarded the King Air Elaine was sitting in the rearmost seat, gazing out the window. Strake said nothing to him for the remainder of the flight.

The weather in Vancouver was light rain falling from low cloud cover and he followed the vectors and altitudes dictated by Vancouver approach with precision, aware of the mountains hidden nearby in the swirling grayness. He captured the ILS and broke out at six hundred feet, the airport just south of the city suddenly materializing as if by magic, and made a light touchdown on the wet pavement.

Strake had a large modern house northwest of the city on several wooded acres in the Coast Mountains looking out over an arm of the bay and massive Vancouver Island beyond. Davis told Cowboy to take one of the two small rooms above the garage.

During the month-long stay Strake hosted two large house parties crowded with a diverse mix of people. They made trips down the coast to Los Angeles and San Diego, Cowboy waiting in the FBOs each time as Strake went off with Davis in tow to conduct business. During his off times, Cowboy explored Vancouver, which he found to be fascinating and beautiful, with many parks scattered among the busy streets and skyscrapers. Along with a rich mix of English, Germans, Sikhs, and Musqueam Indians, there was a strong Asian presence, and he discovered a restaurant he particularly liked amid the glitter of Chinatown.

He went on five-mile runs along the tide-lapped beach perimeter of Stanley Park, which jutted out into the water, separating Vancouver Harbour from English Bay where several freighters were always anchored, waiting to be loaded with grain from Canada's vast plains. It was autumn and front after front swept in from the Pacific to keep the city veiled in mist. He enjoyed his solitary runs and always found Stanley Park, like the other green areas of the city, to be clean and absolutely free of litter.

On a rare sunny morning Davis curtly told him he would be free for the day so he dressed in jeans and a denim shirt and took a cab to Stanley Park for a run on the beach. He had gone about a mile, enjoying the warmth of the sun on his face, when he glanced back to see a man gaining on him with smooth tireless strides. Within a quarter mile the man drew abreast and slowed to match his pace.

"Good day for it," the man said. He was in his middle thirties and obviously fit, dressed in green sweats and good foot gear. He wore a white band that held his longish brown hair back, and large amber shooter's sunglasses.

"Sure is. One thing about all the rain, it makes you appreciate a day like this."

"So they call you Cowboy."

They ran on. He was eyeing the man now. He said, "Do I know you?"

"My name is Nolan Rader. No, we've never met but I know a great deal about you. For example you work as a pilot for Louis Strake, but he seems to be grooming you for more. You're due to fly him back to Teterboro the day after tomorrow."

"Who are you?"

"I'm with the Bureau of Alcohol, Tobacco, and Fire-arms, the BATF, based in D.C. I'd appreciate a few minutes of your time right now. There's a bench coming up just ahead. Let's take a break. Enjoy the view for a while."

"I don't have anything to say to you."

"You don't have to talk. Just listen. What have you got to lose?" He smiled. "Come on. If you don't you'll only wonder what the hell it was all about, right? Ten minutes, no more. Hear me out and then I'll jog away."

"Ten minutes then."

They sat on the iron bench, Rader wiping at his face with his sleeve. He said, "This man you work for. I'm going to assume you don't know the full scope of his business yet. He's a criminal and he's a killer."

"I don't think so. He sells light weapons. It's a legitimate business. He's not responsible for what people do with what he sells."

"Guns don't kill people. People kill people, right? Like the bumper sticker. That's the line he spouts in so many words. But that's not what I'm talking about. I mean he is a killer. Just like that bodyguard of his. Montgomery Davis has a long sheet going back eighteen years. Assault. Loan sharking and protection racketeering when he worked for the Chicago syndicate. Arrested for murder once and weapons charges twice, and he's suspected in two unsolved homicides. He's slippery, though. Only done a total of three years inside during his long and lucrative career. But he's down at the bottom of the food chain.

"Your Mr. Strake, now, he's right up there at the top. His father ran a more or less legitimate business. Louis does not. He may have started out pretty much that way, but since his old man went to the big arsenal in the sky, and since more and more governments have passed more arms control laws, junior has ventured further and further into a lot of gray areas and done more than a few downright illegal deals. The more he gets away with the more he seems willing to try. He's like a lot of your top bad guys. They don't print enough money to satisfy him. He's ruthless and he's cunning. And he *is* a killer."

"If you know all of this, why don't you arrest him?"

Rader put his hands on his knees, leaned back on the bench, and tilted his head slightly to look at the sky. He said, "They killed fifty million people in the Second World War. How many conflicts would you say there have been since? I mean those in which significant numbers have died."

"I don't know. Maybe a hundred."

"That's more than most people would estimate. There have been three hundred major conflicts—in places like Lebanon, Biafra, the Yemen, Katanga, Cambodia, Argentina, and so on—that have killed a total of twenty-five million people. Let's put that in some perspective. Imagine Fenway Park filled to capacity—a vast sea of faces.

"A hit squad comes in and starts killing them all. Every last fan. Every man, every retiree, every pregnant mother, every child. They shoot some, blow some up, make some kneel in front of pistols The squad works hard but it still takes hours. Then tomorrow they fill up the park and do it all over again, and the next day, and the next. They keep it up seven days a week. For two years. That's how many have died in major conflicts since the Second World War. And the vast majority of those human beings, folks not so different from your friends, your relatives, the skinny kids you see on a playground who couldn't even spell politics, have died—and an untold number of millions have been wounded—by light weaponry. Rifles, pistols, submachine guns, mortars, shotguns, grenades. The sort of merchandise Worldarms has been marketing."

Rader paused and then said, "Name one of the biggest recent wars."

Cowboy said, "I don't know. Desert Storm?"

"That little fracas only killed four hundred Allied troops and maybe ten thousand Iraqis. Fact is, every year since Desert Storm this tired old planet has seen an average of ten conflicts that have *each* killed ten thousand or more. Georgia, Sudan, Tadzhikistan, East Timor, southeast Turkey. In under a two-year span *half a million* Angolans died from war or war-related starvation in the most brutal ways you can imagine.

"Oh, I know there are festering feuds and deep-rooted political and ideological and religious differences among people all over the place. Differences that can't easily be resolved, some that may never be resolved. But when you take a country, or two bordering countries, where there are already intense arguments and you sprinkle a couple hundred thousand AK-47s, a few million rounds of ammo, and maybe ten thousand grenades into that pot it more often than not will boil over into bloody carnage. Everybody stops arguing and they just start shooting.

"The shooting doesn't have to go on for long before violence becomes a way of life. And life becomes cheap. People think that can only happen in some podunk country you can't even point to on a globe. But it can happen anywhere. There are over two hundred and ten million guns circulating in the States and six million more are produced or imported every year. We're beginning to see more drive-by shootings in the ghettos, Interstate gunnings just because somebody gets pissed off in traffic, more homicides out there in the suburbs. Your average Joes can get concealed carry permits all over the place. Look around the world and see where too many weapons have led other countries. The Rwandan Army casually killed thousands of civilians, anybody even remotely suspected of disagreeing with them, using AK-47s routed to them through Egypt. In the Iran-Iraq war they sent children out in waves across mine fields. Can you imagine that? Kids in rags blown to bits like so many small animals just to clear mine fields. Can you hear them screaming?

"Take Colombia. They've been fighting internally for so long it's routine now. Kids are born into it so they don't know anything else. Leftist guerrillas against right-wing paramilitary groups supported by the remnants of the drug cartels and to hell with whoever gets in the way. There are a hundred thousand well-armed private security guards in the country. A million permitted weapons and maybe five million illegal ones. A family argument, a shouting spat over traffic, a debate over a soccer match, any incident can turn into a shootout in a heartbeat. In a six-year period there have been a hundred and fifty thousand homicides, only ten percent prosecuted. In Cali and Pereira upper-class teenagers ride around at night shooting beggars, the homeless, drug addicts, and prostitutes from their cars for sport. In Bogota the police kill the same kinds of people—the *deschables* or the disposable ones—but they call it social cleansing. The U.S. arms the Colombian National Police with more sophisticated weapons so the guerrillas want upgrades, too. Keeps the black market demand right up there.

"You know why your boss has been to Venezuela three times in the past six months? He's been black-marketing guns, ammo, and night vision equipment to a particular well-financed Colombian guerrilla army through a Venezuelan contact. He bought a load of government-owned AR-15s in Panama from corrupt officials a year ago, for example, and recently smuggled them into Venezuela labeled as drilling equipment on a container ship. The Venezuelan thugs he's been dealing with got them across the border into Colombia. A Venezuelan investigative reporter named Armando Ramirez found out about the deal and was about to put the story out when Strake and Davis killed him. Not had him killed, but I mean *killed* him, up close and personal. We don't think it's the first time something like that has gone down. You see, I don't think your Louis Strake is completely sane."

"This is interesting and educational, but I'll say again, if you know all of this to be fact why isn't somebody arresting him?"

Nolan thought for a time, gazing skyward, then said, "Sometimes our government does things that are near impossible to understand. Do you remember when they hired the Mafia to get rid of Castro? That was a case in point. How about funding the Contras through the Sultan of Brunei? Old stuff, right? How about a little more recent stuff? How about fifteen of the nineteen Nine-Eleven hijackers being Saudi? But we aren't supposed to think about that, are we? Got to have all that Saudi oil, right? What if the hijackers had been from North Korea or Iran? Politics and international dealings have gears within gears. Who the hell are we to figure it all out?"

"What has all this got to do with Strake?"

"Not much, after all, I guess. Just rambling. As far as Strake goes, knowing and proving are not real close cousins. This is where you come in. We think you're a basically honest dude. We need somebody on the inside who's willing to feed us just a little information. Who Strake meets. Where he goes and when. Small crumbs he drops here and there."

"You're wasting your time with me."

"True loyalty these days is a real rarity. It's downright refreshing to witness. But misplaced loyalty doesn't make any sense. Your boss is moving more and more in the underground, down where the sun doesn't shine. He specializes in South America but has dealt all over the world. He bribes government officials, pays off customs people, doles out percentages to a number of criminal contacts all over the place. Brokers all kinds of shady deals. There's a whole international underground economy now that trades in designer drugs, product knock-offs, raw gems, computer chips, toxic wastes, a lot of valuable contraband, and guns.

Always guns. There are entire networks of ghost companies and we-don't-kiss-and-tell banks for laundering the
proceeds. Your boss is right down there in the thick of it.
Dealing in death. The longer you work for him the more
you'll see that.

"Anyway, suppose we leave it this way." Rader pulled
a plain business-sized card out of his fanny pack. There
were no names on the card, just three hand-printed phone
numbers. "Here's how you can reach me at any time, day
or night. The top number is my cell phone. The second, the toll-free one, is my office. The last is my home.
Use a pay phone. I may not answer but just tell whoever
does that you're Cowboy and you need to speak with me.
Nolan Rader."

"I really can't help you," he said.

But he took the card.

20

DURING THE FLIGHT BACK TO TETERBORO STRAKE ONCE again came up to take the copilot's seat. There had been no further mention of the incident with Strake's wife.

Strake said, "I've been giving you a gradual education in my business, of course. I need someone to handle some aspects of it routinely. You have demonstrated an aptitude for it. What I have in mind will mean an eventual increase in salary. You will continue to fly, and will schedule your other new responsibilities as you can. Do you have any problems with that?"

He thought for a moment, scanning ahead for any traffic, and then said, "The flying has been exceptional. I don't think this plane could be in much better shape, and my salary is already generous. I have no complaints. The business intrigues me, I have to admit, but I have some reservations about selling weapons. I do believe basically that people kill people, but it seems to me that guns make it a whole lot easier for them."

"I thought we'd had this conversation," Strake said

evenly, his eyes dark and brooding. He stared off into the hazy sky and went on, "Humans persist in the pretense that they are somehow inherently noble. The reality is we are predators to our cores. The most effective, most efficient predators ever to inhabit this planet. Killers of every other species on the planet and of each other by the millions. Our own government is responsible for Dresden, Hiroshima, and Nagasaki and the deaths of uncounted innocent people. Why are we so reluctant to admit what we are? It's the reason we admire other rival predators—the lion, the wolf, and the eagle. Sports teams are not named for rabbits or doves. Violence runs in us like a current just under our skins. With the right provocation any one of us can become violently enraged in an instant, with or without a weapon at hand. You have certainly experienced flashes of it. Everyone has. Conflict is at the dark heart of all our drama—our vicarious other lives—and the more intense that conflict the more fascinating we find it to be.

"How many riots, how many indiscriminate homemade bombings and lead-pipe kneecappings and piano-wire garrotings and bare-knuckle beatings have been perpetrated in the name of one political or religious belief or another? Gather a group of humans and infuse them properly with religious or ideological zeal and what they can accomplish in the way of devastation can be awe-inspiring. There's no better modern example than Nine-Eleven.

"In World War Two the Allies were continually confronted by rabidly suicidal Japanese who were willing to fight hand-to-hand to the last man just to defend one worthless jungle outpost or another.

"In the 1860s Paraguay fought against Argentina, Brazil, and Uruguay simultaneously in a senseless and utterly hopeless contest. The entire country fought to the bitter end, often with nothing more than razors lashed to poles. Before the war the population was 450,000. At the war's end there were only 221,000 left alive, and only 14,000 of those were men. The availability of or lack of weaponry had nothing to do with their desire to kill as many of their neighbors as possible by any means, at any cost.

"Weapons have been with us since the first prehistoric human picked up a thigh bone to settle an argument, and our police still carry clubs. There is nothing inherently lethal in a length of hickory. The lethality lies coiled within us. Every last one of us. Weapons can, in fact, serve well as deterrents to violence. The cold war was a protracted nuclear and conventional weapons stand-off, after all, with enough destructive power stockpiled to erase all life from the planet several times over, yet it has ended almost amicably for all concerned. Our own government has doled out heavy and light weapons for decades with the intent of deterring conflicts.

"If you could rid the world of gunpowder tomorrow humans would merely revert to using spears and crossbows and maces. Less efficient, of course, but no less lethal, and they would soon devise better weapons. Witness the relatively recent development of chemical and biological weapons, or tactical nuclear weapons. There are ingenious people working industriously right now to perfect caseless ammunition that will be lighter, cheaper, and more deadly, and on sound suppression through new bullet design, and on compact optical low-light sighting devices.

"I have not invented or refined any weapons. I do not campaign to perpetuate them. I am merely a broker engaged in a trade that will flourish with or without me. What I do is simply conduct business, and there have been more than a few instances when various high-level people in your government have been thankful that Worldarms has existed to carry out transactions they have preferred not to carry out themselves. I do not claim to be a patriot. My motive is profit. That is certainly not unusual. Money allows me to maintain a life style, to sustain my business, and to sign your paychecks. Decide once and for all whether you want to continue receiving those paychecks. Let me know in one week."

With that he got up and went back into the cabin.

Seven days later Strake summoned him to a morning meeting in his office. Seated behind his massive ornate desk, he said, "What have you decided?"

With only his modest living expenses his savings account had been growing nicely and it would not be too far in the future before he would be able to think about striking out on his own with a small charter operation or some other venture. He was not likely to earn this kind of money elsewhere, and flying the immaculate, well-equipped King Air to exotic places had been a keen pleasure. The conversation with Rader in Vancouver had receded into a murky realm of doubtful and unproven events that in any case need not concern him. He had done no real wrong working for Worldarms and intended to do none. He said, "I appreciate the job, and I'm willing to do whatever else I can for the company."

"No more moralistic probings?"

"No."

Strake appraised him for a long moment. He said, "Then I want you to go to Atlanta for a month. Take a commercial flight. Oversee the installation of my new manager in the Walther plant and assist him in any ways you can. I want you to make your own assessment of what needs to be done to lean out that operation. I'll want your opinions on the new manager and on the remaining top executives. While you're in Atlanta the backup pilot can fly the King Air for me as necessary. Alert him before you leave. That will be all for now."

He enjoyed the assignment in Atlanta, immersing himself in it, looking for ways to cut costs and improve efficiency with an objective outsider's eye. The new manager, a portly CEO in his mid-fifties who had been hired away from a small Connecticut company that made hunting rifles, did not seem to resent the presence of an emissary from Strake, and took over the rusty operation affably but firmly, making his leadership felt beneficially within the first week, letting the department heads and employees know exactly what was expected of them and injecting a fresh energy that seemed to be welcomed. The two of them got along well and the CEO was attentive to any suggestions.

At the end of the month Cowboy returned to meet with Strake and give him a detailed written report. Strake immediately sat behind his desk and read through the report, stopping frequently to ask pointed and perceptive questions, not satisfied until he had received exhaustive answers.

Strake gave no indication that he was either pleased or displeased, but he delegated more and more responsibilities over the following weeks.

Three months after the Atlanta assignment, Davis called him at his apartment late one Sunday night and said, "Get the King Air ready for a flight to Venezuela at dawn."

Strake and Davis met him at the all-night FBO, Strake dressed in a neat gray suit and muted tie and Davis looking bear-like in slacks and a black windbreaker. In addition to the usual light traveling luggage, Strake carried a large thick metal briefcase that appeared to be weighty.

Strake handed him a spiral-bound pad and said, "We're going directly to a private ranch about two hundred miles inland, southeast of Caracas near the Orinoco River. There is a narrow but adequate paved three-thousand-foot strip with pilot-controlled lighting. If the weather is bad there is a non-directional-beacon approach that you can back up with the GPS. The coordinates are listed in that notepad, along with the elevation and other details about the strip. The ranch belongs to a former government official, a business associate, so you do not need anyone's permission. We will stop in San Juan for fuel. Make the final destination for your flight plan Ciudad Bolivar, but we will not stop there. Twenty miles from the coast set the transponder code to the one listed in the notepad and press the ident button. Press the ident button again in exactly three minutes, and again exactly three minutes later, then keep the transponder on that code the rest of the way. Do not talk to anyone."

"But I'll need to get clearances and weather advisories from Venezuelan ATC, and what about customs?"

"We are fully cleared already and will be recognized by the transponder code. Any conflicting traffic will be made aware of us. You can monitor the automated weather station at Caracas. The official is ex-military and is high level, and he wishes this visit to be discreet for reasons of his own."

"This is . . . unusual."

"This is an unusual business, as I'm sure you have been discovering."

The man they were visiting could be a retired Venezuelan military officer who was involved in an arms deal on some kind of commission basis from Strake, a cash commission that could be in that metal briefcase, and the official might not want the government to know about it. Cowboy didn't like the idea of flying into the country semi-covertly, but dealings were decidedly different in South America. If Strake was tendering some kind of bribe to this Venezuelan it would only be considered business as usual by most Latin American standards.

After they boarded, Cowboy called ATC to change the final destination on his flight plan from Simon Bolivar to San Juan, Puerto Rico. He would file again from there, listing Ciudad Bolivar as his destination. This Venezuelan must really have some clout if he could persuade somebody in ATC down there to quietly monitor the flight and to cover up a non-landing at Ciudad Bolivar. There were several ways that could be done, he thought. One way would be to convince the civilian controllers that this was some kind of covert Venezuelan military flight.

When they took off from Teterboro in a dingy dawn there was a spaced-out line of heavy thunderstorms, some topping out at 45,000 feet, advancing threateningly northward across Tennessee and the Carolinas and Cowboy was soon busy picking a way among them, relying on the King Air's sophisticated color radar, which showed the huge cells as menacing scarlet otherworldly amoeba-like organisms, and on helpful vectoring from ATC.

The turbulence was on the bad side of moderate and occasionally somewhat worse and he slowed the plane to contend with it. There were frequent joltingly bright flashes not far away embedded in the heavy rain squalls and swirling dirty mists. The air was much less corrugated by the time they crossed the Florida line, and the rest of the flight, including the refueling stop in Puerto Rico, went smoothly. Strake did not come up to the cockpit.

The weather over the Caribbean was good, with only a high thin cloud layer blurring a three-quarter moon as they passed over the Venezuelan coast in silky late evening air between Caracas and Barcelona above the Pan American Highway, which was marked by widely-spaced vehicle headlights crawling along. They were squawking the specified transponder code, the infrequent chatter from Caracas approach giving no hint of their presence. The chart showed the rugged terrain of the Guyana Highlands ahead. Not far away to the southeast somewhere was Angel Falls and ten-thousand foot Mt. Roraima. The provided coordinates placed the private ranch alongside the Rio Caura, one of the Orinoco's main tributaries. The nearest towns were Cabruta and Caicara about fifty miles west on opposite banks of the snaking Orinoco.

He flew directly to the coordinates and keyed the transmitter five times on the given frequency. Twin rows of dim lights winked alive down in the blackness, looking impossibly short from eight thousand feet up. He spiraled down and slowed the King Air to pass a thousand feet above the strip. There was a dimly-lit wind sock that pointed out a light breeze favoring the western approach. The runway was clear but very narrow, no more than sixty feet wide. Trees and brush had been cut back at both ends to provide reasonably unobstructed glide paths. It was not a strip he would have wanted to approach in IFR conditions, with mountains uncomfortably close and a lot of hostile-looking tangled jungle all around. He spotted a complex of buildings among trees on a hillside a half mile from the strip, with lights on here and there.

He set up for a close-in downwind leg, slowing the King Air to a minimum on the base and final legs, the powerful landing lights probing a light ground fog that hung above the jungle, and dropping it in steeply to take advantage of as much of the runway length as possible, ready to pour the power back on for a go-around if necessary. The mains touched down less than a hundred feet beyond the threshold and he immediately reversed the props. There were rough places in the blacktop that looked like they had been patched with tarred gravel. He stopped the plane with just two hundred feet to spare, realizing how tense he had been as he released his tight grip on the yoke.

The hard part was over now. Taking off out of here

would pose no particular problem with only the two passengers and a good deal of the fuel weight burned off. In the wan moonlight he had noted that climbing away to the northeast would keep him clear of the highest terrain. He taxied slowly to a small apron where a Beech Duchess was tied down under an open-walled T-hangar and a white Land Rover was waiting with its parking lights on. He swung it around and shut the engines down, setting the parking brake.

Strake came to the cockpit door and said, "Stay here with the plane. We shouldn't be gone more than two hours. Keep the air-stair closed against the insects." He had the metal briefcase in hand. Davis could be heard back at the left rear of the cabin opening the door that hinged down to create a boarding stairway.

From the darkened cockpit Cowboy watched the two men walk over to the Rover and get into the back seat, Davis carrying a small soft sports bag and Strake carrying the metal briefcase. The driver stayed at the wheel. The Rover started up and moved away around a curve on a narrow gravel road that climbed up in S-turns through dense jungle. He went back through the cabin and closed the air-stair, getting a pleasant wafting of the warmly humid tropical air.

After opening the cockpit vents to refresh the air, he busied himself for an hour updating his instrument approach binders, neatening up the cabin and cockpit, and re-reading a section of the King Air manual to commit some more of the systems details to memory. The darkness outside was heavy, despite the gibbous moon, the runway marker lights having shut down automatically fifteen minutes after they had landed to leave only a few dim landscape lights along the apron and spaced out alongside the gravel track that wound up the hillside to the buildings.

Thinking of the patched places in the runway, he decided to go out and walk the length of the rough pavement to be sure there were no loose stones or other debris that might damage a prop or the turbines on what he was beginning to think of as his airplane. He had a five-cell flashlight which he took outside, closing the air-stair door behind him. He started walking the runway, sweeping the powerful beam from side to side. The jungle was loudly alive with the sounds of night birds and uncountable other creatures, and tendrils of light ground fog hung in the still air between the walls of solid-looking vegetation that were encroaching on the narrow cleared areas bordering the strip.

He had walked no more than a third of the length before the mosquitoes found him. They were like hot needles on the backs of his hands and the flesh of his face that was not protected by his beard, but he brushed at them and walked on, inspecting the pavement, thinking about the possibility of some big creature tracking him hungrily from the darkness.

The sounds of gunshots froze him. Two very quick reports followed by a single heavier shot. Muffled, but coming from one of the buildings up the hill. If he had been inside the plane he never would have heard them. Strake or Davis demonstrating a pistol? But there was something ominous in the series of shots. The two light reports were in haste, followed instantly by the heavier report, then stillness.

It had been an exchange of fire, he knew instinctively, and he broke into a run along the pavement, across the apron and up the hill along the gravel track.

When he could make out the buildings through the trees he switched off the flashlight and slowed to a walk, stepping carefully on the washboarded gravel. As he rounded the last curve he stopped, still well within the shadows, to look over the scene, the flashlight ready as a club if he should need it.

There was no sign of anyone near the buildings, the largest of which was a long low ranch house with a wide porch all along its front. The Land Rover was parked to one side of the circular drive. Another gravel track led away up the hill. There was a dim light in one of the outbuildings, and there were two area lights mounted high up on poles to beat back the oppressive jungle darkness. Somewhere farther up the hill a generator hammered in a steady rhythm.

There were two more startling sharp reports from within the house. No other sounds then except for the jungle creatures and the muted generator.

He was about to sprint for the shadows at the side of the house, intending to get a glimpse inside through one of the windows, when the double screen doors burst open and a man was pushed stumbling out onto the porch. Davis had the man's arms pinned tightly behind him. The man had a full head of white hair and was almost as large as Davis. He looked to be in his late fifties. He was struggling strongly and spluttering in rapid Spanish.

Davis spun him around and clubbed him full in the

face with a massive fist and the man went down as though he had been struck with a baseball bat. He writhed on the porch floor and groaned weakly. Something flashed in Davis's right hand as he strode over to a rope hammock. With a few strokes he cut the hammock down and sliced off lengths of rope. He went back and roughly tied the limp older man in the porch entry, one arm out to each side, hauling him up onto his feet between the entry posts by sheer strength, so the man was finally spread-eagled facing the house, his head lolling on his chest, his legs splayed.

Strake came out onto the porch and immediately slapped the man's face sharply three times. The man shook his head and gazed dumbly at Strake and then at Davis. Strake moved close and asked him something in a low voice. The man shook his head and protested. He was reviving now and he stood awkwardly to relieve the tension on his arms. He shook his head again as though to clear it, the white hair disheveled, a pitiful overweight figure, but not begging. Strake spoke to Davis, who roughly tore away the man's flowered shirt, wadding up some of it and stuffing it into the man's mouth, binding it in place with a strip of cloth tied around his head.

The man's back was covered with densely matted white hair and he was thick around the waist.

Strake loosened his tie and held out his hand and Davis gave him the knife, the blade bright in the porch light. Strake suddenly stabbed the man in the right shoulder and stepped back to avoid the blood. The man threw his head back and screamed against the gag but the sound was muted to a throaty croaking. Strake asked him something again, the jungle sounds and the distance making the words unintelligible. The man shook his head again, vigorously.

Strake stepped in and stabbed him in the left shoulder. The man writhed and tried to stand straighter to diminish the pain and Strake waited for three seconds and then stabbed him in the groin. The man was trembling violently now, the excess flesh around his middle quaking involuntarily, and he was emitting strangled noises. It was obviously agony for him to stand but also agony for him to sag against the ropes. Davis stood to one side watching impassively. There was a wet black slick spreading out on the porch floor. Strake asked him something again. The man could only move his head from side to side weakly.

Cowboy was numbly rooted in place, not believing what he was seeing, unable to move or breathe. Strake held out his hand again and Davis reached under his jacket to bring out a chromed pistol. Cowboy started forward saying, "No, no," in a dry cracked voice that he wanted to be a shout but was barely above a whisper and he moved two lead-footed steps forward to begin running but Strake took deliberate aim at the man's head from four feet away and fired a single shot, the man instantly convulsing and then going limp on the ropes. Cowboy again froze in place, breathing rapidly and shallowly and feeling sick.

Strake scanned the darkness for several long seconds as though he could sense somebody watching, his face hooded in shadow, and then he and Davis went back inside.

Cowboy was stunned by the savagery of what he had seen. He choked down bile as he stared at the limp figure tied to the porch uprights, the head thrown to one side.

Utterly still. He wiped at his coldly damp face with his hand and finally turned to walk dumbly back down the hillside track. If Strake knew he had seen the killing what would he do? Strake and Davis could not fly out of here themselves. But once back in the States Strake might well decide it would be wise to eliminate a witness. He thought, *I could take off myself and fly to Caracas. Tell the police there about it.* But he was in a foreign country illegally, and might well at a minimum be held indefinitely as some kind of accessory. Strake had too many connections here, several of them presumably powerful.

He broke into a run and when he got back to the plane he shut the air-stair behind him and went to the cockpit. He used paper towels to wipe away the sweat, took a slug of tepid water from a plastic bottle, and laid out an instrument approach plate binder on the copilot's seat as though he was in the process of updating it.

It was thirty interminable minutes before he saw the lights of the Land Rover winding down the hillside. It stopped on the apron and the lights went out. Strake and Davis got out of the front seats, Strake minus his tie and holding his suit coat wadded up in one hand, carrying the metal briefcase in the other. They walked quickly to the plane and Cowboy opened the air-stair.

As Strake brushed past him to take a cabin seat he said, "Take off and go back to San Juan for fuel. Leave the transponder off. Don't talk to anyone until you contact Puerto Rico."

"What do I tell San Juan ATC?"

Strake was staring at him intently. He said, "Why are

you sweating that much?"

"I just went outside for about ten minutes to check the runway for any loose gravel. The mosquitoes chased me back at a dead run."

Strake said nothing for several seconds, then, "Tell San Juan that you filed from Ciudad Bolivar, and while they're filling the tanks re-file for Fort Lauderdale. Leave the transponder off until you approach San Juan."

Strake stayed back in the cabin for the entire flight to Teterboro.

The next afternoon, from a pay phone outside a convenience mart near his apartment, he called one of the numbers on the card that he had kept hidden in a dresser drawer. A woman briskly said, "Yes?"

"I need to speak with Mr. Nolan Rader."

The woman said nothing. Within a few seconds the man answered, "Rader. What can I do for you?"

"This is Cowboy. We need to talk."

244

He said, "I saw Strake kill a man."

They were in Nolan Rader's black Explorer parked on a shadowed street two blocks from Cowboy's apartment. It was just after dark and there was a vaporous rain drifting through the casts from the streetlights.

"Where and when was this?"

"On a private ranch in Venezuela, the night before last about nine o'clock their time. These are the coordinates." He handed over a slip of paper. "I watched it happen and I didn't do a damned thing to stop it. I don't know why I didn't. I couldn't."

"You were right there with him when this went down?"

"Not exactly. He had told me to wait in the plane. The ranch house was a mile away up a hillside, through thick jungle. Strake and Davis were driven up to the house. After about an hour and ten minutes I got out of the plane to look over the runway for debris. I heard shots. I ran to check it out and from a distance of maybe three hundred feet I saw the killing. Davis tied the man spread-eagled to porch posts. Strake questioned the man—he was middle-aged, thinning white hair, thirty pounds overweight, five ten or eleven. The man either couldn't or wouldn't tell Strake what he wanted to hear even after Strake stabbed him three times very deliberately and very . . . precisely. I couldn't believe what I was seeing. It froze me. Then Strake borrowed a pistol from Davis and shot the man once in the head. They don't know that I saw it. And there were other shots. At least four. I think all of them were from inside the house, because they were muffled. I have no idea what it was all about, but I don't think they went there to kill; I think something happened there that set Strake off. You were right about him. I've never seen anything as coldly vicious as what he did to that man. I'll testify, sign a statement, whatever you need."

Rader was silent, gazing through the windshield at the slick street and tapping a forefinger on the steering wheel.

"Well, what's the matter? Isn't this what you wanted from me?"

"Hey, take it easy," Rader said. "I'm glad you came to me with this but you have to understand it happened in a foreign country. That makes things tricky. There are jurisdictional questions. What agencies should get involved up here and down there? Right now there's only your word against Strake's, and he's got all the connections and the clout. There's not even any record of him or his plane being in Venezuela at the time of the killing. I'm going to start checking this out first thing in the morning. But it will take time.

"Meanwhile, I'd like you to go on as though nothing's

happened. Keep working for him. Start watching things closely. Be careful if you take any notes. Commit as much as you can to memory. Try to get all the names of people and companies Strake deals with and all the meeting places and times. See if you can find out the names of any banks he uses here and offshore. Any shipments anywhere. Even if the information seems worthless or disconnected.

"This could take a while; I won't lie to you. But now you've seen what kind of degenerate your boss is. I want to hail all over his parade, grapefruit-size, and I'll appreciate your help in making that happen."

"How should I keep in touch?"

"We'll meet weekly as long as we can set it up safely. Call me next Wednesday from a pay phone. Go out for a run, like tonight. I'll check you for any tail and then pick you up. If I need to get to you in a hurry a woman will call your apartment making like she's a casual girlfriend. She'll suggest a meeting at which I'll show up. We'll only do that as a last resort. Are you up for this?"

"I'll give it a while. I don't really know what I'm doing with this kind of thing."

"You'll be fine. Just start gathering all the information you can. And be careful."

They met a week later, Rader picking him up in the black Explorer again as he was out running on a specified street near a postage-stamp-size public park a mile from his apartment.

Cowboy said, "What did you find out about the killing in Venezuela?"

"The man was Enrique Suarez, a former Venezuelan

Army general lately out of favor with the government because of his suspected ties to a Colombian drug cartel, but still with a lot of old powerful friends. They think he was a middleman on a deal Strake had going with a Colombian guerrilla faction, possibly financed in part by another cartel. It looks like one of Strake's shipments of M-16s and ammo got hijacked. Maybe Suarez hijacked it himself, sold the guns to whomever, and made up a story for Strake; we can't know for sure. We think you're right about the murder being spur-of-the-moment, though. Suarez must have told him whatever story and for some reason Strake wouldn't buy it so he killed the dude. Simple as that. They found a long-time Suarez bodyguard dead inside the place, along with the bodies of a middle-aged prostitute who apparently serviced the general on a regular basis, and an ex-army guy with a game leg who cooked and cleaned at the ranch. The prostitute had been beaten to death, probably by Davis. Snapped neck."

"So, what's going to be done about it?"

"I don't know. It's out of my hands. I've told you just about all I know myself. At least all I can tell you. I'll keep pushing for progress reports and fill you in as I get new information. Now, what have you got for me?"

He reached inside his jacket and handed over a six-by-nine spiral pad filled with handwriting. "This is what I could remember or reconstruct from all the way back to the day I went to work for Strake. Trips, dates, people, what I know of his warehouse inventory, everything. I have my flight log for accurate dating. It turned out I knew more than I thought, really."

Rader thumbed through it in the weak light coming in his side window and said, "Is this in some kind of weird code? Just kidding. Your handwriting is even worse than mine, but I'll decipher it. It's good, this is good. We can compare this stuff with intel we've collected from other sources, you understand. Say we already know some bent deal went down in Dallas on a certain day, and now we know from you that Strake and a couple of his buddies were there for sure that same day, you see? So we do some more nosing around with that in mind and maybe sniff out something we can put to good use.

"Just keep it up. Try to get him talking more. Make friends with his secretary or his accountant or maybe one of his part-time goons and see what they know. Do it easy. Be mister casual. Take small steps. Strake thinks he's immune and I'm betting he's getting more reckless. You hang in there and we'll eventually deep-fat fry this guy." He gazed into the distance pensively.

"Why do you say he thinks he's immune?"

"What?"

"You said he thinks he's immune."

"Oh, nothing. I just mean he's literally been getting away with murder and all kinds of other mischief and he must think by now that nobody cares. But believe me, some of us care."

Strake continued assigning routine business matters to him, giving him the use of an office in the warehouse, but remaining guarded about most of his affairs, and when Cowboy tried to cautiously approach Davis he found the big man to be even more closed-mouthed and hostile. But he observed what he could and began filling the pages of another notebook with flight dates and destinations, meetings, overheard parts of conversations, glimpses of office correspondence, and people he happened to see in the offices.

There were twenty-three employees at the warehouse, including the office staff and three shifts of security guards, so it was difficult to do too much digging without somebody noticing.

Strake's secretary Margaret was a matronly woman who worked with a solemnly brisk efficiency. One day when she had gone into the file room adjacent to her office to get him some routine information he had asked for, leaving him alone, he flipped through her Rolodex, noting the names of three independent long-haul truckers and quickly memorizing two names and phone numbers of Bahamian banks. He had just returned the Rolodex to where it had rested and had straightened up beside her desk when she came back in, a file in hand. She scowled at him for two seconds, but he smiled and she seemed to dismiss whatever trace of suspicion had stirred her. He had full access to the warehouse inventory lists so he hand-copied all the items and quantities.

He taught himself how to operate the office computer system and began gleaning some information from it. He assumed that if anyone became too suspicious he would be able to pass off his digging as merely an avid interest in how the business functioned. The pages in another note-book that he kept in the bottom of a dresser drawer in his apartment began to fill.

He was in the small furnished duplex apartment late one gray Saturday afternoon, with his boots crossed up on the coffee table, light classical music on the stereo and a cold beer at hand, reading a Larry McMurtry western novel that he'd found in a neighborhood book store. He had a collection of western novels that included Zane Gray, Elmer Kelton, Max Brand, William W. Johnstone, and L'Amour favorites, some of which had helped pass the time as he had waited in some FBO or another for whomever was paying him to fly at the time.

The bell rang and when he opened the door he was taken aback. All he could manage was, "Well, hello." A cab was pulling away from the curb.

She said, "This seemed like an innocent idea an hour ago, but now I feel absolutely...awkward."

"Mrs. Strake." He realized she'd been drinking.

"I've been out shopping and I thought I'd stop for a while to talk. You've been cordial to me in the past. Maybe I should just go."

"No, please, come in."

She was at that not-quite-drunk stage, taking pains to enunciate clearly and moving with care. She sat at one end of the couch and crossed her legs, resting her purse on her lap. She wore a conservative gray pants suit.

She said, "Do you have a drink?"

"I don't have anything on hand right now," he lied. "How about a cup of coffee or a soft drink?"

"A soft drink then. Please."

He went into the small kitchen and poured a Pepsi over ice, then brought the glass in and placed it on the coffee table. She left it untouched.

The silence stretched out. Then they both started talking at the same time. She smiled and said, "Please, go ahead."

"I was just going to ask how your plans are coming for that art gallery."

She brightened. "I've been working on it." And she raised a long-nailed finger in the air to emphasize the point. "I think I've found the perfect place, near the Billage . . . Village. An old store that's gone out of business, with reasonable rent, considering, and it's large enough for now, with an old high tin ceiling, so it feels even more open. I can see it renovated and well lit with a big central sculpture for focus, and paintings hung in theme groupings around the walls. And on, you know, pa . . . partitions. I have not approached Louis about it yet. I want to be sure I have all of the information straight first. Sometimes he is not the easiest person to talk to." With her fingers held like a comb she carefully raked her blond hair back over her ear to hold it in place. She focused on him and smiled. "You are an attractive man, do you know that?"

"Thank you."

"I think Louis wants to make you his right-hand man or something."

"Did he tell you that?"

"No. I just know it." She shook a finger at him. "But let me tell you something. Don't you ever get Louis angry with you."

"Why do you say that?"

"He can be . . . he can be unreasonable. Dorothy, our maid, said once, 'There is a dark current in him. I think he can be violent.'"

"Have you felt threatened?"

"No, no. You see ours is a marriage of arrangement. He likes to live well. I do, too. I am his showpiece. In return I have fine houses. Jewelry. Travel to beautiful, exotic places. One day I hope to have a child. Why am I telling you all of this?"

"I have an idea," he said with a smile. "Suppose we walk to the corner, to a place called Gina's. We'll have an early dinner and you can catch a cab home from there. I'll just need a few minutes to change into something presentable."

"Do you think I came here to seduce you?"

"No. I think you just might want somebody to talk to. You chose me. That's okay."

She appraised him for a long moment. "This Gina's. Do they have anything besides pasta?"

"Great salads. Good steaks. Lobster tails. I'm buying."

"You don't have to do that."

"I'll slip it in on my expense account."

She smiled. "Then I would be pleased to dine with you, sir."

At the small restaurant he ordered thick New York strips for both of them.

"Well, you were right," she said. "I just wanted somebody to talk to."

"We all need that sometimes."

"I stay in that house too much. I don't have any close family left. Or many friends. I don't drive. One of Louis's people usually drives me when I want to go somewhere. But sometimes I just want to feel free. Like today. Do you know I took a horse-and-buggy ride through Central Park? I went to see a new exhibit at the Guggenheim, and I did some shopping on Fifth Avenue, and then I had a few drinks in a hotel lounge. That's where I got the idea to see if you were home. I looked you up in the phone book."

"I'm glad you did."

"Tell me about yourself. Are you seeing anyone?"

"No one in particular. There's a woman who works at a ticket counter at Teterboro Airport. We go out from time to time."

"What are your plans with Louis?"

"I don't know. I like the flying. I never thought of myself as a businessman. I always thought some day I might start up a small charter operation in some backwater place along the coast. Get a Cessna and give sightseeing rides. Take aerial photos, that kind of thing."

"I think Louis wants to make you some kind of manager."

"He seems to be training me for something. It's interesting."

"Thank you."

"Excuse me?"

"Thank you for understanding, I guess. This is a nice little place."

"The best is yet to come," he said as the waiter brought the salads. "Wait until you try your steak."

The meal somehow consumed over two hours. He

called a cab for her and after she left he walked the streets for an hour, thinking. She obviously had no idea what her husband was capable of. She seemed caught in her marriage, albeit a gilded cage. He resolved to do what he could to protect her even as he worked to help destroy Strake.

The next morning Davis met with Strake in his office.

"She had a long dinner with him at a place called Gina's," Davis said, "a greaseball joint near his apartment. They're good and friendly. I'd say he's probably doing her."

Strake glared at him with pure malevolence for a long moment, then seemed to exert an iron control over himself, looking away. He said evenly, "How long do you think this has been going on?"

"I don't know. Each of the last two weeks she's taken off for a day by cab. She uses the same cab company each time. I talked to them. She goes downtown. The museums. Shopping. I don't know all the places she's been. They could have been meeting someplace."

Strake stared through him, exuding some dank and ancient force. "I want both of them followed. And I want you to inspect his apartment. Go over it very well but I don't want him to know you've been in there."

Davis chose a day when Cowboy would be gone on business to Philadelphia, flying the King Air with the accountant as a passenger. He waited two blocks down the street that morning until he saw the pilot come out of the duplex apartment, get into his Ford pickup, and drive away.

He gave it fifteen minutes and then walked along the sidewalk not looking to either side, a man merely absorbed in his own usual daily affairs, and right up to the front door. Acting as though he was fumbling with a worn key, he inserted the thin tensioner into the cheap old pin tumbler lock, slid in the pick to align all the tumblers, and in short seconds was inside.

Cowboy had to go back to retrieve a forgotten sectional chart and saw Davis going into the apartment. He kept on driving past.

What did it mean? Strake had to suspect he was spying and there was the notebook in his dresser, filled with facts, including more notes and impressions from the Venezuelan murder scene, that would now confirm Strake's worst suspicions.

He made the trip to Philadelphia. To do otherwise would have alerted Strake. When he returned that night he stopped at the pay phone on the corner of his block before going to his apartment. He called Rader's home number. An unfamiliar man answered.

"I need to speak with Rader."

"Who is this?" the guarded voice said.

He hesitated. "This is Cowboy and I need to talk with Nolan Rader as soon as possible."

There were several quiet seconds, then the voice said, "Where are you now?"

"I'm at a pay phone. Why?"

The voice said, "You know the last place you saw Mr. Rader?"

"Yes."

"Go there now. A man will meet you."

He drove to a small urban public park, deserted at this hour, and sat in the pickup by the curb with the lights out. He watched what appeared to be a furtive drug transaction take place a block away. A man walked by with a Rottweiler on a heavy chain leash. Traffic was sparse. Three cars parked within sight at intervals. After thirty minutes he was about to leave when a heavyset man dressed in jeans and a dark windbreaker came along the sidewalk. He knocked on the passenger-side glass with a fat knuckle and said, "You Cowboy?"

He unlocked the door and the man climbed in.

"Where's Rader?"

"Just drive. A van will be following us on and off. That will be my guys. We're going to do a little maneuvering to see if there are any other followers. It will take about an hour to get where we're going. Go west down here on the main drag, then signal for a right at the first green light but at the last minute slip over and turn left."

After a series of tricky turns, twice doubling back, driving through a fast food parking area and then through a strip mall, they finally kept to a route that wound off for many miles into the suburbs through some patchy woods. They circled through a development called Ravenswood Acres and finally stopped in the driveway of a modest ranch house that was indistinguishable from several hundred others in the neighborhood. The heavyset man got out to open the two-car garage and then motioned for him to drive inside. There was no sign of the van that had been following them earlier and apparently serving as rear guard.

They were met in the kitchen by a trim, balding middle-aged man in a business suit. When they were all seated in the living room the beefy one said, "I'm Vincent Teagarden with BATF, and this is U.S. Marshal Wesley Doyle."

"I'll ask again. Where's Rader?"

Teagarden said, "Mr. Rader was . . . a bit overzealous on the matter of Worldarms. He has been transferred to another matter entirely. This is no longer his concern. I understand you claim to have witnessed some sort of confrontation in Venezuela."

"Not a confrontation. A killing. A cold-blooded murder by Strake and Montgomery Davis. You must have everything I gave to Rader about it."

"We've talked, yes. Do you have any reason to believe that this Strake or Davis suspect you've volunteered information to BATF?"

"That's why I called tonight. By chance I saw Davis entering my apartment this morning. I left a pad there with a lot of information about the operation and some notes they can't fail to interpret as meaning I saw that killing. The pad wasn't well hidden. In a dresser drawer. Davis can't have missed it."

Teagarden and Doyle exchanged glances.

Doyle said, "You were followed to that park tonight. Right now we're trying to determine by whom."

"Well, I'd say it's a pretty safe bet by somebody working for Strake, wouldn't you?"

"There's no reason to get upset, here," Teagarden said.

"Look, I've been supplying Rader with a lot of information. He seemed to know a lot more, to have a store of facts concerning illegal activities by Worldarms built up over some time. I saw Strake fire a bullet into a man's brain and I'm willing to testify, sign a deposition, whatever, so why aren't Strake and Davis being arrested? Why do I get the impression they aren't about to be arrested?"

"That's not within our purview," Teagarden said. "All I can tell you is that evidence gathering of this scope can take a lot of manpower and a lot of time. Years even. At any rate, it's neither our concern nor yours any longer."

"Wait a minute. Is Strake arming somebody the Pentagon or the CIA *wants* armed? That's it, isn't it? That's why Rader said Strake considers himself immune. Who are they? A rebel group somewhere ready to take down a dictator the CIA doesn't like? Some paramilitary gang that has promised to take out one of the Colombian drug cartels?"

Teagarden spread his hands innocently and said, "Again, something like that wouldn't fall within our sphere of responsibilities. Any need we have to know. We're here, Marshal Doyle and I are, to help you. That's all we know and all we're charged to care about."

"I'm sure you've heard of the witness protection program," Doyle said. "Also known as WITSEC."

"You're kidding."

"No, sir. I'm dead serious. We have reason to believe your life may be in danger."

"Danger posed by Strake. So why don't you go get him?"

"There are also people Worldarms may be dealing with who could be a threat to you. In any case you will be accepted into the program provided you are willing to abide by certain stipulations."

"And those would be?"

Teagarden said, "I'll let you two discuss what you have to. I'll go check in with our backup guys." He got up, pulling a hand-held radio from a belt clip, and went outside.

Doyle said, "Beginning right now, tonight, we break all the chains that hold you to your present life. Every last one, and believe me there are more than you realize. You don't go back to your apartment or to the airport. You just disappear. You don't ever come back to this area. We'll send a team to get your belongings, but you'll destroy any pictures you have and all of your ID. You'll move several times under different names until we're sure there is no trail left to follow. You will write out in detail a complete history of your life so we can cover all the angles. We know what we're doing and we're very good at it.

"We'll set you up in a new life somewhere. It won't be easy. You'll live in isolation until we have a completely new identity established for you in detail. You will not ever contact anybody you know now, no matter the reason, no matter how good a friend someone might be. You have no close family left as I understand it so that's not a problem. That's usually the most difficult adjustment for many protected witnesses, leaving all but immediate family members behind.

"We'll give you a new birth certificate, a new social security number, new credit cards. You'll have to apply for a new driver's license and test for your pilot's license and ratings. We'll help out with most expenses. I see no pressing reason for you to alter your appearance too radically. Color your hair and cut it short, try to dress differently, and that should suffice. You will live a quiet life and re-port periodically to a Marshal's office in your relocation area. Some day you might be called as a witness. If not, the more time that passes, generally, the safer you'll be, but that's not to say you or we should ever relax the rules. Are you willing to strictly abide by all of that?"

He thought for a long moment, staring at the wall. He said quietly, "What alternatives do I have?"

"Not many. I believe this to be the prudent one."

He had some money that he'd saved over the years. Enough for a good stake. Maybe enough to buy a Cessna. He was through working for Worldarms at any rate, and he had few other significant ties to the area. He had little to lose by agreeing, so he finally said simply, "All right."

"Then we might as well get started," Doyle said. "Do you have a preference for a new name? It shouldn't be even close to that of a relation or to anybody you've ever known."

He thought for a minute.

"Make it Bass," he said. "Sam Bass."

22

THE MODEST HOUSE WAS AT THE TOP END OF A STEEPLY switch-backing graveled lane a mile outside the town of Cherokee. John Hardin parked his ten-year-old high-mileage dark blue Toyota Camry in the tilted yard and set the parking brake firmly. It was November but only mildly chilly today. A tendril of smoke was curling up from the stone chimney to be shredded and swept away by a light breeze. The well-kept house had board-and-batten siding stained gray, with a green metal roof that sloped down and out to cover a full-length front porch. An old but clean Dodge pickup was parked to the side.

He got out stiffly and looked around. There was a rough lush meadow tumbling away from the house for several acres of the mountain flank, revealing a distant view down onto the narrow town in the valley, where lights were coming on as dusk fell. The woods rising up behind the house were thick with stately conifers, whispering prehistoric secrets among themselves as they combed the breeze. The hardwoods had shed their leaves, giving the forest a soft multicolored carpet.

He heard the front door open and turned to see a thin slightly bent old man dressed in silver-belted jeans and a red shirt with colorful beadwork in angular abstract designs flashed across the chest. His coarse black hair was long, streaked with gray, and bound tightly back into a single long braid.

"You can't be selling anything I would need and probably not even anything I would want at my age," the old man said with a wrinkled grin that showed a few teeth gone. His skin looked burnished and well-aged, like the leather of a Second World War flight jacket kept with care for decades, with deep permanent crevices and intricate patterns of etched-in lines.

"You're Mr. Wasituna Lightfoot?"

"That's what they call me. What do they call you?"

"I'm using the name John Hardin."

The old man frowned and peered down at him intently. "You knew my granddaughter, then."

"She said your father Goingback might have been one of the last of the Cherokee witches. Able to read another's thoughts. Did he teach you how to do that?"

"There's no magic to it. When you get older you can sometimes see into people a little clearer, that's all. So many years take a toll but they also bestow a certain wisdom if you only let them. Besides, no white man has come to see me in a long time, and Valerie described a man of your age and size she had met out on that island. A man she had met and chosen. A man who was a good friend to her Joshua. Can you tell me, why did she die in that way?"

"Because of me, sir. They were coming after me."

"And so we were told. We were also told you were dead." The old man appraised him quietly with squinted eyes, finally nodded once, and grinned again. "You move carefully and your face is bruised around your eyes so you have been damaged but you don't look at all dead. Come into my house, John Hardin, and we'll talk."

The breeze was ghosting into the partly-opened front windows in the living room, ruffling the curtains. It was a good home, old and solid and comfortable and reassuring, this home where she had grown up. Where she had played and laughed and asked many questions and made her plans. There was a small hickory fire in the fireplace, muskily scenting the room and dispelling the chill. A fire like many she must have looked into, the hickory scent catching in her hair as she had dreamed her dreams.

The stone wall above and flanking the fireplace had a series of thick pine shelves that held pottery and fine carvings of eagles and animals, and old wood-framed photos. He stared at one that immediately caught his eye, of a much younger Wasituna standing unbent near a waterfall, with his hand lightly on the shoulder of a six- or seven-year-old Valerie in a plain loose dress. She'd had even then a certain wry smile and a spark in her eye that hinted at the proud woman she would become. He felt his throat constrict and he could not speak. He turned away and sat at one end of the couch, the old man seated opposite on a straight chair, his hands on his knees, waiting patiently.

Finally he said, "I shouldn't have come here, but I just needed to tell you that I'm sorry. She thought the world of you, sir. She would offer some bit of advice based on something you'd taught her, or tell me something about her childhood, some good memory that would include you. I know you pretty much raised her, and you did a good job of it. She wanted me to come here to meet you."

"She lives in here," the old man said, and tapped a gnarled finger on his chest. "And she lives on in Joshua and in you. Every parent believes his children and their children to be special gifts to the world, but there was always something a little more in Valerie. A strong, clean light in her soul that everybody who knew her could feel shining out on them. Her light changed those around her, as it has changed you. So her light—her spirit—lives on."

"Yes, she changed me. I'll never get over the loss of her but I'm richer for having known her. I'll always love her."

"Those who you say came after you and instead killed her. Did you wrong them?"

"No, sir. Not really. I saw one of them murder a man. I started collecting information against him, but that didn't work out so I went into the witness protection program. It seemed like my best choice at the time." He found himself saying much more than he had intended, instinctively trusting this old man.

"Under the name of Sam Bass."

"Yes. But partly by chance they located me and then came after me. I should have been much more careful. I was stupid, and it killed her."

"Now you use another name."

"I'm back in the protection program. These bruises around my eyes are from surgery to change my appearance.

I wear contact lenses to change my eye color. I shouldn't be telling you any of this, and I have to ask you never to tell anybody I was here. It could be dangerous for you. I know Joshua is over near Maggie Valley, but I can't go near him. For his own safety."

"Why haven't these men been arrested? The sheriff of that county where she lived, he can't tell me. Nobody can tell me."

"I don't know for sure, but I don't think they will be arrested any time soon. The one I saw do the murder is rich and powerful, with many connections. He may be selling guns to some group the government wants armed. I don't know any way to find out."

"Did Valerie tell you anything about our old ways?"

"Yes. She loved the culture. The long history of your people."

"Many years ago, years before Valerie was born, there was a young Cherokee woman who was brutally abused. Raped." The old man's eyes were young and hard now, look-ing fiercely into a distant past. "There were corrupt reasons why the man who did it was not arrested. But it was the old way of our people, going back generations upon genera-tions upon generations, for the family of one who has been wronged to see justice done. Three of us met and swore an oath. Justice found that rapist. He did not rape again."

His eyes slowly lost their glare and after a moment he said, "You mean to go after these men."

"Yes."

"You mean to kill them."

"I don't know."

"There is no other reason. You mean to kill them."

Quietly, he said, "Yes."

The old man thought for what seemed a long time, then said, "Where are you staying?"

"I took a motel room in town just for the night."

"Go get your things and come back here. You will stay with me for a time. I'm too old and slow to go with you after these men, but there are things I can teach you. How to walk in the woods or anywhere else quietly and almost unnoticed. Some ways to stalk and kill. How to heal and strengthen your body. But mostly how to harden your heart to what you will do. How to scour out all but the killing-will that you must set loose, to call on the ancient cunning you already have sleeping deep inside yourself, so you will act swiftly and surely.

"But you must not let yourself become like one of them, so you must begin to know how—after you have done what you must do—how to restrain the killing-will and to wall it off from your life again. You won't ever forget the great power of it, and it will change you, but you must learn to live with it as though it is a chained bear safely behind a wall. Then you must work to bring love and laughter and compassion back into your heart. My own bear is chained. I can teach you. Yes, I can teach you. Go now and get your things."

Wasituna gave him Valerie's old bedroom in the back of the small house. There were still traces of her. A faded print dress hanging alone at the end of the closet rod. Stacked boxes on the closet floor, and two boxes up on the closet shelf that held the best of her grade-school papers.

He tried to look through them carefully but found the innocence and the raw imagination and the good heart the discolored old papers displayed much too painful. There was a small red cedar box in the top dresser drawer that held costume jewelry, a key chain, and a high school ring. He left it all undisturbed and turned away, his eyes burning.

He got little sleep that first night in her soft narrow bed, staring at the shadowed ceiling for hours and thinking of her. On a summer night with the bedside window open she would have drifted off listening to the wind gathering in the conifers, and she would have awakened in the morning to the pure music of the birds and the clean scents of the forest. When he closed his eyes he could see her and hear her laughter and feel her hair caress his face with a touch as light as a summer breeze, and recall in detail any of the times they had shared. A perfect vaulted sunny day at Kitty Hawk with Joshua. One night when the three of them capered on the beach as the lazy breakers glowed green. A cool windy fall afternoon spent fishing out behind the island in a borrowed skiff.

He had a hundred snapshots of her locked away in his mind and he took some of them out and examined them. Valerie tossing her glossy hair back with a proud lift of her head, the cord in her bronzed neck prominent. Valerie preparing a meal at her kitchen counter, absorbed and serious. Valerie giving him a mock-angry look when he came out with some lame joke. Valerie closing her eyes as she inclined her head and leaned close for a kiss. Valerie gazing with total unconditional love at Joshua while the boy lost himself happily in some imaginary world on the beach.

He could not allow himself to think of Joshua yet. The boy was safe from the evil that had struck out like some monstrous snake to claim his mother. Joshua would certainly be in great emotional pain, feeling lost and alone, but he was safe and that had to be enough for now. *If I can go out there and make a measure of justice for Valerie*, he thought, *if I can neutralize the threat and if I still live, then I'll think about Joshua and how I might ease his pain.*

But that seemed almost impossibly distant, and he knew the old man was right. He would have to banish compassion and all thoughts of a normal life, of long-range hope or plan, of what good things might have been or what good things there might still be. Such thoughts could only weaken his resolve, encumber him, make him fear or doubt or hesitate. So he began to push all such thoughts away, even the sweet memories of her, and he examined from a cautious distance the nature of the evil he would soon confront, drawing on every relevant fact he could dredge up. He looked for weaknesses, for ways that he might invade it. And destroy it.

He went to work on his body the next morning, rising just before dawn to dress in sweats, and easing out of the house. He found a smooth rock the size of a crushed elongated baseball behind the house and it became his squeezing stone. There was a path behind the house that led up the mountain through the woods and he struck out on it at a fast walk, squeezing the cold stone hard fifty times in his right fist, then fifty times in his left, gradually warming it, and back to the right fist.

A thick opalescent mist moved stealthily through the

trees. Birds called above and squirrels scampered over the thick carpet of leaves. The path rose higher and made him break into a sweat, and his leg muscles ached deeply. The indistinct path veered off to the right to follow a natural cleft, then it became much steeper and he had to slow and pick his way around and over rocks and thick roots. It ended in a clearing near the summit, maybe two miles from the old man's house and a thousand feet higher. He was winded and his body hurt badly in several places.

He would use the path twice each day, he decided, early and late, building up his speed until he could run it all the way up and down without stumbling and falling, increasing his stamina and honing his agility and balance. He would carry the squeezing stone at first and then heavier stones in each hand. In the summit clearing he would do stretches and sets of push-ups and sit-ups, and with increasingly heavier stones he would do curls and lifts. The exhaustion of the workouts would clean out his mind and sharpen his focus. He rested briefly, his lungs burning, his side and hip aching. He walked on trembling legs and skidding feet back down to the house, where Wasituna had a pancake breakfast in the making.

"Yes, my walking path is good," the old man said as they ate at his kitchen table, "but it will soon become familiar so then I'll take you to other trails. And when you run with the stones in your hands choose two of much different weights. They will better help test your balance.

"But preparing your body is the easy part. Preparing your mind is much harder. You already have most of what you'll need deep inside you, passed down through thousands of years. There was a time long ago when your ancestors always walked with danger on all sides, from animals and from other humans. So they learned how to smell the danger and see it on the edges of their vision and even sense it with their minds alone. You have that ability within you but it sleeps because you don't use it. You've felt it. When you've walked up to a strange house, or into a darkened room, and you have known with certainty if anybody else was there or if it was empty. Or you have met a man who smiles widely but you have felt his treacherous nature and so have not given him your trust. Or there have been strange times when you have known exactly what is soon to be said or done by another. It is that ancient power within and you can use it to stalk an animal or a man. If you learn to tap into it, as you would tap into a tree for the hidden sap, the power will help make you stronger than your enemies.

"You must also be aware that one among your enemies may have learned to call on that same power, although he may not even realize it himself, so if somehow that one becomes the hunter you will know to quiet your mind and still your body so you don't betray yourself with movement or sound or fear-scent or even thought, until you can become the hunter again."

"It all sounds difficult to achieve."

"I'll help you. But I think you've already begun. When you run the path to the top of the mountain sit down there and be still for a time. Wash out your mind. Push away all regrets, all doubts, all thoughts of tomorrow except how you might set out to do what you must do. Think of how it once was for your nameless ancestors. Their blood runs in your veins. Drive away all emotion, even anger. Above all, blinding anger. Make your heart cold and hardened. Try to hear every single sound in the woods and know what each means. Be aware of every sound you make yourself and always try to move more quietly. Smell the breeze and know all it tells you. Go walk in the town and try to know what the others around you are thinking. If you try hard enough the power will slowly awaken in you. And then you can unchain the killing-will."

During the days he jogged and then gradually ran on the path and helped the old man do chores around the place. He found downed hardwood trees in the forest, used a bow saw to cut them into lengths that he could drag back to the house with a heavy rope looped around his shoulders, then he cut them up and split them to build up a store of firewood, stacking it high between two trees at the edge of the woods behind the house. He repaired and repainted the shed on two long warm days. He stocked the refrigerator and pantry but left the cooking to the old man, who made mysterious Indian dishes using different herbs that he claimed had magical healing powers.

In the evenings they sat by the fireplace drinking an herbal tea. One night the old man asked, "Do you have enough money?"

"Yes. My plane was insured and paid off. The Marshals got the money for me. Over forty thousand dollars."

He began to grow a beard, which he would keep closely trimmed. He put on an old hat and dark glasses and ran down into the town and walked along by the crafts, souvenir, and leather shops, trying hard to read the thoughts of those around him and actually seeming to get fleeting impressions from this person or that one. He went through the museum, taking in every bit of knowledge it offered about the Cherokee people. He didn't engage in any conversations.

The big casino on the edge of town sat at the end of a vast and ugly parking lot to accommodate the lines of tour buses and the hundreds upon hundreds of cars bearing plates from many states, which fed a steady stream of hopeful people into the neon fantasyland inside the low imposing building of massive laminated beams and stone. The action among the rank upon rank of electronic slots and games went on around the clock as the slick operation gathered in millions from the dreamers and offered only ephemeral cold glitter in return. "It's a palace for fools," the old man said of it.

As he worked or ran, pushing his body harshly, he thought of how he might go after them. There had been at least two in that silver Blazer. The one with the bulldog face, the one Marshal Nelson had said was probably the street thug known as Winston. The other had most probably been Montgomery Davis. A third could have been the young one in fatigues who had been seen in the Ocracoke General Store asking about an airplane charter. He had first spotted that Blazer near the store. So find out for sure who and how many had come in the Blazer and then go after them one at a time, he thought.

He would begin with the one called Winston, whose real name Nelson had said was Walter Calzo, from Newark. Strake was different. Strake was most often surrounded by tight security, either in one of his homes or in his warehouse office, and there were often other people nearby, innocent people who could get hurt or serve as witnesses. He had to strike with total surprise when the man was isolated somewhere. If possible make it look like an accident. Gradually he imagined a fitting way it could be done cleanly and with absolute finality. He began turning the raw plan over in his mind, looking for flaws, thinking of specific ways he might carry it out.

Wasituna took him to several different mountain trails, the old Indian usually walking by himself for a time and then waiting placidly in the car while Hardin ran the trails to near exhaustion. Wasituna urged him to buy a pair of deerskin moccasins, which the old man first soaked in water and then instructed him to wear while he ran until they dried on his feet and so fit like his own skin. "You'll feel every stick and rock on a trail," Wasituna said, "so you'll soon learn to place your feet more carefully, even while you're running as fast as you can. The moccasins will make you quieter and more sure-footed. You'll see." He punished and bruised his feet at first, stumbling and slowing on the mountain path, once tripping on a root and falling headlong, painfully scraping his knees and forearms on sharp slate rock. Gradually he learned to run at speed while still placing each foot in the best spots almost instinctively. His feet began to toughen along with the rest of his body.

On a gray heavily misted day after a light snow the night before, five weeks after he had arrived, Wasituna drove him in the pickup over poor back roads to a new

trail a long way from the town on the edge of the sprawling Great Smoky Mountains National Forest. He ran for
miles along the trail as it climbed and fell and climbed
again, forking three times and winding through the rugged terrain. He lost track of time and was on a sustained
runner's high, feeling at times as though he could glide
along the rough ground without even touching it, sweating
freely, his legs sure and strong and his lungs inflating and
expelling deeply and smoothly.

As he climbed on the faint twisting path strewn with
forest debris he ran alongside a narrow swift stream and the
path became even more indistinct, as though nobody else
had been this way in a very long time. The ground became
steeper and more rocky, the stream eventually disappearing into jumbled rocks. Then the trees thinned and opened
onto a foggy meadow surrounded by cliffs on three sides.

He slowed and stopped, breathing deeply, his blood
singing. He stretched his shoulders and torso and dropped
for fifty pushups. He wiped his face with his hand and sat
on a log to rest. He knew he was miles from anywhere. He
could not pick out where the trail went from here. As his
breathing calmed he rested his hands on his knees and stilled
himself, listening intently to the forest all around. There
was a fitful breeze building, rustling through the conifers
up high and at times clattering in the topmost branches of
the hardwoods. The air seemed to warm and thicken. He
could hear drops of mist hitting the heavily-matted forest
floor and tried to pinpoint where each fell. Some small animal, a squirrel or more likely a chipmunk, judging by the
furtive quickness of the movements, suddenly skittered up a

tree, its tiny claws scratching at the bark.

He closed his eyes and tried to pick out other sounds. A particular branch tapping another. The trickling headwaters of the stream that was now five hundred feet off, barely distinguishable from the breeze sounds above. A bird calling plaintively in the distance, higher up on this nameless mountain.

The breeze increased until it was a steady susurration, mesmerizing, sighing throughout the forest. Still with his eyes closed he listened closely and he could pick out what sounded like the soft beatings of wings. Hundreds of wings. Birds wheeling and climbing and settling. But there was a quality of unreality to it and he did not dare to open his eyes because if it was a mere sensory illusion he desperately did not want to lose it. He knew the mists were swirling around him now; he felt it, but he didn't move. There was a startlingly heavy sound behind him. He froze every muscle. Then it came again, moving up on his left now, a dragging shuffle that broke twigs and scattered damp leaves.

It was a black bear. He heard it clearly, its breathing uneven and chuffing, and smelled the rank odor of its matted coat, but he also *saw* it in some strange way even though his eyes were closed. It moved past him, lurching, and there was a glistening runnel of dark blood leaking from a wound in its shoulder. It ignored him as it lumbered slowly on. The moisture on the high cliffs was thickening and flowing down the rugged granite in violet rivulets. The mist-filled meadow was not a meadow but an ethereal lake. A lake that was real and yet not real. There were

ghostly birds above it. Hundreds of them performing exu-
berant aerial dances in the violet mist.

He thought he had pushed her far back in his mind
where she would be safe until he had done what he had
to do, but she stepped out from behind a tree, her back to
him, wearing a dark green robe, her long black hair sheened
with the chilled moist air.

He did not dare move. He called out to her quietly
but she did not turn around, just raised her left hand in ac-
knowledgment and reassurance and moved on. Close by
the lake shore she let the robe fall. The bear moved painfully down alongside her and looked up at her, its paw lifted
and dripping blood. She motioned for it to go on and it
moved awkwardly into the water until only its humped back
and head showed and it was swimming out into the mist.
She entered the water, her back finely muscled, her hair iri-
descent, her skin exquisitely supple. The lake waters flowed
around her waist and the mists swirled and enfolded her
and she called out something but it was lost in the breeze.

He stood abruptly, his heart hammering and his breath
coming in ragged gasps, searching wide-eyed ahead in the
mist, but the bear was nothing more than a black boulder,
the lake just a vale of low-hanging mist. The robe only
a lush patch of moss. And although he strained to hear,
the sounds of the birds were fading into the strengthening breeze.

Shaken, he stood there for a long time, his eyes stream-
ing hot tears, until he dimly realized the light was failing.
He shook his head to clear it and walked back, looking
repeatedly over his shoulder. Then he ran, filled with

heartache, until he cut the trail close by a familiar cliff and suddenly knew his way again. The old Cherokee was waiting patiently in the darkened pickup and said nothing.

Over the next two weeks he went back to the same trail three times but, despite running for hours and following each of the forks, he could never find the particular stream branch or the high meadow—or *Ataga'hi*, the magic lake—again.

Wasituna bought ten boxes of .45 ACP cartridges, a pistol cleaning kit, and a yellowed Army manual from an old white man he knew who owned a gun shop off the reservation, and Hardin took the old Colt that Hank had given him to a clearing deep in the woods. First he spread out a square of canvas on a rock shelf and taught himself how to strip the gun and clean it. He did it over and over, enough times so that he could finally do it with his eyes closed. He felt its heft and balance and practiced with it loaded but without a round chambered, drawing and aiming it, from behind his belt buckle and then from behind his belt at the small of his back, over and over, trying to improve his speed and confidence so he would not fumble it. He spent long hours at it every day, and carried the gun with him at all times, becoming intimately familiar with it, learning to conceal it under a sweatshirt or windbreaker, in a leather fanny pack, or slid into the top of his boot under loose-legged jeans. He learned to draw and aim it with his right hand quickly while standing or seated, aiming with both eyes open and his left palm cupped under the butt to steady it.

He took it back to the clearing day after day and fired it at cans and dead trees. It was startlingly loud and had a kick that jolted his whole arm. The fat slugs could inflict heavy damage on a tree stump. He fired first for accuracy at ranges from ten feet to a hundred feet, then for speed, not using anything to protect his eardrums, getting used to the noise and the recoil, squeezing the trigger for each shot. He learned to reload quickly with the spare magazine, doing it over and over. He carried it with a round in the chamber, the hammer back and the safety on—what they called cocked and locked—and drew and fired, drew and fired, until his hand was sore from it.

He and the old man devised a training run. Wasituna got a stock of plastic gallon and half-gallon jugs from a recycling center. The Indian first went out and placed a dozen or more water-filled jugs along both sides of a particularly rugged stretch of trail. Hardin ran the trail, drawing and firing when he spotted the first jug, moving on and firing when he saw the next, and so on. Wasituna was creative with the placement, using tree forks, swinging some from ropes, partially hiding others behind rocks, putting two close together, varying the range, and keeping careful score of hits, which were few at first but gradually increased until Hardin was getting frequent hits almost instinctively. He kept the gun meticulously clean and it never failed to fire, never jammed. He could see why the Colt had remained in service for so long and had been praised by so many servicemen over those decades. Wasituna had to go back to the gun shop for more cartridges.

One day Wasituna took him hunting with only his best blowgun, a seven-foot length of dried river cane that he had hollowed with care, smoothing the bore until it was slick and true. The darts were sharp six-inch slivers of locust feathered with thistledown. "Too much feathering and the dart will drag in the tube," the old man said. "Too little and it will not fly straight or far." It was an ancient simple weapon, but not easy to make with precision. In the old man's hands it was virtually silent and absolutely deadly to small game. Hardin watched him stalk, flush, and, incredibly, kill a loping rabbit with it. Hardin tried the blowgun but could not control the accuracy. He realized it must have taken the Indian many years to become so adept with it.

That night Wasituna prepared a savory stew with the meat, fresh vegetables, and a concoction of herbs, then they sat in front of the fire while Hardin told him of his killing plan.

Wasituna listened intently and made several suggestions and refinements.

* * * * * *

Hardin's body was rapidly toughening and strengthening, no traces of fat on his frame now, as he maintained and some days increased his workouts, driving himself hard while he tried to cleanse his mind of every last distracting thought.

But there were still doubts. "I don't have any special fighting skills," he told Wasituna one night. "I've never been in the service or trained in martial arts."

"How do you think these men you go after fight? It took two or three of them to come after you, and in the end they failed. They think you're dead. When you go at them one at a time with surprise on your side and the kill-ing-will strong in you they will be dead men. It will not be a contest with rules where skill is matched against skill. You track each one, surprise him, and kill him. You go at them as coldly as they came at you. They will see a dead man coming for them with ice eyes and they will know fear. I've watched you, I've seen inside you, and I know you can do this. You must have no more doubt. Doubt can cripple you."

Wasituna spent hours telling him stories about the feats of great Cherokee warriors, of how, when threatened by the Creeks or others, the seven clans gathered and went on a war footing with a war chief, and how on nights before battles the warriors painted themselves, put on head, arm, and leg bands of otter skin, danced the brave dance near the fires, and sang the war song, so preparing their minds and setting loose the killing-will.

Wasituna said, "Their weapons were round stones lashed with rawhide in the forks of sycamore sticks, sharp-ened stone battle-axes, bows of shaped and smoothed hickory soaked in bear oil and seasoned by fire. They had cane arrows tipped with flint and made to fly true with the help of the sacred eagle feathers, and flint-tipped spears, and slings, and flint knives." In the light from the fireplace his storytelling was hypnotic.

Gazing into the hickory fire Hardin could easily

imagine the fighting that raged through the forest and witness the individual violent clashes and hear the atavistic
war cries. He knew Wasituna was using the stories to help
prepare him for the coming trials.

Early on a sunny Saturday morning in the unusually warm
winter, seven weeks after he had come to stay with the
old man, in the foothills southeast of Boone, he found a
skydiving school operated as a sideline business by an ex-
Airborne man and his wife, Elwood and Francine Osborne.
The tattooed Elwood piloted the jump plane—a ragged-
looking Cessna 182 with its right door and right front
passenger seat removed—and also taught chute packing and
free-fall techniques. Francine was a lithe athletic brunette
who had competed successfully nationwide in skydiving
events and was the more articulate of the two, teaching an
informal ground school on the sport. Her trophies filled a
shelf in the office of their old barn that served as a hangar,
rigging loft, and clubhouse beside the 2,500-foot grass
strip that was flanked by large grassy fields.

There were three other student jumpers there that
morning—a nervous, smiling young couple from States-
ville and a balding middle-aged man who looked like a
minister.

The Osbornes spent the morning teaching the com-
ponents and functioning of the sport parachute—the
rectangular canopy that by directionally spilling air pro-
duces forward speed and is controlled by pulling wooden

toggles mounted on the risers. They went over the fine points of the harness, shroud lines, back pack, and small tightly-packed reserve chute. They explained how the sport rig is operated by pulling the ripcord from its pocket on the chest harness, which pops the spring-loaded pilot chute that serves as an air anchor, dragging a deployment bag out of the pack. The shroud lines trail out followed by the pilot chute, pulling the canopy free from the deployment bag.

The student would be expected to steer the canopy to land as close as possible to the target, which was two white strips of canvas laid out in a cross three hundred feet from the barn. As the ground drew close the jumper would clamp his or her legs together, slightly bend the knees, and pull both toggles all the way down to knee level, which, if timed correctly, would momentarily reduce the rate of descent enough to allow an easy stand-up landing.

They all watched Elwood pack one of the orange-and-white canopies they would use. With a chalk board Francine outlined the various kinds of emergencies that could occur and went over how to handle each of them. Each student would be directed during the jump with the aid of a small helmet-mounted radio receiver.

In turn they practiced exiting the jump plane while it was parked on the brown grass, pivoting out the doorway to place the left foot on a short length of two-by-four clamped to the gear strut, the right leg hanging free, gripping the angled wing strut with both hands. On a signal and radioed voice command the jumper would push off backward, arch the back as much as possible, and spread-eagle.

Since the belly would be the center of gravity, the jumper would pivot forward to fall flat, chest-first, in the stable position, and the static line attached to a seat belt bracket inside the plane would do the work of opening the chute while the student pulled a dummy ripcord from a harness pocket. The chromed handle had a bright red kerchief tied to it so the instructor, watching from the plane above, could see that the student had actually torn it out and not just a patch of shirt front.

"Above all else you need to protect the reserve ripcord handle," Francine told them. "If it should snag on anything and open the chute accidentally inside the plane, the canopy will very probably stream out the door and take you and a good chunk of the fuselage with it. Not a happy thought."

The couple elected to go in the second load, so Hardin and the other man dressed in baggy jump suits and soft-soled boots, readying themselves for the first load. Hardin's much-used helmet was too tight and the boots were too loose. The scratched goggles turned the world yellow. Elwood cinched up the bulky backpack chute harness tightly and said, "You don't want no slack in the rig or you'll think it jerked a knot in you when it opens."

Hardin lumbered to the plane feeling like a trussed turkey. The other man sat on the back seat beside Francine, and Hardin sat on the floor where the passenger seat had been, facing backward, wondering how he was going to athletically swing out the doorway to grab the wing strut and face forward into the wind.

Elwood climbed into the left seat and fired up the old

Cessna. At the end of the grass strip Elwood did a run-up and then pushed the throttle to the panel. The engine bellowed and they jounced over the uneven strip, the wind blasting in the doorway. The ground fell away and they climbed into the chilly blue day, bounding slightly on mild currents.

At 3,000 feet above the rolling ground the view of the nearby mountains was spectacular on this bright day decorated with only widely scattered cumulus clouds. Elwood lined the plane up and made a pass over the target. The merest wisp of a cloud whipped past the open doorway. When the white cross was directly below, Francine tossed out a paper streamer, weighted to fall at about the same speed as a jumper. She watched how far it drifted downwind to land at the edge of a tree line as Elwood banked around in a wide circle. She would adjust the jump point an equal distance upwind. The theory was that the jumper would then drift back with the breeze to land somewhere near the target cross.

Francine was smiling at him behind her goggles while his heart rate climbed to what felt like machine-gun frequency and Elwood lined the plane up for the jump run. At a hand signal from Francine, Elwood reduced the power and the plane began to mush, the wind blast past the doorway diminishing somewhat. "Okay, John," she said over the helmet radio, giving him a thumbs up. "Out you go onto the step."

His heart hammering and his breathing rapid and shallow, he swiveled sideways, put his left foot out onto the step, grabbed the strut with his left hand, said, "Well, what the hell," to himself, and lurched out to grab onto the strut with his right hand. The wind blast was fierce, pressing the goggles tight to his face, the baggy jump suit whipping like a flag in a gale, the plane bounding gently, the prop a gray blur three feet in front of him. He looked down over the strut. Abruptly all the fear drained away and he felt a totally unexpected exultation, a wild sense of freedom.

Francine was looking below, waiting for the exit point to come up, holding her hand spread. Then she looked at him, nodded, and said over the scratchy radio, "Okay, John, push back and spread eagle. NOW." She pointed downward.

He pushed off strongly, arching his back, his arms and legs flung out wide, and he caught a glimpse of the plane receding like a big startled bird. His arched body pivoted forward until he was falling prone. The fall was brief and he felt the jerk of the opening and looked up to see the big gaily-colored rectangle billowing out. He swung twice and then settled down, all the wind and loud plane noise gone now, the ride soft and silent.

He was aware of the far-off drone of the Cessna above, and sounds wafted to him from below—a truck chugging up a hill several miles away, a dog barking, a crow calling sharply. Nothing far down under his boot toes but the soft green countryside. He reached up and got hold of the small wooden toggles and tried a turn to the right, the chute responding instantly and surely. It felt more like floating than descending, but as the ground drew closer he seemed to be falling faster. That was illusion, he knew. He tried to stay upwind of the target until the last hundred or so feet, then he turned for it. Francine, watching from the plane above, told him over the radio to turn back into the wind and get ready to land. He made the turn, still 50 feet up, brought his legs together, and pulled both toggles down to his knees.

It was as though he had put on brakes. The rate of descent declined sharply, and he touched down lightly about 75 feet shy of the target cross, stumbling only slightly before he regained his balance, the chute collapsing in a gaudy billow beside him. The young couple waved excitedly from near the barn, and he gave them two thumbs up. He looked up to see the other student descending under a good canopy, then gathered his canopy in a big loose bundle and walked to the barn.

Over the next three weeks he made seven jumps at the strip, the last a 30-second stable freefall before he pulled his ripcord, with a landing ten feet from the center of the cross. Francine and Elwood told him he was one of the fastest-learning students they'd had in some time. They invited him to join their club and attend the next of their evening meetings, but he didn't go back.

One night by the fireplace he told Wasituna he was ready.

"You'll leave tomorrow?" the old man said.

"Yes. Early. Thank you for all your help. If it goes well I'll be back to see you one day."

"You'll be in my thoughts," Wasituna said, and looked into the flames.

23

WALTER CALZO LIVED IN A NARROW TWO-STORY DUPLEX apartment on a street lined with other nearly identical shoulder-to-shoulder duplexes in Newark not far off of I-95. The address had been right there in the phone book. Late one cold afternoon, Hardin began watching the apartment from a block away in the only parking slot he could find for his car. There was little activity on the street apart from the continual sparse traffic. Two teenage boys flashed past on rollerblades, not looking to either side, weaving expertly, expressions intent. A siren wailed in the distance. An aged couple walked by, bundled in rags, the man pushing a rusted shopping cart that had one wobbling wheel and was half filled with aluminum cans.

Just after dark a cab stopped down the street and a heavy woman dressed in a brown overcoat and with a scarf tied over her hair got out and moved slowly up the steps to the Calzo apartment. She carried a bulging shopping bag and used the step railing to help pull her bulk upward. She used a key to go inside.

At seven-thirty a man lumbered down the apartment steps, looked up and down the street, and stood waiting in the down-glow of a streetlight with his hands in the pockets of his black leather jacket, his breath pluming in the cold night air. It was Calzo.

Within five minutes a white Mercedes with heavily tinted windows stopped and Calzo got into the back seat. The car moved off briskly.

Hardin followed in his old dark blue Camry, staying at least a block back. There was enough other traffic so he believed he wouldn't be noticed easily. The Mercedes took a right turn on a main thoroughfare where the traffic was much heavier, then kept straight for a dozen blocks. It took a left on a side street and after three more blocks it slowed and pulled into the parking lot of a place called the Little Italy Lounge. Hardin drove on by slowly and stopped at the next intersection at a red light. He canted his rearview mirror and saw three men get out of the Mercedes and walk toward the canopied lounge entrance.

He found a parking slot in the next block and backed into it to wait. At eleven-fifteen the three men came out of the lounge and drove away in the Mercedes. Hardin started the cold Camry and drove back to his motel.

He watched Calzo carefully for the next two days. The big man seemed to have no particular schedule and no job. He drove his own car, a late-model green Trans Am that was garaged out behind his duplex apartment, to some kind of meeting in a house out in a suburb, went into a barred- and glass-fronted pawn shop on a Newark back street where he angrily harangued the owner for fifteen minutes, the owner obviously cowed, worried, and anxious to please.

He made several brief stops at small Newark business-es ranging from a butcher shop to a hardware store, spent two afternoon hours in a pool hall, and returned to the Little Italy Lounge on the second night, riding in the same white Mercedes, this time with only the driver.

Hardin considered attacking Calzo in the lot of the Little Italy Lounge or outside his house, but there were always too many people nearby. Breaking into the man's home was out because of the wife. He needed to find out more about Calzo. His habits. His haunts.

Late the next afternoon Calzo wheeled a square green trash container out to the curb. There were several other similar containers curbside along the street. An hour later, as dusk was falling, Calzo and his wife left in the green Trans Am.

Hardin drove three blocks away and parked near an alleyway where two derelicts were sharing a bottle of wine on the steps of a run-down rooming house. He offered one of the men ten dollars to swap his tattered camo jacket and dirty red ball cap for Hardin's new heavy windbreaker.

"Hey, sure thing, Sarge," the man said. "Listen, you make it twenty you can have the pants, too."

"Just the jacket and cap, thanks."

As he walked away he heard one of the men say to the other, "You sit anywhere in this freakin' city long enough you'll see one of every freakin' kind, you know?"

Dressed in the jacket and cap and affecting a slight limp he walked down Calzo's street. He picked up a plastic bag from one of the trash containers and half filled it with rags and cans to give it some bulk. He poked through two more containers before he came to Calzo's container.

There were people on the street but nobody paid undue attention to him. He had become one of the legions of faceless, nameless, urban creatures who live in the shadows and exist by whatever means they can, and who are all but invisible to the rest of humanity. He opened the lid and used his pocket knife to slit two of the big trash bags, releasing a foul, almost overwhelming odor. Holding his breath as much as possible he picked through the contents, a mixture of garbage and miscellaneous refuse. A *Woman's Day* magazine. An empty Jim Beam fifth bottle. A brief letter to Maria Calzo from some woman in Florida. A wadded-up grocery shopping list. A burned-out light bulb. There were a few receipts but nothing that yielded any useful information.

Then he turned up a damp, well-thumbed Cabella's fishing and hunting catalog addressed to Calzo, with several of the page corners bent back. One marked-up page listed Leupold, Alaskan Guide, and Tasco rifle scopes. Another page had a pair of hunting boots circled. There was nothing else in the trash that helped, and he was spending too much time here. He closed the lid and slowly moved on along the street, eyes downcast, limping, stopping to dig through another trash container before he turned the corner at the end of the block and headed back for his car.

Two nights later he again followed Calzo and the other two men in the white Mercedes to the Little Italy Lounge. This time he waited until the trio came out at eleven-ten

and drove away. He gave it fifteen minutes and then got
out and walked to the lounge. The interior was dim except
for the well-lit bar with its glittering ranks of bottles ar-
rayed against an ornate mirror.

There were maybe a dozen customers scattered at tables
and in booths. A thin brunette waitress sat tiredly on the
end bar stool. The muscular bartender was hip-leaning
against the inside of the bar, his big arms crossed, looking
up at a basketball game on a wall-mounted TV. A black-
haired woman in what looked like a wet red painted-on
miniskirt got up from a booth she was sharing with another
woman, walked unsteadily to the jukebox, dropped in
change, and punched a number. An island beat blared out,
then Jimmy Buffet began loudly singing "Margaritaville"
and she went unsteadily back to the booth swiveling her
slick hips and snapping her fingers. She spotted Hardin
and smiled at him. He smiled and nodded back.

He walked over and took a padded stool that was
ergonomically designed to swaddle the drinker for hours
on end, nestled up to a slanted, padded bar. There were
luxury cars not as comfortable and comforting.

The bartender glanced at him and said, "Yeah, friend
what'll it be?" as he turned his attention back to the game.
"Well, take the damn shot, stupid, before they yank the
damn ball away from ya *again*."

"I'll have a shot and a beer," Hardin said. "Draft."

The bartender tore himself away from the game long
enough to say, "Well, okay, there, friend. We like serious
drinkers around here." He poured a generous shot, deftly
drew a beer from the tap into a frosted glass, and made

change, all with frequent glances up at the TV. "That freakin' thirty-nine's gonna lose this one all by himself," he said to no one in particular, "and I'll be out fifty bucks. Dammit."

"Tell you what, Jake," the waitress said. "From now on will you let me know who you're betting on like a day beforehand? 'Cause then I'll bet on the other team and it'll be like a sure thing for me. When's the last time you won?"

"I can't remember," Jake said. "Shoot, *shoot*, for Crissake. The clock's runnin' out...ah, dammit. Well, there goes the game."

"Sorry your team lost," Hardin said. "Hit me again here, will you?"

"Sure thing, friend. You're either celebrating or soaking your sorrows. Love or money won or lost; which is it?"

"Celebrating, I guess. Coming back home after a long time gone. This was my old home town."

"Well, I don't know where you been, friend, but if you're happy to be back here it must have been pure hell there."

"Hey, this is the Garden State, isn't it?"

"Any freakin' gardens around here I haven't seen 'em," the bartender said.

"I got a tomato plant on my fire escape," the waitress said.

"Freakin' thing'll die of air pollution," Jake said. "Anyway, friend, welcome home."

"There used to be a guy I'd see around," Hardin said. "A big guy named Walter Calzo. They called him Winston. Does he ever come in here?"

The bartender instantly became wary. "What did you

say your name was, friend?"

"Leo Heath."

"That bastard." The black-haired woman in the tight red miniskirt had slid onto the stool next to Hardin, bringing a musky scent of perfume and excess makeup. "That fat bastard Winston," she said. "You just missed him, Mister Leo Heath. He was in here with those two other hoods he hangs out with. You say you're like a friend of his?"

"Hell, no," Hardin said. "He was only one of the guys I remembered. A tough guy. As a matter of fact he had a run-in with a friend of mine and my friend took a beating. One of those things you don't forget."

The bartender leveled a look at the woman and said, "Maybe you ought to keep your mouth shut, Rose. You've had more than a few tonight."

"Hey, I ain't afraid of Winston, that fat bastard."

"Look, I didn't mean to start anything here," Hardin said, smiling. "It's not important. I was just making conversation, you know? Rose, why don't you let me buy you and your friend over there a drink? What are you having?"

She smiled sexily and raised a plucked eyebrow. "Margarita on the rocks for me, white wine for Sarah. This time salt my rim, will you, Jake? Leo, why don't you come on over and meet my best friend?"

"You kids go ahead," the waitress said, "I'll bring the drinks."

"Thanks," Hardin said as he left the soft embrace of the bar stool.

"Don't mention it. I'm like a sucker for romance," the waitress said dryly.

Rose slid into the booth and patted the seat beside her. Hardin took it.

"Meet Leo Heath, a real gentleman, I bet," Rose said, "and this is Sarah, my best friend."

"He's cute, too," Sarah said with a woozy grin. She was displaying a square yard of pillowy cleavage, her sprayed blond hairdo had partially collapsed, and her makeup seemed to be slipping like a hillside just before an avalanche. She said, "So, what do you do for a living, Leo?"

"I sell sporting goods. Boots, tents, fishing rods."

"I bet you make good money at that," Rose said.

"I do all right."

"So, are you like married or what?" Sarah said. "Little wife and half a dozen rugrats at home?"

"Never been married. What do you ladies do?" The waitress had brought their drinks and was setting them out on napkins, and saying to Hardin, "Now there's a silly question, Ace. You should probably ask, like, what *don't* they do."

Ignoring the waitress, Rose said, "Sarah's a sexy secretary and I'm a cashier. We both work for Sullivan Auto Parts and Salvage. Nine stores in five cities. Big deal."

"We're gonna call in sick tomorrow," Sarah said. "We already decided. Screw 'em if they like can't take a joke, right, Rose?"

"Do you ever go to Atlantic City, Leo?" Rose asked.

"Never have, but I've always wanted to. Do you like it there?"

"It's *fantastic*," Sarah said. "There are lights everywhere and nobody hardly even sleeps. They have like these great shows, and the food and the drinks are practically free. I mean good drinks, too, not watered down like they are here. That's why I only drink wine here."

"And there's always the chance you'll get rich rich *rich*," Rose said. "You've just got to be at the right slot at the right time, you know? I mean it could happen to anybody. One pull and you can win a car or that big plastic box of cash they have in the lobby of this one place. I have this friend Sammy? He bought a book that tells how you can recognize the slots that are just about ready to pay off, and how to outsmart the blackjack dealers, and what numbers are the best to play in roulette and stuff. I'm telling you, this book is like just about impossible to find because all the casino owners got together and tried to keep it from being printed. They don't want people knowing all those secrets. Sammy says the man who wrote it? They evicted him from both Las Vegas and Atlantic City because they were afraid he'd win too much. Sarah and me are gonna read up on it and then go on another one of those bus tours to Atlantic City."

"Watch out, Donny Trump, here we come," Sarah said.

"The two of you will clean them out," Hardin said, smiling. "I'm glad I met you before you get rich. Otherwise you probably wouldn't talk to me after you do."

Both the women giggled and sipped their drinks.

"Listen," Hardin said to Rose, "I'm sorry about mentioning that guy Calzo earlier. I didn't mean to spoil your night out."

"That fat bastard, pardon my English. He comes in here tonight, Leo, he comes in here with those other two goons tonight like always. Like the three Hoodkateers. And they sit there at that table and right away they start like hitting on us."

"Talking about us like we're just a couple whores, you know?" Sarah said.

"Winston, he finally comes over and sits down right where you are," Rose said, "while those other two bastards are laughing. He starts putting his hands all over me. I told him to fuck off or his wife's gonna get a phone call, you know? He gives me the mean eyes like I'm supposed to faint right here. Then the chief goon Nicky, he goes, 'Come on, Winston, knock it off, the bitch ain't worth it,' and so lardass gets up and goes back to the table. He acts like he's some kind of Mafia big shot but he's just another dumb bone breaker. He doesn't fool me. I've been knowing him for years. I could like tell the cops a thing or two about ol' Winston, let me tell you."

"I thought he used to be a hunter or something," Hardin said.

"If you call shooting deers in some kind of deer zoo great sport," Sarah said.

"We heard them talking about that for about an hour," Rose said. "The brave hunters. They're going to some big place in upstate Pennsylvania, I forget the name of it, where they raise the deers and you pay a heavy fee so you can shoot yours. They guarantee you get to kill one."

"They probably tie one to a post that's got like a sign on it says deer," Sarah said with a laugh, "and then lead you over to it by the hand."

"Maybe they spray-paint a target on it for you," Rose

said, giggling. "Shoot it here or here but don't shoot it there or you'll have a hole in your steak."

"Did they say when they're going?"

"Next week, I think," Rose said. "I guess that's when zoo deer season starts."

"And you don't know the name of the place?"

Rose frowned and tried to focus on him, getting a little suspicious. "Just some kind of big fancy hunting club. Why?"

"No reason. Just curious. It looks like you girls could use another drink." He motioned for the waitress and asked Rose what her favorite gambling game was.

She was heavy-lidded now and her friend Sarah was not far behind. They were both slurring some of their words.

"Craps," Rose said. "It's real exciting, but it goes like so fast it's hard to follow, you know? You can wooze...lose big-time and just like that." She tried to snap her long-nailed fingers. "Leo, what you say after this drink we go get something to eat?"

"Sure, ladies. Do you know a good place?"

"You bet," Sarah said. "You got a car, Leo? We took a cab here so we wouldn't have to worry about driving home after."

They went to an all-night diner for early breakfasts, Sarah looking even more disheveled in the harsh light. Rose was drunk and nodding. After they ate he drove Rose to her apartment first and Sarah helped him get her inside and comfortable on the couch. Her miniskirt rode up while Sarah was slipping her shoes off. There was a small tattoo of a rose on her inner thigh. She was snoring lightly and she looked worn, vulnerable, and bereft of hope. Hardin got a pillow and a sheet from her bedroom and covered her up. Then he drove Sarah home and left her at her door with a kiss on her heavily made-up cheek and an empty promise to see her again soon at the Little Italy Lounge.

The next morning, with a pocket full of change, he found a pay phone in the corner of a convenience store parking lot and started calling hunting clubs in Pennsylvania at numbers supplied by information, asking to confirm a reservation for Walter Calzo.

The Beechwood Sporting Association covered six hundred rolling, posted acres of fields and woodlands in northwestern Pennsylvania, some of it adjacent to the Allegheny National Forest. The staff raised pheasant, partridge, doves, rabbits, and deer for the pleasures of the guests. The accommodations were log cabins, each plushly furnished and screened from its neighbors by careful rustic landscaping. Staffers in a log lodge prepared excellent meals and box lunches, sold gear and ammunition, and rented out such items as fishing rods, rifles, and shotguns. A basic three-day deer hunt cost $3,000 per person and results were guaranteed.

If a guest happened to kill his or her buck or doe on the first day or two there were other pursuits depending on the weather, including cross-country skiing, snowmobiling, tennis, chip and putt golf, indoor swimming, horseback riding, and serious drinking, all at extra fees, of course. Since this was a private club there was no need to observe legal hunting seasons.

A half hour before dawn a Beechwood guide had used a flashlight to lead Walter Calzo along a path to a deer stand that the guide claimed was one of their best, a log bench atop a low boulder that protruded from a hillside, lightly screened by brush and with a commanding view of a wooded vale about 100 yards out where there was a stream that had been dammed to create a small pond. A salt lick near the pond had been not-too-cleverly disguised as a tree stump. Particularly tempting forage had been planted near the pond. Calzo could see none of this yet because it was too dark, but the guide described it like he was reading from a color brochure. The guide left him with a small canvas shoulder bag packed with a thermos of coffee, soft drinks, sandwiches, and two hand warmers.

Like all guides and hunters at Beechwood, Calzo was dressed in a blaze orange winter jacket and an orange billed cap with ear flaps, along with good boots, heavy pants, and orange shooter's gloves to ward off the cold. He sat on the bench with his Winchester Model 70 Classic .30-06 left-hander bolt action rifle across his ample lap, a cartridge from the five-round magazine chambered and the safety on. With the scope the rig had set him back over $1,000 but it was deadly accurate and hit like a pickax. He knew the ballistics by heart. The rifle fired one of his favorite bullets, a Springfield soft-nose 150-grain Power-Point notched around its metal jacket so it would instantly blossom like a gray flower when it hit living tissue. The bullet would be moving at more than half a mile per second when it blew out of the 24-inch rifle muzzle. All the way out to

400 yards the drop would only be 27 inches and the ve-
locity would still be 1,700 feet per second, so it could still
hit with 967 foot-pounds of punch, plowing a half-dollar-
diameter tunnel through muscle, flesh, and bone. From
here to the pond off there in the murk, if the guide was
right about the range, the bullet would hardly be slowing
down, would rise just over two inches, and would hit with
over 2,200 foot-pounds. One hell of a smack.

The log bench had a back rest so he relaxed. He unzipped the jacket enough to dig a fat greenish cigar out of
his inside pocket. He clamped it between his teeth but
didn't light it.

The air was still but as the sky turned gray and the
trees and pond began to emerge from the darkness a light
breeze came up, blowing down-slope at his back, which
meant he was upwind of the pond and any deer coming
that way would probably smell him.

"Phuck," he said around the cigar, thinking *I might as
well eat a sandwich.* He pulled a ham and cheese out of
the canvas pack and rested the cigar on the edge of the
bench seat. He had both cheeks full and was thinking
about moving around the pond to a spot between two trees
over there that looked pretty good when a man stepped
out from behind brush just downhill to his right and he
damned near choked on the sandwich.

He coughed heavily and spat to the side and said, "Hey,
asshole. You don't want to get shot you don't come up on
a man like that."

But there was something bad wrong here. The man
was dressed all over in Realtree camo. He was holding an

un-scoped lever action rifle across his chest, his finger inside the trigger guard. His eyes were shadowed by his hat brim. He stood there real still, his legs apart, like he was ready to make a fast move. Was he wearing fucking moccasins? He wondered if he could get the Winchester up off his knees, hit the safety, and shoot before this asshole could swing down on him and pull. In the distance a rifle went off twice. A semi-auto.

He tossed the rest of the sandwich aside carefully and said, "Well, you ain't a guide or a hunter here or they'd make you wear orange. So, who the hell are you?"

"That was smart," the man said. "Saving your night vision until I took off and I was right over you."

"What?" Winston said, but then he knew and he went still inside. He reached for the cigar slowly, very carefully got his Zippo out of his side coat pocket, and lit up, blowing out a small bluish cloud.

He put the lighter down on the bench and said, "You made a hell of a splash. Didn't think you'd get outta that. I hit you?"

"In the hip."

"Good. You here tryin' to kill me? Have a shoot-out? Is that it?"

Hardin watched the big man carefully, ready to shoulder the rifle and fire. He'd bought the Marlin .30-30 in a Harrisburg Wal-Mart for $265 and had practiced with it at short range for three hours two days ago in an old sand pit he'd found deep in the woods. He had a soft-nose deer round chambered, the hammer back and the safety off.

Winston showed no change in his bulldog expression.

Just sat there pulling on the cigar.

"I want to know who planted the bomb in my Jeep."

Around the fat cigar Winston said, "Why the phuck should I tell you anything, asshole?"

"It killed a woman I knew who had nothing to do with Strake or any of you."

"Look. You gonna do something here or you wanna talk all morning, asshole."

"Tell me who planted that bomb. If it wasn't you, maybe you'll live."

Winston thought for a moment as he studied Hardin intently. Then he slowly removed the cigar with his right hand, inspected the glowing end, and said, "I hated that skinny fuck from the time we picked him up. Talks in a little kid voice and don't know when to shut up. A ex-Marine fuzzhead. Name's Donny Loomis. Supposed to know all kinda fancy shit with stuff like grenades and C-4. Got this big stainless Sig Sauer cannon. He probably sleeps with it between his legs. Lives upstairs in a warehouse in Brooklyn someplace near the docks. Place looks like a rat hotel."

"So Strake sent Montgomery Davis, this Donny Loomis, and you."

The old man had told him one night by the fireplace, "Watch the eyes; because it has been said they are the windows to a man's soul. It's true. But it is not such a simple thing to do. You must look deeply, deeply, to see a man's soul. Watch, and you'll know what that man is going to do."

Winston looked away to the side, seemingly unconcerned, took a careful pull on the cigar and plumed the smoke upward, then settled his dark eyes on Hardin. "I always liked a good cigar," he said, suddenly snapping it spinning, pin-wheeling sparks, straight toward Hardin and quickly grabbing up the Winchester, feeling surely for the safety. All he needed was for this guy to focus on the cigar for a fraction of a second before reacting.

But Hardin had been staring coldly into the big man's eyes and was ready. He totally ignored the cigar even as it struck the ground not far from his feet. He was already swinging the 30-30 down smoothly and time seemed to slow as he focused all his being on aiming and firing accurately and his rifle kicked his shoulder just as Winston pulled his trigger half a heartbeat too early, the crack of the supersonic round loud close by Hardin's ear. Hardin's bullet flew true and caught Winston in his broad chest just to the right of the heart, plucking a black dot into the blaze orange. Winston slammed against the bench back, stiffened, and groaned, "uuuuuk" weakly, his rifle sliding out of his grasp, his chest spurting dark redness. His head tilted back, the whites of his eyes showing. He seemed to slowly deflate, and toppled sideways off of the bench.

Hardin slowly lowered the rifle. He stood frozen, his right eardrum numb. He didn't have to look closer to know the man was dead. The dew-damp woods seemed unnaturally still. He fought off an engulfing, dizzying wave of nausea.

And then he ran, swiftly and quietly, alert for fellow hunters, only a fleeting shadow in the woods.

It took him forty minutes to get back to where he had left his car in a grassy turn-off by a dirt road in the Allegheny Forest. He drove by a circuitous route back southeast, stopping only once at a remote bridge across a wide brown river to throw the rifle and his remaining six cartridges into the water.

24

TEN DAYS LATER HE RENTED A ROOM BY THE WEEK IN A run-down back-street motel, a place where the Pakistani management looked nobody in the eye and asked no questions and where there were furtive happenings far into the blackest hours. The furnishings were frayed and stained and the room stank of cigarettes and a dozen kinds of despair.

There was no listing for Donny Loomis in the Brooklyn directory in the motel's dirty office. Information said the number was unlisted. He began asking around near the docks in corner groceries, gas stations, and bars. He spent two days at it but nobody knew anything about a Donny Loomis.

Past midnight he came out of a filthy side-street establishment that had no apparent name, just a red neon BAR sign hanging from a rusted bracket bolted to the brick above the door. He was dressed in a lined nylon jacket and a ball cap against the cold. A half block from him in the darkness, between him and his car, there were four figures grouped under a streetlight. Those buildings along the narrow street that weren't gutted were heavily barred at their sightless windows.

He was about to cross the street to avoid the group and get to his car when one of them said clearly, "Hey, you. White boy. You in the wrong neighborhood, heah, ain't you?" Two of the others uttered short derisive laughs. One of them was softly punching a fist into a palm as though merely keeping warm.

I could just go back into the bar and wait, he thought. He looked at them and then walked up to stand twenty feet from the group. They were now arranged on the sidewalk to block his way. They all wore red bandannas, voluminous jeans, and oversized brown leather flight jackets with dirty fleece collars and cuffs. "I'm looking for a man," he told them. "Name of Donny Loomis. White. Thin. An ex-Marine. Talks in a high-pitched voice."

Ignoring the question, one of them said to his friends, "You think this here white boy's some kinda law?"

"Naw," another one said. "This ain't the Man. The Man be crazy come down here this time a night all by hissef."

"Maybe he ain't the Man but he shore be crazy. Maybe we ought to make him pay like a toll an' use our sidewalk. You know whose turf this be, muh'fuckah?"

"I guess it's yours. I'm not here to challenge that. I don't have any fight with you, but there's something you ought to know."

"What that be, muh'fuckah?"

He pulled his hands very slowly and deliberately out of his jacket pockets. He had the .45 in his right hand, cocked and locked. All four men stopped all movement. He held the gun casually down at his side. "Like I say, I don't have any fight with you. I've practiced a lot with this thing and I'm good with it. It's cocked. I don't like paying street tolls but I might pay a hundred for some information I need. Then I could walk away and there wouldn't be any blood on this sidewalk. Yours or mine."

A low-slung violet car with dark tinted windows sped past, its bass speakers thudding into the heavy cold air trapped between the brick buildings.

Two of the men started to ease hands inside their jackets so he slowly brought the .45 up to level it from the waist, freezing them all in place.

The tallest of them had so far said nothing, just standing motionless at the back of the group. Now he said, "You're talkin' to the Bones, mister. What you want this Marine for?" The other three held their positions. The two kept their hands close to their open jacket zippers.

Hardin focused on the tall one, the obvious leader. *You'll die first,* he projected to the man.

"I heard he knows about some things," Hardin said calmly. "Maybe deals in some things. There's an item I might want to buy from him."

"Way I heard it," the tall one said, smiling, "that dude likes fireworks. Big fireworks."

"That's what I heard."

"Information 'bout a man like that oughtta be worth a couple hundred."

"It's worth a hundred to me, no more. If you don't know anything I'll find out somewhere else."

"Let's see the hundred."

"I'd have to see everybody's hands first. And then I'd have to hear what you have to say before I give it to you."

One of the men with his hand now inside his jacket had hard black eyes and a long scar on his cheek and was standing with his feet apart, ready to make a move. He said evenly, "What we could do is we spread out a little and then maybe I show him what it feel like to catch a nine in the knee."

Hardin said, "The thing Army men used to like about this gun was you hit a man anywhere and he's out of it. Maybe you'll be the first here."

"Chill, Mustafa," the leader said. "This guy coulda just gone back in the bar when he seen us. That tells you somethin'. Business be a little slow. A extra hundred wouldn't hurt none. Let's all take it down a notch." The two let their hands slide down to their sides, the one with the hard eyes pulling his hand out of his jacket slowly and then flexing his gloved fingers like claws.

Hardin lowered the .45 but didn't take his eyes off of the leader. He reached for his wallet with his left hand, flipped it open, and thumbed out the corners of two bills from the back that he knew were fifties, nipping them between his teeth while he returned the wallet to his pocket. He held the bills in his left hand at his side.

"How much more you figure he got?" hard-eyes grinned and said.

"You'll never know," Hardin said coldly. He knew they could probably sense whether or not he would shoot if pressed. That might be his only advantage, all that was

holding them in check. He had it locked into his mind
that he absolutely would shoot to kill if any of them showed
a gun.

The leader said, "Crown Street off of Lafayette. Lives
upstairs in like a warehouse. Not our turf. But you best
watch how you go knockin' on his door. Might not be too
healthy, I hear."

Hardin took two steps sideways and slid the two bills
under the wiper on a parked car. He pointed at the street
behind him and said, "I'll cross the street now and walk
that way."

Hard-eyes said, "This be you lucky night, muh'fuckah."

He crossed the street and walked backward for forty
feet, the .45 still held at his side. He turned and walked
quickly to his car and drove away.

*₀*₀*₀*₀*

For three days and much of the nights he parked two or
three blocks from Crown, then walked the dingy streets in
dark clothes, keeping a wary watch. There were few people
in the area. He got lucky the fourth night as the sun was
setting. He saw a man who matched Donny's description,
right down to a camo jacket and pants, walking along
Crown Street to enter a run-down brick building.

The former warehouse was in a blitzed area not far
from the docks. It looked as though some time ago an effort had been made to salvage several blocks by converting
the old brick buildings into ground-floor business spaces
and studios for photographers and artists, judging by the

remnants of signs, with loft apartments on the second floors, but the effort had obviously failed miserably. Broken windows, piles of refuse, blown-out streetlights, and splashes of angry graffiti served as warning to any other redevelopers not to try something that foolish again.

The area was so devastated there were not enough people to hide among while trying to observe Donny's loft for any length of time, so he abandoned the idea of planning an outside ambush. Instead he decided to carry through with what he had told the gang bangers and try to get close to Donny by offering him a business deal. He parked halfway along the block and watched the loft for almost two hours, until he had the feeling that Donny might be in for the night.

He got out and locked the car, making sure nothing tempting was left on the seats. He was wearing jeans, a ball cap to shadow his face, a dark windbreaker, and thin driving gloves. He walked over to the steel door that Donny had entered and used the heel of his gloved fist to pound on it.

He waited a minute and pounded again.

After another half a minute the door creaked open three inches against a heavy chain lock. It was dark inside but Hardin caught the darkly glinting outline of an automatic hand gun.

A high-pitched man's voice said, "Yeah. What?"

"Are you Donny Loomis?"

"Who's asking?"

"I'm John Hardin. I'm alone. I was told I might be able to buy something from you."

"Who told you that?"

"A man who runs with the Bones, over on Franklin Street."

"What are you looking to buy?"

"Let's call it a special kind of fireworks."

"I don't know you and I don't know anybody in the Bones gang. You could be a cop."

"I'm not a cop of any kind. There's somebody else who told me about you. A guy from Newark named Walter Calzo. They call him Winston. An ugly son of a bitch."

"Winston sent you to me? I didn't think he was a big fan."

"He's not. The fact is he doesn't like you much, but he says you know a lot about things that make loud noises."

There was no response.

"Look," Hardin said, "I'm willing to spend some money with you if you can help me out. Why don't you let me come in and we can talk?"

More silence. Then Donny said, "Okay. Here's how we'll do it. You lace your fingers and put your hands on top of your head. That's the way. Stay like that." The door closed and reopened just enough to let him in, Donny using the door for partial cover but not standing too close to it, and making sure that Hardin saw the big stainless automatic. "Come on in and stand over there with your back to me. Keep your hands on your head and spread your legs. More. Okay, hold it right there."

Donny closed and locked the steel door, moved up behind him, and patted him down thoroughly, finding and removing the .45 stuffed under his belt at the small of his back. "Old timer," Donny said of the gun. "But it's still a good side arm. You're not carrying any I.D. and no money. Why is that?"

"I left my wallet locked in the car and hidden pretty well. This looks like it could be a bad neighborhood."

"Okay, keep your hands on your head and go up those stairs. The door's open at the top."

Upstairs there was a large loft, with a kitchen in one corner, a bedroom area partially screened in another corner, the door to a bathroom, a dining area merged with a living area that had a furniture grouping. Area rugs. None of it was expensive but it was all neat and clean. Spartan. Donny used his shining automatic to motion toward the couch. "You can take your hands down and sit there."

Donny slid his own gun back into the shoulder holster he wore. He took a straight armchair facing the couch on the other side of a heavy oak coffee table. He ejected the magazine and the chambered cartridge from the .45 and put it all on the coffee table close to himself. "So talk to me."

There was a cold feral intensity to the slim man, and the eyes, devoid of emotion, seemed to mask a hair-trigger ferocity.

Hardin blanked his own emotions, calming himself throughout his mind and body, projecting absolutely no threat, as the old man had patiently taught him to do over many long hours, if he should ever find himself in the presence of such an innate killer as Donny.

"I've got a situation," Hardin said. "There are these three people who will be together at an out-of-the-way place soon. It would be in my best interests if these people weren't around much longer." Building the lie. Believing it himself. Seeing three shadowy men he wanted to kill. "I don't want to use a gun. They'll all be armed. I need something quick and effective. I want a grenade." Seeing himself tossing a grenade into their midst. Seeing them freeze in shock and fear.

Donny showed no change of expression. He said, "Something like that would cost a lot out on the street and it would probably be old junk."

"How much would one cost from you?"

"If I had something like that it would cost seven hundred. No dickering."

"It might be worth almost that much if it was untraceable."

"You think I'd sell anything that could point back to me?"

"No, I guess you're smarter than that. Can you help me or not?"

Donny gazed at him coldly and intently for several seconds and then said, "Stay right there." He got up and went over to a footlocker that was against the wall. He opened it, removed several items and placed them on the floor, rummaged inside, and came back carrying something in each hand. He sat back down in the armchair.

He looked at the grenade cupped in his right hand. It was smooth and round, about the size of a baseball. "This is your US standard-issue M 68 impact frag. American as apple pie. You know how to use it from watching the movies. It's got a wire clip as a backup retainer for the safety lever. You take that off when you're getting ready for action. Then you hold it in your fist with the safety lever clamped down against the body of it. You can pull the ring pin and hold onto the grenade all day if you want, as long as you keep the safety lever clamped. When the time is right, you lob it, the safety lever flies off while it's in the air, and within two seconds, still while it's in the air, the impact fuse arms, so it goes off when it lands. That's partly to prevent any attempt at toss-back from your target. Say for any reason the impact fuse doesn't work, like it lands on thick grass maybe, or in mud, then a pyro time fuse takes over and it goes bang in anywhere from three to seven more seconds anyway. The throwing range is forty meters if you've got a good arm, and the casualty radius is fifteen meters."

He looked at the other grenade cupped on his left palm and said in his childlike voice, "This is a DM 51 West German model. Ring-pin and safety lever just the same but no impact fuse, only a four-second timer. It's got a removable plastic sleeve on it. Without the sleeve it does the work by pure blast. Slip the sleeve on and you've got three thousand eight hundred little steel balls packed on there. The HE charge makes a steel shower out of the balls. Either one of these bad boys will clean out your attic, but I'd recommend the DM 51 because it gives you more time to take cover after you throw. Unless your targets are trained military they're not going to even think about tossing it back at you, at least not anything like quick enough, so there's no real need for an impact fuse. Neither one of these is traceable because they both—"

The suddenness and ferocity of the attack took Donny completely by surprise. Hardin heaved the coffee table up and onto Donny, knocking him backward out of the chair. Donny lashed back blindly with the speed of a snake, launching an expert side kick that caught Hardin solidly on the thigh and another fast kick that grazed his ribs, then Donny was scrambling backward dropping the grenades and reaching for the automatic in his shoulder holster, but Hardin had raised the table again and he brought it down with brutal force. There was a wet crack that was Donny's upper right arm breaking and a thud as his head bounced hard off of the floor, and he went limp. Hardin pulled the table away and grabbed up the stainless automatic.

He stood there breathing hard with adrenaline coursing through him, watching Donny, but there was no movement except shallow breathing. He put the automatic in his left jacket pocket and he found the .45, its magazine, and the ejected cartridge, all of which he put in his right pocket, his hand shaking badly. He righted the coffee table, which now had a cracked leg, and put the grenades on it.

He went over to the footlocker, looking for rope, but he found a roll of duct tape. Better yet. He stood the wood armchair up and heaved Donny onto it, propping him while he carefully taped his forearms tightly to the chair arms, his head lolling slackly on his chest. Then he sat back on the couch, ten feet away, and waited, taking out the .45 and reloading it. He brought Donny's automatic out and laid it on the table. He was still wearing the thin driving gloves, so he had no concern about leaving fingerprints anywhere.

In a few minutes Donny's head jerked and he opened his eyes. He moaned and said, "Arm. I think it's broken."

"Yes."

"Why...ah, God it hurts. Why you doing this?"

"A bomb you rigged in a Jeep in North Carolina killed a woman who never even knew what it was all about."

The thin man's expression did not register any understanding as the seconds stretched out. Then his features betrayed surprise under the pain. He shook his head convincingly and said, "Look, I don't know what you're talking about, man."

"I know you did it, Donny. Calzo told me all about it. He didn't like you. Calzo is dead."

Donny looked from side to side as though searching for some way out. He licked his lips, squinted up at Hardin, and said, "But that wasn't supposed to happen. Man, it was a job, you know? I just did what they told me. Just a job."

"I understand that."

"Look, there's money."

"Where?"

"In the kitchen. Refrigerator, in the back. Almost ten thousand. In a coffee jar. Go look. Take it, man."

Hardin went in and found the money and stuffed it into his pants pockets, leaving the jar. Then he swept cans and dishes and pots out of the cabinets, strewing them onto the floor. Not looking for anything but trying to make it look like somebody else had been searching the place. Somebody looking for weapons or cash.

He went back into the living area. Donny was struggling desperately against the tape but stopped. Hardin pulled off the bedding and rifled through the dresser drawers. Then he pulled the contents out of the footlocker and threw them onto the floor, finding two more grenades.

He looked around the loft and went back to stand to one side of the armchair, out of reach of Donny's boots.

Donny moaned again and said, "You get the money, man?"

"There are two ways we can do this," Hardin said, picking up the M 68 grenade from the coffee table. "I can walk over to the door and take off the clip and pull the pin and throw this back into this room. Or I can give you a chance. Do you want a chance?"

"You don't have to do this. I just did what I was told. Look, I'll do anything you want. A guy named Strake ordered that job. You want me to waste Strake for you?" The words were a high-pitched, tumbling plea.

"Do you want a chance or not?"

Donny looked at him with wide terrified eyes. "What . . . how . . . how you going to give me a chance?"

Hardin took the duct tape and made a single tight wrap around Donny's left wrist, leaving a flap across his palm. He removed the other tape from his left forearm. He took the M 68 grenade and slipped off the clip. He put the grenade against Donny's collarbone and pressed his head down so he was clamping the safety lever with his chin. He held Donny's head there, pulled the ring pin, and placed the pin on the coffee table.

Hardin said, "Hold the grenade there while you get the tape off and you'll live."

"'ait . . . 'ait," Donny said through clenched teeth. "'iss's nurder . . . iss . . ."

"It's a chance," Hardin lied. "It's not much of a chance, I admit, but it's a better one than you gave the woman in that Jeep, isn't it?" Then he walked out, locking the upstairs door and the downstairs steel door behind him.

"Jeeeesiss . . . uh, Jeesiss," Donny said through his teeth, trying furiously to think, his heart going like crazy.

He worked his little finger under the tape flap, managed to pinch it with his third finger and pulled and it came free a little. *Good, good.* But he was sweating now and his fingers were slipping. He tried again and a little more came free but it wasn't going to work. It wasn't *fucking* going to work. His face was sweating and his collarbone was hurting and his chin was going numb. Sweat ran down the side of his nose in an itching trickle.

The bed, he thought. *If I can get to the bed, kick a pillow off on the floor. Drop the grenade on the pillow. That should keep the impact detonator from going off and give me some seconds. Then kick myself across the bed and down on the other side.* The bed was built up with a solid platform underneath it, so it should shield him.

It could work. Had to.

The metal of the grenade was warming against his slick skin. His chin was going more numb. He clamped down harder. Straining his neck muscles.

He set his feet, left foot forward, right foot back under the chair, and carefully stood in an unsteady crouch, lifting all the weight of the chair with his left arm, the right front chair leg knocking against the floor, his right arm on fire, but he was standing. Then, very carefully, he started moving, inching along in the crouch toward the bed.

It was so far away.

Halfway to the bed the grenade slipped and he clamped

down even harder and said, "Nooooo . . ." and then he started moving faster. *Got to get to the bed. Got to—*

The smooth grenade began sliding and he froze his legs and moved his head down frantically trying to stop it, saying, "Nononono—" but it turned and the safety lever sprang up free in front of his eyes with a little ping and he clamped the grenade for a second longer just below his collarbone and then it squirted out and as he was frozen there in the crouch he watched it fall toward the hardwood floor . . .

Hardin was parked a block away on the other side of the street, looking backward through his open side window. He saw the flash inside the loft and the windows blossoming out in a bright glittering cloud a fraction of a second before the sound reached him, echoing off of the buildings.

He started the car and drove away slowly.

25

HARDIN CALLED FROM A PAY PHONE.

Duane Kelly answered, "Yes."

"You're flying for Louis Strake?"

"That's right."

"I have a proposition for you." He was trying to disguise his voice, speaking slowly and in a lower than normal register. "A good chunk of money in return for a small favor."

"Who is this? You sound a little familiar." Kelly was the man Hardin had recommended to Strake as a backup pilot.

"You don't need to know that."

"I don't get involved in any tricky stuff."

"You did once. But this isn't smuggling. Nothing anywhere near that risky or difficult. Just a simple favor."

"But not legal."

"That depends on how you look at it. Why don't we meet for twenty minutes and talk about it? You don't have anything to lose."

"How much money are we talking about here?"

"Five figures."

"Just for a little ol' favor."

"That's right."

"Where did you want to meet?"

"There's a place near the Teterboro Airport called the Starlight Lounge. Do you know it?"

"Yeah. Used to be a good place to go but not lately."

"Park as close as you can get to the far back corner of the lot tonight at eleven. Leave your passenger side door unlocked. I'll get in and we'll talk. What are you driving?"

"A red BMW rag-top. Brand new."

"Heavy payments."

"Tell me about it. But you only live once, you know?"

"Eleven o'clock then."

Hardin parked in the dark lot at ten-thirty and waited. The BMW showed up at five before eleven and pulled into a slot at the far back corner. There were only half a dozen other cars scattered over the lot. Hardin gave it ten minutes, then slipped out of his car. He had removed the dome light bulb. He was wearing driving gloves and he pulled on a black ski mask. He went up behind the BMW and quickly slid into the passenger seat.

"*Dammit*, I knew you were coming and you still scared the crap out of me," Duane said nervously. "What's the mask for?"

"It's best for you if you don't see me." Trying to disguise his voice, the wool mask helping.

"Already I don't like this deal."

"It's not complicated or dangerous for you. We'll pay you twenty thousand dollars for a favor. Five right now, the rest after you've done the favor. We'll mail you a key to a storage locker in the Teterboro terminal." He had decided it might be a good idea to lead Kelly to believe more than one person was involved in whatever was going on.

"It must be a pretty big favor. A little more than introducing you to my sister, I'll bet."

"Do you have a backup pilot for Strake's plane?"

"No. Not yet. I'm supposed to be looking for one."

"We need you to make copies of the hangar and plane keys and leave them in the FBO pilot's lounge hidden under the base of the weather TV console; the base is hollow. That's so you and I don't have to meet again. We know you take Strake and Montgomery Davis on fairly frequent routine southern flights. We know he usually likes to take off well before daylight. We want a scheduled flight with just Strake and Davis aboard to Georgia, Florida, the Bahamas, or South America. A late-afternoon or very early takeoff, well before dawn, would be best. As soon as a flight like that is scheduled you call me. If I give you the go-ahead, you come down with sudden food poisoning. About two hours before takeoff you call Strake or Davis and say you can't make it but you know a good pilot who can take over, maybe serve as a backup from now on."

"What do I give for a name?"

"You tell them Vinny Stratton, who flies Baron and King Air charters out of Baltimore, with two thousand hours in King Airs."

"Is that you? I swear you're familiar somehow."

"Not your concern. You just have to sound very sick and tell them Stratton is in town, available, and competent, and you can send him over to get the plane ready immediately. We need them firmly convinced, and we don't want to leave them enough time to run any kind of check on Stratton. You call me again when it's solidly set up."

"So what's the rest of it?"

"That's it. Then you stay in your apartment for at least twenty-four hours so it looks like you're really sick."

"I mean why? Why are you doing this?"

"Again, not your concern. Maybe we want to get Strake alone and propose a business deal. Maybe Stratton just needs the job as backup pilot."

"And maybe you don't really want to screw my sister. I think I can safely assume Strake isn't going to be happy about this and he can be a mean mother. What if he decides this is all my fault?"

"He won't. Don't worry about that."

"Suppose somebody like the FAA starts asking uncomfortable questions at some point down the airway?"

"Make up a simple story. You happened to meet this Stratton in some bar the night before the takeoff. He told you he was a King Air pilot and wrote his cell phone number on a napkin. You never checked his credentials; why should you? He's average height, black hair, about one-eighty. When you took sick you recommended him. End of your story. That's all you know. You can't even remember his cell phone number."

"Why do I think this is going to turn out badly?"

"Once again, it's not your concern. Will you do it or not?"

He thought for half a minute, looking out across the

dark lot, tapping a finger on the wheel. "You say you've got five with you?"

Hardin pulled out a plain thick white envelope with a number printed on it and placed it on the dash. "My beeper number is on this. When you call it I'll call back within twenty minutes. When it's all set up I'll put the storage locker key in the mail."

"So that's it."

"Not quite." He pulled a small recorder out of his pocket along with a folded paper. He handed Duane the paper and a small squeeze light. "I've recorded this conversation and the one over the phone. That paper details our agreement. I'd like you to sign it."

Kelly read through it and said, "Who sees this?"

"Just me unless you try to upset our apple cart. Then Strake's people, the FAA, the media, everybody."

"There's always a catch, isn't there?" He read the paper, reluctantly signed it, and handed it back. Hardin carefully refolded it and slid it into another envelope.

"Oh, I get it. You want my prints on it, too. That's pretty devious."

"Like I said, nobody ever has to see this but me. Don't worry about it."

"You know, most of the trouble I've gotten into over my life has been because I like high living," Duane said pensively, caressing the steering wheel. "Maybe I ought to sell this money bucket. Cut up two or three of the charge cards. Move into a smaller apartment."

"But you won't."

"No," he said and smiled sadly. "No, I guess I won't."

Nine days later Kelly called the beeper and Hardin called back in fifteen minutes from a pay phone.

"Did you get the keys?" Kelly said.

"Yes."

"There's a flight scheduled for next Thursday. Strake wants to go to the Bahamas. Leaving Teterboro at four in the afternoon. Just him and Davis."

"That will make the arrival after sunset. It's not legal to fly a private plane in the Bahamas at night."

"That depends on who you are and who you know and where you're going. He's going to a private island called Blue Coral Cay and he says he'll take care of the details. The return flight is on Friday afternoon."

"What about a flight plan?"

"I'm not supposed to file one at all if the weather is VFR. If it's instrument conditions I'm supposed to file for Jax as the destination. When I'm getting close to Jax I call and change it to Hilton Head or St. Simons and cancel the flight plan, then just turn off the transponder and divert at low altitude for the islands. He said to plan on staying below ten thousand to the coast, then below 2,500 over the water. Pilot controlled lights at the island strip."

"All right. Set it up."

They talked again on Thursday two hours before the scheduled flight, Hardin calling back from a pay phone near the airport.

"Did you have any problems?" he asked Kelly.

"No. At least I don't think so. Since a few details about this flight aren't exactly legal, Strake wondered how a replacement pilot would take to it. I told him this Stratton really needs some extra money right now because he owes a bundle, and that there are rumors he's been involved in some pretty tricky stuff before, but that he's supposed to be a top-notch pilot. I told him it wouldn't be a problem. I'll be honest, I tried to make it sound like I don't really know this guy all that well, to cover my ass. I told him Stratton could swing by here to get the keys and have the plane ready to go on time. Strake wasn't happy, to put it mildly, but he told me to go ahead and arrange it."

"Okay. That storage locker key will be in the mail."

The plan was simple.

Hardin would get to the plane enough ahead of time to hide his parachute in plain sight. The Para-Cushion backpack had been made to serve as a cushion as well, and was at most only two inches thick, that in the lumbar area. With the harness folded around behind it and a tailored piece of sheepskin slipped over it nobody would suspect it was anything other than a custom seat-and-back cushion. The .45 would be in his flight case along with a roll of duct tape, right behind his seat. Not having to file a flight plan simplified things. He would keep inland, fly south, and depending on the local weather, would choose his spot on the sectional chart.

By dusk they would be over sparsely populated southern Georgia and on autopilot. He would allow enough time so he could get out the .45, use it to disarm Davis and Strake, and tape them into their seats. If either one of them tried to fight he would simply shoot. He would disable the radios and transponder by smashing them in with the butt of the .45 in case the men should get loose later.

He would drop down to 5,000 feet and slow the plane. Then, with the course set southeasterly but while still over land and close to his chosen spot, he would drop the airstair door and jump. The high T-tail would allow an easy exit. He had a small flashlight, a compass, and a knife taped to the chute harness. On the ground, he would get rid of the chute, walk to U.S. 17 or an I-95 interchange, and hitch a ride north. The King Air would fly on autopilot toward distant Africa until it ran out of fuel and then it would begin a long last dive down to the sea.

And Valerie's death would be avenged.

He stopped only long enough to swing by a mailbox and drop in the envelope containing the key for Kelly, who would find the agreed-on money, right to the dollar. He wore the driving gloves so there would be no prints. He left his old car in the long-term storage lot, walked to the hangar carrying the cushion and his flight bag, and prepared the King Air, pulling it out onto the apron with the electric tow cart and then closing up the hangar.

The plane was as immaculate as ever and already had a full load of fuel. He did a careful walk-around out of long habit. He made sure the cockpit was arranged according to plan, took off the driving gloves, and stood on the pavement waiting near the open air-stair door, watching the planes, mostly light business twins and singles, taking off and landing. He was wearing a captain's hat, a blue blazer, blue slacks, a white turtleneck, and large aviator transition glasses, now tinted dark in the light of the lowering sun. His beard was neatly trimmed. He slipped a dime-sized wad of cotton in each cheek against his lower teeth to help disguise his voice.

The weather was pretty much VFR all the way down the coast but a strong storm front was rolling in from the west. There should be just enough time to get down over Georgia before the winds and rains hit.

The dark blue FBO shuttle van pulled up and stopped fifteen feet from the King Air. The driver got out and slid the big rear door open.

Louis Strake and Montgomery Davis got out. They were followed by another man who looked to be fit and in his mid-thirties, dressed in a black suit with a white shirt and a string tie, and with a long braided blond pony tail.

And then Elaine Strake got out of the van.

Hardin was shaken to the core. Strake was walking toward him, preoccupied and scowling. "I'm Louis Strake," he said, not offering his hand. "Kelly explained this flight to you? The special requirements?"

Hardin cleared his throat and said in his practiced altered voice, "Yes, sir. No flight plan. Cruise below ten thousand to the coast and then drop it down. Destination is a private strip on Blue Coral Cay."

"There's been a change. Two more passengers as you can see. We'll go to Blue Coral first and spend tonight. Tomorrow morning we'll fly to Treasure Cay and stay two days at my cottage there. Do you have any problems with that?"

"No, sir."

Strake looked at his watch. "I want to be airborne within fifteen minutes." He walked up the air-stair into the cabin. The van driver was piling the luggage to one side of the air-stair so Hardin began loading it into the aft cabin bay, standing aside while the other three boarded.

Davis carried a metal briefcase with him. He hesitated when he first looked at Hardin, then he frowned to himself and went up the air-stair. Elaine did not look at him at all, and the other man just nodded, unsmiling, and climbed up into the cabin last.

The King Air had club seating in the front part of the cabin—a pair of plush leather seats along each side of the aisle behind the pilot's and copilot's seats, opposite each other across a small fold-down table. To the rear of the club seats there was another seat on each side of the aisle. Strake was seated directly behind the pilot's seat, facing aft, with his opened briefcase on the table, reading some papers. The third man sat across the aisle, also facing aft, a paperback book in hand. Davis sat opposite him, facing forward. Elaine was sitting in the right back seat looking out the window, lost in her own thoughts.

Hardin closed the air-stair, moved up the aisle, sat on the Para-Cushion, pulled the headset on over his captain's hat, and buckled up. He could feel eyes on him and he turned his head to see Davis staring at him intently. Hardin smiled slightly and turned back to begin his checklist.

The plan was out of the question now, of course. There was absolutely nothing he could do but pilot the flight to the Bahamas and back, saying as little as possible, keeping to himself, doing nothing that drew attention.

He fired up the turbines and called Teterboro ground control for taxi clearance. He followed a Comanche single and a Baron along a taxiway and when the tower cleared him for takeoff he swung out onto the runway, lining up.

He pushed the power levers to the stops, the big props spinning up to become light gray discs and the plane gathering momentum quickly, the tire-marked pavement rushing by beneath them. As the airspeed needle swung past one hundred miles per hour he gave the yoke some back pressure and the nose wheel lifted off. The mains rumbled along for another two seconds and then the plane was airborne. He held forward on the yoke a bit and trimmed to counter the pitch-up tendency, hit the gear retract and the wheels tucked up in a fast four seconds, and they climbed away with a high deck angle at almost 2,000 feet per minute.

He followed the vectors from Teterboro departure scrupulously, with the green transponder light winking each time they were swept by the ground radar. Released from Teterboro air space and with the transponder switched to the all-purpose VFR code of 1200, he levelled off at 9,500 feet, a mile above a yellowish haze layer, where the air was much clearer. He trimmed for cruise and the airspeed increased to 300 miles per hour. The King Air thrummed along smoothly and some part of his mind marveled once again at the precision, power, and docile handling of the sleek six-ton ship.

He flew offshore and took up a southerly course that would roughly parallel the coast and appear on any inquisitive radar screens as though they were headed for Florida. He knew they were now just one of hundreds of low-level radar blips, some of which were military in and near the Military Operations Areas and the restricted areas, those planes only occasionally in contact with civilian ATC, if at all. There were also many private flights ranging from student practice sessions to business singles and twins, a lot of them not on any filed flight plans and only in contact with local airports.

Unless he did something stupid to draw attention to the King Air it would be no particular problem to drop down at the right time and place, switch off the transponder, which would reduce their radar image to a dim un-coded blip, and slip on over to the islands. They would be arriving over Blue Coral Cay not that long after official dark, so anyone who happened to spot their faint blip on a screen would likely dismiss them as only a late-arriving private inter-island flight of no concern.

The afternoon sky was serenely beautiful in contrast with Hardin's gut-churning inner turmoil. To the east the sea was already darkening as the sun sank lower into the haze. Off to the west a long sporadic line of angry-looking clouds signaled the approach of the predicted storm front.

He had not programmed Blue Coral Cay into the GPS so he reached back into his flight case for a sectional chart. For no particular reason he decided to bring the gun closer, so he sandwiched it between two partially unfolded sectionals and brought it into his lap. Then with his left hand he slid it down beside his seat, to the floor on the left side, leaving one of the sectionals to cover it. He opened up the other sectional and studied it.

Blue Coral Cay was a kidney-shaped island two miles long at most, one of many islands dotting the sea between Grand Bahama and Andros. Blue Coral was surrounded by several tiny islets, and off to the southeast there was a pair of long slender islands called Big Sandy Cay and Little

Sandy Cay. The larger of the pair had a short airstrip at one end and a small group of buildings at the other. He had a handbook on the Bahamas in his flight case so he got it out.

There was only a paragraph about Blue Coral that said the place was private and to be avoided. It had a large residence on a low bluff and a cluster of outbuildings, all close by the 3,100-foot paved strip. Unauthorized landings were strictly prohibited to the extent that an unwary pilot might find the runway obstructed by spaced-out steel barrels.

He fed the coordinates into the GPS, which took a minute to digest the information and then obligingly displayed the range, the desired track over the planet to get there, and the ETA. The suggested course angled away off to the left because it was the direct line there over the ocean, so he inserted a position ten miles offshore of Sapelo Island, midway along Georgia's mostly desolate coast, as a waypoint. He would fly to the fix abeam Sapelo, drop down to 2,000 feet as though planning to land at Brunswick or somewhere else along the coast, then switch off the transponder and make for Blue Coral Cay. He didn't want official attention drawn to this flight any more than Strake did.

As they flew farther south the sun became a ruddy striated neon ball in the haze blanket and there were occasional lightning flashes in the bowels of the low black clouds prowling closer here and there along the western horizon, but the air along the coast was still mostly clear and absolutely smooth.

He sensed movement in the cabin behind him and

turned his head to look out the windows across the empty copilot's seat as though scanning for traffic. In his peripheral vision he saw Davis move up to sit across from Strake and beckon him closer to listen. They talked in a huddle over the small fold-down table for several minutes. The pony-tailed man across the aisle paid little attention, absorbed in his paperback book.

He began losing altitude slowly as the marshy river-laced shoreline of Georgia slid by on the right, the meandering waterways black. The city of Savannah lay off ahead on the right, lights already twinkling here and there in the growing dusk. Beyond it there was not much of civilization until the small city of Brunswick a hundred miles down the coast.

There was a three-quarter moon high up to the east, already growing bright.

A few minutes later Davis moved up the aisle into the cockpit, drawing the heavy curtains closed behind him. He sat in the copilot's seat and buckled his belt loosely. Half-turned in his seat, he stared at Hardin intently for a minute.

Hardin moved the right earpiece of his headset aside and said, "Yes, what is it?"

Davis reached over and took the sunglasses off of him carefully and held them up to the wan sky light. "Plain glass. So you don't need these to see." He was speaking in a low voice. Nobody back in the cabin would be able to hear him over the engine noise. He leaned close. "Contacts. You're wearing contacts." He sat back for several seconds and then said, "Tell me something. Was that Indian slut a pretty good fuck?"

Hardin reacted like he had been punched hard in the solar plexus, glaring at Davis, his hands bunching into rock-hard fists on his knees.

"I thought so. How have you been doing, Cowboy? Take it easy. Let's not make any quick moves. He reached over and patted him down and worked a hand behind his back feeling for a belt weapon. "Wait a minute. What's this?" He squeezed the edge of the Para-Cushion and felt along it. "This wouldn't be a parachute would it, Cowboy?"

He felt under the pilot's seat and down inside the flight case. "Sure it would be. What did you figure to do? Shut down the pressure system and then ease it up high enough to put us asleep while you went on your oxygen? Then aim the plane out to sea and jump, that about right? Well, I have to give you credit. You almost pulled it off. But once I study a man I don't forget him. Call it a sixth sense. And you couldn't know Elaine and Buster would be along on this flight, because that was a last-minute thing. So maybe your plan was trashed anyway, wasn't it?"

Hardin just looked at him. The Sapelo waypoint came up and the plane banked gently under the guidance of the autopilot to take up the heading for Blue Coral Cay. Davis was startled by the turn, but recovered quickly. "So you got out of your plane and made it to shore. I should have figured for that. But sometimes you think things have gone your way just because you wanted them to, you know? They gave you tinted contact lenses. Dyed your hair some. Did some plastic work here and there. Then the beard, and the glasses. But they can't change the way a man moves or thinks. They say some of the old African hunters could tell a particular lion or an elephant from a mile away, even after years had gone by. Somebody should have studied how they did that."

He spat out the small cotton wads and said, "Why did you order the bomb put in the Jeep? There wasn't any need. You could have just yanked out the distributor wires."

"We all make mistakes. That one was regrettable. But what's done is done. If it's any consolation, the man who set the charge is dead. Or do you know he's dead? Well, I'll be damned. You did it, didn't you? Again, I'm impressed. Donny was not an easy man to take. But look, before this gets out of control, I've just had a talk with Strake. He would rather his wife didn't know anything about all of this. I think I can assume you don't want her hurt, either. So after we land we'll wait until they're out of the plane and then you and I will take a walk. It turns out you're not really much of a threat to us, and your affair with Mrs. Strake, well that was a long time ago now. Strake is willing to chalk that one up."

"There was no affair."

"Whatever you say. Anyway, Strake is willing to give you some serious money to just go away. How does fifty thousand sound?"

Hardin said nothing.

"Like I say, when we land, you and I will take a walk. I'll see that you get your money and a boat ride to Nassau. Be smart. Take the offer and go away."

Hardin thought, *If I take a walk with him on the island, I'll get a bullet in the back of the head and a boat ride out to feed the reef sharks.* He hesitated for thirty seconds, then said, "I guess I don't have much choice."

"Good. Good. That's the way we thought you'd see it. You just fly the plane, then, and think about how you're going to spend all that money. I'll sit right here to keep you company the rest of the way. If we get bored we can reminisce about old times." He snugged up his seat belt.

The darkness was gathering fast now as the vastness of the green-black sea passed by below, the moon growing brighter. He realized he had not switched off the transponder so he did it now.

Neither man said anything for many long minutes. Hardin felt hollow-headed and remote and he couldn't seem to focus his mind on anything. Blue Coral Cay was drawing closer at nearly 300 miles per hour.

Hardin thought of his days with old Wasituna Lightfoot, and a peculiar calm began to seep into him as he pushed aside his blinding anger and fought to quell the fear that was threatening to turn his gut to gruel and steal away his reason.

And he began to think.

"Why are you descending?" Davis said.

"We're getting close." The plane was out of autopilot now. "And the lower we are the less likely we are to attract attention on somebody's radar."

He leveled out at 1,000 feet and peered intently ahead and as Davis also focused on the sea ahead he reached out and turned the brightness down on the GPS until the numbers faded out. After another minute he pointed ahead and said, "There it is."

There was a black hump on the sea ahead, with other lumps in the area ranging from dots to larger abstract shapes, the blue moonlight glimmering on the shallow sea among them. The one he was pointing at was still fifteen miles away.

"We'll go straight in," he said. He tuned the primary radio to the silent emergency frequency of 121.5 and turned the volume up to maximum. There was a burst of static but he used the squelch to stop it. Then he switched the radio from the headset to the cockpit speaker.

Davis watched his moves but obviously had no idea what was go ing on. A cockpit is a bewildering array of esoteric gadgetry to anyone not schooled in it, and this cockpit was more complex than many.

He rehearsed it all in his mind as he banked to the right and then back to the left to line up with the long axis of the black mass ahead, the moon swinging around to about eleven o'clock. As it began to look more like an island and less like the humped back of some prehistoric monster he selected approach flaps, turned off the propeller synchrophaser, and pulled the torque back to 1,000 foot-pounds per side, watching the airspeed bleed off to 160 miles per hour.

He let the plane sink smoothly.

Now he could make out trees on the island, silhouetted against the lesser shadows of the sea, and he turned on the powerful wing tip landing lights, startling Davis with the sudden glare.

"We're fast," Davis said. "Isn't this way too fast?"

There was the runway ahead, beginning almost at the

shoreline, and he made a slight correction to align with it. There were three light planes parked on scrub grass alongside the strip, one of them an old Cessna Cardinal. He squeezed off another 200 foot-pounds and the airspeed inched down to 130 miles per hour.

The gear warning horn silencing switch was on the left power lever and he had already flicked it off. The gear remained retracted.

Davis had his right arm out straight now, his hand braced on the top of the instrument panel, staring ahead into the brilliance.

In quick succession Hardin switched off the cabin and cockpit lights and the avionics master and shut off the fuel flow to both engines, which kept spinning as though nothing had happened, running on the residual fuel.

As the King Air sped in over a swath of coral that glowed like old bones in the landing light glare and the threshold flashed by fifty feet below, Hardin used his left hand to push the yoke forward and his right hand to snake out and uncouple Davis's seat belt buckle.

Davis said, "*Wait.* What . . ."

The plane slammed down onto the pavement on its belly, the big props digging up gouts of pavement and curling back on themselves, the belly grinding, the plane skidding and slewing wildly and the noise deafening, the violent deceleration easily flinging Davis's big body heavily against the yoke and the instruments and the slanting windshield.

The impact had set off the automatic Emergency Locator Transmitter and the whooping wail issuing loudly over the emergency frequency from the cockpit speaker added to the din.

The plane ground to a stop, rocked up once, then settled back and was still, the ELT signal shrieking out of the speaker at earsplitting volume, one of the landing lights crazily aimed skyward outside, the only glow in the pervasive blackness.

The man with the pony tail ripped aside the cockpit curtain, his face white and shocked, and shouted "What the f—" but Hardin already had the .45 in his right hand and he swung it back with all his strength, catching the man a glancing blow on the side of the head and driving him back to slump in his seat.

Hardin clawed his seat belt buckle loose and pivoted out into the cabin aisle, starting to drop as some part of his brain screamed that he would be outlined against the only light, which was coming in through the shattered windshield, but it was too late and there were two flashes in the darkness that he couldn't hear and the right earpiece of his headset disintegrated and there was a searing burn across his right collar bone. Then he was down low in a crouch.

Elaine was letting out terrified hoarse screams and whimpering in the darkness off to the left. There was a lightening at the rear of the cabin and a furtive shadow and he knew that Strake had opened the air-stair and fled.

Hardin lurched down the aisle, his leg hurting but not broken, he knew. He paused long enough to see in the dim light that Elaine looked terrified but seemed unhurt. She had been securely belted in. There was little danger of fire now. He half fell down the stairs onto the pavement, going down onto his knees and getting up and moving in a half run.

Strake turned back and fired and Hardin raised the .45 and fired just as Strake went down but he wasn't hit, only stumbling and falling flat out onto gravel, then scrambling for some low sparse trees and rolling over onto his side.

Hardin limped over to him, the .45 aimed out stiffly with both hands. Strake was on his side, both hands clamped onto his knee. "It . . . something in it ripped when I fell . . . hurts." He grimaced and rocked onto his back. His gun was on the sand three feet from him.

Hardin lowered the .45 down along his right side and said, "What is that? It looks like a little .25 automatic. That's really funny."

Strake's eyes were glittering black marbles, the hatred radiating from him in the eerie glow from the landing light. He said, "Money. Enough to live the rest of your life."

"Go ahead and pick your weapon up."

"No." His eyes were as hard and depthless as those of a tensed cornered rat.

"All right," Hardin said, and fired the .45, sand spouting up near Strake's feet. Strake did not flinch. His eyes became slitted and he hissed. Then he scrambled for the gun, grabbing it up and aiming it. And Hardin fired deliberately and accurately three times.

He went over and looked down at the body, the .45 still aimed at it, the blood roaring in him, nothing in the world but himself and the hot gun and the ruined body.

The voice seemed a long way off but then it clarified. From behind him. "I said I've got a gun on you. Don't move a damned hair. I can blow out your spine before you get half turned around. Believe it."

Hardin went still.

"Okay," the man said. Hardin knew it wasn't Davis. Had to be the one with the pony tail, the one Davis had called Buster.

"I don't give a damn about Strake," the man said. "I never liked the prick, anyway. I'll assume you've got a good reason for all this. If you're through killing him just let the gun fall out of your hand."

Hardin said, "No."

"What?"

"No. If you wanted to shoot me you would have. I'll keep the gun down by my leg but I won't shoot unless I have to. I have nothing against you. I'm going to turn around slowly now."

The man stood with his feet apart, aiming a large revolver at his face with his right hand. The side of his head was blackly wet with blood. He held the shiny metal briefcase in his left hand.

Hardin said, "Is Elaine all right, Buster?"

"Davis is dead. A broken neck, I think. I got the woman calmed down some and told her to get into the head and stay there for at least thirty minutes no matter what she hears outside. She's not hurt. That damned siren is still going off in there."

"What do you want?" He used his free hand to take off the remains of the headset.

The man said, "This isn't Blue Coral Cay, is it?"

"No. It's called Big Sandy Cay."

He held the silver briefcase up a little and said, "There's more than a million in here. Bribe money for somebody Strake was going to meet. I was only along as some extra security. I can break into one of those airplanes over there and hot wire it but I can't fly it. I'll pay you two hundred thousand to fly us over to Florida. We just ditch the plane over there someplace and then we each go our own way. Don't take too long thinking about it. I could still put a hole in you and take my chances on finding a boat. I don't see any buildings or lights anywhere nearby, but somebody sure as hell must have heard the shooting. We don't have all night. What's it going to be?"

The ragged storm front would be rolling in over Florida and Georgia. The rain would mask them, but he would have to find a hole somewhere to let down. Find some little strip that was closed for the night. Then he could walk. Get to a bus station in the morning and buy a ticket north. Elaine would be left alone in the plane, but she wasn't hurt. She'd be found, and she would have Strake's fortune left to console her.

Hardin said, "Make it three hundred thousand. You count it out while we're in the air, and I put it in my pockets. We get rid of the guns. Just drop them out the window. I'll drop mine first. Then you. If you decide not to do it I'll just point the plane at the ocean."

Buster looked at him for long moments. He shrugged. "Okay. Okay. I can't run a damned boat, anyway. But do you think we could hustle it along here?"

"I have to go back into the King Air to turn off the ELT." He also needed to get his flight case and the Para-

Cushion and wipe his prints from everything he could remember touching.

"Sure. Then you pick up Davis's gun, put a few holes in me later and take it all."

"No. I don't want it all, and I don't want anything more to do with guns and killing. But come into the plane with me if you don't believe that."

Buster thought about it. "Okay. Now, we can start a fire and get out the marshmallows here. Tell scary stories. Look at the stars. Or we can clear out. You want to get moving?"

26

THE OLD MAN WAS SITTING IN HIS ROCKER WATCHING the fire, the flames laced with long-ago memories, some of them sweet and heart-swelling, some sinister and soul-crushing. The phone rang six times before it stirred him and he got up.

"It's done," the voice said.

The old man was quiet for a moment, then he said, "Good. Her spirit will rest. And is your bear chained and not a threat to anyone else or to you?"

"Yes. Thank you for all you did."

"We will not speak of it again. Come to see me some time."

"I will. You take care."

* * * * * *

The day was warm and rich with clean earthy scents. New-mown hay and sun-heated pine. It was a modest white clapboarded cottage with a front porch, by a narrow dusty road on the side of a hill near the mountain-ringed town of Maggie Valley, surrounded by patches of forest and wind-rippled meadows fenced with split rails and fieldstones and decorated with nodding, incredibly delicate spring wildflowers.

He parked the six-year-old Jeep Wrangler that he had bought a week ago in the driveway and nervously wondered what to do next. He had shaved off the beard and his hair was dyed its natural black. The contact lenses were back home in the medicine cabinet. He was dressed in a new red shirt, jeans, and new goatskin ropers. He gathered his courage and got out and walked halfway to the cottage. He stopped, his heart hammering. Took a deep breath. He went up the steps onto the porch and pushed the old bell button.

Combed his hair back with his fingers.

Nothing happened for long seconds and then the door opened behind the screen door and Josh stood there looking up at him through the screen with a face devoid of boyish innocence. Utterly empty of the strong joyful current that should be flowing in him at his age.

"Hi, Curly. It's good to see you, boy."

Josh frowned and then his face lit up and he whispered, "Sam?"

There was some awkward confusion for both of them, getting the screen door out of the way, and then he went down onto his knees and Josh flung himself at him and he fell sideways onto the porch and they were both laughing and crying.

"My goodness, Joshua, what—" A middle-aged Indian

woman appeared in the doorway and froze at sight of the spectacle on the porch. She watched for a few seconds and then smiled widely and wiped at her eyes with her fingers.

Sam propped himself up on one hand and then stood up. Josh was adhered to him, thin arms and legs wrapped around him, laughing and crying against his shirt collar.

"I'm . . . I'm sorry, ma'am. Josh and I . . . old friends. Sorry . . . barge in like this. I just . . . just had to see him. I . . . I should have call—" But he couldn't speak any more, wiping at his own eyes with his shirt cuff, his other arm supporting Josh.

"No. Don't be sorry, mister." She smiled broadly, tears bright on her dark weathered cheeks. "Don't you be sorry. That boy's soul was withering away no matter what we did. Dying. Now he's alive again. Just that quick. You come see him any time you want to. Thank God." She held the screen door wide. "Come in. Please come in. I'll have lunch set out in a few minutes and my husband is coming in from the garden and I guess you'll just have to stay because I don't see how we can pry this boy loose of you, anyway. Oh, thank God."

* * * * * * *

He parked the Jeep in a far corner of the lot in the early evening. He was wearing the contact lenses and a blond shaggy wig under a dirty backward-aimed ball cap, a frayed jean jacket, and worn sneakers.

The matronly white-uniformed woman at the reception desk gave him what she probably assumed was a smile and asked him to sign the register. After he filled in the information line with block printing, she looked at it, frowned even more, and said, "Roy Gaskill. So you must be here to see Hank and Hattie. I don't believe I've seen you here before."

"I've been away for some time."

"Well, I'm sure they'll be happy to see you. I don't remember when they've had a visitor who's a family member. They're in Villa Fifteen." She pointed at a layout of the Shady Grove facility on the wall. "As you can see the hallways form a pentagon, with all of the villas on the inside. You go down this hallway, then take your first left, and left again at the end of that hallway. Then Villa Fifteen is just down a little way on the left. Do you need someone to show you the way?"

"No, thanks. I'll find them. I want it to be a surprise, anyhow."

"All right, then. You can go through that glass door over there into the hallway but you'll need one of the attendants to let you back out. Just push the buzzer. That keeps some of our residents from wandering off. If you have any questions there are attendants at each of the four intersections near the emergency exits. You'll have to come back here to the entrance to sign out. You can go through the villa out into the interior courtyard, if you'd like to take a little walk with the Gaskills. There are benches and shuffleboard courts. It's really quite pleasant. Visiting time ends at eight o'clock."

There were a few residents shuffling along the hallway dejectedly, most in pajamas and robes, all their attention focused inward. He walked the full length of the perimeter hallway, then came back to the intersection the receptionist had pointed out on the layout. There was a white-uniformed young freckled woman with short-cropped hair at the attendant's desk behind a glass partition that had a speaking hole in it.

He said, "Excuse me, ma'am."

"Yes. What is it?"

"Well, I was walkin' by Villa Sixteen down there and I overheard this woman—I think her sign said Miz Toomey—hollering about real bad indigestion or something. She sounded pretty bad off."

"Oh, dear. I'll go and check in on her right away. Thank you."

He walked a few steps to a vending machine and bought a Coke as the young woman hurried off down the hallway and entered Villa Sixteen.

He stepped quickly into her cubicle, opened the top drawer in her desk, and found a small cabinet key in the pencil tray. It opened the cabinet behind her desk and inside he found a neatly labeled key rack. One said EMERG. EXIT #2. He took that one, re-locked the cabinet, and put the small key back into the desk. He was walking along the hallway when the young woman came out of Sixteen and said, "She seems to be resting comfortably now."

"Hey, good. The lady had me worried there."

He waited until she was back in her cubicle with her back turned and then knocked on the door to Villa Fifteen.

Hank opened it two inches and said, "Yeah, what is it?"

"Let me in quick, Hank."

"You a friend of Bo's?" Hank let the door swing open.

He closed the door behind him, ducked to pop out the contact lenses and drop them into his shirt pocket, and took off the cap and wig. They were in the small kitchen/dining room.

"Well, I'll pure be danged," Hank said, smiling. "Wait a minute. Let me go get my bottom teeth. Mother? Look who's here." He ducked into the bathroom and came out adjusting his dentures. "In here," he said. "She's in here, and he grabbed his arm and led him into the tiny living area. Hattie was seated in a stuffed chair, half dozing. She looked old and defeated. There was no interest in her faded blue eyes when she glanced up at him. He went down onto one knee and took her withered hand. "Hello, Flutter," he said. "Aren't you glad to see me?"

She focused and smiled and said, "Roy? Oh, it's you, isn't it?" And she reached out and enveloped him in a pleasantly musty hug.

"Roy, I didn't think you'd ever get back to visit us. My land, I'll have to fix you something to eat. Hank? Go put the kettle on."

"Mother," Hank said with a grin, "that's the best smile I seen on you since that quack took you off those half-dozen medicines. Son, your friend Bo sure helped us out a lot after you left, but one day a ranger come along and that was the end of it. Bo's been to see us three times since."

"I know. I talked to him a week ago."

"Did you finish that job you had to do?" Hattie asked.

"I did. And I made a little money. I put a good down payment on a place up in the mountains. Just outside a small town called Maggie Valley. It's not fancy. It's a three-bedroom log house about sixty years old, up high at the end of a gravel road, on ten acres of land with a lot of woods. It needs a little work. Well, okay, a lot of work. There's a screened porch and a good view off over the hills. You can see maybe thirty miles. There's mist in the valleys at sunrise. The hawks ride the updrafts all day long. You can hear the mockingbirds and the whippoorwills and the wind in the trees at night. The nearest neighbor is a quarter mile away. A person could hide away up there and nobody would know. A man could sit out on that porch and play music and sing all afternoon and nobody would even care. I've got a guitar and I'm going to take lessons. The thing is, three bedrooms are way more than I really need."

"Oh, it sounds so beautiful there," Hattie said.

"Don't you get it, Mother?" Hank said, smiling. "Roy's here to break us out, ain't you, Roy?"

"There's a small church you might like in the valley. A great country restaurant. And there's a really good clinic there." He held up the key and smiled. "This fits Exit Two."

Hank took on a sly expression. "Mother, we need to start packing. They'll do a Villa check at eight but you can hide in the closet, Roy. The Guard Witch takes a cigarette break in the staff head about once an hour, so Exit Two will be clear for about ten minutes then. Plenty of time for us. Dang, Mother, we can be long gone by nine tonight and they won't even know it before breakfast."

He said, "Meanwhile, Flutter, I could sure use a cup of tea."

"Hank," she scolded. "Didn't I tell you to put the kettle

on?" She got up smiling and busied herself in the kitchen.

"We can earn our way, son," Hank said. "You know Hattie can sure cook, and I can be handy around a place. We won't be no trouble."

"Hank, you and Hattie saved my life. I've been missing that fiddle of yours, and Hattie's skillet corn bread. You'll be welcome to stay for as long as you want. And there's a young boy I want you to meet who could use two more good friends."

When Hattie came back in carrying a cup of tea Hank gave her a wrinkled grin and said, "Well, here we go again, Mother."

She smiled back, a glint in her eyes, and said, "Don't forget to bring a pencil and paper. We'll have to start making a buy-or-borrow list."

* *_{*} * *_{*} *

He met the woman late in the afternoon at the Asheville Airport. She was a tall blond built like a Nordic queen. She had shoulder-length hair tied back with a red scarf, and was wearing a dark blue skirt with an impressively breast-filled white blouse. She had a black briefcase by her feet as she prepared a cup of coffee for herself at the FBO courtesy snack table.

He walked over and said, "Hello. You're Susan Davenport?"

She smiled like a sunrise and said, "Yes. The Stilleys sent me. Maybe we could go over there by the windows and talk a little?"

"Sure thing."

She picked up the briefcase in one hand and her coffee in the other and he followed her. A young red-headed woman behind the service counter beamed at him and he nodded back. There was also a handsome and muscular shaggy-haired young man with piano-key teeth behind the counter. He was wearing BP coveralls. He said, "Mrs. Davenport. The plane is topped off for you. Checked the oil. It's ready to go."

She gave him her radiant smile and said, "Thank you. That was fast."

She sat on a sofa facing out the tall windows, put her coffee and briefcase on the low glass table, and gestured for him to take a seat beside her. He did, at a respectful distance. He said, "You flew in?"

She nodded, sipping coffee. "Yes. That 182 over there."

The plane out on the apron looked new, with glossy white paint set off with backward-sweeping burgundy and gray stripes. It looked like his old Skyhawk only bigger. The 182 had a reputation as a good short-field load hauler with plenty of power and tame handling. He said, "That's a nice-looking plane you've got there. What year is it?"

"It's a 1986 model but you'd hardly know that. It's been gone over nose to tail. Rebuilt 230-horse Continental O-470, injected and turbocharged. Reworked prop. The Horton STOL kit. Full IFR panel. Three-axis autopilot. New paint and a gray leather interior. It will tolerate an out-of-shape driver up front, three 200 pound passengers, and baggage stacked to the roof without exceeding the CG limit. Unless somebody's hauling gold bars it's pretty tough to bust the gross load limit. And it handles like a pilot's wet dream. You can practically operate it out of a Burger King parking lot."

"Well, I envy you," he said.

"I don't know why you should. It's yours."

"Excuse me?"

"I just flew it over from Raleigh-Durham for you. Executive Aero. I own the company. I deal in top-quality used Cessna singles and light twins. I don't believe I've seen a better 182 than that one right there. I found it in Colorado, owned by a rancher who could afford to have it his way. I traded him up to a cherry 310."

"I don't understand."

She drew a sealed envelope out of her briefcase. "I'm supposed to give you this."

He opened the envelope and unfolded the note, which said:

Dear Sam:

We still think of you as Sam. Give us a while to get used to your real name.

That newspaper reporter Ira Cohn and his girl-friend Samantha helped us find out a lot about you and about Josh's family. We decided we want to help Josh however we can, and we left word with Valerie's aunt and uncle to get in touch with us if you ever showed up to see the boy, which we knew you'd do if you were alive. Ira Cohn had a strong hunch you were. After you did show up the aunt kindly gave us your address and phone so Ms. Susan Davenport could get *in touch with you. (How about those hooters!)*

The airplane is yours. Don't even think about saying no. Osprey was insured and we wanted to use the money for this. We belong out on our deck with our feet up, sipping salty dogs and looking at the ocean, not out there plunging around on it. When we want to go back to New England we'll drive the Mercedes. Or get you to fly us.

Remind us to tell you the one about the handsome author and the beautiful book critic.

Thanks for giving us these priceless good days we're living now. Come see us when you can.

Ralph and Adele Stilley

He shook his head, re-read the letter, smiled, and said, "Well, I'll be damned."

"So," Susan Davenport said. "All I need is your signature on some paperwork and our business will be done here. There's even an insurance binder so you can fly it right away if you want. The keys are in it." She pulled a folder out of her briefcase, spread papers out on the glass table, and handed him a pen with the name of her business on it. "Every place there's a red X, please."

He leafed through everything, dutifully signing at all the Xs.

She glanced at his last signature and said, "That sure is an unusual name. Keep the pen. I have a rental car and I'll be spending a night or two at the Sheraton, looking this area over for potential business." She looked at him speculatively and raised an eyebrow. "Why don't you let me buy you dinner to celebrate?"

"Thank you, but I really need to get back home before too late and I've got a buy-or-borrow list I have to try filling first at the all-night Wal-Mart in the city."

"A buy-or-borrow list?"

"Sorry. It's sort of a private joke."

She smiled radiantly and offered her hand for shaking, "Suit yourself, then. Here's my card. If you have the slightest problem with the plane, call me. And the next time you land at Raleigh-Durham, look me up."

"Thanks. I'll do that."

As he was walking out on the apron to the plane and Susan Davenport came up to the service counter, the red-headed girl behind the counter said, "Gee, who was that guy? Those gray eyes really, like, get to you. He reminds me of, like, a wolf or something, you know?"

Susan said, "He's just another cowboy pilot, honey. And he's a little long in the tooth for you."

The young man had the name "Kevin" stitched on his coveralls.

"Kevin," Susan said, "Why don't you show me yours and I'll show you mine?"

"Excuse me, ma'am?"

"Why don't you show me your fuel ticket and I'll show you my credit card?"

"Oh. Yes, ma'am."

"Tell me something, Kevin."

"If I can, ma'am."

"What time do you get off work around here?"

* * * * * * *

He did a leisurely walk-around and could not find a flaw. He sat on the soft rich-smelling leather inside and leafed through the operating handbook, noting all the numbers. The plane was immaculate. With it he would be able to start up a small charter operation much sooner than he had hoped. He had a little money left after setting up the $150,000 trust fund for Joshua. Enough to get an inexpensive brochure card printed, send out some letters, and cover operating costs and living expenses until the charter work began to pay off.

He closed the door, belted up, switched on the tail strobe, shouted "Clear," clamped the brakes, and keyed the starter. The engine fired immediately and the prop became a fluttering gray blur. He called clearance delivery and they told him he could taxi. He did a run-up at the hold line and when the tower cleared him for takeoff he swung out to line up precisely with the dashes and pushed the throttle smoothly to the stop.

With the engine at full bellow and the plane coming alive under his hands he accelerated down the runway, faster and faster until the wheels broke free with only a gentle tug on the yoke and he felt the old familiar shot of euphoria as he ceased to be a gravity-shackled human of the weighty Earth and became a creature of the vast ephemeral sky.

He trimmed for best rate of climb, banked away toward the west, and leaned back in the seat. The sun had already rolled down beyond the Blue Ridge, shadows gathering among the glowing buildings and on the car-lit roads and in the folds of the ancient forested hills below, the sky all around painted like an old Cherokee blanket.

There was a clean bright patch in a high band of cirrus and he aimed for it, climbing strongly.

Chasing the sunset.

The End

**A SPECIAL PRESENTATION OF
MICHAEL BERES' NOVEL,
THE PRESIDENT'S NEMESIS**
ISBN#1932815732
ISBN#9781932815733
Platinum Imprint
US $24.95 / CDN $33.95
Political Thriller

CHAPTER 1

AT PRECISELY THE same time on two consecutive nights, the large black vehicle moved slowly through the darkness of the parking lot below Stan's window. It could have been a Lincoln Navigator or Chevy Suburban. The headlights and taillights and side marker lights gave it a general shape, a large sport utility vehicle. He was certain it was the same vehicle both nights. If the vehicle appeared a third night this would be very curious indeed.

The first night, when the vehicle parked in front of the garbage dumpsters on the far side of the parking lot, Stan thought it might be a police vehicle, detectives on a stake-out. But why with the lights on? That first night he stood at his front window until the vehicle drove away. Slowly at first, until it got to the apartment complex entrance. Then fast, heading south around the curve on Elmwood Drive, taillights disappearing between the gas stations at the crossroads.

1

Stan saw the same vehicle again the next night, parked in the same spot with its lights on. As he stood at the window that second night, he saw two figures in the front seat. The passenger got out on the far side next to one of the garbage dumpsters. Only the top half of the passenger was visible moving toward the front of the vehicle. Small head, short hair, large shoulders, a man. The man lifted the lid of the garbage dumpster and placed something inside, or simply reached inside. Then back into the vehicle. No courtesy light on while the door was open, so Stan could not see faces. And like the previous night, the vehicle drove slowly out of the lot, then fast once it was on the road.

On two nights in a row at exactly one in the morning a vehicle had visited the garbage dumpsters in the parking lot and Stan's curiosity began to torment him. If he didn't stay up late every night he would never have seen it. But he did stay up late. Sometimes watching television—switching between the classic movie channels or the Biography or History Channels. Sometimes at his computer surfing the Web. If he didn't stay up so late and have such an idle mind he wouldn't have concocted dozens of reasons for two men driving up to a garbage dumpster at one in the morning and tossing something in.

Stan really hadn't seen much of the driver, only that there was one, but because of the police stakeout idea he assumed both were men, both wearing overcoats like the guy who had gotten out and gone to the dumpster. Maybe they lived somewhere else, one of those new subdivisions way south, and were too cheap to pay a scavenger service.

But a more enticing possibility was FBI agents checking someone's garbage. So why hadn't he seen a flashlight? Last night the man with large shoulders opened the lid, reached inside, then closed the lid gently with both hands. No noise, no package visible, like the man was reaching in to touch the garbage, to see if there was garbage. Crazy.

Tonight, the third night, Stan had prepared for the vehicle's arrival. He'd switched off the television at twelve-thirty and turned his lounge chair toward the window. As he sat there he thought about kidnappers picking up a ransom. But if that were the case, the man would have snatched up the ransom package and jumped back into the vehicle. And if the man had been putting something into the dumpster, what would it be? Garbage. A guy from the apartment complex who works nights, rides in to work with another guy because they both drive gas guzzlers and want to save money. A disc jockey and engineer doing the before-dawn shift at a radio station.

"Hey, man. You gonna stink up my vehicle with garbage again?"

"Only 'til we get to the dumpster. I'm too lazy to walk it over."

Stan rose from his chair and walked to the window. Should be in bed instead of spying on guys who'd laugh like hell if they knew a crazy bastard was watching them. But he needed to see if the vehicle returned tonight. A large vehicle tricked out with oversized wheels and maybe some other gadgets. A vehicle for someone with money to burn, or a vehicle for official business. He stared at the rows of cars and sport utes and pickups in the lot. But all of these seemed too small. He leaned close to the window looking at the vehicles parked at the far end of the lot. One vehicle parked beneath a yellowish overhead light in the distance looked like a big sport ute, but the distortion of the window glass and the distance made it impossible to tell. He waited.

Then, although the back entrance to the complex was not visible, Stan could tell that a vehicle had driven in because of the dip of headlights. Instead of a black sport ute, a large black car appeared from behind the last apartment building and turned toward him. High beams on. He backed away from the window out of the glare and watched the car approach. Once inside the complex it did not stop until it reached the garbage dumpsters. The car had come from the road, had turned into the complex for one purpose—to park at the garbage dumpsters across the lot, not more than fifty yards from his second floor window. On previous nights it had been a sport ute, tonight it appeared to be a limo.

Stan hadn't realized he was backing up until his chair bumped against his calves. He stooped down, heard his knees crack, and watched for movement inside the limo. He knelt on the floor balancing himself, his hands on the windowsill. He thought about gangsters, hit men sizing up a hit. Or maybe terrorists hiding out in apartments nearby, preparing for an attack. He was about to reach for the phone on the end table when an orange glow appeared in his peripheral vision.

The big sport ute that had been parked at the far end of the lot beneath the overhead light had moved out and was coming this way, only its parking lights lit. Maybe the police were already watching. Maybe someone else had seen the limo and now there would be a sport-ute-limo confrontation. The sport ute with oversized wheels had a spotlight mounted on the driver's door. He waited.

The sport ute's parking lights lit up the bumper of the limo ahead. A foot apart, limo and sport ute stood motionless. Limo with headlights on, sport ute with an unlit spotlight.

A man got out on the far side of the sport ute and walked quickly to the limo. Big shoulders, small head, just like the man from the previous night. Still no courtesy light inside the sport ute, and now no courtesy light visible inside the limo as the man opened the rear limo door and a tall thin man got out and stood next to the big-shouldered man. The tall man raised his hand. Not like a stickup, not like a wave. Like the Pope giving a blessing. Then the big-shouldered man opened the dumpster and the thin man lifted something in. At first the package had been hidden by the limo. But as the man lifted it in, Stan saw the shopping-bag size of it for an instant before the lid was closed.

The tall man got back into the limo, and after the other man closed the door he returned to the sport ute. Then the two vehicles drove slowly out of the lot, and when they turned onto Elmwood Drive sped through the curve in one swift movement like a snake. Just before they disappeared between the darkened gas stations, the headlights of the sport ute came on.